ALSO BY JOSHUA HENKIN

Swimming Across the Hudson

Matrimony

Matrimony

Joshua Henkin

PANTHEON BOOKS, NEW YORK

Copyright © 2007 by Joshua Henkin

All rights reserved. Published in the United States by Pantheon Books,
a division of Random House, Inc., New York, and in Canada by
Random House of Canada Limited, Toronto.

Pantheon Books and colophon are registered trademarks of Random House, Inc.

Library of Congress Cataloging-in-Publication Data

Henkin, Joshua.
Matrimony : a novel / Joshua Henkin.
p.   cm.
ISBN 978-0-375-42435-9
1. Marriage—Fiction.   2. Man-woman relationships—Fiction.   I. Title.
PS3558.E49594M38 2007
813'.54—dc22   2006103202

www.pantheonbooks.com

Book design by Wesley Gott

Printed in the United States of America

First Edition

2   4   6   8   9   7   5   3   1

For Beth

Northington, Massachusetts

"Out! Out! Out!" The first words Julian Wainwright ever spoke, according to his father, Richard Wainwright III, graduate of Yale and grand lubricator of the economic machinery, and Julian's mother, Constance Wainwright, Wellesley graduate and descendant of a long family of Pennsylvania Republicans. Julian, the first Wainwright in four generations to be given his own Christian name. Julian's father would have liked another Richard Wainwright, but Julian's mother was a persistent woman and she believed a child of hers was entitled to his own identity and therefore his own name. And so, at fifteen months, in a car ride back from Martha's Vineyard, Julian, who until then had not said a word and had given his parents every reason to think language would come slowly to him, uttered these words in rapid succession: "Out! Out! Out!" Not once, not twice, but repeatedly, until the words became a chant and it was obvious that for reasons all his own he didn't want to return to New York City, to his parents' apartment on Sutton Place.

Now, seventeen years later, he had gotten his wish. It was 1986, and he was starting his freshman year at Graymont College, a small liberal arts school in Northington, Massachusetts, two hours west of Boston. An alternative school, according to the Graymont brochure, on whose cover there appeared a picture of Rousseau sitting next to a cow. Henri Rousseau? Jean-Jacques Rousseau? The students didn't

3

know, and they didn't seem to care. The only thing that mattered was that they were at Graymont, in the middle of whose campus stood a shanty protesting college investments in South Africa, a shanty so large it could fit practically the whole student body inside it. According to one upper-class math major, more nights per capita had been spent sleeping inside the shanty at Graymont than in any other college shanty in the United States.

At Graymont, if you wanted, you could receive comments from your professors instead of grades, and on the application for admission there was a "creative expression" section that, according to rumor, one successful applicant had completed by baking a chocolate cake. "Hash brownies!" a student said. "The guy got the dean of admissions stoned!"

Julian's own creative expression section took the form of a short story he'd written. At thirteen, he'd met his hero, John Cheever, standing on the steps of the 92nd Street Y, and ever since then, ever since he'd gotten John Cheever's autograph, Julian had known he was going to be a writer.

But that would come later, once classes had begun. Right now, Julian waited in his dorm room to greet his new roommate, a young man from New Jersey who had assured him over the telephone that he was bringing the largest stereo system Julian had ever seen. It was going to take the two of them to carry it up the stairs.

Julian's roommate was right. The promised stereo system, when it was delivered, looked like an intercontinental ballistic missile. It was a stereo system paid for by Ronald Reagan and built by the United States Pentagon and directed at Mikhail Gorbachev and the Soviet Politburo, a stereo system that could blow the Russians out of the sky and turn them into a mushroom cloud.

Wandering about the room, trailing wire behind him, Julian's roommate was contemplating where to put his electric guitar, his boom box, his microwave, his toaster oven; he was, Julian thought, a tangle of electricity. "This school is wild," his roommate said. "Some of the guys on campus wear skirts."

"They do?"

"They're hoping to transcend the boundaries of gender. Mostly they're just trying to get laid. There are naked parties here. People come to them without any clothes on."

"Completely nude?"

"In the winter, I guess, they wear shoes and socks. It gets pretty cold here." Julian's roommate was dark-haired and thickset, and he had brought with him piles of pressed shirts and trousers, each of them separated from the others by a white piece of tissue paper, as if they had come directly from the dry cleaner. He was hanging them up now, smoothing them out with his hand. "You think those guys pee in the shower?"

"Which guys?"

"Jared and Hartley. Bill. Stefan." Julian's roommate gestured to the room down the hall. "Hartley's the kind of guy who pees in the shower."

In the bathroom now, Julian glanced warily at the showers. There were two stalls for six guys, each with a white piece of plastic hanging down from the rod but not quite reaching the floor.

"It's bad enough to pee in your own shower," his roommate said. "But in a communal shower?" He looked up at Julian. "You don't pee in the shower, do you?"

"No," Julian said. From time to time he had. Didn't everyone?

"I had this roommate in prep school who peed in the sink."

"You didn't," Julian said.

"Swear to God. When I was using the bathroom and he needed to go, he'd just climb up on the sink and pee in it."

"That's disgusting."

"All the same, I think I'll be wearing flip-flops in here." Again his roommate gestured to the room down the hall, as if to reassure Julian it wasn't him he mistrusted.

"Here come the PCC-ers," his roommate said. Through the window, Julian could see a group of students walking across the quad. They wore blue badges and name tags and held red and black satchels. They were upperclassmen, Julian's roommate said, recent graduates of a weeklong training course in reproductive health, purveyors of information about pregnancy and sexually transmitted disease, and in their satchels they carried the tools of their trade: leaflets, condoms, dental dams, and spermicide in all flavors.

Julian said, "The PCC-ers?"

"Peer Contraceptive Counseling. First night at school, they come talk to you. It's all part of in loco parentis."

"There are dozens of them."

"Like flies," his roommate said.

That night, as his roommate had predicted, everyone in Julian's entryway met with four members of Peer Contraceptive Counseling, each wearing a PCC badge and name tag and holding a red and black PCC satchel. In freshman entryways across campus, upperclassmen had descended, wearing these very same badges and name tags and carrying these very same satchels.

Julian listened to a beautiful young woman named Nicole demonstrate how to use a dental dam. What exactly was a dental dam and why was Nicole wearing one? She appeared to be covered in Saran Wrap. Now Nicole's colleagues, Brian, Ted, and Simone, were trying on dental dams as well. Several of the boys began to laugh, but the girls nodded knowingly, as if they'd spent their whole lives in the company of dental dams.

Soon it was time to taste the spermicide.

"There's nothing to be afraid of," Nicole said, uncapping a tube of spermicide and squeezing a little onto her finger. She stuck her finger into her mouth, then passed the spermicide to Ted, who stuck his finger into his mouth. Everyone was eating spermicide.

"It's fruit flavor," Nicole told the freshmen. "It's supposed to be eaten."

She asked for volunteers from the students, and when no one raised a hand she chose Julian.

Julian stood up. Was he supposed to stand up? Did you eat spermicide sitting down or standing up? Nicole was only a junior, but she seemed so much older than he was, so wise to the ways of the body

6

and to the various flavors of spermicide and to the reasons there should be various flavors of spermicide.

"Would you like passion fruit?" Nicole asked. "Or strawberry?"

"Strawberry's good," Julian said.

Nicole handed him the spermicide.

"Don't worry," Nicole said. "It goes down smooth. It tastes like strawberry bubble gum."

Julian squeezed some spermicide onto his finger and stuck it into his mouth.

"How does it taste?"

It tasted terrible. Like strawberry bubblegum but with extra chemicals. It had a sloppy, grainy texture. Julian nodded in approval.

The session lasted an hour and a half, and at the end of it all eighteen freshmen from Julian's entryway were sent off with a contraceptive loot bag that included spermicide, dental dams, and condoms, miniature red and black satchels of their own taken from the larger satchels the PCC-ers carried with them. Carefully, seriously, respectfully, the girls took their satchels upstairs to their rooms, while the boys tossed the contents at one another and dissected them, and Hartley, from across the hall, filled his condoms with water and jettisoned them out the window into the courtyard, seeing if he could get them to explode.

Julian's roommate said, "I'm telling you, that guy pees in the shower."

"Could be," Julian said. He went into his bedroom to unpack.

The reason Julian had come to Graymont, the only reason, as far as he was concerned, that anyone should come in the first place, was to study fiction writing with Professor Stephen Chesterfield. In the course catalogue the class was called "Fiction Writing Workshop," but Professor Chesterfield hated the word "workshop," which sounded like a church meeting, hated it, especially, as a verb ("Will my story be workshopped next time, Professor Chesterfield?"), the use of which was grounds for expulsion from his class.

If you were lucky enough to have been admitted in the first place.

Applicants to Professor Chesterfield's class had to submit a writing sample and they were required to answer the following question: "Do you now, or do you ever intend to, write material geared for the U.S. motion picture industry located in Hollywood, California?"

Poor Professor Chesterfield. His only novel, published twenty-five years ago before the onset of his now famous writer's block, had been sold to Hollywood, and Professor Chesterfield had been flown out to California to meet the screenwriter and the director and to witness the proceedings on the set. Nobody on the set got along, and in the end Professor Chesterfield's novel never made it to the screen. Some people said it was Professor Chesterfield's own fault. Displeased with the script, he acted brutishly, threatening the screenwriter, the director, the actors themselves. It was the darkest period in an already dark life, and in the wake of his trip to Hollywood, Professor Chesterfield's bout with writer's block began.

"Do you now, or do you ever intend to, write material geared for the U.S. motion picture industry located in Hollywood, California?" Julian suspected that F. Scott Fitzgerald himself wouldn't have been admitted to Professor Chesterfield's class if he'd said he wanted to write a screenplay.

Destroyed by Hollywood, Professor Chesterfield returned to Graymont, to his students, who watched more and more movies and read fewer and fewer books. Scrutinizing their stories, he could see the camera panning, the jump cuts and dolly shots, all the things that had ruined him. Worse, his students had taken to writing words such as "bang," "pop," and "splat," as well as nonwords masquerading as words, such as "kaboom," "yikes," "glunk," and even "arrrghhhh," often followed by multiple exclamation points. And in case the reader didn't understand, the student would use capital letters: "ARRRGHHHH!!!!!"

Worst of all was "kerplunk," which a student of Professor Chesterfield's had used the previous year. A character had fallen off a horse, and then, in a paragraph all its own, came the single word.

"Kerplunk."

So in the fall of 1986, the first thing Professor Chesterfield did after placing his papers on his desk was approach the blackboard and write, in all capital letters though without exclamation points, the following rule:

THOU SHALT NOT USE THE WORD
"KERPLUNK" IN YOUR SHORT STORIES.

The first of what would prove to be 117 commandments written on the blackboard that year.

Professor Chesterfield was fifty-seven years old, but he had a lithe, sinewy build and a full head of hair, and he walked about the classroom in his signature dark blazer and Stan Smith tennis sneakers with the agility of an athlete. Julian had heard that he still played pickup basketball and that the reason he walked around the classroom— as much as a mile during the course of a single class, according to the calculations of one former student—was to stay in shape for the basketball court.

THOU SHALT NOT UTTER THE PHRASE
"SHOW, DON'T TELL" WHEN DISCUSSING
ONE ANOTHER'S SHORT STORIES.

Rufus McCoy appeared stricken. Rufus was a freshman from Delaware, and he had so desperately wanted to get into Professor Chesterfield's class that after handing in his application he went straight to Professor Chesterfield's office and begged to be admitted; he actually got down on his knees and said, "I beg of you, sir." Until this point, Rufus had not only believed in "Show, don't tell," he believed in it with the fervor of a religious acolyte. In fact, it was practically the only thing he believed in when it came to creative writing. "Why not?"

"Because it's a lie." Professor Chesterfield was sitting on his desk, his legs swinging back and forth, and between his left thumb and forefinger he held a cigarette. There were rules against smoking in Graymont buildings, but Professor Chesterfield didn't care about rules. The only rules he cared about were the ones he wrote on his blackboard.

"In what sense?" This was Astrid, who had a semicircle of silver studs in the rim of her left ear and wore a thick layer of black lipstick. She gave off an air of wounded toughness.

"In the sense that it's not true. Tell me something," Professor Chesterfield said. "Where would Proust be if he weren't allowed to tell anything?"

"Proust?" someone said, sounding as if she'd never heard of the man.

"Or Flaubert. Or Stendhal. Or Dickens." For a time, Professor Chesterfield had succumbed to convention and spent the first day of class going around the room, allowing the students to introduce themselves. These were known as ice-breakers, but Professor Chesterfield didn't like what was beneath the ice. The students told one another who they were and what books they were reading, and these were always books Professor Chesterfield hadn't heard of, and once he had, he regretted it.

He approached the blackboard.

THOU SHALT NEVER USE PASS-THE-SALT DIALOGUE.

"What are you talking about?" Astrid said.

"Here," said Professor Chesterfield, "is a representative smattering of student dialogue: 'Hello, how are you, I'm Bill, I'm Ted, nice to meet you, nice to meet you, too, shall we go to the theater, what street is it on, I'll be there at seven-thirty on the northwest corner, see you there, pronto.' Ladies and gentlemen, I beg of you, turn off your tape recorders. If your characters need salt, just give it to them. Don't make them have a discussion about it."

"Never?" said Rufus, whose characters liked to have discussions about everything.

"So," said Professor Chesterfield, "when might a character reasonably say, 'Could you please pass the salt'?"

Julian raised his hand. "If it characterizes him. Say you tell me your father just died, and I say, 'Could you please pass the salt?' It shows I'm not listening to you."

"And you are?"

"Julian Wainwright."

"Congratulations, Wainwright, you win!"

"Quadriplegic," said Carter Heinz, who was sitting languidly in the back of the classroom, his feet propped on his desk.

"Pardon me?" said Professor Chesterfield.

Carter had a baseball cap pulled down over his eyes so it was hard to tell whether he was awake or asleep. He wore a look of aloofness and superiority, which attracted Julian, who was hoping to appear aloof and superior himself. "Let's say you're a cripple," Carter said. "Paralyzed from the neck down. So I say to you, 'Could you please pass the salt?' "

Professor Chesterfield began to laugh. Slowly, his laughter built until the classroom vibrated. "That's the most brilliant thing anyone has said all year."

The year was all of thirty minutes old.

Now it was time for the in-class writing exercise. Professor Chesterfield asked the students to describe a greasy spoon, first from the perspective of someone angry and then from the perspective of someone lovelorn. No mention was to be made of anger or lovelornness; the descriptions themselves were to do the work.

"A real-life greasy spoon?" Astrid said. "Like Denny's?"

"Or IHOP?" Rufus said.

For the next half hour Professor Chesterfield sat unflinching on his desk as if he'd been cast in plaster; he looked scarily dead. Finally, his features thawed and he collected the students' exercises and began to read them. But no sooner did he pick one up than he appeared to tire of it and he moved on to the next one. He laid the exercises across his desk like pieces in a jigsaw puzzle.

"What does 'lovelorn' mean, anyway?" someone asked.

"It's when you love someone," Rufus said, "and they don't love you back." There was a longing, dolorous tone to Rufus's voice. He appeared to be speaking from experience.

Professor Chesterfield read from Sue Persimmon's exercise. Sue was blond and full-figured, and she was staring raptly at Professor Chesterfield, but she had written, literally, about a greasy spoon and only now had she realized her mistake.

"'The spoon was very greasy,'" Professor Chesterfield read. "'Megan didn't want to eat from a spoon that had so much gunk on it.'"

Professor Chesterfield read from Rufus's exercise. "'Bill picked up his fork and knife, looked warily around him, and cut into his collared greens.' Rufus," Professor Chesterfield said, "kindly undress your vegetables."

Professor Chesterfield read from another exercise. "'Tom's French toast stared back at him, uncomfortable, indignant.' What we have here, ladies and gentlemen, is a piece of indignant French toast. I've never seen one of those before, but then it's a new year."

The students looked up mutely.

"Class dismissed," Professor Chesterfield said. He motioned to Julian and Carter to stay behind. "I like you guys," he said. "You're the only two students in the class with even an ounce of talent. Not that you have much of it."

"No, sir," Julian said.

"Are you two friends?"

"Don't know him," Carter said.

"Well, you should get to know each other."

Outside the classroom Julian read through his exercise. Professor Chesterfield had written one word on it. "Sophomoric." On Carter's exercise there was one word, too. "Pusillanimous."

"Jesus," Julian said.

"Well, fuck," said Carter, and he crumpled up his exercise and fired it across the hallway, where it landed in the trash can.

The next morning in the courtyard Julian saw Carter leaning indolently against a tree. Julian was tall and thin, with straight dark hair that fell across his face. Carter was squatter and more compact, but he held himself in such a way as to make a person think he had no shape at all. He had short-cropped blond hair and a tiny scar above his upper lip.

"So we're supposed to be friends," Julian said.

"Papal decree," said Carter.

"'Sophomoric' and 'pusillanimous.' Do you know what those words mean?"

"They mean Chesterfield thinks we suck."

"Actually, he likes us," Julian said. "Why else would he bother to criticize us? You heard what he said. The only two students with any talent."

"He said we didn't have much of it."

"But more than anyone else."

They walked across campus, and outside the student union whom should they see sitting on a park bench wearing a broad-brimmed straw hat but Professor Chesterfield himself. "Hello, Heinz. Hello, Wainwright."

The next evening they saw him again, outside the Bison Bar and Grill. Professor Chesterfield was wearing another hat, this one made of felt, and he tipped it at them in greeting. "Well, hello," he said, and disappeared inside.

At Safeway the following afternoon they found him bent over the frozen food examining the turkeys. His cart was filled with a quart of skimmed milk, a head of lettuce, a tomato, and twenty, maybe thirty cans of cat food.

"The man has a cat," Julian said.

"I doubt it," said Carter.

"Then why's he buying cat food?"

"Who knows?"

They spotted him the next day in the English department where he emerged from his office followed by Sue Persimmon. Sue looked every bit as pretty as she had in class, except now she appeared tousled, as did Professor Chesterfield. Professor Chesterfield went jauntily up the stairs, taking them two at a time, blond, sloe-eyed Sue Persimmon in her white sundress and silver anklet trailing amiably behind him.

"I bet they're having an affair," Julian said.

"How's that possible?" said Carter. "The semester's just begun."

"Maybe he works fast."

They saw him yet again, this time at the gym, where Professor Chesterfield was holding his own in what appeared to be the over-forty game of pickup basketball. He was surprisingly agile-footed. He had a dead eye from the outside and he played exuberant, harassing defense; no one wanted to be guarded by him.

The next week, however, he limped into class with a cane.

"What happened to you?" Astrid said.

Professor Chesterfield hoisted himself onto his desk and removed a dog muzzle from his briefcase. "Some rules." There was, he explained, an almost unbearable urge on the part of the student writer to explain his short story as the class discussed it. This wasn't to be permitted in his classroom. "Someday, when your stories are published in *The New Yorker*"—a ludicrously gigantic smile crossed Professor Chesterfield's face, as if the thought of his students being published in *The New Yorker* were too outrageous to entertain—"you won't be able to stand over your reader's shoulder and tell him what you meant. For that reason, the writer won't speak until after his story has been discussed."

In many writing classes, the students sat in a circle and the professor guided them as they expressed themselves. But this wasn't, Professor Chesterfield said, how he conducted things. His students spent their whole lives expressing themselves, through word and deed, and in his classroom, at least, a moratorium would be placed on expressing oneself.

Professor Chesterfield read from Cara Friedberg's story, which was called "The Great Tragedy." At the beginning of the story, a young woman was breaking up with her boyfriend at a pizza joint. In the middle of the story, a young woman was breaking up with her boyfriend at a pizza joint. At the end of the story, a young woman was breaking up with her boyfriend at a pizza joint. Twenty-three pages of breaking up with your boyfriend at a pizza joint, and then there was a twenty-fourth page on which the young woman, ruing her decision to break up with her boyfriend, goes back to find him. Regrettably, her boyfriend has departed, and in her frenzied search for him she gets mown down by a bus. The young woman is dead; where can the story go? Nowhere, not least because the story has been written in first-person. But it goes on anyway, for one final sentence, in a magical stroke of narrative reincarnation: "I lay there cold and lifeless in Sean's arms; rigor mortis had started to set in."

"Karen Friedman," Rufus said, already breaking Professor Chesterfield's rule against expressing himself. He was referring to Cara's protagonist. "It's pretty close to Cara Friedberg, don't you think?"

"Does this matter?" Over the years, Professor Chesterfield pointed out, his students focused on the smallest, least crucial details and ignored everything else.

"I find the story unbelievable," Astrid said.

Julian nodded. He found many things unbelievable about the story, not least the climactic bus accident.

"I like the last sentence," Rufus said. He read it aloud. " 'I lay there cold and lifeless in Sean's arms; rigor mortis had started to set in.' "

"What do you like about it?" Professor Chesterfield asked.

"The semicolon."

"It's an excellent semicolon," Professor Chesterfield agreed. "In fact, throughout the story Cara uses semicolons properly, and for that reason I'm going to give her an A in the class."

"You are?" said Rufus.

"It's been my experience," Professor Chesterfield said, "that the average college student thinks of the semicolon as a very large comma. But Cara doesn't, so I will give her an A. In fact, I will say this right now: whosoever uses semicolons correctly in this class will get an A for the year."

"No matter how bad the writing is?" Rufus said.

Professor Chesterfield was so uninterested in grades that one time when a student came to complain about a C, he changed the grade to an A before the young man could even finish talking. "As for this particular story, it's a dead character speaking in the last sentence, but it's a dead character who knows her semicolons."

Next came Simon Pelfrey's story, which was called "Strumming in the Zone." There was time travel in the story, and though the story didn't say so explicitly, the characters, Julian surmised, were intended to be werewolves. At the very least, they were extremely hairy human beings. They spoke in what seemed like English, except that periodically the letter "z" would appear, orphan-like, in the middle of a sentence. It was as if Simon had committed the same typo over and over again.

"It was an experiment," Simon explained when it was his turn to speak. "I'm writing experimental fiction."

"God bless the American teenager," Professor Chesterfield said, "and his experimental fiction." The previous year, he told the class, one of his students, in her own idea of an experiment, had written a story about a husband and wife, only at the end of the story the reader learns that the wife isn't a wife but a cat. "Fooled you," the writer seemed to be saying. Professor Chesterfield tried to explain the difference between writing fiction and telling a riddle. On the blackboard he wrote, "THOU SHALT NOT CONFUSE A SHORT STORY WITH A RUBIK'S CUBE."

"What was the experiment?" someone asked Simon.

"I was wondering that myself," Professor Chesterfield said.

"The letter 'z,' " Simon said, "is the last letter in the alphabet. I was trying to say something about endings." He looked up at Professor Chesterfield. "The letter 'z' appeared in my story exactly a hundred times. I imagine that casts things in a different light."

"What about your characters?" Julian said. "Are they supposed to be werewolves or people?"

"I left it open," Simon said. "I didn't want to bias the reader."

"Well, thank you, Simon," Professor Chesterfield said. "Thank you for sharing." He gave the muzzle an affectionate squeeze.

He approached the blackboard.

THOU SHALT POPULATE YOUR
STORIES WITH HOMO SAPIENS.

"And one more thing," Professor Chesterfield said. "Would everyone please stop writing the same story?" According to Professor

Chesterfield, the male students always wrote about fathers and sons going hunting together and the females always wrote about depressed young women who curl up into a ball.

"What's that supposed to mean?" said Sue Persimmon, who seemed to take this personally.

Julian looked knowingly at Carter. Maybe that was what had happened in Professor Chesterfield's office. Sue had curled up into a ball.

At the end of class, Professor Chesterfield asked Julian and Carter to stay behind again. "There's a lot of bad writing here."

"The worst," said Julian.

"It's easy to be a critic, isn't it, Wainwright?" Professor Chesterfield got up from his desk and, without limping, walked across the classroom and out the door, leaving his cane and muzzle behind him.

That first semester Julian spent a lot of time watching. He watched his classmates as they walked to and from class, the sets of feet going up and down the steps of Thompson Hall, the air emerging from everyone's lungs as the weather got colder. He watched the cigarette smoke, and the dust that flew up at the clapping of mittens, and he felt buoyed by it all.

In those fall months, he took to befriending the municipal workers in Northington, and soon he knew the names of the local policemen and firemen, of the meter maid, whom he greeted, "Good morning, Elaine," saluting her as he passed. He would buy milk and orange juice and Pepperidge Farm Mint Milano cookies from the local grocers in town, alternating among them, like a man spreading his largesse. But he went most often to Mr. Kang, the Korean grocer, who, when Julian came in, would tell Julian about his childhood in Korea; then Julian, holding a carton of milk in each hand, would tell Mr. Kang about his own childhood.

On one of his morning walks Julian found a stray Beagle who took a liking to him and followed him on the footpath back to campus, staying outside his dorm and bleating until Julian didn't have the heart to leave him outside. There was a tag with the owner's name around the dog's collar, and when Julian called Mr. Quincy to pick the dog up, Mr. Quincy was so grateful he thrust a fifty-dollar bill into Julian's hand and refused to take it back.

A few mornings a week Julian began to walk Mr. Quincy's Beagle, and then other dogs, too, and soon he could be seen walking along the streets of Northington with eight or nine dogs at his side, Retrievers, Collies, Shepherds, a St. Bernard, and Mary, his favorite, an aging Newfoundland who trailed the rest of the pack like a den mother and who, like Julian, seemed filled with the spirit of discovery, turning her head from side to side like someone perched on a parade float. Mary was so big a few of the Northington children thought she was a bear until Julian assured them she was a dog, and he allowed them to feed Mary scraps of meat, which he carried in a cellophane baggie inside his knapsack.

Sometimes, late at night, on the way back from a movie or simply alone walking through town, taken with the sense that his life was romantic, that the life of a young man at college was the only life to live, yet filled at the same time with a melancholy whose roots he couldn't unearth, feeling unappreciated, turned down by some girl, Julian would stop at Mr. Kang's grocery where he would find Mr. Kang tending to the fruits and vegetables. Mr. Kang used a hose that sprayed a mist so fine Julian could practically see the individual particles of water. Inside, Mrs. Kang was at the cash register examining a bulb of fennel. Julian thought he would like nothing better than to own a grocery, he and some future Mrs. Wainwright, the two of them tending the fruits and vegetables, late nights in the storeroom in back, punching the keys on their matching calculators. Other times, however, there was nothing he would have liked less than to be hovering over the produce in the growing cold, and he would comfort Mr. Kang with the fact that he'd be closing at midnight whereas the Korean grocers in New York City were open twenty-four hours a day.

"New York's the city that never sleeps," Julian said. He started to sing—"New York, New York, it's a hell of a town"—and as he did, he thought about the Korean grocers in New York City, the one in his parents' neighborhood next to the pizza place on Second Avenue, how everyone ended up in their own niche, the Korean grocers and the Israeli taxi drivers and the old mustachioed Italian men selling cherry and rainbow ices in Central Park, as if the whole thing had been ordained by some invisible force. He thought about the Irish girl who served him vanilla milk shakes at the diner at three in the morning, the construction men perched high above midtown, and George, the elevator man in his parents' building, who, when he got off at midnight, took the subway back to Queens. Walking along the streets of New York, Julian liked to stare into the windows of people's apartments and contemplate the lives that went on inside, the way he liked to contemplate Mr. Kang's life, his life outside the produce store, his life with Mrs. Kang. "I have to go home and study," he said.

"It's too late to study," said Mr. Kang.

"That's the problem. I've only just started." Julian shook Mr. Kang's hand and waved at Mrs. Kang inside the store. Then he wended his way back to campus, holding a bag of Golden Delicious apples Mr. Kang had given him for free, and as he walked toward the college gates he ate an apple down to the core and then he ate another one.

So Julian and Carter were becoming friends. But Julian couldn't tell whether Carter liked him. It came down to this: Julian was a rich kid from New York City and Carter wasn't. According to Carter, Graymont was filled with rich kids from New York City, and Carter was from California, just outside San Francisco, and he had no interest in New York City. He equated Graymont with New England and New England with wealth and wealth with New York City and New York City with bullshit, and Carter hated bullshit, he'd grown up in a place utterly devoid of bullshit, in a completely bullshit-less town.

No bullshit in San Francisco? Julian had been to San Francisco, and there was plenty of bullshit there, even if it was different from the bullshit in New York. Carter was from the suburbs, besides. The suburbs were *all* bullshit.

In Carter's opinion, everything was more impressive on the West Coast. There was a great cultural divide that flowed with the waters of the Mississippi and cast its shadow across the Rocky Mountains and the Mojave Desert and accounted for the fact that in creative writing class Carter was the only one who didn't take notes and, in general, all the other students cared and he didn't. His first day at Graymont, Carter showed up in torn blue jeans and scuffed boots made of alligator leather and with several days' growth of beard on his face. That first semester, he would walk across campus with his sneakers untied, his blue jeans frayed, his shirt not fully buttoned, running his hand through his hair as if he were in a permanent state of having just woken up.

But if Carter didn't care, why, right now, was he asking Julian to read his short stories, and why was he standing in Julian's room watching him like a voyeur? Carter's stories were good—they were *really* good, Julian thought—but when Julian told Carter this, Carter just shrugged.

According to Carter, there was a sexual abandon where he had grown up that helped account for the fact that he'd lost his virginity at thirteen whereas Julian hadn't lost his until much later. "And thirteen was late," Carter said.

Often, Julian felt Carter didn't have time for him, but then Carter would show up at his dorm and they'd go play pickup basketball, and late at night they'd walk to the Store 24 or stop for cheeseburgers and onion rings at the Bison Bar and Grill and then go play poker with the guys down the hall. After Professor Chesterfield's class they would return to the dorms and Carter would ask to see Julian's stories. Carter liked Julian's stories and he liked Julian himself, and one night, drunk on beers and having smoked some pot, Carter admitted that the reason he talked so much about the West Coast was that he missed home, he missed his mother and father, and he found the East Coast daunting, the history of it, the wealth, New England especially, where he'd gone to prep school on scholarship for a couple of years before returning home and graduating from his local public school. That was why he had come to Graymont, to show himself he wasn't intimidated by New England and by people like Julian who came from New York City and had lots of money and had been to places he'd never been to, such as Europe. And although it was true he'd lost his virginity, it hadn't been at thirteen, and when Carter told Julian this he looked as if he were going to cry.

Now the empty beer cans were collecting on the floor and Carter was saying, "I love you, Wainwright, I love you, man," and he hugged Julian so hard he almost knocked the wind out of him. Really, Carter said, they were going to be writers someday. "You're a fucking sophomoric, pusillanimous writer, both of us are, the only two talents in the class." Carter was laughing, and then it seemed he was going to cry, and now, embarrassed, he said, "Hey, you *dork*!" and he kneed Julian hard in the leg.

Then they went camping together. They were in the car, and Carter was talking about virginity again. According to him, a girl could get her virginity back.

"Retrieve it?"

"In a manner of speaking."

"How?"

"Surgery," Carter said. "It's for born-agains, mostly. Doctors are reinserting the girl's hymen. You know how on a movie set a guy gets shot and there's blood all over the place but he's really just bleeding ketchup? Well, it's the same idea. A girl gets a new hymen but it's not really a new hymen. It's a fake new hymen."

"Made of ketchup?"

"Made of who knows what. It's mostly for born-agains, like I said. Some kind of Pentecostal medical ritual. Not that you'd have to be a born-again. But why else would you do it?"

"Why would anyone do it?"

"I have no idea."

At the campground where they pitched tent, Julian was learning new things about Carter, such as the fact that Carter could imitate a loon. Carter was so eerily adept at imitating a loon that when Julian closed his eyes he thought Carter was a loon. So did the loons themselves. Carter was leading them in a chorus of calling.

"That's fucking fantastic," Julian said.

Carter shrugged. "I've got perfect pitch. I was born with it, I guess."

"I can do this with my tongue," Julian said. He curled up his tongue into three segments so it resembled a cauliflower.

"That's excellent," Carter said.

"It's retarded," said Julian.

"Sure it's retarded. But it's also excellent."

For dinner, Julian and Carter grilled hot dogs, and they wrapped corn and potatoes in tin foil and tossed them into the fire and ate those, too. By the time he was done eating, Julian felt so full he could barely move and he beached himself on the hood of the car. He lay on his back, his arms spread to the sides, looking at the sky through a knot of branches. "The thing about hot dogs is, once they're inside you the pieces come back together again. It's like they're guided by some magnetic force."

"Hot dogs," Carter said, "are made entirely of cow testicles. Except for the parts made of pig testicles."

"I don't doubt it," Julian said.

Carter handed him a stick with five roasted marshmallows on it. "You know what marshmallows are made of?"

"Some other kind of testicles?"

"I suspect so," Carter said.

In the tent that night they talked about the fact that they were two guys who weren't half bad-looking, so why were they camping alone?

In Carter's opinion, it all came down to evolutionary biology. How else could you explain Henry Kissinger who, if the rumors were to be believed, was a lothario. Anyone who had seen Henry Kissinger recognized in him a familiar figure from their past, the kid from their high school class who was smarter than everyone else but who didn't have any friends. Henry Kissinger had orchestrated the Vietnam War. He'd bombed the Indochinese and lived to tell about it to the tune of twenty-five thousand dollars a speech. Never mind the starving children in Ethiopia and Cambodia. If any evidence was needed that the world was an unjust place, all one had to do was consider Henry Kissinger's sex life. Henry Kissinger was ugly and corrupt; he was a war criminal. But he was a war criminal with sex appeal.

Julian said, "Maybe girls like it when you bomb people. You know, maybe they find it erotic."

"That's part of it," Carter said. "Henry Kissinger's older than we are, right?"

Julian nodded.

"He's older than we are, he's wealthier than we are, and he's more powerful than we are, so girls like that. They're looking for someone to protect their offspring. They think they're looking for something else, but they don't have a clue. It's the same with us. We like girls who are hot."

"Certainly."

"Well, we *think* we like girls who are hot, but subconsciously, *evolutionarily,* we like girls who are fertile."

"A hot girl is a fertile girl," Julian said.

"The problem is, the fertile girls don't like us back. Evolution's got us by the balls." Carter looked up at the inside of the tent, as if hoping it would provide an answer to their predicament. "The one consolation is Henry Kissinger is having empty sex."

"You think?"

"Definitely. Guys like Henry Kissinger who were what they were in high school spend the rest of their lives compensating. Nothing makes Henry Kissinger satisfied."

"Not even the sex?"

"I'm telling you," Carter said, "the man's unhappy. He's very depressed."

But Carter himself was depressed. At least that was what Julian thought as Carter's story "Boat People" was discussed in class. Because Professor Chesterfield, instead of doing what he usually did, which was allow the class to attack the story before following with a more sustained attack of his own, forbade all discussion of Carter's story and read it aloud from start to finish, after which he said, "This story is brilliant, it's publishable."

But later, in the dorms, Carter seemed so glum it was as if he hadn't heard the praise.

"The world's greatest curmudgeon called you brilliant, Heinz, and all you can do is sulk? Do you know what I'd give to have Chesterfield say my story is publishable?"

"Then I wish it had been you."

"Oh, come on."

"Who cares how well I write? I'll still be mopping people's floors." As part of his work-study package, Carter was required to clean the dormitory bathrooms of the very students he went to class with. It didn't help—it made matters worse, in fact—that Julian refused to let Carter clean his bathroom, that he even volunteered to join Carter on his work-study days and, bucket in tow, help him mop the floors and brush the toilet bowls of the students down the hall. "What's with the noblesse oblige?" Carter said. "Who do you think you are? The welfare state?"

Then winter break came, and when Carter said he wasn't returning to California—he couldn't afford the ticket, he admitted—Julian insisted he come home with him. "At least come for Christmas dinner," Julian said. "My mother's an amazing cook."

On the drive to the city, Carter was silent, pretending to sleep, and no matter how hard Julian tried, he couldn't get Carter to talk to him.

When they arrived in New York, Julian, hoping to impress Carter, took him to the Empire State Building, where they rode the elevator to the observation deck and dropped quarters into the telescopes. "Oh, man, I can see Europe," Julian said, and Carter said, "You're facing the wrong direction." Julian fed more quarters into the telescope, and now, pointing the telescope at the building across from them, he said, "Oh, man, that girl's naked," and for an instant he had Carter fooled and Carter stepped forward to look through the telescope.

Then they were down the elevator and into a cab, which expelled them into the maw of Grand Central Station. Across from the newsstand, the shoeshine men were huddled like supplicants at the businessmen's feet. Grand Central Station looked resplendent on Christmas Eve, a young woman like a marsupial carrying her baby in a pouch, a man returning home with a baguette from Zaro's, everyone headed to where the holiday would take them. Julian so wanted to be a part of it all that he sat down in front of a shoeshine man, only to realize he was wearing sneakers. He didn't care. He would have the shiniest sneakers in all of New York. He gave the shoeshine man a five-dollar tip and he and Carter went back uptown, where late that night, on a friend's rooftop, they looked down at Manhattan shimmering beneath them. They drank a few beers and were playing cards, and Carter seemed more lighthearted than he'd been all day, for he was tossing bottle caps off the roof, shouting "Merry Christmas!" to the pedestrians seventeen stories below them.

But the next morning, Carter was sullen again.

"What's wrong, Heinz? Bee in your bonnet?"

"No."

"Freshman slump? Overcome by ennui?"

At Christmas dinner, Julian's father, in a jacket and tie, sat at one end of the table, and Julian's mother, in an evening dress, sat at the other, and Julian and Carter, on opposite sides, sat in the middle. Two candles in silver holders had been placed at the center of the table and Julian's mother had folded the napkins in such a way that they appeared to be standing and bowing to you. Julian's mother was lovely, with limpid green eyes and auburn curls, and Julian caught Carter staring at her.

Julian's father peered at Carter from behind horn-rimmed glasses. He was a robust man with a thick chest and an expression of impenetrability, and his hair, which was black with flecks of gray, looked as if you couldn't have mussed it up if you'd tried. "How are you enjoying college?" he asked Carter.

"It's all right."

"What classes are you taking?"

Carter listed them. "Anthropology, Spanish Two, 'The Biological Bases of Human Behavior,' and 'Fiction Writing.' That's how I know Julian," he said. "From fiction writing class."

"Do you like writing fiction?"

"It's okay."

"Whether he likes it or not," Julian said, "he's the star of the class."

Carter, reddening, stared down at his plate.

"What have you been writing?" Julian's mother asked.

"Just some short stories," Carter said, and it was clear that he didn't want to talk about this.

"Where did you grow up?" Julian's father asked.

"Sausalito, California," Carter said. "Just north of San Francisco."

"And your family still lives there?"

Carter nodded.

"What does your father do?"

"He's in business."

"And your mother?"

"She's a librarian."

"Tell me about Sausalito," Julian's father said, and Carter, holding his fork in the air, a piece of ham impaled on it, appeared not to know what to say. So Julian's father coaxed him along, asking what the population of Sausalito was and whether there was any local industry, and Carter, who didn't know the answer to these questions, responded with a mumble and a shrug, as if the fact that he didn't know the population of Sausalito meant he couldn't possibly live there.

Later that night, lying in his old bunk bed, Julian said, "I should have warned you about my father. He's the Grand Inquisitor."

Carter was quiet.

"Sometimes I wish he'd just cease and desist."

"I take it you don't like him," Carter said.

"Oh, he's all right," said Julian. "I love him, I suppose. He's my father, after all. Not that I see him very often." Through his bedroom window, Julian could make out the Pepsi-Cola sign on the banks of the East River and, behind it, Queens. He could hear Carter breathing in the bunk bed beneath him.

"I can't believe you grew up here," Carter said. "This apartment's amazing."

"It's all right."

"Are you kidding me? Do you have any idea how high the ceilings are? And the moldings? They look like something Michelangelo carved. If I ever have this kind of money, you can be sure I'll appreciate it."

"I appreciate it," Julian said, but Carter was silent, and Julian could tell he didn't believe him.

Across from him, he could see the coin machine his father had bought him, years ago for his birthday. It separated the coins by denomination; then you arranged them in rolls and took them to the bank. From the start, his father had tried to teach him about finance. He wanted Julian to grow up to be an investment banker, to take over the firm from him.

"Sure, I grew up wealthy," Julian said, "but my father was at work until midnight and I'd have traded it all if he just came home for dinner a few nights a week."

"Lots of money, little love?"

"I suppose. It was basically me and my mother and I liked it most of the time. I had a classic Oedipus complex: I wanted to kill my father and marry my mother. But I also had it in reverse, because in a way it was my father I missed most. I wanted us to play sports and card games, do father-and-son kinds of things, but that hardly ever happened. My father wanted me to go to Yale. He was hoping I would be him in miniature, but I wasn't going to be that, and even if I had, we wouldn't have spent any more time together."

"What about your mother?" Carter asked. "Did she want you to go to Yale, too?"

Julian shook his head. "If I'd been a girl she'd have wanted me to go to Wellesley, but as it was I'd have had to go in drag."

"Your mother's beautiful," Carter said.

"I guess." Julian had heard this before and it made him proud, but also vaguely uncomfortable. He slid out of bed, with Carter following him, and padded down the hallway.

In the kitchen, he took out a cup that said *té* on it. He opened a drawer and removed his old baby bib, which said *bébé* across the front. "My mother's pretentious," he said. "She majored in French in college, but that's no excuse. Do you know what she called the stroller she used to wheel me in? A *poussette*." He guided Carter into the guest bathroom, where the faucets said "c" for *chaud* and "f" for *froid*. He was the only child in America, he liked to say, who grew up thinking "c" stood for "hot."

But now, back in bed, he was enveloped by fonder memories, of the school lunches his mother had packed for him, the cucumber and Camembert sandwiches in their Baggies, the Granny Smith apple slices that accompanied them. He thought of the times his parents had traveled, how his mother would write him before she and his father left so he would receive a letter on the day they departed. Every afternoon when they were gone he would wait impatiently for the mail to arrive. He still had the letters his parents had sent him, the blue *par avion* envelopes with the airplane on the outside that he'd unsealed with his father's gold letter opener.

"My father had a younger brother," Julian said. "His name was Lowell, and when my father was four and Lowell was three they were playing catch in front of the house and Lowell got killed by a hit-and-run driver. My father never talks about it—I've never heard him mention his brother's name—but it changed him forever. At least that's what my mother says."

"Do you doubt it?"

"No," Julian said. "I'm sure it's true. It's just hard for me to imagine my father as a four-year-old." He leaned over the bed, and from where he was lying, all he could make out was Carter's face in the dark, the pale oval like a moon. He glanced down the hall to the row of closets, each with a mirror on the outside; if you opened the closet doors and lined the mirrors up you saw yourself replicated many times over. Sometimes even now he would arrange the mirrors that way, half expecting to see his former self reflected back at him instead of the young man he had become.

"I don't get it," Carter said. "Why, if you were an only child, did you sleep in a bunk bed?"

"I wanted a sibling," Julian explained, "and I thought if I got a bunk bed my parents might fill it." In the dark, he could see the posters on the walls, the newspaper clippings and pennants from the 1970s, the photographs from *Sports Illustrated* of Walt Frazier, Earl Monroe, Jerry Lucas, and Bill Bradley. "Heinz?"

Carter was silent.

"Have you gone to sleep?"

"I was just thinking," Carter said.

"About what?"

"How I'm staying over at your apartment and I guess we've become good friends, but you really know nothing about me."

"How can you say that?"

"Do you realize how different my parents are from yours?"

"Tell me about them," Julian said. "Your mother's a librarian?"

"For elementary school kids," Carter said dismissively.

"At least it's books. I can't remember the last time my father read a novel. My mother probably reads a couple of novels a year, but they're not the kinds of books you and I would read."

"My mother shows six-year-olds what a card catalogue is. I wouldn't romanticize it." Carter looked up. "Do you think you understand me, Wainwright?"

"I hope I do."

"Because I'm not sure you ever will."

"Try me, then."

So Carter began to speak. He had grown up in Marin County, he explained, where all his classmates were richer than he was. And money was only part of it. His friends' parents were on the faculty of U.C. Berkeley, they were board members of the San Francisco Ballet, they were partners at Morrison & Foerster and other prominent law firms. It was even worse when he got to prep school. A tenth-grader when the other students had already been there for a year, a scholarship kid, and everything about him said he was from somewhere else. "According to the school brochure, the students came from thirty-seven states and fifteen foreign countries, but everyone I met was from New England, and they looked at me the way they looked at everyone from California. As if we were tarot card readers. A bunch of B actors like Ronald Reagan."

"Is that why you left prep school?"

Carter shook his head. "In the end I adjusted. It's always been that way. I suspect I'll be adjusting for the rest of my life."

"Yet you went back home."

"That's because the more successful I became at prep school, the more I felt like I was betraying my parents. I knew I'd end up hating where I came from. I already hated where I came from, but this was worse. I was becoming haughty."

"So you returned to California?"

"And for a month my mother didn't stop crying."

"Why?"

"Because she wanted me to get the best education possible. I'll tell you what my childhood was like, Wainwright. Vocabulary quizzes at the dinner table. Summers spent at Johns Hopkins in this program for the gifted. My mother was so committed to saving money for my education that she bought me reversible clothing. She figured she was getting two items for the price of one, but I refused to wear those clothes."

"And your father?"

"He was off in his own world, attending to one of his get-rich-quick schemes."

"What does he do?"

"A little of everything." Carter described his father's jobs, and these, he said, were just the ones he could recall. He'd been in the Laundromat business, the stationery business, the restaurant business, the liquor-transporting business, the furniture business, the grain-exporting business, and the pasta-making business. Finally, when Carter was in high school, his father settled into running a marginally profitable company called So Much Hot Air that took people for rides in hot air balloons over California's Mount Tamalpais.

"So Much Hot Air," Julian said. "I like that. It's clever."

"That's the problem," Carter said. "My father sits around trying to be clever instead of actually making a living. He dreams about becoming rich. I dream about becoming rich, too, but I'm going to do something about it."

"So that's why you're at to Graymont? To become rich?"

"It's as good a reason as any." Carter looked up. "Graymont's like prep school all over again. But then, you wouldn't understand."

"Why's that?"

"Because if the kids at Graymont are rich, you, Wainwright, are the richest of all." And with that wealth, Carter said, came an indifference to wealth that only the wealthy could afford, a sense of entitlement, and a way of being in the world that was utterly at ease. He might have been good at affecting indifference, but Julian's indifference came as naturally to him as breath itself.

"So you have me figured out," Julian said. "Is that what you're telling me?"

"You think I'm wrong?"

Lying on his back, Julian watched his shadow move across the ceiling. "I'd like to meet your parents," he said. "Maybe I'll come out to visit California."

"Sure," Carter said.

But Julian knew it wouldn't happen; Carter would make sure of it. Carter would no more invite him to California than he would invite him to Neptune.

Carter's breathing had steadied, and now, when Julian looked down from his bed, he saw Carter with his eyes closed, asleep.

The first real snow of the year fell, and the students came out of the dorms for a snowball fight, freshmen and sophomores against juniors and seniors; but then the teams shifted, alliances were fluid, everyone was friend and foe. Julian pelted people and they pelted him back. Someone had taken Graymont and shaken it up; he felt as if he were living inside a snow globe.

In town, he guided his dogs to where the path had been cleared, so the snow in Northington wouldn't look like the snow in New York City, all sludge and mud and urine. Now that it had gotten colder, Mary, the Newfoundland, had gone into hibernation. She was consuming less meat, her metabolism had slowed, and Julian, standing in front of Mr. Kang's grocery, fed the leftover scraps to the other dogs, letting them lick the juice from his fingers.

Mr. Kang's store was quiet, and soon Mrs. Kang had come outside and was making a snowman in front of the grocery. She had on a down coat and red wool mittens, but her head was uncovered, her hair loose. She put features on the snowman's face: Brussels sprouts for the eyes, radishes for the ears, a carrot for the nose, and a snow pea for the mouth. Then she went inside to pack vegetables for Julian: a head of cauliflower, arugula, tomatoes on the vine, and purple kale, which he'd never tried before. He said goodbye to Mr. and Mrs. Kang and headed with his bag of vegetables slung over his shoulder back to campus.

Perhaps, he thought, he should become a vegetarian. If he stopped eating meat, he'd eat more vegetables; he'd help Mr. Kang make a living. In the cafeteria, however, they were always serving bacon, and he loved bacon. What justification was there for eating bacon that wouldn't also justify eating dog, eating Mary herself, and the thought of that sickened him. So he ate his bacon with a heavy heart, not getting as much pleasure from it as he normally did. He ate vegetables, too, more of them than usual, sitting in the cafeteria, trying to make it up to Mr. Kang, while outside the snow began to fall again in the courtyard.

Suddenly Carter had met a girl. Her name was Pilar, which was, Julian had to admit, a sexy name—an appropriate name, Carter pointed out, because it was attached to a sexy person.

Carter had met Pilar in the college dining hall. "At breakfast," he said.

Breakfast! The college boy's forgotten meal! Why, Julian wondered, was he always skipping breakfast?

"French toast," Carter said sagely. "Next to the big trough of maple syrup."

"She was standing behind you in line?"

"In front," Carter said. "Ladling."

"Breakfast people are boneheads," Julian said.

"Not Pilar."

"What are you telling me? You asked her out on a date?"

"Not a date."

"Then what?"

"We're going to hang out."

"When?"

"Tomorrow night."

"In the dorms?"

"At the bar."

"But it's not a date?"

"A date's official."

"And this is?"

"Unofficial."

"Meaning what?"

"Meaning it's casual, Wainwright. It's practically inadvertent."

The next night Carter showered, combed and mussed his hair, and prepared to leave for the Bison Bar and Grill where he would inadvertently run into Pilar and inadvertently hang out with her. In his jeans pocket he placed a roll of condoms in case, at the end of the night, they should inadvertently have sex.

"You're being presumptuous," Julian said. "You act presumptuous with a girl and you end up hoist with your own petard."

"I'm not being presumptuous," Carter said.

"So let's say you get lucky with this girl and she makes it known she wants to sleep with you. What do you do then?"

"I take out my condoms."

"Mistake."

"Why?"

"Because Pilar, who yesterday you met for the first time, just a nice girl who likes maple syrup on her French toast, your fucking *classmate*, Heinz—Pilar sees you take out your condoms and she wants to know one thing."

"What's that?"

"Do you carry those condoms with you all the time or did you bring them just for her? Which means you're in trouble."

"Why?"

"Because if you brought them just for her, she thinks you think she's easy, which means she won't be easy, even if she really is."

"So I tell her I carry them with me all the time."

"Then she thinks you're a slut."

"But I can't be a slut," Carter said. "I'm a guy."

It was a good non-date, Carter told Julian; he'd been having an excellent time hanging out with Pilar. But at the end of the night, perhaps because of his exuberance, or in a chivalric rush to pick up the tab, he removed from his jeans pocket not just his wallet but the condoms as well, the spool of them cascading onto the table.

"What did you do then?" Julian said.

"I apologized," said Carter. "It was the only thing I could think to do."

"And then?"

"I invoked you."

"*Me?*"

"I said you were my best friend and you warned me not to bring condoms. I told Pilar you were a cautious guy."

"You, on the other hand, throw caution to the wind."

Carter shrugged.

"So that was it?" Julian said. "The date's over?"

Carter shook his head. Pilar, he explained, scooped up the condoms and placed them in her pocket. Then she walked over to the jukebox and put on a song. She was standing with her back to him, and her jeans were on so tight he could see the outline of his condoms through her back pocket.

"So she's torturing you," Julian said.

"You might say that."

"Well, you deserved it, Heinz."

Carter smiled. "So I'm sitting at the table nursing my beer, and Pilar comes over and drops the condoms in front of me. 'Class is over,' she says."

"I don't get it."

Carter smiled. "She was just fucking with me, Wainwright! Having a good time!"

"And then?"

"Then we left the bar." As they walked up the hill, Carter told Julian, their arms touched. Then Pilar was resting her hand on his shoulder. Then she was taking him back to her dormitory.

Soon Carter was staying at Pilar's most nights, sleeping there with such regularity that, upon interrogation, he was forced to admit he kept an extra pair of tennis sneakers in her dorm room, and a toothbrush, too.

"A *toothbrush*?" Julian said.

"To brush my teeth with."

"I understand that."

Upon further interrogation, Carter acknowledged it wasn't just a toothbrush and a pair of tennis sneakers he kept at Pilar's, but underwear, socks, mouthwash, dental floss (since when had Carter become so preoccupied with his teeth?), a couple of novels for bedtime reading, a pair of track shoes (Pilar ran cross-country and she and Carter had started to run together), nail clippers, a few T-shirts, and a box of Q-tips.

Worst of all, Carter and Pilar had bought a toaster oven together and they could be found late at night heating kippers in it.

"So what are you telling me?" Julian said. "You got his-and-hers toaster ovens?"

"Not his-and-hers. Just one."

Then the three of them went out together, and Julian understood why Carter was spending so much time with Pilar. Pilar wasn't just a pretty girl who liked maple syrup on her French toast; she could talk about literature, for now she was engaging Carter and Julian in a discussion of Joseph Conrad.

Then Carter and Pilar were talking about Julian, almost, it seemed, as if he weren't there. "Julian thinks words are erotic," Carter said.

"Well, they are," Pilar said. "At least they can be."

Emboldened, Julian explained to Pilar that there were certain words he liked. "Sullied," for instance. And "jejune."

" 'Jejune' is a good one," Pilar said.

"Or 'pelt,' " Julian said. He liked "pelt" as both a noun and a verb.

"Julian likes 'sexual congress,' " Carter said.

Julian shrugged. He couldn't remember having told Carter this, but it was true; he liked "sexual congress."

Soon there came across the faces of Carter and Pilar incipient looks of distraction. There were repeated glances at watches. At eleven o'clock, there commenced between them an astonishing assortment of signals and tics, a kind of lovers' Morse code. At eleven-fifteen, the yawning began.

"Time to rock 'n' roll," Carter said.

"You bet," said Pilar.

Was the sex really that good? Or was this just what happened when you found a girlfriend? You grew progressively more sleepy?

It was worse than that, Julian discovered. Carter and Pilar wanted to get back to the dorms so they could watch *Nightline*.

"Ted Koppel?" Julian said to Carter the next day. "How old are you, Heinz?"

"Nineteen."

"You're nineteen years old and you've got your Ted Koppel and your his-and-hers toaster ovens. When did you become so domestic?"

"What's wrong with domestic?"

Julian couldn't answer him. He was domestic, too, if that meant waking up late and eating his meals in the dining hall, hanging out in the dorms watching sports on TV, playing poker with the guys in the room next door. He was jealous, that was the problem—jealous of Carter for having met Pilar, and jealous of Pilar, who now spent more time with Carter than Julian himself did.

Julian and Carter had a game. They would sit with the freshman face-book and argue over who knew more of their classmates. Then Carter would decide he hated his classmates, at which point Julian realized he hated them, too. The facebook was dog-eared, especially page 47, where, in the upper right-hand corner, was a photograph of Mia Mendelsohn.

Mia from Montreal, Julian called her.

"She's dreamy," he said.

"She would appear to be."

"What do you mean?"

"You can never be sure until you actually see her."

In her photograph, Mia from Montreal had dark curly hair, and she wore round wire-rimmed glasses that gave her a look of contemplation. On her face there appeared the beginnings of a smile, and Julian thought he could make out a single dimple in her left cheek. "She's for me," he said.

Then he saw her in person, at a party. The band was playing a song by the Police, but Mia from Montreal wasn't dancing to the Police. She appeared to be dancing the rumba.

"I spoke to her," Carter said the following week. "Mia from Montreal!"

"You're kidding me."

"Not only that, I walked her across campus."

"Tell me she was going your way."

Carter admitted it: she was going his way.

"She's not your typical Canadian," Carter said.

And what, Julian wanted to know, was your typical Canadian? Carter had a theory about everything, and almost invariably that theory was false.

"It's the well-known phenomenon," Carter said, "of the inferiority complex masquerading as the superiority complex. The obsessive focus on Canada? National health insurance, bilingualism, the Québécois?"

"That's what you talked about?" Julian said. "The Québécois?"

"Actually, we didn't even mention Canada."

Now Julian was confused.

"Wainwright," Carter said, "do you like ankle bracelets?"

"Does she wear one?"

Carter nodded.

"Then I like them."

"What about stockings?"

"Hate 'em."

"She does, too."

Where, Julian wondered, had they walked? To a department store?

Carter said, "She's got a nice figure, but she doesn't flaunt it. It's almost like she's a girl who doesn't have sex."

"A prude?"

"More like a girl who's saving herself."

"For what?"

"That special someone."

"I doubt it."

"Exactly. She's not really saving herself. She only seems like she is."

"But why?"

"Because she's sophisticated. Mia from Montreal doesn't call attention to her body. She's hot by not being hot. That's how the heat gets generated."

Julian saw her again, this time in the laundry room. He hoped she didn't notice that next to him, clearly in his possession, was a package of fabric softener. He had a book of stories by Ernest Hemingway, and he placed the book on top of the fabric softener, to balance the picture out.

Mia from Montreal sorted her clothes at her feet. There was a colors pile and a whites pile, and Julian thrust his face into his book so she wouldn't think he was staring at her laundry.

Periodically, though, he glanced at Mia herself, who was even more beautiful than he remembered. She was wearing blue jeans and a gray V-neck T-shirt, and her hair was up in a bun.

"I think you know my friend Carter," he said.

Mia nodded. "Carter's great."

"The very best," Julian said. Then, wanting to make sure Mia didn't take this literally—he, Julian, after all, was the *very* best—he mentioned Carter's girlfriend, Pilar.

A black bra strap stuck out from under Mia's T-shirt, and she fingered it idly, then brushed a wisp of hair from in front of her face.

"I saw you at this party," Julian said. "You were dancing the rumba."

Mia laughed. "I used to dance in high school."

"The rumba?"

"Sure."

"Are you Cuban?"

"Jewish."

"You can't be both?"

"I guess you can." Mia peered through the window at her rotating clothes, giving the washer a baleful look as if her laundry disappointed her. "I was even religious briefly."

"Really?"

"An Orthodox Jew, if you can imagine that." Mia grabbed hold of a T-shirt and held it up to him, showing him the name tape sewn into the collar. "There I am," she said. "Mia Mendelsohn."

"Are you related to Felix Mendelssohn?" Julian asked.

Mia laughed. "I can't even keep a tune. In Hebrew school, I had to sing in the Passover pageant and the teacher told me just to mouth the words."

"The Passover pageant?"

"It's like the Christmas pageant, but with the Ten Plagues. I was a locust."

"A singing locust," Julian said.

"A lip-synching locust," said Mia. She had forgotten almost all her Hebrew, she told Julian. When she was small, her mother used to clean out her ears with a washcloth and tell her what she found inside. French toast. Marmalade. Cauliflower. Roast beef. That was where her Hebrew was, beneath the archaeological layers of her. "In Hebrew my name means 'Who is God?' So I guess that makes me a born agnostic."

"You know what my name means in Welsh?"

"What?"

" 'He travels heavily amongst the goats.' "

"It does not!"

"I come from a family of Welsh goat herders."

"You do?"

"If you go back far enough." Julian's great-grandfather had been born in Wales, but Julian himself had never been to Wales and his experience with goats was limited to a visit to the Bronx Children's Zoo, where he'd grabbed the billygoat's leg and refused to release it. "My parents were born here. So were my grandparents. My father's just a regular American money launderer."

"Your father's a criminal?"

"Not technically." In high school, Julian had had a classmate whose father was rumored to be an actual gangster. Now, that was the kind of criminal father he would have liked to have. "My father and I argue all the time."

"About what?"

"Ronald Reagan, the Equal Rights Amendment, that sort of thing. My father says the ERA would have led to coed bathrooms."

"Would it have?"

"I'm not sure." He paused. "Do *you* think the ERA would have led to coed bathrooms?"

"I don't know."

"Me, either." Now he felt foolish. "I mean, who cares about coed bathrooms?"

"Not me."

"My father's insane," he said.

"Everyone is," said Mia. And now, as they stared at the laundry in the dryer, as they watched their clothes flip over themselves, they listed what was insane at Graymont, starting with the laundry itself, the dearth of washers and dryers and the number of quarters you needed to do the wash, and soon they had alighted on the cafeteria food, the Sloppy Joes served every Sunday night in Commons, the tortuous lines for the salad bar. Then they moved on to the library and the gym, the reserve stacks at McMillan, where you weren't admitted, so you had to wait for the librarian to get your book ("I mean, it's a library," Julian said. "Don't they understand the meaning of 'browse'?"), the wait for the Nautilus machines and the byzantine process to sign up for them, and now, circuitously but inexorably, they had wound their way back to the laundry: did it really have to be so laborious?

Suddenly, though, Mia had switched course. She was talking about the ways good fortune shone on them, how they were at Graymont, a fine college, and their parents were paying for their education. There were people starving in Ethiopia, or holed up in the Nicaraguan hills. What were the odds of their being alive in the first place, because when her parents got together, in that act of love, what were the chances she'd be the result of that? "Oh, God," she said, "is that not the most banal thing you've ever heard? That things could have been different?"

"Well, they could have been."

"Do you think it's the laundry?"

"What?"

"You and me here in the basement and there's no air? Maybe it does something to your brain cells."

"Could be."

"Still, it's important to remember how big the world is. There are cities in China with over a million people that you and I haven't even heard of."

"I was never good at geography," Julian admitted.

"Even if you were." Mia removed her clothes from the dryer. She was standing next to Julian now, folding her T-shirts and jeans. She pointed at his book. "Tell me about Hemingway."

"You haven't read him?"

"I have."

So Julian told her about the metaphor of the tip of the iceberg. According to Hemingway, the tip of the iceberg implied the whole iceberg; what you left out was as important as what you left in. "Less is more," he said.

"Is it?" Mia was sitting on the washer, smiling at him—a flirtatious smile, he thought, or perhaps he was just imagining it. Maybe she was right about the air in the laundry room; maybe it did something to your brain cells.

Mia drove so fast it was astonishing she'd made it to college; Julian couldn't believe she was still alive. *Drive faster,* he thought, even as he held on to the plastic handle above his seat.

Mia said, "You know how they tell you to accelerate into turns? Well, I just accelerate into everything."

They were driving into Boston, where Mia's grandparents had lived when they were alive. Mia loved Boston, she told Julian, though mostly she loved it because she'd loved it as a girl; she saw the city through a child's eyes.

They drove through old mining villages, past junkyards and parking lots. A single tube sock clung to the limb of a tree; a woman's pink camisole dangled from a clothesline. In the middle of a field stood an abandoned school bus; graffitied on the exterior was STANLEY FUCKED DONNA GOOD. Soon came the signs of encroaching industry, trucks rumbling past them, the Worcester skyline ahead.

"So this is what I do," Mia said. "I drive."

"Where to?"

"Anywhere. I came to college to get away from things, and now that I'm here I'm getting away some more." She looked up at Julian. "And what do you do?"

"I drive with you."

All around Boston, everywhere they walked, it seemed to Julian they were surrounded by park rangers, some giving tours, some just walking the streets the way he and Mia were. Mia walked the way she drove: fast. He had trouble keeping up with her.

They stopped at King's Chapel Burying Ground, where John Davenport and John Winthrop were buried. At the Granary, where they went next, you could see the tombstones through the metal gratings. John Hancock was buried there, as were Paul Revere, Samuel Adams, and Benjamin Franklin's parents and siblings.

"Are you taking me on a tour of colonial cemeteries?"

"Why not?" Mia said. She was reading a plaque. "Mother Goose is buried here."

"You mean she's real?" Julian had thought Mother Goose was a cartoon character.

"She was a writer," Mia said sunnily, "just like you."

In the North End, on the corner of Hanover and Parmenter Streets, stood a cluster of wooden arrows: "Roma." "Milano." "Venezia." "Capri." "Genova." Julian and Mia stopped into a specialty store where Italian women sliced ham for the customers and filled jars with Sicilian olives.

Then they went back across town, to the Public Gardens, where *Make Way for Ducklings* was set. A row of bronze ducks lined the walkway. There was a pond in the middle of the gardens, and a bridge above it where two boys in Puma sweatshirts were playing tag. A Chocolate Labrador trotted across the bridge, wearing a red bandanna around its neck. Trees grew out of an island at the center of the pond, and on the periphery stood a statue of George Washington on a horse. A man was reading *Make Way for Ducklings* to his daughter.

"Life imitates art," Mia said.

It was lunchtime, so they went across the street to pick up sandwiches, turkey for Julian, roast beef for Mia, and between bites Julian explained that he'd been reading about supertasters. It was an actual scientific category, he said. Supertasters were different from other people. Their tongues were denser; they had more taste buds. "Say you like Brussels sprouts," he said.

"I do."

"And I don't. But when we eat Brussels sprouts, are we eating the same thing and just responding differently, or are our taste buds actually registering something different?"

"Is that a philosophical question?"

"I think so."

But before she could answer him, he had moved from philosophy to English usage. He was listing the idioms he used to get wrong. He'd said "no holes barred" instead of "no holds barred" and "deep-

43

seeded" instead of "deep-seated." "It's 'home in on,' " he said, "not 'hone in on.' Like a homing pigeon." Why, he wanted to know, was it "the whole nine yards" and not "the whole ten yards"? It took ten yards to get a first down. Or "have your cake and eat it, too." It was no trick, he said, to have your cake and eat it. The real trick was in reverse, to eat your cake and still have it. That was what the idiom should have been: "to eat your cake and have it, too."

"Or 'long in the tooth,' " Mia said. "What does that mean?"

"Old."

"But why? Do our teeth get longer as we age? Are we destined to become beavers?"

They walked through Beacon Hill, Mia's grandparents' old neighborhood; Mia was taking him to see their house. Her grandparents were on her mind, she said; they always were when she came to Boston.

"There are lots of antique stores here," he said.

"This neighborhood used to be old money," Mia explained. "Now it's porcelain frogs and wooden Dachshunds."

"Were your grandparents old money?"

She shook her head. "They weren't new money, either. But they got by."

They passed another antique store, and a pub, a pizza place, a post office, a leather shop, and now, off Charles Street, on Pinckney, on Revere, they were winding their way through the neighborhood, along the silent residential streets. A light went on in a living room, then flickered off. A Jaguar pulled out of a driveway, the sound of its engine hushed, guttural, and low. In a garden out back, two girls in slippers were walking a rabbit on a leash. The mansions stood sentinel on the hill, winking at them in the diminishing sunlight.

"There it is," she said.

"What?"

"My grandparents' house."

"Oh."

"Anticlimax?"

"No."

"It's nothing special. It's a house. It's got a roof and floors, some plumbing."

"It looks nice," he said, but then he felt bad because all he could see were a few shuttered windows and he didn't wish to sound insincere.

"An old woman lives there now," Mia said. "You know what I think? They should make a law that after a person dies their house has to remain empty for a while. Let it lie fallow. Come," she said, "I'm being macabre." She took him by the sleeve and they walked off.

They strolled on Newbury Street and Boylston and Newbury again, past Newbury Comics and the department stores and the Boston Public Library, heading west toward Kenmore Square and Fenway Park and, beyond that, Boston University. Commonwealth Avenue was like a European boulevard, with high-domed buildings and wide promenades. As they walked along it, rain started to fall, lightly at first but then harder. They were getting poured on now. They had neither the inclination nor the will to seek cover; they ran and ran, past Gloucester and Hereford, kicking up puddles as they went, their sneakers sloppy and rain-drenched, the canvas sticking to their socks. They crossed Massachusetts Avenue and now, on the corner, they bent over like sprinters catching their breath.

Mia's hair was matted to her forehead; it stuck in clumps against her neck. A drop of rain rolled down her chin, and Julian brushed it off with the sleeve of his windbreaker.

They drove home soaked, as if someone had thrown them fully clothed into Boston Harbor. When they stopped at the turnpike to get their ticket, Mia twisted the water from her hair. As she drove on, Julian fell asleep to the rhythm of the car, his nose, his whole face, pressed against the window.

"Let's go out to dinner," Mia said. She told him she knew of a good place to eat, elegant but not too elegant; she hated restaurants where the waiter pulled out your seat for you. Julian agreed; fancy restaurants made him uncomfortable.

They ordered a bottle of wine and quickly dispatched it. Julian felt a warming come across his face. He liked wine, though he knew nothing about it. Textures and aromas, nutty wines, fruity wines, which wines should be drunk with which foods: all this meant nothing to him. He didn't want to know about wine; he just wanted to drink it. He had an image of himself standing barefoot in some vineyard where his only job was to trample the grapes. His fingers and toes were purple—his whole body was—and Mia was with him; she was there to trample, too. "Tell me something about you."

She laughed. "Are we getting to know each other?" She took a sip of her wine, and when she put down her glass the imprint of her lips was on the rim, an exact mold of her mouth. "I like watching you," she said.

"Tell me something else."

"I want to kiss you." She rested her hands next to her plate. Her forearms were tawny, bare, and slender, but also with a firmness to them, a heft of sinew. A single white candle sat between them, the wax dripping to the table.

"Do you always kiss your dates?"

"If I want to," she said. "If they want to kiss me back."

He leaned across the table and so did she, their bodies hovering above their pasta bowls and the tiny saucer of olive oil with red pepper flakes swimming in it.

"You're a very handsome man."

He laughed.

"Why? No one's ever called you handsome before?"

"No one's ever called me a man." Her fingers were touching his, lightly, lightly, and his fingers were touching hers back.

At the dorms, Julian asked his roommate to vacate for the night. "I need privacy," he said.

"But I live here."

"Technically."

"Not technically. In fact."

"Then think of it as one of my peremptories." It was like jury duty,

46

he explained. The lawyers could dismiss a certain number of jurors without giving any reason. He ushered his roommate out the door.

Was it possible for a person to exist without sleep? According to *The Guinness Book of World Records,* the longest anyone had gone without sleep was eleven days. Laboratory mice died when deprived of sleep, yet when an autopsy was performed the cause of death could not be determined. Apparently the mice had died from lack of sleep, but you couldn't see it clinically.

Their first week together, Julian and Mia stopped sleeping. They were coasting on adrenaline, Mia said.

"On libido," said Julian.

Banished from his room that first night, Julian's roommate hadn't come back the second or the third. Mia felt bad for Julian's roommate, but not so bad, she told Julian, as to want him to return. She and Julian were alone, and they made love where they wanted to, in Julian's bedroom, in the common room; they even made love on Julian's roommate's beanbag chair. To be nineteen and making love wherever you wished: this, Julian thought, was how a person should live. Mia was sprawled naked next to him, peaceful, recumbent on the beanbag chair, her eyes half closed, her hair touching his; the vinyl felt cool along his neck. The dorm was quiet, and above them he could hear a fly buzzing against a bare lightbulb. There was a candle on the shelf, and he got up and lit it. He lay next to Mia in the hollow imprint his body had left. She started to drift off.

"You can't fall sleep," he said. "It's against the rules."

"I'm cold," she murmured. She took a blanket and spread it over them. She turned on the TV, where a kung fu movie was playing, and they watched it idly for a few minutes, then muted the sound and read to each other from books they chose randomly off the bookshelves. Julian read to Mia from *The Adventures of Huckleberry Finn,* and Mia read to Julian from Freud's *Totem and Taboo* and from *Thirteen Days* by Robert Kennedy. They even took turns reading about photosynthesis and the Krebs cycle from Julian's roommate's biology textbook.

Mia kissed Julian. She kissed his toes, his knees, his elbows. She kissed the tiny tuft of hair above his butt. It was four-thirty in the morning and they hadn't slept the night before. You got to the point when you were so tired you couldn't make a decision. You couldn't stay awake and you couldn't go to sleep. Before long, you were starting to hallucinate.

Finally they fell asleep, and when they awoke the next morning Julian said, "Thomas Jefferson was in my dream last night. He was my student. I was Thomas Jefferson's professor."

Mia looked at him dubiously.

"Jefferson came in to complain about his grade. I'd given him a B-plus on the Declaration of Independence."

"A B-plus!"

"That's exactly what Julian said. He wanted at least an A-minus."

"Thomas Jefferson!" Mia said. "You have very arrogant dreams." She placed her foot behind Julian and pushed him over her leg so he tumbled backward to the floor. As he fell, his legs kicked up and his testicles did, too. "Be careful," she said. "I was on the wrestling team in high school."

"You were?"

"Field hockey," she said. "Close enough."

"Come," he said. "Let's shower."

She stepped into the stall and raised her face to the water, holding her hair in a fist behind her head. He took her by the shoulders and drew her close to him, feeling the press of her nose against his face.

Afterward, in class, he missed her already and he'd only just seen her. When he saw her again she said she'd missed him, too. She loved everything about him, she said: the tiny dimple on his right elbow, the way his hair was so straight coming down over his forehead, all of it dark brown, almost black except for a little patch of blond above the left ear. "I'm one-two-hundredth albino," he told her. She loved his toenails, she said, and the way in his sleep he wrapped her hair around his fingers. That was how she liked waking up in the morning, with her hair twirled taut around him.

·   ·   ·

48

It went on like this, the weather getting warmer and the afternoons extending into what had been evening, the oak trees in full bloom above the dormitories, casting their shadows across Christ Church. The clocks had been moved forward (*Spring forward,* Julian thought, *fall back*), which pleased him, an extra hour of daylight; he'd have been happy to have Daylight Saving Time all year.

He went with Mia everywhere, even to her classes. He sat in on her sociology seminar and she joined him for his history survey, "Europe from the Inquisition to World War I." They ate their meals together, and late at night they picked up chili cheese dogs and chili cheese fries from the grill downstairs and fed quarters into the pinball machines and video games, which they pressed up against, hoping to get a little extra English, jabbing their fingers against buttons and joysticks.

Mia gave him a key to her room, and she would find him flipping through her books, trying to discover what she liked to read. "Be careful," she said. "Someone else might think you're a voyeur."

"But you're not someone else. You're you."

One time, she found him in her closet, rustling around. He held up a pair of shoes and clapped them against each other.

"Are you becoming an archaeologist?"

"*Geologist,*" he said, showing her a pebble he'd extracted from her shoe.

She had loved him from the start, she said, when after their first night together he met her on the steps of McMillan Library with a Swiss cheese–and–avocado sandwich he'd made for her. How had he known she liked avocado? "Why wouldn't you?" he said. But had he known that as a girl she had eaten as many avocados as she could in order to plant the pits? She would sing to her avocado plants because they were supposed to grow better that way, but she had such a terrible voice, maybe that was why they hadn't grown. Had he known that, the singing part?

Yes, he said, he did.

"How?"

"I intuited it."

"You're perfect," she said. She loved the taper of his calves, and the

feel of his hair, and the fact that he called his dorm room the Wainwright Hotel and left Peppermint Patties on her pillow.

Julian took Mia to meet Mr. Kang, who was standing where he always
was, outside the grocery, like a maître d'.

Mr. Kang shook Mia's hand, then went to get his wife. Although
Julian hadn't said anything, Mr. Kang seemed to understand who Mia
was, and Mrs. Kang seemed to understand as well.

"My wife will get vegetables," Mr. Kang said, and Mrs. Kang ran
off, with Mr. Kang close behind her. Their backs were to them, and all
Julian could see was the movement of their hands from the produce
bins and back again; it looked as if they were doing exercises.

"They must like you," Julian said. "They only give free vegetables
to people they like."

"I think it's *you* they like."

"If you're lucky," he said, "they might throw in some fruit."

They walked slowly up the hill carrying their shopping bags, and
when they turned around they saw Mr. and Mrs. Kang waving at the
bottom of the hill, and with their free hands they waved back.

In writing class, Professor Chesterfield said, "What's with Wainwright? He appears to be in la-la land."

"Wainwright's in love," Carter said.

Professor Chesterfield began to clap. Slowly, singularly, he was
applauding Julian. "So, Wainwright, is it true?"

Julian shrugged.

"I've been in love," Professor Chesterfield said.

"You have?" said Rufus.

"There's no sadder sight in the world," Professor Chesterfield said,
"than a young man who's fallen in love."

Carter seemed to agree, for afterward in the dorms he was calling
Julian Loverboy, saying, "Well, look who's walking down the hall, Mr.
Wash My Clothes at Every Opportunity." It was as if Carter thought

Julian had contrived to meet Mia in the laundry room, as if he believed cleaning your clothes were compulsive and he'd caught Julian at it.

They would stay up late, Julian, Mia, Carter, and Pilar, eating chips and burgers and playing Hearts, a game Carter loved, and never more so than when he played with Julian and Mia, because he always won.

"Carter goes for the throat," Pilar said. "You'd think he'd die if he didn't win."

"You mean I wouldn't?" Carter laughed and Pilar did, too, and you could tell Pilar liked this about Carter, his ferocity, and the fact that he won.

Soon they switched to poker, which Carter usually won at as well, though Pilar won a couple of games herself. She jumped up and did a victory dance, and she and Carter ran a lap around the lounge, after which Carter did hurdles over the couch. Then, hand in hand, they departed, humming a tune as they did so.

Soon Julian and Mia left, too, to see horror movies in Pickens Hall—*Earthquake, The Towering Inferno, Carrie, The Exorcist*—which now that finals were approaching were the only movies showing on campus.

"It's a school of sadists," Mia said. "Can't they show a romantic comedy?"

As the movies played, she and Julian fell asleep in the quiet of the auditorium while beyond the walls their classmates were falling asleep, too, in the library, on the sectional couches. The voices on the screen dissipated, incorporating themselves into Julian's and Mia's dreams, and soon another movie had started and they began the process all over again, falling asleep with their fists in the popcorn, their fingers trailing through the butter.

They returned to Julian's dorm and fell asleep for real, and in the morning when he awoke Julian found Mia where he'd left her, sprawled on her stomach, looking beautiful still, the edge of his pillow tucked inside her mouth.

At Graymont, the longer you'd been at the college the farther away from campus you lived, for housing was laid out in clusters, with the freshmen at the epicenter, in the Commons, and the sophomores in a circle surrounding them, and the juniors set even farther back, most of them in off-campus housing. It was like the rings around Saturn, Julian thought, until, when you were a senior, it was as if you weren't in orbit any longer and you lived far enough away from school that you made no pretense of going to class.

It was the fall of their senior year and he was living with Mia; in the room next door lived Carter and Pilar. It was a huge house, nominally a co-op, in that there was a shopping rotation and monthly meetings, but the four of them weren't interested in living cooperatively and had joined because the bedrooms were enormous and out back was a landscaped garden with a hot tub raised in the middle of it. They would stay in the hot tub so long they'd nearly fall asleep, and one time Pilar did in fact fall asleep, listing to the side like a canoe before keeling over and toppling in, only to be rescued, coughing, by Carter.

It was a temperate October night and they were lounging in the tub, the four of them illuminated by lanterns strung from the garden walls. Mia lay on her back in the water, warming herself in an imaginary sun. It was the proper way, she claimed, to say goodbye to college, naked, warm, as if the water itself might transport her to wherever life after college led. "Soon we'll graduate, and I imagine we'll have to wear clothes to work. They have dress codes out there, don't they?"

"It will be a concession," Julian agreed, "but if I have to wear clothes to get out of this place, so be it." He wanted to hurl himself into the world, where there were no papers or exams, no professors lecturing him.

"The problem with the real world," Carter said, "is you have to have a boss." Carter was determined never to have a boss, but the more resolute he became the less it seemed possible, and thinking about this made him morose and, to his surprise, nostalgic for college. Though at the same time, he said, he was sick of school. He had always been partial to academic shortcuts, but now that he was a senior he was taking evasion to new extremes. He had started to write what he called beyond-the-scope-of-this-paper papers, in which he would begin by listing all the things he wasn't going to write about. He had already handed in a paper that spent the first seven out of fifteen pages outlining the issues he wouldn't address, and his goal was to visit on some unsuspecting professor a paper composed entirely of things he wouldn't address and to receive an A for not having addressed them. "I'm taking pity on my professors," Carter said. "They probably get bored with the usual stuff." In sociology class, one of Carter's classmates had accidentally left his paper lying on his desk, and Carter, seeing that the paper began with the words "Throughout history," had affixed in the margin: "Throughout history I've been reading papers like this one."

Now, lying in the hot tub, Carter said, "Let's take a drive."

"Where to?" said Julian.

"You name it."

Pilar said, "The world's our oyster, Carter?"

"I don't know about the world," Carter said, "but we can start with western Massachusetts."

But the four of them remained floating in the water while beyond the garden walls sat Julian's green Saab, gleaming in the coop's floodlights. Over the summer, he and Mia had driven the Saab cross-country, up into the Badlands, then west through Wyoming, Montana, and Idaho, before turning south and heading back. They had intended to buy a used van and drive it until it wouldn't go any longer, but once Julian's parents saw the van in question, they handed him the keys to their car. Still, the understanding had been that Julian would return the car at the end of the summer. So he was startled, and delighted, when Labor Day came and it was simply assumed he'd take the Saab up to school. "Squatters' rights," he told Mia.

Now, up on campus, Julian had made clear that Carter and Pilar could drive the car as well, and other friends, too, were allowed to borrow it if they needed to run an errand. Julian was rich but he was generous, and he, Mia, Carter, and Pilar could be seen caravaning to campus—"Here comes the Wainwrightmobile!" Carter would call out—depositing themselves in a parking lot near class.

Other times Carter would take his motorized scooter (he'd been home over the summer, working in Oakland, and the scooter had been his reward to himself) and Pilar would hop on and he'd drive her to campus.

Pilar was more cautious than Carter, and she was always telling him to drive carefully, which made him only more headlong. "Don't worry," he told her. "I've got a hard head."

"A dense one!" she yelled into his ear, holding on to him as they zipped along the roads, past Main Street and Union and West University.

Later, with the four of them reposing in the hot tub, passing around a hollowed-out apple Carter had fashioned into a bong, Pilar said, "A person can get to class without doing wheelies, don't you think?"

Julian shrugged beneath the water. "Carter has a reputation to live up to."

"That's right," Carter said. "Evel Knievel goes to anthropology class."

Pilar made a show of being exasperated. She was tall and thin, with eyes the green of a soldier's uniform and a fine, delicate nose that seemed always to be pointing somewhere. Her features were constantly moving, she had a high-alert face, and she was beautiful, Julian thought; they all did.

"Eventually, Carter's going to crash that thing and I'll end up as some poor college-girl widow. A twenty-one-year-old Jackie O."

Carter shook his head. "What's going to happen is we'll both be dead and the school will have to mourn us together."

"That's Carter's dream," Julian said. "To have the college flag at half-mast and him in heaven spitting down on everyone."

Carter said, "It would almost be worth dying just for that."

"He does have a death wish," Pilar said.

But later, alone with Julian in their bedroom, Mia said Pilar protested too much. Pilar liked having a boyfriend who drove a scooter, even liked the fact that he drove it helmetless and insisted that she ride helmetless, too. "Carter has this theory," Mia said, "that the safer the world gets the more we need to find new risks. It's like we have this allotment, and one way or another we're going to spend it." She and Julian were reading in bed, idly glancing up from their books. "The thing about Pilar is, you know how she's always deferring to Carter, giving him the spotlight? Well, secretly she has a plan for him."

Julian agreed. Carter had started to dress differently, with fewer holes in his blue jeans, less alligator leather, and now that he'd moved in with Pilar he seemed like a striver, as if suddenly he thought all this could be his.

"When we go out to dinner," Mia said, "have you noticed how Pilar watches him hold his fork? She's always saying things like, 'Perhaps you'd like to try the mallard.'"

Pilar had grown up in Washington, D.C., and in Greenwich, Connecticut, where everyone wore white on the tennis court and no one wore it after Labor Day, and she had been to debutante balls even if she hadn't been a debutante herself. Mia had assumed Pilar would end up in law school—both her parents were attorneys—so when she told Julian that Pilar had a plan for Carter, what she meant, she said now, was that Pilar would get Carter to go to law school, too.

"I doubt it," Julian said. "Everyone goes to law school. That alone would make Carter not do it."

But soon October became November, and as everyone prepared to return home for Thanksgiving, the senior class was overcome by anxiety. The career counseling office extended its hours, so that when Julian walked past at nine at night he would see some classmate huddled over a book of résumés, anxiously contemplating his future. Julian was mildly anxious himself, but Carter, it was obvious, was more so. He kept a calendar on the wall above his bed and he had begun to use that calendar as a countdown to liftoff.

That night, the four of them were eating dinner at Bamonte's, where the first Wednesday of every month was Wig Night: everyone who showed up wearing a wig got to eat at half price. Carter, seeing the thatch of dark curls pasted to Julian's head, said, "Look at Wainwright, he's wearing a poodle." Carter's own wig was bright orange, and he was also wearing oversized clown shoes, which he waved about like flippers.

"I'm wearing lynx," Mia said. "Or is it otter?"

"Watch out for PETA," Julian said.

Mia fingered the ropy tendrils. "Actually, it's pure synthetic. Woolworth's special, for nine-ninety-nine."

Pilar wore a blond wig, and she sat sipping her Coke, saying that if another person asked whether she was Marilyn Monroe, she would have a fit. "It's not like there aren't other blondes out there."

The waiter gave them the once-over. He was wearing a wig himself, and the effect was of a sandy-haired Rastafarian.

They chewed silently while Bamonte's pumped out songs from the jukebox and everyone beneath their wigs had started to sweat. Carter looked pensively at his watch as if he were checking not just the time but the number of days left in college. "All right," he said, "fess up. What are you guys doing when you graduate?"

Although the subject preoccupied them, they'd avoided talking about it until now. Even alone, the two couples had been leery of bringing it up. Were they making plans together or apart?

"I've thought about architecture school," Mia admitted. "Or anthropology."

"Mia's made it through the A's," Pilar said.

Mia laughed. "Sometimes I think I could do almost anything."

"What I want to do is nothing," said Carter.

Julian said, "I plan to write."

"That's one way of doing nothing," Carter said.

Mia's father wanted her to get a Ph.D.—"He thinks without one you're not really educated"—and Pilar acknowledged she was considering law school. Mia mentioned the Peace Corps, and Carter said, "What about Wainwright?"

"Julian can come along. We can do the Peace Corps together."

Carter laughed. "Have you ever been camping with Julian? He brings an inflatable mattress." Carter removed from his bookbag a stack of papers. "Look what I stole from Career Counseling." It was the Myers Briggs personality test. You answered a series of questions, and depending on your answers you were placed into one of sixteen types, which helped you choose a career.

"You actually took one of those tests?" Julian said.

"They're based on Carl Jung's typologies," said Carter. "You've read Jung, haven't you?"

Now, as if to prove what he thought of career counseling, Carter shredded a page of the Myers Briggs test, leaving a heap of confetti on his pasta plate. But then Mia was saying, "Come on, Carter, try it out on us." So, over tiramisu and cannolis, Carter read from the remaining pages. " 'Yes or no. You find it difficult to express your feelings.' . . . 'You often think about humankind and its destiny.' . . . 'You believe the best decision is one that can be easily changed.' . . . 'You find it difficult to speak loudly.' . . . 'You prefer to isolate yourself from outside noises.' . . . 'You feel involved when watching TV soaps.' . . . 'You value justice more highly than mercy.' . . . 'You are almost never late for your appointments.' . . . 'Your desk, workbench, etc., is usually neat and orderly.' . . ."

After every question their voices rang out, and Carter, pen in hand, made a show of writing down what they said, though they all knew he wasn't keeping track.

Soon the check came, and Carter signed the credit card slip "C. Myers Briggs."

Now, back at the co-op, Julian exclaimed, "God bless Carl Jung!" and they all deposited themselves into the hot tub, the four of them naked except for their wigs.

"May we never graduate!" Pilar said and, one by one, Carter released the remaining pages of the test. The group of them watched the paper float away, the ink melting in the bubbles and the heat, and they closed their eyes and passed around a beer and declared their intentions not to think about the future.

But later that night, Julian saw Carter sitting alone in the garden.

"Want to take a ride?" Carter said, offering Julian a seat in his own car.

They drove through town and out of Northington, the car gliding over the road. "Are you kidnapping me?"

"We keep going straight," Carter said, "and we hit California." Rain had begun to fall, and Carter turned on the windshield wipers. There was a series of red lights, and then the traffic cleared and what was left before them was farmland, cows and horses dappled in the moonlight.

"What's going to happen when we graduate?" Carter said. "I can't believe you don't take this seriously."

"Heinz, you're not going to turn into a pumpkin."

To the sides of the road stood bushes and a few evergreens; most of the trees had divested themselves of leaves, and the bare branches rose and fell in the wind, like arms being raised above someone's head.

"So you want to write fiction," Carter said. "Is that what you're telling me?"

"You know I do."

"That's not really an option for me."

"Of course it is."

Carter looked over at him. "So you go sit in a café in Paris? Or Kyoto, or Prague, or wherever they're doing it now?"

"That's not what I had in mind."

"Writing is for rich people."

"Investment banking is for rich people. Writing is something else."

"You're a trust fund kid," Carter said.

"Maybe so," said Julian. But if Carter believed that was who he was at heart, he didn't know anything about him.

Ahead of them, a raccoon stepped onto the road, and Carter swerved around it. He cracked open the window and a breeze came in; there was the scent of sea and lilac. "Do you really think we'll be friends in ten years?"

"I hope so," Julian said.

"My father's always saying that college is the great equalizer. Here, we're all taking the same courses and eating the same meals. But then we graduate and gravitate toward our own kind."

"In that case," Julian said, trying to lighten things, "you better make a lot of money."

"I'm thinking of doing that," Carter said.

"You'd be good at it, I suspect. The fact is, I haven't seen anything you're not good at."

Carter tapped his hand against the dashboard, nodding purposefully to the beat.

"If you want to resent someone," Julian said, "you should resent Pilar." Pilar's father, Theodore Brodhead, had worked in the Kennedy and Johnson administrations. He'd been in attendance at President Johnson's fifty-seventh birthday party when the White House chef made a cake decorated with the symbols of the Great Society. Pilar's father had eaten Medicaid.

"Maybe I do resent her," Carter said.

They were quiet now, and as the fog settled onto the road it was as if they were driving through bags of fleece. The gas needle had dropped and there were no signs anywhere and Julian was afraid they might run out of fuel. "We should probably head back. The girls will be waiting up for us."

Carter spun the car around, and Julian thought of him and Pilar on his scooter, Carter spending the risk he'd been allotted.

"Did you ever think you'd still be with Mia? Three years after you started to go out?"

Julian shook his head. "What about you and Pilar?"

"Not a chance. Before Pilar, I hadn't been with anyone for more than three months."

"We're the last ones standing," Julian said. "The only two couples still together from freshman year."

Julian heard a popping sound, then the whispering ululations of night. A deer stood at the side of the road, looking at them inquisitively. The rain had stopped, and on the pavement lay a puddle of gas rippling out in reds and purples. Carter opened the window and let the breeze in. Julian could see the sign for Graymont.

"Looks like we made it back," he said. "Tell them to call off the search party."

"Listen," Carter said, "we've got the rest of this year. It doesn't matter what happens after we graduate."

"No one's going anywhere, Carter. Wherever I am, you can pick up the phone."

Thanksgiving came, and a gloom settled over Mia. She was Canadian, so Thanksgiving wasn't her holiday, and every year its arrival impended earlier: the row of plastic turkeys dangling from a wire above Main Street, strung up by workers the day after Halloween; the annual Thanksgiving ball announced each autumn in *The Graymont Clarion* with more drawn-out ceremony; the Pocahontas Piñata hanging from a tree next to Thompson Hall, waiting for classes to end and the students to eviscerate it.

Yet her reaction surprised her, for she wasn't someone who usually felt excluded, and with the approach of Christmas, not her holiday either, she joined in the campus Secret Santa rituals without resentment or regret. But Thanksgiving was different, and Canadian Thanksgiving felt like pallid consolation. She could have embraced Canadian pride and its attendant disdain for the United States, but that struck her as banal, a pose; in high school, when she'd traveled over the summer on her Eurail Pass, she had steadfastly refused to be one of her country people who sewed the Canadian flag onto their backpacks. The truth was, she considered herself an honorary American. Her parents had been raised in the United States, and although she'd been happy growing up in Montreal, she'd always borne a dim resentment over how her family had ended up there. Her mother had once said that Thanksgiving was her favorite holiday; these words had made an impression on Mia, who had come to see distilled in her mother's love of Thanksgiving the pattern of her parents' journey and of their lives in general, her mother following her father to Montreal, abandoning her career—she'd been studying for a Ph.D. in classics—so he could accept a job teaching physics at McGill. Twenty-five years later, her father had little but contempt for the United States, which he saw as two hundred and fifty million people content to do nothing but eat Big Mac after Big Mac. For him, Joe McCarthy equaled Vietnam equaled McDonald's equaled Disneyland equaled Ronald Reagan calling in the National Guard in 1968.

Yet it was in the United States that Mia's parents had met, in graduate school, at Harvard, less than two hours from where she was now. In coming to Graymont, she saw herself as reversing her parents' course, returning to the place where her mother had grown up and where she'd visited her grandparents over school vacations. From the start, Northington had felt like home to her, but then Thanksgiving would come and leave her feeling displaced. This, her senior year, there had been talk of staying on campus and celebrating Thanksgiving with friends, but when Carter joined Pilar in Connecticut, she resolved to go with Julian to New York.

Mia liked Julian's parents, but she felt acutely that this wasn't her family and, worse, that it wasn't really a family at all. In her mind, Thanksgiving involved a throng of children surrounded by uncles, aunts, and cousins, and she felt bad for Julian and his parents, for their feeble approximation of a Thanksgiving meal, the four of them sitting around a turkey too large to consume, engaged in what felt like play-acting. Living alone must have been like this, the pretense of laying out a table for one's own solitude, and she thought, depressingly, that if she ever lived alone she would subsist on Cheetos and late-night pizza, that she would always be eating off Styrofoam.

Later that night, in bed with Julian, she said, "I found tonight depressing."

"The meal?"

"Everything. It's not your parents, Julian. God knows they're nice to welcome me." Outside, she could hear the keening of an ambulance, then a choir of voices waxing and subsiding. Julian's figure was lumplike, his breath expelled from the pillow next to hers, the smell of turkey and candied yams.

At the window now, Julian pressed his hands against the glass, leaving big mitts of condensation. "What do you think? No sneaking around this year?"

It had come as a shock to her that his parents hadn't set up the guest room as they always did, that they'd helped carry her suitcase into his bedroom. No one said anything, but it was understood: this year they were allowed to sleep together. "We're twenty-one," she said. "Officially adults."

When Julian visited Montreal, they never had to sneak around at night; from the start, her parents had let them stay in the same bedroom. Even when she was in high school, her parents had allowed her to sleep with her boyfriend. So it surprised her to miss the old ritual, she and Julian whispering late at night with his bedroom door locked, the sleepless whiling away of the hours as they stood half-clad in front of Julian's window looking down at the people dotting York Avenue. Mia felt in a deep way that she was growing up, that she'd become an adult without having realized it. Already she and Julian alternated holidays, Thanksgiving and Christmas in New York, New Year's and spring break in Montreal. "Where do you think you'll be next Thanksgiving?"

"I don't know," Julian said. "How about you?"

"Me, either." She loved Julian—she'd never doubted it—but she wasn't sure what this translated into now that they were graduating. She tried to imagine the two of them married, a lifetime of dividing holidays. In a way she could envision it all too easily, but the exercise was speculative, undertaken in the same curious, abstracted way she'd always done it, with any boy she'd ever been with. She'd never really given marriage much thought, and the more time passed the less seriously she took it, as if the fact that she was getting older, closer, presumably, to actually getting married, no longer accommodated the fantasy. She'd read that most college students met their spouses in college, but "college students" included junior college students and state college kids from Oklahoma and Nebraska, and she understood that people like her, at schools like Graymont, didn't marry their college boyfriends. Doing so seemed fantastical and quaint, not all that different from marrying the boy next door or even from the dimly exotic world of dowries and arranged marriages, of parents conscripting the town elders to marry their children off, as had been done for her great-grandparents in Eastern Europe. "What happens, happens," she liked to say. But sometimes she wondered what was *going* to happen. With the exception of the year after she graduated from high school, the year she spent in France, everything she'd done had been a matter of course: school, school, and more school. It had always struck her as uninventive, all that studying, but now, finally, when she had to invent something, she wasn't sure how to do it.

"You can drive up with me tomorrow if you'd like." She was going home to see her parents in Montreal.

"Do you want me to?"

"I always want you to, Julian. You know that."

But the truth was she was content to go alone, and Julian, seeming to sense this, allowed her to. It was what she'd done the last couple of years, spending Thanksgiving with Julian's family, then going home for the remainder of the weekend.

It was after midnight when she arrived. Olivia stood in the kitchen with her back to her, washing dishes. She had headphones over her ears, she was in her leotard, and her hair, pale as butternut, rested wet on her shoulders.

"Olivia," Mia said. "Sweetie."

Olivia spun around. Her sister the dancer—she even extinguished the water with élan—and Mia had an epiphany: this was what she would do when she graduated. She would move back to Montreal and get to know her sister, not simply in the way she'd known her before she left home, when she was seventeen and Olivia was twelve and knowing Olivia was the least consequential thing she could imagine.

But she realized this wouldn't happen. She didn't want to move back to Montreal, and Olivia would be a senior next year—she was thinking of going to Juilliard, or maybe, to her parents' consternation, simply moving to New York—with her own indifference to attend to.

"Look at you," Mia said. "In your leotard at one in the morning."

Olivia took a fistful of her hair, as if to wring it out. "Mom and Dad think I've turned the house into a gym."

"No pain, no gain?"

Olivia raised her hands above her head and did a pirouette.

"How are you, Ol?"

"I'm all right."

"And Mom and Dad? Are they still driving you crazy?"

"They've turned it into a science."

"You'll be getting out soon."

"Not soon enough."

Olivia had begged Mia to apply to McGill. But Mia had never seriously considered McGill and she quietly dismissed Olivia's pleas as the exaggerated entreaties of a twelve-year-old. And maybe they'd been that. Though now Mia wondered whether, if she'd stayed in Montreal, things might have been easier for Olivia, who fought with their parents, especially their father, over her increasing commitment to dance. What they were really fighting about, Olivia said, was that she wasn't as good a student as Mia was. Their father had been the valedictorian of every school he'd attended; he'd never gotten a B in his life. But Olivia's grades were middling, and every time she brought home a report card her father was baffled anew.

Mia held up two turkey sandwiches in Baggies. "Look," she said. "Smuggled across the border from Manhattan."

"Zabar's?"

"Wainwright's. They're leftovers from Thanksgiving. Julian's mother packed them for me."

"How *is* Julian?"

"He's good."

"So when is he going to come rescue me?"

"What do you mean?"

"He could take me to New York," Olivia said. "Do you think he'll let me rent out his bedroom?"

"Olivia, what would you do on the Upper East Side? It's all ladies with frosted hair wearing beaver stoles. Believe me, it isn't SoHo."

"It isn't Montreal, either."

"A city that doesn't know how to make a bagel?" Montreal bagels were dipped in sugar water and cooked in ovens. They were more like doughnuts, Mia understood, but since she liked doughnuts she liked these, too. The fact was, Montreal's denizens claimed their bagels were the best in the world, and St.-Viateur Bagel had become a tourist destination. They weren't, however, to Olivia's liking. Olivia was always saying that someday she, too, would move to the United States and share an apartment with Mia—in New York, or San Francisco, or Chicago, or New Orleans, anywhere but Montreal.

"Eat up," Mia said. Julian's mother had placed toothpicks in the sandwiches, and the bread looked anchored to the plate.

Now, watching Olivia perched on a stool, her legs like a foal's dangling down from her, Mia realized her sister had lost weight. "You look so thin."

"Dancers need to be thin."

"So do anorexics."

Olivia removed a carton of milk from the fridge. "I'm not anorexic, if that's what you're asking."

"You promise me?"

Olivia dutifully ate her turkey sandwich. Then, for good measure, she finished the last couple of bites of Mia's sandwich, too. "Are you happy?"

Mia smiled at her.

"I have to go," Olivia said.

"Where to?"

"Off to throw up my food."

"Olivia!"

"I'm only kidding."

Later, wandering sleepily through the house, Mia found Olivia's door closed, the music playing low, the quiet murmur of her sister on the telephone. Tacked to the door was a "Hazardous Waste" sign

Olivia had filched from the high school chemistry lab. It was the bedroom of a teenager, when Mia still remembered the frills and bows and stuffed animals, the blue-green tank that housed Olivia's turtle, which she'd named Rocket, after Maurice "The Rocket" Richard. Their father was a die-hard Montreal Canadiens fan and Mia and Olivia had become hockey fans, too. Before the games, they would walk around the house in their Canadiens jerseys in anticipation of a night in front of the TV. "My hockey Martians," Mia's mother called them. "One of these days, you'll be watching the game wearing ice skates."

That weekend, it was for hockey that Olivia emerged from her bedroom and they all stayed up late in front of the TV. The rest of the time Olivia was gone, and it was just Mia and her parents, her father with *The New York Review of Books* and the *TLS,* her mother reading a novel, Mia going through old mail. Collapsed on the couch, in the house she'd lived in her whole life, Mia felt as if everything else had receded and the world, not unpleasantly, was shrinking in on her, swaddling her in its silent diversions.

Back at school, she studied for her finals in the college library, alternating between the carrels and the sectional couches, which, like the treadmills at the gym, now generated long lines of waiting students.

"It's rush hour," Julian said. It was one in the morning. Someone had tacked a sign-up sheet above the couches with the words "Orchestra Seats" in bold letters, and people had started to sign their names on the list.

"It's crazy," Mia said. She found tests insulting; she believed in learning for learning's sake (Graymont purportedly did as well; that was the idea behind the pass-fail option, which she, to her regret, had declined), but the words sounded trite to her, uttered by generations of students before her who nonetheless took their exams with the same mute resentment she felt.

"It's flash card time," Julian said, unfurling a sheaf of flash cards and waving them in front of her.

"Anthropology?" Mia said.

"How about Semiotics? Or Western Civ?"

Back at the house, they found Carter and Pilar with their own set of flash cards, which Carter flung like Frisbees across the garden. "It's an art installation," Carter said. "I've gotten funding from the NEA."

With finals approaching, the four of them had started to play backgammon. Carter would stand in the hot tub and place the board on his head and the rest of them would play as if he were the table.

"I've got a flat head," Carter reasoned. "I'm good at balancing things."

"Carter has a lot of useless talents," said Pilar.

Carter smiled dolefully. "Am I pathetic or what?"

"Pathetic and bathetic," Julian said.

"What's the difference?" said Pilar.

"Pathos," Julian said, "is the sight of Heinz with a backgammon board on his head. Bathos is when he capsizes." He shoved Carter off-balance, sending him and the backgammon board careening into the water.

"Julian's going to be a teacher," Pilar said.

"Not a teacher," said Carter. "A schoolmarm." He removed the backgammon board from the hot tub and wrung his hair out all over it.

That night, in bed, Julian and Mia played backgammon themselves, falling asleep in the middle of a game, and when they awoke the next morning, the backgammon pieces were strewn across the mattress.

Julian laid the red pieces along his stomach. "I'm a pepperoni pizza."

Then the phone was ringing, and Mia, still half asleep, trundled across the floor to get it.

It took Mia several moments to understand what he was saying; her father was so elliptical and obscure. He spoke of a *development,* of a *growth,* as if this were a parking structure or an economic chart, when he was talking about her mother and she had a lump in her breast. A *malignant lump,* Arthur Mendelsohn was saying over the telephone—the biopsy had already come back positive—and Mia still wasn't sure she'd heard this right, so she asked him to say it again. "It's malignant?"

"Yes."

"I'm driving home right now." Already she was calculating the time it would take, the miles and traffic flow, whether the police would be out and how fast she could drive, how she hadn't packed her clothes yet but maybe she could get home by dinner.

"You'll be home in two weeks, darling. Take your finals and then come home. You have winter break to be with Mom."

"Finals?" There was no argument she needed to muster, nothing more she had to do than echo that preposterous six-letter word.

"It would be best."

"For whom?"

"For you," he said. "For all of us. It's what Mom wants, too."

"She told you that?"

"Yes."

Mia didn't believe him. It was best for her to be sitting in the library while her mother was back home with breast cancer? Best for her to be reading the English Bible and Plato and St. Thomas Aquinas and Aristophanes and whatever else she was supposed to be reading for Western Civ? "I want to speak to Mom."

"She's asleep," her father said. "She's resting."

"Is there going to be a mastectomy?"

"Yes."

"Chemotherapy and radiation?"

"It looks like it."

"Mastectomy is surgery."

"I know."

Was her mother really asleep? Or was she next to her father, listening in, too frightened to talk to her? Sometimes when Mia called home, her parents would both get on the phone and Mia, not realizing this, would think she was talking to just one parent and would suddenly hear the other's voice. That was what she wanted now. She needed to hear her mother. "Which breast is it?"

"What?"

"Which one has the lump?" She wanted to know this; she had no idea why.

"The left one."

"Are you sure?"

"Yes."

"Oh, Christ," she said, and hung up.

Mia ran out of the house and into the garden, and not knowing what to do, she came back upstairs, with Julian trailing her.

She called her father back. "What stage is it at?"

"What do you mean?"

"Cancer goes in stages, Dad. One through four."

He didn't say anything.

"Maybe they don't know yet."

"Probably not," her father said, buoyed, it appeared, by the doctors' ignorance. Her father was an idiot, she thought; for a genius, he was a fool.

"Mom might die," she said.

"You have to believe," said her father, a man so atheist he found the word "believe" contemptible, a man who generally believed in nothing save for the fact that there was nothing to believe in.

"All right." She stifled a sob. She'd disappointed him, and herself. She was letting them all down by saying—by even thinking—her mother might die.

"People recover from breast cancer all the time."

"I know," she said, trying to sound hopeful.

Now her father was telling her about an obituary he'd read for a woman who had lived to be a hundred and thirteen. An illiterate, her father said, her obituary in a newspaper she couldn't even read, yet she was the longest documented survivor of breast cancer. She'd lived cancer-free for eighty-five years.

Mia was silent. If her mother lived cancer-free for eighty-five years she'd be a hundred and thirty-four. Let her mother live till seventy, Mia thought, and she'd get down on her knees and thank God.

Now her father was saying she had a choice. She could go about her life as if everything had changed, or she could act as though things were normal, which was what he and her mother hoped she would do.

"But things aren't normal," Mia said. "Isn't that what cancer is, Dad? Abnormalities of the cells? 'Proliferations,' as you like to say? You're the scientist around here."

"I'm a physicist," Arthur Mendelsohn said calmly, "not a biologist."

"I'll fail my finals," she said, half prediction, half threat. "I'm switching my status to pass-fail."

"Mia . . ."

"I'm enrolling pass-fail retrospectively."

"Retro*actively*," he said.

"Whatever." She knew what the words meant. Now wasn't the time for a vocabulary lesson. "Did you tell Olivia?"

"Last night."

"And?"

"She's scared. We all are."

But her father didn't sound scared. He sounded collected and imperturbable, as he always did. And maybe, Mia thought, that was a good thing; someone had to play that role in the family. "Daddy," she said, "promise me something."

"What?"

"Promise me Mom isn't going to die."

"I promise."

She started to sob. It was days, it seemed, before she stopped.

Later that week, she talked to her mother, and her father was right; her mother didn't want her to come home, either, not until the semester was out. So Mia stayed at school, sullenly passing the time, feeling like an orphan, only worse, because she had a family and they didn't want to see her and her mother was at home, sick.

"I'm worried about you," Julian said.

"Don't be."

"You need to talk to someone." He took her in his arms, in a grip so strong she thought she might asphyxiate. She felt her heart beat against him like something caged in, wings batting, slapping against themselves.

She called her mother again, but the conversation was unsettling, for her mother didn't want to talk about the cancer, which left them nothing to talk about. "Speak to me, Mom. Are you all right?"

"Yes, sweetie. I'm just tired." Her mother started to cough, and when she spoke again her voice was raspy, as if dice were being shaken in her throat. "I fell asleep for a few moments."

"It's three in the afternoon." It made Mia wonder, *Has the cancer spread?*

"I'm up all night," her mother said.

"Worrying?"

Her mother was silent.

"You need to get some sleep, Mom."

"I sleep during the day."

Then there was more silence, and Mia realized her mother must have hung up, or maybe she'd fallen asleep again, because a recording came on saying the phone was off the hook and there was an incessant beeping like a car alarm.

That night, Mia lay in bed with Julian and they tried to have sex, but she couldn't do it. She raged at herself for even thinking about sex and she raged at her mother for having gotten sick and she raged at Julian for simply being there, for falling asleep while she remained sleepless. "Oh, God, why am I burdening you?"

"You're not burdening me." He folded her in his arms, tied her in the lanky ribbon of him, and everything was all right while he was holding her. But then he left for the library, to do the things he needed to do, and she started to come unbound.

One night, she woke him at four in the morning and got him out of bed. Naked next to her, he stood in the shadows rubbing his eyes.

She said, "Punch me."

"What?"

"Hit me in the stomach."

"Are you insane?"

"I want you to hit me."

"I can't."

"Why not?" She wanted to feel something. Or not to feel something. She wanted to prove she was tough.

And when he just stood there not doing anything, she said, "Okay, then I'll hit you."

On this, he relented. He tightened his stomach muscles and she hit him, once with each fist, and then again and again. Then they got back into bed and fell asleep, and in the morning it was as if she had forgotten about it.

The next couple of days she pretended to study while Julian went to the library to look up articles about breast cancer. He flipped through the bound copies of *The New England Journal of Medicine* and *Science* and *JAMA* and *The Lancet,* copying the articles that mentioned new treatments.

Then Mia was going to the library, too, where she looked up breast cancer in the medical encyclopedia and typed "cancer" and "breast" into the computers. There was "bilateral breast cancer" and "osseous metastatic spread" and "malignant neoplasm" and "histologic sub-types" and "suboptimally debulked disease" and "electrophoresis" and "neoadjuvant chemotherapy" and "thrombocytopenia" and "tumor cell necrosis" and "erythrocyte count" and "lymphadenopathy." She had no idea what these terms meant, couldn't figure out whom these articles were intended for, certainly not for people like her, and with the change jingling in her pockets, she went downstairs to the copy machines, feeling like a laboratory mouse running through this maze of journals and dictionaries, through this web of incomprehensible jargon.

She laid out the articles on the floor of their bedroom and stamped on the pages as if they were bubble wrap. Then she removed her T-shirt and bra and stood half-naked in front of Julian, hands on her hips, staring at him. "Look at me."

He did.

"Look at my breasts."

"Okay."

"Well?"

"They're nice."

"*Nice?* Julian, you don't get it, do you?" Everyone she knew had breast cancer. There had been her high school history teacher, and her music appreciation professor first semester at college: one week she was in class, and the next week she wasn't. And Cynthia, her friend back home, whose mother had endured what lay in wait for Mia's mother, the enervation and nausea, the wasting away, the hair falling out, the vomiting.

Mia took her finals, quietly, perfunctorily, without complaining or changing her status to pass-fail, and without caring in the slightest.

Now she was home over winter break, sitting in the hospital room across from her mother, who was recuperating from surgery. Her mother dozed off.

"Do you want me to come back later, Mom?"

"No, darling, stay." Her mother had a hospital bracelet on, a pale plastic thing yoking her wrist, like half a set of handcuffs.

Joan Mendelsohn was small-breasted, and Mia had imagined that as long as her mother was dressed she might not notice the difference. But now she was so intent on not looking at her mother's chest that it was all she could look at. She glanced away, and when she turned back she focused on her mother's hair, which was gray and unkempt, shooting out in all directions like stalks of hay.

"I haven't had a shower," her mother said.

"Here, Mom, I'll help you."

In her bra and underwear, Mia stood behind her mother while she showered, hands pressed against her mother's shoulder blades. She closed her eyes and soaped her mother's back and arms, thinking her mother had lost weight, praying that this was the last of it, that after the chemotherapy and radiation the cancer would be gone. "Are you okay, Mom? Is the water too hot?" But her mother was too weak to answer. She ran the shower scrubber across her mother's buttocks, down the backs of her thighs to her ankles and toes, soap dripping off her mother and onto her as she squatted at her mother's feet. The steam had fogged the shower up and all that was left was the feel of flesh and skin.

Mia guided her mother back to bed, doing her best to make her comfortable, but seeing she was as comfortable as she could be, she just hovered over her. "I don't want to go back to school," she said.

"It's vacation, sweetie."

"I mean ever. I'm going to spend all my time with you."

"I'll be asleep a lot," her mother said. "What will you do then?"

"I'll watch you." Mia folded back her mother's sheets. "You used to watch me sleep, didn't you, Mom? When I was a baby?"

Her mother nodded. A neighbor of theirs had a child who had died of SIDS, and after that Mia's mother would spend the night reading beside Mia's crib, looking up every few minutes to make sure she was still breathing. Sometimes she would place a finger directly beneath Mia's nostrils so she could feel the air coming out. "I counted the days until you turned one."

"Why one?"

"Because that's when the risk of SIDS diminishes."

"And then you stopped worrying?"

Her mother smiled. "Then I moved on to other things."

"Talk to me, Mom. Tell me stories." And as Mia, her eyes closed, listened to her mother, she kept thinking, *Tell me again, tell me again,* conveyed back to when she was small and prunelike, when her mother drove her to day care past the hospital where she lay now, just another building stitched to the sky, a backdrop to the day that lay ahead of her. "Mom," she said, "will you ever forgive me?"

"For what?"

"I was so insolent."

"Oh, Mia."

"Don't you remember what I was like as a teenager? We fought all the time."

"I thought it was a requirement that a girl fight with her mother."

The worrywart, Mia and Olivia had called her, for the smoke alarms and carbon monoxide detectors she installed in the house, the fold-up ladders in closets in case the family had to escape, the fire drills they were forced to participate in. What other teenager, Mia thought then, was required to run fire drills in her own house? From the instant she was born, she'd been preparing to leave. My little wanderer, her mother had called her. Summers at the beach when she was four, and already she was running off. So her mother tied a piece of twine around her wrist. "Stay in touch, pumpkin," her mother said.

"We'll fight again," her mother said now. "I'm looking forward to having many more fights with you."

"I don't want to," Mia said.

"In that case, we don't have to."

Mia stared out the window, at the trail of traffic winding through the city, the vehicles so close to one another it seemed as if they were attached.

"I bumped into Glen's mother last week," her mother said.

Glen had been Mia's high school boyfriend. Her mother had loved him, though Mia herself hadn't managed to love him, at least not the way he had wanted her to. Yet he was bighearted and handsome, and

Mia liked watching him hit tennis balls on the local clay courts and in his varsity tennis matches after school. Sitting with her mother in the hospital room, feeling that everything from the past was better than the present, remembering how fond her mother had been of Glen, Mia thought she should have stayed with him, that as much as she loved Julian, he didn't know her mother the way Glen did and, she feared, he never would.

"Do you remember when I used to knit?" she said. "I made a sweater for Olivia."

"It was beautiful," said her mother.

"It was a little misshapen, but it was all right."

"Why did you quit, darling?"

She didn't know. She'd abandoned knitting like everything else, convinced it was time to move on.

"I'll need a wig," her mother said.

Mia nodded.

"I don't want to wear one."

"You don't have to, Mom." When Mia was a girl, her mother had made her wear hats in the winter. According to her mother, people lost forty percent of their body heat through their heads. Every year the figure went up. First it was forty percent, then it was sixty percent, then it was seventy-five percent. It was as if her mother worked for the hat industry.

"Your hair will grow back," Mia said, and because she wasn't sure of this, she said it again.

There were flowers beside her mother's bed and several more vases on the windowsill. The only cheerful place in a hospital, her mother had once said, was the obstetrics ward. Recalling this, Mia excused herself to go to the bathroom, but instead she went upstairs to obstetrics. The babies lay like take-out orders beneath the warm lights, the boys with blue hats, the girls with pink ones, everything determined already; Mia, hating this, swore that if she ever had a baby she'd have the pinkest boy in the world, she'd have the bluest girl. Her mother was wrong—obstetrics didn't make her happy—and she ran back downstairs to her mother's room.

She thought of the nausea that would accompany the chemotherapy. She had never seen her mother throw up. When she got fevers and stomachaches as a girl, when she came down with the flu, when she awoke at three in the morning and vomited, her mother cleaned up after her. That was what it meant to be a mother. And now Mia felt nausea herself.

A week later they got the news. Her mother's cancer had spread to the lymph nodes. She would begin chemotherapy immediately.

Julian drove up to spend New Year's Eve with her, but they went to bed before midnight, and were it not for the fireworks outside her bedroom window, she wouldn't have known what day it was. She heard a distant hooting, like owls celebrating some nefarious feast, and she lay in bed as one o'clock passed, and then it was two and she was still sleepless. She could see the tropical fish swimming in circles in their tank, casting their aqua glow. "Those things never die," she said. "I neglected them in high school and my parents still neglect them. I think they're essentially unkillable." She could hear the rain falling on the roof, tapping its relentless code. "Look at you," she said. "Your feet stick out."

"I'm too big for the bed," Julian admitted.

Her mother was down the hall, recovering from the chemotherapy; a new round would begin tomorrow. Her father and sister were focused on the details, which was a way to occupy themselves, she understood, but she didn't want to discuss the details. She just wanted them to admit how frightened they were, but it seemed they weren't able to. And maybe she wasn't, either. Last night, she'd stood silently with Olivia in the kitchen, and then she blurted out, "I love you," and Olivia blurted it back. A discomfort settled between them, a shame almost. What freighted words those were, reserved for so few people sometimes it seemed they were never to be used at all. She recalled being a child, four, five, six when she said those words to her teachers and classmates, when it seemed there wasn't anybody she didn't love. Then a hardening set in, a calcifying of the heart, and you didn't love anyone any longer, or at least you didn't say you did, so that now she couldn't remember the last time she'd said those words to anyone besides Julian, when there were other people she loved, her family, certainly.

She nudged Julian out of bed and they shambled in their pajamas through the house. She felt desperate for him to know her better, felt a conviction that despite having been with her for three years, he didn't apprehend her at all. From her parents' bedroom came the sinister whirr of the white-noise machine. She felt somnolent, guiding Julian through a haze from which she feared she would never emerge.

They stood in her father's study, where built-in bookshelves rose from the floor to the ceiling, with a library ladder that rolled along a track. And there she was, in the photo on her father's desk, poised between her parents at a McGill graduation, holding a 7 Up aloft. The faculty brat, surrounded by books. She and Olivia used to play a game, Guess the Number of Books in Dad's Study, like Guess the Number of Jelly Beans in the Jelly Bean Jar.

In the den, she flipped on the TV. Only three hours after the fact, Times Square looked abandoned except for the garbage. Now the countdown was being replayed, and the TV, a small black-and-white number with a broken antenna, started to go fuzzy. "You think *this* is bad," she said. When she was growing up, her parents' TV had been even smaller and her father had used a metal hanger to function, sporadically, as an antenna. Her parents had kept the TV in the closet, taking it out only for special occasions—they liked to watch *Masterpiece Theatre* and *Upstairs Downstairs*—so that the status quo ante, as her father liked to say, was with the TV in the closet. Though late at night, when she was supposed to be asleep, she would emerge to find her father watching hockey games on tape delay and she would sit down and watch with him. When she was small, her father liked to explain hockey to her, not just the rules of the sport but the physics of the game, the strategic use of angles and the way the puck caromed off the boards, and it seemed to her listening to him that the ideal hockey player was really a physicist.

She handed Julian a stack of papers. "Look what I came across when I was poking around. My mother's half-finished dissertation."

It was on onionskin paper, so gossamer she feared it would crumble in his hands.

"What did she write about?"

"Ancient Athenian coinage." Mia stared down at the typed pages. "What a fucking shame."

"To write about ancient coins?"

"No," she said impatiently. "That she never finished it. It would have taken her another year. Two, at most."

"She told you that?"

Mia nodded. The assumption had been that her mother would finish her dissertation when she got to Montreal and then, who knew, maybe there would be a classics position at McGill. But she never went back to her graduate work. It was one of the things Mia had fought with her about. Mia had sworn she would never be like her mother, would never abandon the city she loved and relinquish her career for her husband's.

In the basement, she and Julian swatted a Ping-Pong ball back and forth. They went at it silently, the ball hitting the paddle and the table and the paddle again. Then they climbed the stairs and wandered around the same rooms they'd been in before, moving mindlessly about the house like rodents trundling across a cage.

Opposite her bed, Sigmund Freud looked down at her paternally. How curious, she thought, to grow up with a poster of Freud in her bedroom when all her friends had plastered their walls with the heartthrobs of the day. Freud had begun his career as a hypnotist, and Mia had been obsessed with hypnotists; there had been one at every Bar and Bat Mitzvah she attended. She would come home from those parties and swing a pendant in front of her parents' eyes, chanting "You're getting weary, you're getting very, very weary" until her parents, utterly unhypnotizable, insisted that she stop.

She was crouched in her closet, rifling through boxes. "Hebrew School," said one. "Synagogue," said another. "My Jewish archives," she told Julian.

"You really could read this?" He flipped through the papers with Hebrew lettering on them.

"I still can," she said. "Sort of."

"My girlfriend the Orthodox Jew."

There was a Hillel at Graymont, and she had gone a couple of times to Friday night services, but she found them uninspiring, so she never returned. It had all started with those Bar and Bat Mitzvahs, the hotel ballrooms and the hypnotists, the celebrant's name emblazoned on the dessert mints. A charade, her father said, retrieving her from one of the parties. He was right, Mia thought; she was convinced this wasn't Judaism as it was intended. But she didn't know how Judaism was intended, and she felt suddenly, at age twelve, a disconnection from her faith and past so profound she couldn't believe she'd never experienced it before. So she joined the local Jewish youth group and came under the sway of an Orthodox rabbi, and soon she was going to synagogue every week.

She'd driven her father crazy by becoming religious—that, she suspected, had been her real motive—and there had been a protracted battle over her wish to unscrew the lightbulb on Friday afternoons so she could open the fridge on the Sabbath without turning on the light. She unscrewed the lightbulb and her father screwed it back and she unscrewed it again, until her mother intervened and removed the lightbulb, which meant she'd won: there was no light in the refrigerator. And that was how it stayed, even when, a year later, she stopped being religious. Perhaps the lightbulb had been lost, or maybe everyone had just gotten used to a dark refrigerator.

"And your mother?" Julian said. "She went along with all this?"

"She was amazing." And now, hearing that white-noise whirr from her parents' bedroom, voices, indecipherable, escalating and diminishing, Mia started to grow teary-eyed. She had resolved for the new year not to cry anymore or, at the very least, to cry less than she had been, and she was already breaking her resolution. The year she was religious, her mother had walked with her to synagogue, three miles there and three miles back, because Mia didn't travel in a car on the Sabbath, and her mother sat with her through the services despite not being religious herself. Her mother purchased kosher meat for her, and two new sets of dishes, one for dairy and one for meat. And earlier, before Mia became observant, her mother had gone with her to the Oasis of the Occult and had lain down in the magician's box as she'd requested. Her assistant, her beautiful mother, the lady she sawed in half. "Things are only going to get worse," she told Julian.

"How can you say that?"

As if what she said made a difference. It was superstition, this belief that hope had any bearing. Yet she knew she had her own superstitions, for in a way her pessimism *was* her hope. She would prostrate herself before the god she didn't believe in, humble herself to the point that she couldn't be any more lowly, for how could you lay waste to someone who had so utterly given up hope?

"My mother wants me to shop for a wig with her."

"Are you going to?"

"I'm scared. What if I don't recognize her?"

"Of course you will."

"Julian, I want you to come with us."

He hesitated.

"Please? Do it for me?"

At the store, above the cash register, sat rows of torsoless heads with wigs perched on them. In front of Julian, an Orthodox Jewish woman was examining a wig, her six children holding hands behind her, linked like sausages. Next to them stood Mia's mother; her hair was already starting to fall out, and filaments the color of wheat had landed on her jacket.

Julian watched Mia's mother choose a wig. Then Mia was crying and Mia's mother was, too, and Julian felt like crying, also, listening in on this family that wasn't his, making their despair his own.

"You look good," he told Mia's mother. "Really, you do."

Then Mia seized his hand, was clutching him by the elbow, and Mia's mother was holding him, too, and he was guiding them out the door and into their car, Mia's mother's wig in its box like a cake on her lap as he drove the two of them home.

.   .   .

January of their senior year of college: the calm before a storm so savage it would deposit her in places she didn't know existed. The doctors were saying the treatment was working. The tumor had shrunk; it was too early to say "remission," yet that was what they implied.

Then February came, and as snow pummeled campus, leaving everyone in drifts, there arrived the news that her mother's cancer had spread to her spine.

And in March to her liver.

An organ a month, Mia thought darkly, and it was true what people said; nothing was more unendurable than the waiting. The doctors tried new kinds of chemotherapy, but all these did was make her mother weaker. There was an experimental therapy, but her mother didn't qualify, and another one, interferon, she couldn't endure, and so she was removed from the protocol.

Mia wanted to drop out of school, but her parents wouldn't let her. She staggered to class, and once she was there she couldn't recall having arrived. She was like a drunk driver who had left the party and woke up the next morning not remembering how she'd gotten home. She didn't care whether she went to class, but she needed to go somewhere. Often Julian would find her wandering like a lunatic on the streets, and he would skip his own classes to accompany her to hers. She had stopped sleeping, and the bags under her eyes were so dark it looked as if someone had hit her.

Often now, she drove Julian's car into Worcester and Boston, and sometimes north toward New Hampshire and Maine, with no destination in mind, letting the gas needle dip perilously close to empty. Once a week, she attended a support group for people with a parent who had died of cancer.

"Your mother hasn't died," Julian said.

"I know that."

"What would she say if she knew you were doing this?"

"I want to prepare myself."

"By pretending? Do you talk at these meetings? Do you actually say your mother has died?"

"You don't have to talk if you don't want to."

"But do you?"

She didn't answer him.

"Why are you doing this?"

"Because it's the only cancer support group I know of. Find me a support group for people whose mothers have breast cancer and who are supposed to pretend they're going to college, and *fine,* I'll go to that one."

"You're spying on other people's pain."

"Jesus Christ, Julian, going to these things makes me feel better. Doesn't that count for something?"

"Of course it does."

"Well?"

She let him take her back to their room and put her into bed, but he found her an hour later walking down Main Street in the rain, without a raincoat or an umbrella, her shoes waterlogged, mud coating her ankles. Holding his raincoat above her head, he guided her back to their room and into a warm set of clothes. He made her a cup of tea and placed her damp and mumbling into their bed where; still wet himself, he ran a towel across her body.

Now, more and more, people gave her a wide berth, even her friends, who, not knowing what to say, chose not to say anything.

"Pilar's awful," she told Julian. "The way she stares at me, it's as if I threw up on her tennis whites."

"Her intentions are good."

"Well, the road to hell . . ."

She found Carter one night alone in the co-op kitchen, warming up food in the microwave.

"You want some ravioli?"

She shook her head.

"They're Chef Boyardee."

"Is that supposed to be an inducement?"

Carter shrugged.

"I'm not hungry," she explained.

"In general?"

"No."

"A person has to eat."

Now Carter was doing the dishes. Mia watched the movement of his shoulder blades as he worked the sponge, the pumping up and down of his clavicle.

"My mother had breast cancer," he said.

"She what?"

He was silent.

"You never told me that."

He was scrubbing pans and pots that were already clean, doing his best, it was clear, to seem occupied.

"Is that all you're going to say?"

"I'm sorry about your mother."

"I mean about *your* mother."

"I don't know what you want me to tell you. I was six when she was diagnosed, and they cured her. I barely even remember it."

"You're so fucking laconic, aren't you, Carter?"

"It's probably encoded in my DNA."

"You don't really believe that."

"That we're genetically programmed?"

"Oh, forget it," she said. She didn't want to have a debate right now about nature versus nurture.

"We think about you a lot," Carter said. "Both me and Pilar."

"Pilar," Mia snorted.

"She's terrible with illness," Carter said. "Her appendix burst when she was a kid and she spent two weeks in the hospital. When people are sick she gets the heebie-jeebies. You should see what she's like when I have the flu."

"My mother doesn't have the flu," Mia said evenly.

Carter looked at her as if to say, "Exactly."

What, Mia wondered, did Carter want her to say? That she forgave him and Pilar their discomfort? She felt suddenly that they weren't her friends, that despite all the time they'd spent together, they'd never really cared about her. She wished she were at a big university, but here at Graymont everyone knew her, and when she entered a classroom she could hear the whispers, could see people averting their eyes.

Carter had cut his hair short, and as he leaned against the refrigerator the back of his head reflected off the metal. "I'm so sorry," he said. "If there's anything I can do . . ." He reached out to hug her. But his arms felt limp around her, and now, stepping away, he shrugged apologetically. "You take care of yourself, Mia." Then he was out the door and into the garden.

Over spring break, home in Montreal, she sat down, finally, with her mother's doctor. "Your mother doesn't have much longer," he said.

Still, his words didn't shake her, not until her father said them, too, her father who knew nothing compared with the doctors but upon whose resolve she had come to depend. From the start, he had insisted that statistics didn't matter, the stage of cancer didn't matter, what the doctors said didn't matter. The only thing that mattered was that he didn't believe his wife was going to die. Mia had never seen him cry before, and now, seeing him cry at last, she realized her mother would die soon.

She turned her mother's hospital room into a shrine. She unplugged the lamps and lit candles and incense and put on tapes of Native American oboe music and covered the walls with photos of the family. She scoured her parents' cabinets for the vases she'd made for her mother as a girl and brought them to the hospital and put flowers in them. Then she lay in bed with her mother and read poems to her.

"Come back soon, sweetie."

"I will."

"Promise me something."

"What?"

"Swear to me you'll take care of Olivia. You're stronger than she is. You'll be all right."

"What about me?" Mia wanted to say. "Who's going to take care of me?"

.   .   .

Back on campus she ran into Pilar, who wore a look of such carefully wrought compassion it was as if she'd painted it on. In anthropology class, Mia's professor had said they lived in a death-denying culture, for sickness had been banished to the silent confines of the hospital, whereas in other cultures it was less feared. That, Mia thought, was what Pilar should do. She needed to immerse herself in death so as to overcome her fear of it. Though Mia realized she needed to do that, too.

"I'm so sorry," Pilar said, but before Mia could respond, the words came spooling out of Pilar: at least Mia was getting the chance to tell her mother goodbye.

"Tell her goodbye?" Mia said. "Do you think that's what I want to do?"

"I mean . . ."

"Just stop, Pilar. Please."

Someone else had said the opposite ("At least you don't have to see your mother suffer for too long"), and Mia said to Julian, "If another person starts a sentence with the words 'At least,' I'm going to throttle them."

"Ignore Pilar," Julian said. "She doesn't know what to say."

Mia lay down and took a nap, and when she awoke she said, "Come with me." She led Julian out of the co-op and over to campus. They entered a dormitory and went down to the basement, where she held open the door to the laundry room.

"I don't get it."

"Don't you remember?" she said. "This is where we met. Spring of freshman year."

He nodded.

"Julian, I want us to get married."

He didn't respond.

"I thought you loved me."

"You know I do."

"And we were going to get married eventually."

He'd assumed this himself—he'd allowed himself to hope for it—but neither of them had brought the subject up.

"I don't know how much longer my mother will live. I so want her to be there."

And the idea bloomed in him that she was right. They would get married on campus after they graduated. They would celebrate with their families while her mother was still alive.

Ann Arbor, Michigan

Battened down in his bulky winter coat, a backpack slung over his shoulder, Julian trudged through the snow amid the throng of students heading south on State Street. He and Mia lived in Kerrytown, the graduate student ghetto, but not being a graduate student himself, he felt a vague contempt for his neighbors, for the person he might have been had he become a graduate student. Many of Mia's classmates lived in Kerrytown, a constellation of them arrayed over a few square blocks, between Ingalls to the east and, to the west, Detroit Street, where Zingerman's Deli stood and where you could see the workers at six in the morning preparing food for Ann Arbor's early risers.

The neighborhood extended south, where Julian was headed now, bent forward like a pugilist, taking on the weather. The wind blew hard against his face; he was late to meet Mia for lunch. He passed the student co-op and the rows of squat apartment buildings and wood-frame houses. A "For Rent" sign was covered with snow, the name of a local realtor obscured, and in the distance, on the corner of Washington Street, the diner, Olga's, stood boarded up, though all the other storefronts were occupied. Beyond Olga's lay Park Avenue Deli and Stucchi's and the university apparel store and a cluster of coffee shops—Gratzi, Caribou Coffee, Espresso Royale, Amer's—each seeming to have spawned the next.

Farther up State Street, the undergraduates could be seen in swarms, standing in their fraternity and sorority sweatshirts, the boys in backward baseball caps, the girls sipping Diet Cokes in Einstein's Bagels, everyone along North University on this Monday after a football Saturday dressed in maize and blue. Julian himself, four years removed from college, had become a devotee of Michigan sports. A lifelong sports fan—one of his earliest memories was of the Mets' trip to the playoffs in 1973, the improbable victory over Cincinnati, the brawl between Pete Rose and Buddy Harrelson, before the heartbreaking loss to the A's—Julian had taken a break from spectator sports at college. There were no intercollegiate teams at Graymont, just club athletics, the level low enough that Julian himself had been the starting shooting guard on the Graymont club basketball team, whose games, he liked to say only half jokingly, involved playing but not keeping score. Now, having landed at a Big Ten university, if only as a spouse, he was reliving the college sports life he'd never had. In the fall of 1991, when he and Mia had arrived in Ann Arbor, there had also arrived five eighteen-year-olds—the Fab Five, they would soon be called—who would take the Michigan basketball team on a trip to the NCAA tournament finals, and then do it again their sophomore year. Now three of them had turned professional, but their mystique still hovered over campus, and Julian, who had never seen these players off the basketball court—this was another difference between the University of Michigan and Graymont: at Michigan, athletes rarely went to class—nonetheless had come to think of their arrival as coincident with his own, as if the six of them had decided to attend Michigan together.

But today he stayed clear of North University, avoided State Street entirely as it became more commercial, and cut up east on Huron. He turned past Rackham with wistfulness and regret, for it was at Rackham, in the reading room on the second floor, that he went in the evenings to write, and his writing wasn't going well.

He was working on a novel, and the book was spinning away from him, doing things he hadn't been prepared for. It was becoming bigger than he'd intended, but in the process, paradoxically, it was also becoming smaller, a bramble of sentences with no clear direction, time moving forward with insufficient purpose. The day they graduated from college, he and Carter had been awarded Graymont's creative writing prize, along with a check for a thousand dollars each, and though Julian understood that the world was littered with creative writing prizes, enough people had told him he was good that he had come, tentatively, to believe it. But the praise didn't buoy him; if anything, it left him dispirited. On graduation day, Professor Chesterfield had said, "I expect great things from you, Wainwright," and Julian already felt, moments after graduating from college, that he was letting people down.

"I make no promises," he had said. But the truth was he'd made a promise to himself, to have a publishable novel by the time he turned twenty-five. He'd told no one this except for Mia, and now, at twenty-six, no closer to that goal than he'd been at twenty-two, he wished he hadn't told her, either, for it seemed to him that the very act of setting this goal, of believing he could publish a novel so young, was proof that he wasn't a real writer. He believed he would improve as he got older, but other times he wasn't so sure. He saw himself at thirty-five, forty-five, fifty-five, not knowing how to do it any better. It was a mystery, he suspected, what distinguished those who made it from those who didn't, and he feared he was missing that essential something. This was what drove him to work harder, was, in fact, the reason he'd left the apartment late today, for as the morning had waned, he'd felt a small breakthrough coming on. But the breakthrough hadn't come, and now he was late to meet Mia.

They were supposed to have lunch on the other side of campus; he would have to sprint to get there on time. But he didn't want to sprint in the cold, his backpack thumping against him. He was feeling prickly, besides, because this morning Mia had told him not to be late and had reminded him of her busy schedule.

"I have a busy schedule, too."

But Mia didn't say anything, and he knew what that silence meant, and he resented it.

Two teenagers in down coats were pelting each other with snow;

each had an arsenal of a dozen snowballs at his feet. One of the boys was protected by a tree, but the other had ducked behind Julian and was using him as a human shield.

Now Julian was at the entryway to the Michigan League, where, standing sentinel in front, was a snowman so precisely rendered it looked more like sculpture than like snow. On its head was a University of Michigan hat; oversized sunglasses were perched on its nose.

Julian headed down the long corridor of the Michigan League, passing notices for dance performances and chamber music concerts. The Glee Club was performing on Friday night. When his parents had visited, he and Mia had taken them to the Michigan League to see Arthur Miller's *The Crucible,* and during intermission his father had said that *The Crucible* was the most frequently performed play in America and that for every performance Arthur Miller received a royalty check. But what Julian heard his father saying was that he should write something like *The Crucible,* that if he was going to be a writer he might as well make some money at it. Julian, fuming, considered telling his father that he was making art, not selling widgets. But even as he thought this, he knew it was possible his father was saying nothing of the sort, that he was simply making an idle comment about Arthur Miller.

He was on campus now, crossing the Diag. Ahead of him lay East University, Church Street, Forest Avenue, and Washtenaw; to the south were Monroe, then Hill and Packard. He knew all the street names in town, even the obscure ones, the little cul-de-sacs where he rarely had reason to go, for when he and Mia first moved here he'd walked purposefully through town memorizing the street names. He was compensating, he understood, for he was hamstrung when it came to sense of direction. Yet he continued to have faith in himself. He and Mia would be invited to someone's house for dinner, and he would convince her to follow him down the wrong street, the two of them getting lost on Ann Arbor's Old West Side.

Unwarranted confidence, Mia liked to say, was a quintessentially male attribute. She was T.A.-ing this semester for the abnormal psychology course, and she found the girls smarter than the boys. Yet the girls talked less, and when they did their voices rose at the end of their sentences so that they appeared to be asking questions even when they weren't. The boys, on the other hand, were transported on the billows of their own bluster. One, in particular, a young man from suburban Detroit, spoke with such authority about assignments he hadn't read that Mia had to remind herself that he hadn't in fact read them.

Yes, Mia thought, when Julian wasn't leading her somewhere she didn't wish to go, his errant internal compass had its charms, and she would have been more forgiving if it didn't come attached to a corresponding disregard for time. Julian would agree to meet her for coffee at two but wouldn't show up until two-fifteen. He said he had a dialectical approach to time, which sounded to Mia like rudeness masquerading as Marxism. The answer, she decided, was to start without him. So now, when Julian arrived for lunch, he found her at a table, her hot dog and a basket of waffle fries already in front of her.

"Did you give my seat away?"

"I tried."

"No takers?"

"Come here," she said. "Kiss me."

Mia's dark hair hung in front of her face, and as Julian brushed back her curls, the word "schoolgirl" came to him, which, technically, he supposed she was, though she was twenty-five and had already earned her master's degree. Her mouth tasted of mustard and relish. "I'm sorry," he said.

She gave him a look of exaggerated admonishment. "I told you I was in a rush."

"You have to be at the clinic?"

She nodded.

He dropped *The Michigan Daily* onto the table, open to the classifieds. "Someone's selling tickets to Friday night's game."

"Go Blue," she said. This was the University of Michigan chant, and what it lacked in imagination it made up for in brevity. When Mia had gotten into graduate school, her father had bought her a University of Michigan sweatshirt, and though she'd never been one for school spirit, she had worn the sweatshirt when she visited home so her father wouldn't think she'd left it in mothballs. Walking around Montreal, she must have been accosted half a dozen times by strangers shouting "Go Blue!" at her. She'd forgotten: there were more alumni of the University of Michigan than of practically any other university in the United States. She and Julian had been to a few Michigan football games, but once November came and the temperature dropped, it was oppressive to sit for three hours in the cold, and they both enjoyed wandering along Main Street on football Saturdays, seeing the town emptied of its inhabitants. She preferred basketball, besides. She had grown up attending hockey games with her father, who could turn a Canadiens game into an educational odyssey. Julian, on the other hand, disapproved of talking during games, and Mia, whose research in psychology focused on children, liked to think of them as toddlers engaged in parallel play, cheering the home team, shouting at the visitors, but never directly engaging one another. She had become a Michigan basketball fan herself. It was she, after all, who had seen Chris Webber ("the fabbest of the Fab Five," she liked to call him) outside the Brown Jug, a coup, she told Julian, who needed no convincing. During time-outs, she and Julian would discuss what was happening in the game. They would indulge in beer and frozen yogurt and try to answer the trivia questions that appeared on the scoreboard above half-court. Sometimes Julian would supplement them with questions of his own, and Mia would attempt to answer those, too. Julian had asked her to name college teams with nonplural nicknames, and she had come up with the Harvard Crimson, the Stanford Cardinal, and the Alabama Crimson Tide. There were more, Julian said, but when he offered to tell her she refused; she had never been someone to give up easily.

In line now, Julian scanned the lunch options. Red Hot Lovers was an old-fashioned hot dog joint, and what Julian liked best about it was the free condiments. Sauerkraut, Clancy's Fancy Hot Sauce, sharp mustard, yellow mustard, honey mustard, ketchup, steak sauce, celery salt, relish, barbecue sauce, pickles. Julian had always been a sucker for free food. At the all-you-can-eat sushi place in Northington, he would stuff himself until he got sick, on the grounds that each additional piece of sushi was free. Now, in Ann Arbor, he and Mia would stop at Zingerman's to taste the scone bits laid out in baskets and the olive oil arrayed in tiny porcelain bowls. In the sandwich line, they would ask for tastes of soup—of the yogurt cucumber, which was Mia's favorite, and the cream of tomato, which Julian preferred. Julian ventured that they could have subsisted exclusively on Zingerman's tastings, but they didn't want to feel like freeloaders. So they usually bought something, a muffin or a sandwich or, more frequently, just a pickle, which for seventy-five cents came twisted in a Baggie. Julian would get a sour pickle and Mia a half-sour one, and when they reached the midway point they would switch.

Julian came back with his bun piled high.

"Is there even a hot dog under there?"

"One day," he said, "I'm going to order just the condiments."

"How was your morning?" she asked.

"Shitty."

"Writing didn't go well?"

He shook his head.

"I'm sorry."

"In the end, it doesn't matter."

"What do you mean?"

"If you screw up with a patient, the person's life is at stake. The only damage I do is to imaginary people. And to the principles of good art."

"Oh, Julian." Mia wanted to offer him encouragement, but all she could come up with were bromides. She wondered whether he was temperamentally suited to be a writer. Often he would become restless writing at home and he would go to Angell Hall, to the computing center, so he could be in the presence of other people and the clicking of hundreds of keyboards. She'd suggested he meet other writers to discuss ideas, but writing, Julian said, wasn't about ideas. In the end, there was no one to talk to except the work itself, and even in the midst of Angell Hall he would be overcome by solitude.

Then there was rejection, which Mia understood was the writer's lot. Julian took rejection harder than most. Or maybe it was she who took his rejections hard; she was very protective of him. Julian would send out his short stories for publication and he would receive them back in his self-addressed stamped envelopes, often with nothing more than a form rejection slip. He sent them to *The Atlantic* and *The New Yorker* as well as to the literary journals, most of which Mia hadn't even heard of. But these journals received thousands of submissions a year, so that the chances of being published in one were minuscule.

Yet at twenty-six, Julian had already published three short stories in literary journals. "You see?" he said when his first story was published. "I'm not half as bad as you thought I was."

"Julian! I never said you were bad." But she hadn't said he was good, either. Julian had called her the toughest critic he knew; their relationship had been built, he liked to say, on nights out at the movies freshman year, on shared discernment and good taste. But Mia was tired of good taste; she'd grown up in a tyranny of it. The right authors (Tolstoy and Henry James), the right composers (Mozart and Brahms), the right directors (Bergman, Godard, and Fellini). *"De gustibus non est disputandum":* her father used to quote those words to her, but every statement of his, every gesture, made clear that he didn't believe they were true, and there was no better proof of this than that he always quoted in Latin. The fact was, there *were* better and worse tastes, and Mia's mother in her less emphatic way had agreed.

The other thing Mia had learned was never to show your homework to the people you love. Growing up, she'd fought with her father over her term papers (he wanted her to revise, and to do further research), over her interest in the sciences (she had aptitude in physics, but she'd been determined not to display that aptitude), and over the occasional B+ on her report card. Long ago, she'd resolved not to value herself for her work, or to value others for their work, either. Now, in graduate school, she didn't show Julian her research papers and she didn't ask to see his fiction. "Aren't you curious?" he would say, and she said, Yes, of course she was, and she would agree to read something he'd written. But once it was in front of her, she couldn't concentrate on Julian's story, fearing her own judgments. In moments of repose, she vacillated between thinking Julian was a good writer and thinking it didn't matter whether he was a good writer. But sometimes she wondered whether she really believed this. What if he wasn't a good writer, and what if it did matter? So she was glad he'd decided not to show her his novel. She wanted to like it—she believed she *would* like it—but she thought it best to like it from afar.

"When's your appointment?" he asked.

"One-thirty." She had been awarded an internship at the university health clinic and had started to see patients. When her mother got sick Mia had gone into therapy, and although seeing a therapist wasn't a requirement for graduate school, most of her classmates had been in therapy, and those who hadn't been were looked at askance by those who had. Becoming a therapist without having been in therapy was like trying to teach swimming without having been in the water. But being a patient took you only so far; now she was in the therapist's chair, and the only qualifications she had were three years of coursework and a T.A.-ship in the abnormal psychology lecture. She was getting on-the-job training, which made her think of medical school graduates, who started their residencies every July and caused patients to postpone surgery until after the summer. Yet she found she had a knack for the job. She was hardworking and she listened well; she believed she was helping her patients.

"And after that?"

"I'm going to the gym."

"We could play racquetball." Julian had been a squash snob when they met—he called racquetball "squash for dummies"—but the year after they graduated Mia convinced him to give racquetball a try, because that was what she had, a racquetball racquet, found in her parents' attic when she was cleaning up after her mother died. She liked seeing Julian in his goggles. They looked like spacemen, the two of them, playing racquetball together. The court's walls were white, but dark ball marks pocked the walls, and she and Julian were adding to the mosaic.

In the wake of her mother's death, she had been too incapacitated to make plans, so she and Julian stayed in Northington. She wait-ressed three nights a week at an Italian restaurant downtown, and during the day she worked at the Graymont registrar's office, up the hill from where she and Julian lived. Julian took a bartending course, and soon he was serving drinks to the students whose transcripts she was processing. At home, he put his new skills to use, making cock-tails for him and Mia, dropping paper umbrellas he had purloined from the bar into drinks the color of gumballs. He would place his hands behind his back, one drink in each, and say, "Choose a hand," and the hand Mia picked would hold her drink for the day.

"Quiz me," he said.

"What's in a Harvey Wallbanger?"

"One ounce vodka, four ounces orange juice, half an ounce Galliano."

"And an Alabama Slammer?"

"One ounce sloe gin, one ounce Southern Comfort, three ounces orange juice, one ounce amaretto."

"Make me something blue," Mia said, and Julian mixed her a drink he'd never made before, something that, for all she knew, he had con-trived at that moment, but it tasted good either way. "What's that?"

"A Julian Wallbanger."

The next day he told her was serving her an Alabama Mendelsohn.

"My very own drink." But it tasted remarkably like a Harvey Wall-banger to her, and when she pressed him, Julian admitted it was a Harvey Wallbanger and he'd simply changed the name.

In bed at night, they read novels to each other, and once, when Mia had the late shift and wasn't coming home until after he went to sleep, Julian called the restaurant and read to her over the telephone. Mia laughed, pretending she was writing down a take-out order, but when her boss began to stare at her she said she had to go.

Waiting up for her, Julian would flip through the student tran-scripts she had brought home. He invented a game in which she would read aloud from the students' application essays and letters of recommendation and he would try to guess their college major. Then she would open *The Northington Free Press* and describe the houses that had been sold, and he would attempt to guess the sale price. A couple of times he got the price right and he thrust his arms in the air and declared himself the real-estate king, as if by guessing the correct price he'd won the house itself.

Then Mia would feel bad because how, she wondered, if her mother had just died, could she be playing games like these? Already there were times when she was happy, when she and Julian would look out the window of their apartment, hearing the quiet vibration of traffic on the street, and she'd be filled with serenity. In bed with Julian as he read to her, or drinking the cocktails he'd mixed, or simply flipping through take-out menus, she'd be overcome not by joy, exactly, but by something quieter than that, a contentment she felt most profoundly when doing something as inconsequential as choosing take-out orders. But this feeling didn't last long because contentment, she believed, was a betrayal of her mother. She wanted to move on, yet every sign that she'd done so compelled her to turn back.

Now, at Red Hot Lovers, she picked at her French fries, trailing them through a puddle of ketchup. Out the window, a man was shouting into a microphone. A born-again. There was a rotation of them, warning people of impending doom.

Behind the counter, the cook was dropping French fries into sizzling oil. One of the hazards, Mia thought, of having been a waitress was that you could never eat out innocently again. Once, at the restaurant where she'd worked, a fellow waiter had tasted the melted cheese on a customer's onion soup, and when he handed the soup to the customer, a long filament of cheese ran from the soup bowl to the waiter's mouth. The man the waiter was serving turned out to be the provost of Graymont, and the next day the waiter was fired. "Poor Ian," Julian said. "Caught with the provost's cheese in his mouth." After that, Julian would pretend he was Ian, and he would serve Mia a salad for dinner and stand with a napkin over his shoulder and a piece of romaine lettuce dangling from his mouth.

Mia gestured in the direction of another table, where two students were eating lunch. "Do you hear their accents?"

Julian smiled at her. It was Mia who was always telling him he was an East Coast snob, the New Yorker who thought there was nowhere but New York. Those initial months in Ann Arbor, that whole first year, in fact, she'd felt obliged to be a Michigan booster, for they had come to Ann Arbor because of her and he'd agreed to the move only reluctantly. Even now, she found herself pointing out how good their life was, as if obliged to defend Michigan's virtues.

Still, it was hard to get used to those Michigan accents.

"You're one to talk," Julian said. He liked to make fun of Mia's Canadian accent, how she said "Montreal" as if it were spelled "Muntreal." "Muntreal," he would say. "Like Muenster cheese."

Mia looked at her watch. "I've got to go," she said. She leaned over and kissed him on the mouth.

It was a sunny December morning, and Julian was seated in Caribou Coffee, holding office hours. His students' final papers were due next week and he'd made the mistake of having them write first drafts, so he now had to read two papers from everyone, and there were eighteen students in his class.

When someone asked him what he was doing in Ann Arbor, Julian liked to say he was the Merry House Husband. Student spouse, he called himself, for that was how he gained access to the college gym and purchased tickets to Michigan basketball games. But the truth was, he was now an official employee of the University of Michigan; he was teaching a section of English composition and was scheduled to teach another next semester. He should have been grateful, for the rest of the composition instructors were graduate students in English and all he had was a bachelor's degree. It was official university policy not to allow people like him to teach undergraduates, but official university policy, he discovered, was one thing in February, another thing in August, and when enrollment spiked over the summer the chair of the English department turned to him.

He had been given an office, a cubicle in the basement of Angell Hall, which he shared with the other composition instructors, whose job was to negotiate among themselves who would hold office hours when. But it was dark and cold in the basement of Angell, and Julian wanted to dissociate himself from the university, from the very idea that he was a composition instructor. He believed a writer was supposed "to live," which in his mind meant "to do manual labor," to work on a construction crew or on a fishing boat and get up before dawn to write. The problem was, he didn't have much experience with manual labor and, if he was honest with himself, he wasn't good at it.

Worse, he was a stickler for good grammar and proper syntax and he feared he was well suited for the job. The head of the composition program had been at it for twenty-five years, and whenever Julian saw him in the elevator, his brow etched with fatigue, his right shoulder slightly lower than his left from having carried his briefcase for so many years, he saw a future version of himself.

His first three years in town, Julian had worked at Shaman Drum Bookshop on State Street. At Shaman Drum, he stocked books and tended to the register and, along with a graduate student in art history, helped run the bookstore's readings series. Down Liberty Street was Borders Books, and during breaks from writing, Julian would check out the "New Fiction" section at Borders, then stop in at Shaman Drum to greet his old coworkers. Standing in front of the W's, he would picture his own book there; listening to someone read at Shaman Drum, he would imagine himself reading. But no sooner would he do this than he would rebuke himself. Fantasies were for fools, he believed; the only thing that mattered was hard work. Superstitiously, he told himself that the way to succeed was to believe you wouldn't, that only someone convinced of failure had a chance of success.

At the next table, another composition instructor was meeting a student, and beyond her sat two English graduate students holding novels on their laps. Each department commandeered a café. The English graduate students were at Caribou, the anthropologists at Gratzi, the historians at Espresso Royale. Everyone would remain at their appointed location, and then, after a few months, they would tire of it and, like migratory birds, they'd move on.

It was ten-fifteen, and Trilby, Julian's favorite student, was late to meet him. This surprised him, for Trilby was generally so punctual he worried something had happened to her.

Then Trilby breezed in, clapping her mittens against each other, tall, august, walking briskly between the tables, removing a wool cap to reveal an unfurling cascade of blond curls, her cheeks pale with little blotches of ruddiness, her eyes the blue of agate. "Julian, I'm so sorry."

"Dog ate your homework?"

"What if I told you it was the cat?" A number of times, Trilby had regaled Julian with stories about her roommate's cat, who seemed to function metonymically for Trilby's roommate herself: high-pitched, sharp-taloned, venomous. Trilby placed her bookbag on the table. "Actually, I was taking care of Helene."

"Ah," Julian said, "the roommate." Then, fearing he'd been insensitive, he said, "Is she all right?"

"She'll live," Trilby said.

"Well, that's a start."

"I had to take her to the hospital with alcohol poisoning. I've never met a person who vomits so much. When it's not beer, it's bulimia."

"My wife's studying to be a psychologist," Julian said.

"No offense to your wife, but Helene needs more help than that. If I were her parents, I'd cart her back home to Wisconsin."

Julian didn't doubt Trilby was telling the truth. But she was also, he suspected, capable of embellishment; she was a born raconteur. Besides, her account squared too neatly with her own prejudices, so that her roommate—the subsisting on Diet Coke, the passing out at fraternity parties, the waking up with guys she couldn't recall having met—seemed less like an actual person than a stand-in for everything she disapproved of at college.

Trilby had grown up outside Syracuse ("Every place I've lived," she told Julian once, "it's been snowy and cold"), with a poet mother (Julian had seen a few of Trilby's mother's poems in *The New Yorker*) and a painter father. Her parents had named her Trilby after the character in the Du Maurier novel, which, she told Julian, her friends would have thought was a joke, if only they'd understood it. "No one reads where I come from," Trilby said, and when Julian, only half kidding, said, "No one reads where I come from, either," Trilby said, "No, you don't understand."

In Trilby's high school, there had been nothing to do but have sex and watch football. (Trilby had grown up in a town that lived for high school football. "And that was the adults," she told Julian. She was so impassioned in her aversion to sports that Julian didn't have the heart to admit he was a sports fan himself.) And so she'd done her best to play along. But when she was a senior, she applied early to the University of Chicago, because it was a good school, but also because in a ranking of party schools it had come in dead last.

Yet as soon as she got to Chicago, she was miserable. The weather was freezing, she told Julian, but in a different way from how it was freezing back home, and Hyde Park felt rarefied and alien. She stayed in Chicago for three semesters, then spent the next couple of years bumming around Europe. First in Stockholm and then in a small town an hour outside Oslo, she worked off the books as a bar waitress. Finally, when she returned to the United States, she decided to enroll at the University of Michigan. It was a good school and she was used to the cold, and Michigan accepted her credits from Chicago without hassle or complaint.

"But then you were forced to study with me," Julian said.

"I wouldn't say *forced*."

"I would."

"Okay," she said, laughing. "But it's been the best thing that's happened to me."

The first time she came to Julian's office hours, Trilby was surprised, she admitted, to be enrolled in composition. Even if she'd been a freshman, she would have regarded composition with barely suppressed disdain. She had placed out of composition at the University of Chicago, and this, paradoxically, was what prevented her from placing out of it at the University of Michigan, which wasn't interested in giving her credit for work she'd done in high school. But now she was a junior, having spent two years abroad, which made her four years older than the rest of Julian's students. She was closer to his age than to theirs, and this flustered him. Or maybe it was the fact that she was so pretty and he, as the teacher, wasn't supposed to notice. He worried the other students would think he was playing favorites, but at a certain point it became comical: whom else was he supposed to favor? Trilby was so much better than her classmates that they appeared to regard her as Julian's assistant. It was possible she was a genius, he thought. It was also possible she just seemed that way compared with his other students, who were respectful and well-meaning and by and large not unintelligent but next to whom Trilby appeared as enormous—she was, in fact, five ten—as Lionel Trilling.

Perhaps, Julian thought, Trilby looked at him the same way. Maybe she was comparing him with the rest of the room and not to her other professors. Whatever the reason, instead of resenting him, as he thought she might, she had come to respect him, to like him, even, and he, in turn, liked her back.

Yet too often he would forget that she was his student and there were things he wasn't supposed to say to her. Trilby seemed to encourage this; it was as if she wanted him to cross a line. Now, sitting across from him at the café, she said, "Can you believe class yesterday?"

"So you thought things got out of hand?"

"*I'll* say."

"Chalk it up to December. Everyone's got vacation on the brain."

"College," Trilby mused. "It brings out the solipsist in the best of us."

"And sometimes not the best of us," Julian said, and there he was again, having been drawn into Trilby's trap, commenting unfavorably on his students.

The purpose of Julian's course was to teach the students essay writing: how to come up with a thesis statement and defend it, how to write an introduction and conclusion, how to make good transitions from paragraph to paragraph. This was, he understood, an important skill, but over the course of the semester it got stultifying to read so many such papers, and so for a few weeks he'd had his students writing personal essays. He had even, one week, encouraged them to write fiction, an idea Trilby had taken him up on, and she'd produced a small, affecting story about a woman whose husband, much younger than she, dies suddenly, a narrative meditation on grieving. Julian copied the story and handed it out to the class, but they hadn't been impressed.

"I guess you can't please everyone all the time," Trilby said when she next saw Julian in office hours.

"Don't listen to them," Julian said. "That story was terrific."

Occasionally, the composition instructors would hold meetings and the conversation would invariably turn to the poor quality of student writing. Julian, who had as much bad writing as anyone else, nonetheless felt self-conscious joining in the lament, a bunch of twenty-five-year-olds complaining about college students. Besides, if anything, he found the student responses to one another's work more disheartening than the work itself, for it was always the best writing that they appreciated least and the sentimental, cliché-ridden papers they gravitated to. Once, flummoxed by a student's response, Julian— he would later regret having been so peremptory—simply said, "I'm sorry, Steven, but you're wrong," and ended all discussion.

This was why he decided, after Trilby's story, that it was best not to continue having his students write fiction, best, even, to discontinue the writing of personal essays, which were near enough cousins to fiction anyway. It was all too close to home, having his students write creatively—he wondered how Professor Chesterfield had managed to do it—and he was torn between being aghast at how bad their work was and worrying that when he was eighteen his own work had been as bad, or, worse, that it still was as bad but that he was too close to what he wrote to realize it.

Yet even argumentative essays could become personal. Yesterday, discussion had broken down when two football players argued that student athletes should be paid for playing college sports. A drama student said that if student athletes were paid, student actors should be paid as well. Soon everyone was calling out about their own experience, and it was in a brief break in the shouting that Julian heard Trilby murmur, "Enough about me; what do *you* think about me?"

Now, at the café, she said, "You know what you should do? Put a moratorium on all first-person pronouns. From now on, no one can use the word 'I' in their papers."

"If I did that," Julian said, "there would be other problems."

Trilby shrugged. "What would Descartes say if he were alive now? 'I have an opinion, therefore I am'?"

"Well, well, well."

"I know," she said. "You should make me go up to the blackboard and write a hundred times, 'I will not be such a snot-nosed student.'"

"You're not snot-nosed."

A drop of apple cider hung on Trilby's lip, and presently she licked it away. She brushed a filament of curls behind her ear, only to have them fall down again. "Do you have other students coming?"

"The whole crew."

"Okay," she said, "then let's talk about my paper."

"Your paper's terrific," he said. "Your first draft is better than other people's second drafts."

She looked at him mildly, as if to say, "Damning with faint praise."

"All right," he said, "it's better than *my* second draft."

His response didn't fluster her. She had confidence, he thought, perhaps too much of it. Earlier in the semester she had written about *Roe v. Wade,* and though she was pleased with how the Supreme Court had decided, she faulted Justice Blackmun for a weak opinion, the implication being that if she herself had been on the Supreme Court a woman's right to choose would have been more firmly buttressed. Strong words from a twenty-three-year-old. Yet she had managed to say them without arrogance. There was, in fact, a vulnerability to her, a tentativeness, even, to how she was looking at him now.

She said, "I'm giving myself a crash course in jurisprudence. I'm writing about moral desert. One 's,' not two." She fingered the handle of her cider mug, tapping it a couple of times.

"I know," he said. "I read your paper." He held it up for her to see. It was studded with check marks.

"Humor me," she said. "Let me revise."

"Okay," said Julian. He was all for revision. He believed it separated the real writers from the dilettantes.

Trilby was writing this time about affirmative action and, more broadly, about the idea of merit. She was arguing not simply that university admission wasn't an entitlement but that human beings didn't own their endowments, that intelligence and diligence were qualities people exhibited but didn't in any moral sense deserve. She was using Kant, Mill, Rawls, and Dworkin, some of whom Julian hadn't read himself.

"So you're telling me you have seventeen more of these?"

Julian nodded ruefully.

"I'd hate to know your hourly wages."

"They're even worse than you think."

"So why do you do it?"

"It's a long story," he said. It was eleven o'clock, and students were passing in and out of the café. It was rush hour, Julian thought, and this was Ann Arbor's subway.

"Tell me."

"First of all, my college creative writing professor recommended me."

"You couldn't have said no?"

"It would have been hard. This friend of mine thinks something Freudian is going on. That my professor is a father substitute."

"Is he?"

"It's possible."

"And second of all?"

"My wife wanted me to take the job. Which is a long story in its own right."

A biscuit had come with Trilby's cider, and she was nibbling at it now, leaving a trail of crumbs across the table. "Sometimes I feel bad that this is what you do, teaching composition to college kids. It seems beneath you."

"Nothing's beneath me," Julian said balefully.

"Oh, come on."

"I know," he said. "Self-pity isn't attractive."

"Don't you worry it can infect you? Day after day with the commas and semicolons?"

"It's my job," he said. "Besides, I worry I'm good at it. And there's a beauty to precision, don't you think?" Trilby of all people had to know what he was saying. From the start, he'd counted on her to give examples to the class. She wrote on the blackboard, "The children who are good will get candy," followed by "The children, who are good, will get candy," and explained the difference to everyone. When he lamented his students' punctuation, when he noted that they reflexively placed commas between adjectives, she wrote, "My first beautiful wife," followed by "My first, beautiful wife," and distinguished between the two. Seeing her standing in her black boots and jeans, her blond hair tucked like a scarf into her turtleneck, hearing the sound of the chalk pressed against the blackboard, Julian thought he might be a little in love with her. Trilby was beautiful—how could he not notice?—but in the end she'd won his heart because she knew the difference between "which" and "that."

"I used to like to diagram sentences," she said.

Julian thought of his own adventures in sentence diagramming, late at night in his childhood bedroom looking out at the East River. "My wife thinks I'm a schoolmarm," he said. "I'm the guy reading the *Times Magazine* who exults when they mistake 'forego' for 'forgo.'"

"At least you're not a prig about it."

"I hope I'm not."

Trilby canted her head as if trying to get a better look at him. Her hair brushed across the table.

"Mia tells me I seduced her with Strunk and White."

"Did you?"

"I guess I did. On our first date, I gave her the highlights of my childhood malapropisms. 'No holes barred' instead of 'no holds barred.' 'For all intensive purposes.'" He shrugged. "I was eighteen."

"When I was eighteen . . ." Her voice trailed off.

"What?"

"It's not even worth going into." Trilby looked around her, at the clusters of her classmates in repose. "Clearly I've come to the wrong college. You should see how guys try to seduce you here."

By the door, in the shadows, a young man was standing in an orange parka. A student of Julian's. Trilby rose from her seat. "I'm sorry I took up so much of your time."

"Trilby, come on."

She was standing above him, holding a mitten in each hand. "You want to know the real reason I was late today?"

"Sure."

"I was in the Hopwood Room."

"What's that?"

"It's where the creative writing program's offices are. You've never been there?"

Julian shook his head.

"They have a whole table of literary journals. I was reading your story. The one in *The Missouri Review*."

"It's in there?"

"I loved it," she said. "Would you believe me if I told you I cried?"

He was silent for a second.

"Look at you," she said. "You're blushing. And don't tell me it's because of the cold." She held up a compact for him to see.

"I don't take compliments well," he admitted.

"Well, your story was wonderful," she said. "I wish I could write something like that." She wrapped her scarf around her neck and turned to go. "Take care of yourself, Julian." Then she walked through the café and out the door, disappearing down State Street.

Now another semester was under way, another composition class, another set of papers. Occasionally Julian ran into Trilby on the street and they stopped to talk for a few minutes. "You've spoiled me," he said. "My students this semester seem like dolts."

"Probably because they are," Trilby said, and then, seeming sorry for having been so uncharitable, she said, "I'm sure you have some good ones."

One time she suggested they get coffee, but so far, at least, they hadn't done so, and the more time passed, the less likely it seemed that they would. Now, when they greeted each other on the street, they rarely stopped to talk.

It was February. Snow piled high on the ground, and Julian, who had finally managed to liberate his and Mia's car, had, after the last storm, capitulated to the drifts. The apartment building they lived in had sixteen apartments but only eight parking spots, and now that he'd secured one, he considered leaving the car there for the rest of the winter, which in Ann Arbor could run well into April; eight inches of snow had fallen on April Fool's Day last year. Their car looked, Julian thought, like a woolly mammoth. All the cars in town did, rows of mammals frozen in mid-step, these lumps lining State Street and South University, an occasional headlight protruding. "We should just blowtorch the car and ride around in snowmobiles."

"It's not the snow that I mind," Mia said. "It's how gray everything is." At the clinic, there had been a rash of new patients. Second-semester blues, Mia's supervisor said. Mia wondered whether it was seasonal affective disorder; she hadn't seen blue sky in over a week. *Sit under a sun lamp and call me in the morning.* That had been the joke going around the clinic.

"I'm not crazy about the snow, either," Julian said. Even as a child, he'd looked forward to snow only in the hope, usually dashed, that school would be closed. He treated the snowball fights and the erecting of snowmen and the sledding in Central Park as ways to make the best of a bad situation, and he would think of swimming pools and the ocean off Martha's Vineyard, of the summer months that lay ahead.

Even now, sometimes, he wondered whether he should have followed Carter to California; he was made for the weather on the West Coast. But Mia hadn't wanted to move to California, and for Julian, too, California seemed alien and far away. Besides, Carter acted so superior about California. He would send Julian postcards on the front of which appeared the sunset over Half Moon Bay, or whales at Point Reyes, or the coastal highway winding past Big Sur, and he would sign off, "From the land of volleyball and Golden Retrievers, where the weather comes just as you order it." The more Carter effused about California, the less appealing the state became to Julian, though days like today, with the wind-chill factor near zero, were enough to make him wonder.

He was down the hill from his and Mia's apartment, picking up food for a dinner party. Mia's friend Sigrid had passed her comprehensive exams and a group of them was celebrating.

Sigrid had an air of composure—a good quality, Julian believed, in a budding psychologist, and in human beings in general. It made sense, he thought, that Sigrid had taken her comprehensives first. In a way, her passing her comps was a celebration for the whole class, because it now seemed possible that they would pass, too.

The exams were an unsparing, day-long ordeal, with an oral and a written component. Going before the firing squad, Mia called it; her own execution was just a few months away. She'd been spending every night in the graduate library and, when that closed, moving next door to the undergraduate library before coming home exhausted at one in the morning. She was drawing perilously close to the all-nighter, an experience she thought she had left behind at college.

There was something about movement, Julian believed, that prompted the creative juices to flow, for he found inspiration when he was driving or running or merely taking a stroll through the Arboretum. Cooking had the same effect; maybe one kind of creativity begat the other. Growing up, he'd never been much of a chef, but he'd begun to cook when he got to Ann Arbor. Mia would come home to find him with flour across his face and herbs from the windowsill lined up in glasses, Julian with baking soda in one hand and baking powder in the other, unsure what the difference was. He appeared unable to distinguish between a garlic clove and a garlic bulb, because one time Mia found him peeling clove after clove of garlic—the recipe had called for three cloves but Julian was peeling three bulbs—and he suspected his error only once he saw the recipe was supposed to take an hour and he'd spent an hour just peeling the garlic.

Another time, Mia found him in the kitchen chopping onions, his racquetball goggles clamped over his face. "Cooking as sport?"

"Onion eyes," he explained. He had tried placing the onions in water, but that hadn't worked, nor had chewing on bread or chopping the onions next to a flame, which were other methods people had suggested. So he settled on his racquetball goggles. Other implements had already proven versatile, such as his postage scale, which was doing double duty as a food scale, except now his mail had started to smell of cheese.

Sometimes the recipe said "twelve baby carrots or two carrots peeled," but twelve baby carrots never equaled two carrots peeled, and he'd be lining up the carrots next to one another, trying to guess the right amount. Or "eight ounces of apple." Was that before you peeled and cored the apples or afterward? He bought a large spice rack, but he didn't know much about spices, so, without regard for what they were, he moved alphabetically through the supermarket spice section, sweeping jars into his cart like a looter.

Over time, however, his meals had improved, and in the psychology department, at least, he'd gotten a reputation as a good cook. Sigrid and her boyfriend, Ivan, who ordered out for pizza and Indian food more than they cared to admit, had been pleased to learn that Julian would be cooking dinner tonight.

Home now, Mia said, "What do I smell?"

Julian unveiled the food for her: lamb brochettes with North African spices, shiitake mushroom bread pudding, endive salad with warm sherry vinaigrette.

"You're amazing, you know."

Julian shrugged. "Any idiot can read a recipe."

Not this idiot, she thought. If it weren't for Julian, she, too, would have been ordering takeout every night.

She was in their bedroom changing clothes when he called out, "Can you set the table?"

In her bra and underwear, she laid out the knives and forks. She put a wineglass at each place setting. Julian stood hovering beside a pot of boiling water. Presently, he stuck his head inside the fridge—to look for something, Mia assumed; or perhaps merely to cool off.

She was pulling a black turtleneck over her head, and she spoke to him through the fabric. "How do I look?"

"Headless."

"And now?"

"Beautiful."

To go with the turtleneck, she was wearing a white chiffon skirt. It was a billowy getup and it flounced around her. She didn't generally dress this way; usually she wore pants and simple tops, sweaters sometimes, a lot of straight lines and angles. But this was a special occasion, and she wanted her attire to announce it as such. She had put on lipstick and eye shadow and was wearing earrings. It felt strange to be dressed up in her own home, where she spent much of her time in sweatpants, often in nothing at all.

She stood in front of the mirror pinning up her hair. "Look at me," she said. "I'm twenty-seven, and I'm going gray."

"No, you're not."

She picked out a strand and showed it to him. "You see?"

"You look the same as you did the day I met you."

"Well, that's not true," she said darkly.

The guests arrived together, Sigrid and Ivan leading the way, followed by Francine and her boyfriend, Saxton, with Will trailing the pack, holding hands with his girlfriend, Paige.

Will held up a bottle wrapped in felt. "It's Dom Pérignon," he announced.

A chorus of admiration rose from the group, and Paige said, "Will blew his whole stipend on it."

Will shrugged. "How often does a girl get to pass her comps?"

Sigrid was at the center of the room, and the rest of the group orbited around her. She had curly auburn hair and was wearing a cashmere cardigan that was auburn, too. The effect was to make her luminous, as if, having passed her exams, she'd been lit up.

"Let me start with a beer," she said. "It feels like I haven't had one in months. It's as if I've been pregnant."

"Don't say it," Francine said. "Passing your comps is like giving birth."

"More like taking a dump, I'm afraid."

"You're next," Will reminded Mia.

They were sitting in clusters, and the way they held themselves, the ease of conversation, reminded Julian of college. It made him nostalgic for a time when everyone was just dropping by, the cheeseburgers and onion rings eaten on dorm room floors, the hastily organized surprise parties, the years when time unfurled illusorily before them, when there was nothing to do but celebrate one another.

With one hand, Julian took everyone's coats, and with the other he passed out bottles of beer. "Grad student, grad student, grad student," he said. "Do they produce anything else here?" Sigrid, Francine, and Will were Mia's classmates, and their partners were graduate students, too, Paige in anthropology, Saxton and Ivan in comparative literature.

"The imagination gets constricted in this town," Ivan said. "It's either grad school or go work for GM."

Saxton dug into the plate of baked Brie, then passed it around to the others.

"So this is how you know you're a grad student," Mia said. "The couch sags so low you can't get up."

But soon, with the promise of dinner, they managed to disentangle themselves from the furniture and, starting to get drunk, they deposited themselves around the table, with Sigrid at the head.

"Happy birthday, Sigrid!" someone called out, and buoyant, blithe, and lighthearted, the liquor spreading through them, they joined in a chorus of "Happy Birthday," though it wasn't really Sigrid's birthday.

Julian brought out the salad, and Francine, rising, said, "Can I help?" But Julian declined all offers of assistance. He liked Mia's classmates, but when the conversation turned to shop, as it often did, when someone referred to something that had happened in class, when a piece of gossip was proffered about one of the professors, he felt, not excluded, exactly, but as if he were hovering on the periphery, looking in through a window at the festivities going on inside. He liked going to parties, but once he and Mia were actually at one it was she who had the better time, for she was more adept at small talk than he was. Friendship—the very idea of it—assailed him. There were people in Ann Arbor he had gotten to know and could, with pleasure, grab a beer with, but there was no one with whom he'd established a true kinship. Most of the people they socialized with were Mia's fellow graduate students, and though she encouraged him to develop his own relationships with them, when he found himself alone with one of them he realized how much he relied on her to grease the wheels of the friendship.

"Eat," Sigrid insisted.

So Julian sat down. But then he was up again, bringing out the lamb and the bread pudding and pouring more wine and beer.

Now everyone was talking about the future of clinical psychology.

"What I fear," Sigrid said, "is that twenty years from now we'll be looked at no differently from soothsayers and phrenologists."

"The quick fix," Will said, bemoaning what they all bemoaned: the growing dominion of psychiatry and medication, the rise of HMOs, behavior modification, short-term therapy.

"Half my students are on Ritalin," Francine said.

Mia agreed. Medication now functioned as an excuse. People's computers no longer crashed. If someone didn't show up to class, if they handed in a paper late, they blamed it on their medication.

Sigrid said, "What are we doing in this discipline?" They'd gone into psychology for various reasons, but at least some of them had chosen the field because by the standards of a Ph.D. it was practical; there was the promise of a job. And there were still jobs, to be sure. But they could see it already, in the academic journals, in the popular press. The battering Freud had taken in *The New York Review of Books*, and barely a letter in his defense. The primacy of the brain over the mind, the focus on neurotransmitters and chemicals, the idea that talk therapy was unscientific and soft, when, Jesus, Will said, the relationship went both ways. Hadn't anyone read the latest studies? That talk therapy worked and, what was more, that the mind affected the brain, not just the other way around?

The group nodded: Will was preaching to the choir. Yet they felt worn out, and at Michigan, especially, they believed they were victims of a bait-and-switch. The psychology department had been rooted in the analytic tradition, but in the last few years its focus had changed.

A couple of graduate students had transferred to more analytic programs, and Francine, who was planning to do analytic training, had for a time contemplated transferring, too. Mia wondered where this left her, for her own inclinations were analytic.

"Soon you'll be like the comp lit students," Ivan said. "Unemployed and unemployable. And then you'll really have to go work for GM."

"No joke," said Paige. She was a steward for the graduate student union, and negotiations for a new contract had stalled. In the halls of Rackham and Angell there was talk of a strike.

"Well," Sigrid said, lowering her glass, "suddenly passing my comps doesn't seem like such an accomplishment."

"But it is," Francine said, and Julian, sensing some celebratory object was needed, brought out the cake. Saxton got up and poured everyone more wine and Ivan reached into his bag and removed a video. Soon the group had migrated across the room, bivouacking themselves on the couch, sprawling across the floor, and Will was saying, "When the night's over, someone's going to have to roll me home."

Then the video came on, fuzzy at first, but soon the picture was in focus, O. J. Simpson in his Ford Bronco, leading the police on his slow-motion chase. The trial had begun, and outside the computing center in Angell Hall the blacks congregated in one area and the whites congregated in another and the whole thing was depressing. But now, with Paige on the recliner drifting off to sleep and Sigrid rising to get more cake, they all seemed to have agreed not to talk about this, and they watched reverentially from the cocoon of Mia's apartment as O. J. Simpson made his slow drive along the freeway.

"It's been almost a year," Ivan said, "and Sigrid still can't get enough of it."

Sigrid shrugged. She had a weak spot for the tabloids in the supermarket checkout aisle, and for *People* magazine.

"There are worse sins," said Will.

Saxton clicked on fast-forward, trying to get the video to adjust, so that the Bronco would go at normal speed.

Francine emerged from the bathroom. "It's Valentine's Day!" she reminded them. On the table, the cake lay in half-eaten clumps, the icing smeared like putty across the flatware, and Francine drew a heart in what was left of her cake and licked the icing off her finger.

Finally, the champagne was brought out, but at this point everyone was too drunk to appreciate it.

"Drink the champagne before the beer," Paige said. "That's the lesson for the day."

Soon Ivan announced that it was one in the morning and he had to teach in a few hours. He led the group into the bedroom where the coats were laid out, and the women kissed and the men gave each other handshakes that evolved into hugs, and Saxton called out, "A dollar for the coat check!" and one by one, as if walking down a receiving line, they handed Julian a dollar.

Now, with everyone departed, Mia leaned over, holding her head. "I thought I'd learned not to drink so much."

"We learn and we forget," Julian said.

The guests had helped clear the table, but if anything the dishes were in greater disarray, for they were more spread out now (one had been placed on top of the bookshelf—by Saxton, Mia presumed: he was six four), and a coffee cup, still half full, had landed on the rim of the bathroom sink, directly beneath the toothbrushes.

"We should invest in a dishwasher," Mia said.

"That would be you." Julian placed an apron over her head. Ceremoniously, he guided her to the sink.

"I can't."

"But you said you'd do the dishes."

"Done in a moment of weakness." Mia threw herself onto the couch; the apron hung like a cloak around her. "Have mercy on me, Julian. I have to teach tomorrow."

"I do, too."

"And my comps are coming up. You heard what Will said. I'm next."

"Your comps aren't for another three months."

"Every day counts. Just because Sigrid passed doesn't mean I will."

But Julian didn't doubt that she would pass. She was the golden girl of the department. That was what everyone called her, and though she protested, he understood that it was so.

He carried a couple of water glasses into the kitchen, then brushed the crumbs from the counter. When he turned around, Mia was directly in front of him, so close they could have kissed.

"Please?" she said.

"You're not the only one who's tired."

"I understand."

He drained the wineglasses into the sink, then turned on the disposal. "Every day counts for me, too."

"I know it does."

He looked at her levelly. "I've already taken up a lot of the slack."

"And I appreciate it." She tapped a plate against the lip of the garbage, sending the food toppling in.

Soon, however, she had departed the kitchen, and when he saw her next, she was in her tank top and underwear, getting ready for bed. "If you put a gun to my head, I couldn't do the dishes now. I'll get up early tomorrow morning and wash them."

But now, with Mia in bed, as he sat at the computer trying to write, Julian could feel the dirty dishes piled behind him. If he'd had a study, he could have closed the door and let the dishes lie there, but he and Mia lived in a one-bedroom apartment where the living room and dining room were also the study. Mia would have suggested he go to the computing center, but it was two in the morning and snowing out, and the computing center was fifteen minutes away. When they moved to Ann Arbor, he'd proposed that they rent a larger apartment, but Mia hadn't wanted to appear rich. So they'd overcompensated, living in sparser quarters than most graduate students did. She'd been overcompensating, too, with her comment tonight—"So this is how you know you're a grad student. The couch sags so low you can't get up." He'd been with her when they'd gotten that couch; they'd bought it used from a departing student, and though he hadn't objected to doing that, it had seemed to him that she was making a point and he'd had half a mind to tell her to stop slumming.

He turned off the computer and went into the kitchen. It would take him an hour to complete the task, and he seethed as he settled into it, the water scalding his hands, the steel wool abrading him. Oh, for a dishwasher! For a bigger apartment! He let his mind wander to the political, to the fact that Mia's friends envied her his cooking, the way he helped out at home; if their roles had been reversed, if he'd thrown a party for his friends and Mia had done the cooking and then, because he was tired, she'd been left to clean up, there would have been a noxious aspect to the evening and the guests would have partaken of the meal with quiet disapproval.

When he got into bed, Mia reached out to touch him.

"You're not asleep," he said.

"I was for a while."

"Did I wake you?"

"No."

The numbers of the alarm clock flipped over, peeling back from themselves like molting skin.

"How did your writing go?"

"It didn't." In the dark, he was beginning to make out the edges of her, like a photo floating in fixer.

"Tomorrow will be better," she said. "It's what you always say. The bad days are investments in the good ones."

"I did the dishes," he said.

"Oh, Julian. You didn't have to. I said I would do them in the morning."

"I couldn't go to bed with the place looking like that."

She was on top of him now, and he felt a swelling within him. He didn't want to be angry with her, but he also didn't feel like having sex. That was a difference between them. When they fought, she saw sex as a way of making up, whereas he saw making up as a prerequisite for sex. Though occasionally he'd succumbed to her entreaties.

"Did you have fun tonight?" he asked.

She nodded. "How about you?"

"It was all right."

"The food was great," she said.

"I'm glad." His eyes had adjusted to the dark, and now his dresser and nightstand appeared before him as if covered in a gray cloak.

"My friends like you a lot," she said. "It gets tiresome hanging out just with other graduate students."

He felt it coming on again, that feeling of what-am-I-doing-here? But he knew what he was doing here; he was here because Mia was in graduate school. And the next move would be for him: they'd agreed on that.

"Not that they'd like you any less if you decided to go back to school."

"What do you mean?"

"Those people would be lucky to have you here."

"What people?"

"Michigan's MFA program. You've already published some of your stories. They'd be crazy not to take you."

"But I don't want to get my MFA. Can't you understand that? I've already been in enough writing workshops."

"Okay," she said. "Forget I even mentioned it."

He went into the bathroom and washed his face. A squirrel had alighted on the windowsill, and another was behind it, leaving prints across the snow. He rearranged the shower curtain. It had a map of the world printed on it, and he and Mia would play a game where they would close their eyes and point to the map and that would be where they would take their next vacation. One time, he spun her around and she pointed to Albania, and since that didn't seem like the best vacation spot, she went again, only to land on Sudan. Michigan wasn't marked off on the map, so Julian had marked it off himself, writing "Ann Arbor" in indelible ink and next to it an asterisk with the words "You are here."

Back in bed, he listened to the radiator beat out its tune, the syncopated rumble like the sound of something scurrying. Above him, his and Mia's shadows were pressed against the wall, like figures in a cutout.

"I got an offer for next year," he said. "The department wants me to teach another composition class."

"Julian! Why didn't you tell me?"

"I'm telling you now."

She leaned across the covers and kissed him. "Come on," she said. "Why so glum? Don't pretend this isn't great news."

"I guess it's better than not being offered it."

"Which would have been inconceivable, mind you."

"I only have a bachelor's degree," he said. "They could have gone back to the rulebook. Decided protocol was protocol."

"But you're better than everyone else."

"I don't care if I'm better than everyone else. It's not what I want to be doing in twenty years."

"What do you want to be doing in twenty years?"

"Writing," he said. "I just want to be more successful at it."

Mia liked to say she could have opened a psychology clinic for the exclusive treatment of Nobel Prize winners. Julian suspected she was right, but he couldn't help feeling that if he were as good as they were he would really know how to appreciate it. When people asked him why he wrote he told them the truth: he had to. And no matter what Mia said, he thought if he were successful he'd be happy, for there was a sorrow so deep in him he couldn't excavate it and he believed he could uproot it only with acclaim. And if he went deeper than that, if he tried to excavate the wish itself, he suspected he wrote for his parents. They had always been distracted, his father at work, his mother in an emotional cloud cover he couldn't penetrate. Perhaps it was the lot of only children, spending so much time in the company of adults, pressed, in his case, into the service of parents who hadn't managed to give him what he wanted. Or maybe he wanted too much. He'd written for his parents when he was a boy—in a way, he still wrote for them—and the sad thing was that his parents weren't really interested in fiction, certainly not his father, who in another of his hapless, well-intentioned gestures had secured for him for his sixteenth birthday an inscribed copy of *Atlas Shrugged,* which Julian accepted with perfunctory gratitude, doing his best not to betray what he thought of Ayn Rand. For years he'd told himself he would publish a novel and at long last his parents would celebrate him. Though another memory settled on him, of a breakfast one morning when he was a teen-ager, his father across from him with *The Wall Street Journal,* Julian announcing that he'd written a short story and his father saying so idly, so inattentively it was possible, Julian realized, he hadn't really heard him, "I wouldn't begin to know how to write a short story." Maybe that was when he'd decided to become a writer.

"I'm not talking about fame," he told Mia. "Just a measure of success. You must want that, too. A feeling that you're doing a good job."

"I just worry you're setting the bar too high."

"All I want is to publish my novel. Is that so unreasonable?"

She didn't think it was. But it concerned her how long it was taking him. She felt as if he were on a ride, and that by being married to him she was on that ride, too, lassoed by his despair. She'd spent her life around artists. There was Olivia, of course. And her mother had painted when she was younger and for a time had thought about going to art school. Now Mia herself was married to an artist, and at a certain point, she believed, persistence became pigheaded; it was just a way of kidding yourself. Julian hadn't reached that point, but she didn't know if she would still think so in five years, or ten. She'd been relieved when he started to teach composition. It felt like a real job to her. For a time she'd suggested he go to law school and write on the side. It was what Carter had done; but he'd given up writing entirely.

Now, though, lying next to Julian, Mia resolved not to bring up graduate school again. She felt grateful to him for having come along, for having loved her as long as he had. Thank God she'd found him, because where would she be now if she hadn't married Julian, if she'd graduated from college and her mother had died and it was just her alone, without anyone?

She made love to him, while outside the sky was lightening; in another hour it would be dawn. When Julian came, he gave a little squeal that delighted her.

Afterward, they lay next to each other on their backs, listening to the sounds of their breathing.

"Penny for your thoughts?"

She didn't respond.

"Is something wrong?"

She sat up in bed, feeling his toes against hers, the knobby Braille of his ankle. "When Francine mentioned it was Valentine's Day today, I realized I'd forgotten about it."

"I did, too."

"And it's understandable. We're both busy, and I know the whole thing's a creation of Hallmark. But it makes me wonder whether something's missing."

"With us?"

"You love me, Julian, don't you?"

"Of course I do."

But she felt unsettled nonetheless. It had been four couples at dinner tonight, but she and Julian were the only ones married. It had been that way from the start, for at first she'd been the lone married member of her graduate class. When she was introduced to her classmates during orientation week, she'd resisted telling them she was married, but eventually they found out and they wanted to know why she'd been hiding it.

And then she wondered whether she *had* been hiding it. When she and Julian arrived in Ann Arbor, it had been only a year since she'd gotten married, but already the wedding was a fog to her. She hadn't wanted to receive gifts when her mother was dying. She had opened a few of the cards, most of which were offers of condolence as well as congratulations; in their fumbling attempts to express some honest sentiment they made her embarrassed for the card writer, and after reading a few of them she couldn't go on. Instead of gifts, she and Julian had asked people to donate to a charity in their name, but most of the guests sent gifts anyway, and the few they opened were bowls, which she and Julian arrayed carefully about their apartment in Northington, conscious that they were setting up a home together. But the bowls looked wrong wherever they were placed, so she returned them to the closet with the other unopened gifts. Occasionally they would look inside that closet as if peeking at a life they had chosen not to live, and they would remind each other that they had to write thank-you notes. Finally, Julian wrote eighty-five thank-you notes in a single weekend, though he and Mia still hadn't opened most of the presents, so he could write only vague thanks for the person's generosity.

When they moved to Ann Arbor, they finally opened the rest of the gifts, which made Mia feel as if they'd just gotten married and it was permissible, finally, to celebrate. But the gifts meant little to her. There were more bowls and plates, some cookware, a waffle iron, a fondue set, the kinds of things people gave to suggest a new, shared life. But she and Julian had never been fondue- or waffle-eaters and it seemed forced to become them just because they were married. Besides, they had gotten married so long ago it was hard to connect the gift with the event, and so they did what they had done in Northington: they placed the gifts back inside the closet.

"Sometimes I wonder whether we made a mistake," she said now. "Getting married how we did."

"Shotgun?"

It had been a practical matter, but did it have to be *so* practical? She, in particular, had treated the wedding rituals with disdain, as if she were above it all. In Ann Arbor, she was the person friends turned to with their marriage proposal story, thinking that she, being married herself, would understand the flutter. She knew the story about the hidden engagement ring that beeped in the metal detector and how the man had to convince airport security not to make him empty his pockets. She knew the story about the jeweler who hadn't produced the ring on time and had to deliver it at midnight to the hotel. But when someone asked her about her own wedding proposal, she had to admit there hadn't really been one.

"None?"

"Not in the traditional sense." She couldn't tell the truth—she disapproved of marriage proposals—because she was talking to someone who had just been proposed to. Back then, she'd given everyone an earful, about how she and Julian would get married as they wished to. If anybody was going to propose, it would be she, because she found it detestable that the woman was supposed to wait. But she didn't wish to propose, either. Marriage was a decision she and Julian had reached together, and to turn it into a question a person asked on one knee smacked of playacting. She was no more interested in an engagement ring than in a proposal—this, too, she found repugnant, as if the groom were purchasing the bride—and she considered diamond rings garish. She didn't see why the bride was supposed to wear white, when no one was a virgin any longer. When someone said to her, "Don't you want people to know who the bride is?" she said, "I'll be the one up front next to the groom." It was her wedding, she explained, and she would wear a red dress if she wanted to. And she wouldn't walk down the aisle carrying flowers, because she didn't carry flowers in general and to do so on her wedding day felt contrived. No matter that the florist told her that in twenty-five years she had never seen a bride not carry flowers: all the more reason, Mia thought. She wasn't interested in doing what everyone else did. In fact, everyone else's doing something was grounds enough not to do it.

She wrote the wedding invitations by hand because it was more personal that way. Besides, the printed invitations always came from the parents of the bride, the wedding itself thrown by them as if they were paying off the groom's family. And the announcement in *The New York Times:* she disapproved of that as well, your résumé paraded for the world to see, as if in a breeder's catalogue, and she made her parents promise not to send an announcement to the *Times.* The garter belt—there would be none of that. As for the wedding cake, which the groom was supposed to feed to the bride as if to an infant: she saw no reason to have a wedding cake at all.

"I never thought of you as so political," a friend said to her.

She hated that word "political," the way it was used as a billy club to make you seem shrill when what you were saying was so sensible it shouldn't have needed repeating. It wasn't a question of politics, it was a question of her dignity, and of Julian's too, and if defending her dignity was political, then she was more political than she'd realized.

"Are you changing your name?" someone asked her.

"Yes," she said tartly. "I'm changing it to Julian."

She reminded herself that the wedding was just a party, and she made Julian promise that they would celebrate the anniversary of their first night together as much as they celebrated their wedding anniversary. "Even more so," she said, because that was when their relationship had begun and the wedding was just an affirmation of what was already true. She and Julian bought matching mood rings, which they wore in the month leading up to the event, and on the actual day they were accompanied by Mary, the Newfoundland Julian had walked at college, acting as ring bearer, lumbering down the aisle with the rings inside her mouth, to the guests' amusement and applause. Slimy, saliva-coated rings, but they were her and Julian's rings and it was their wedding. It was exactly as she'd wanted it.

So why now, lying next to Julian, why, after a dinner party that had gone well, was she smarting? Perhaps, she thought, she should have gotten a wedding gown. At the very least, she wished she hadn't worn that red dress again because now it was as if the wedding had been diluted and the dress was just an outfit she'd worn to a number of parties, several of which she couldn't recall. She didn't want an engagement ring, but the rings she and Julian had gotten had long ago been put away in a drawer—they weren't going to wear mood rings indefinitely—and hadn't been replaced by anything else. She wished she hadn't refused to videotape the event, especially since a friend of theirs had offered to do it unobtrusively with a handheld camera. She had seen a talk show that featured women who couldn't get over their wedding day. When the women's husbands left for work, the wives put on their wedding gowns and secretly, like alcoholics, spent the day watching their wedding video. But was that the only choice, either watch your videotape all day long or not have a videotape at all? Because looking back, all she could remember was the blur of her and Julian walking down the aisle with Mary shambling in front of them.

"Would you have married me if I'd proposed?" she said now.

"What do you mean? You did propose."

"But I didn't ask you formally. No one got down on one knee."

She got out of bed and kneeled before him. "Will you marry me, Julian?"

He laughed.

"Come on. Tell me you'll marry me."

"I'll marry you," he said.

The next day, they went to a jeweler and purchased rings, simple silver bands for each of them. But the gesture felt past due, as if they'd bought clothes for someone who had already outgrown them.

And Julian, walking through town the next few weeks, found himself playing with his wedding ring. He'd never worn jewelry before and he couldn't get used to it.

Late one night he ran into Trilby. She looked perplexed, as if she'd discovered something new, and Julian assumed this was because she'd caught him leaving the local sports bar. It was only after a few seconds that he realized she was staring at his left hand.

"You're wondering about my wedding ring?"

She nodded.

"It's a long story," he said.

She smiled at him. "You're full of long stories, aren't you?"

But before he could respond, she had turned to go. He watched her walk down William Street to Cottage Inn Pizza, where she opened the door and stepped inside.

Berkeley, California

Julian had lain down across three empty seats, a pillow propping his head up, but now that the movie was starting, he sat up and inserted his earphones. There was an individual TV in front of each seat, and he had spent several minutes watching the little airplane move incrementally across the screen. He'd finished off his meal, a mushy chicken number with orange sauce that he nonetheless had consumed appreciatively. Whenever he flew, he felt as if he were a child once more—back then, he used to insist on being taken up to the cockpit to meet the pilot and check out the controls—both grateful and amazed that you could eat or watch anything so high in the air.

When Mia's mother was alive, her parents used to fly separately for the children's sake, and on the way to the airport this morning Julian had said, "If your parents really wanted to be safe they should have taken separate taxis and boarded the same plane. The fact is, you're safer on a plane than in your own bathtub."

"Well, it's what my mother wanted," Mia said. "And I hope you'd do the same for our children."

The real argument was that Mia hoped to have children someday and Julian wasn't sure he wanted to have them. They were thirty-one now. They had been in Ann Arbor for eight years; for the last three years, Mia had been writing her dissertation. Her research was on children who had lost a parent, and maybe that was why the work was slow going: it depleted her. Or maybe she'd been infected by Julian; they were the world's two slowest writers. She had no idea when she would finish, but she knew she eventually wanted a child. Julian, on the other hand, didn't want to think about children until he was done with his novel. When the subject came up on the way to the airport, a gloom settled over the car and they rode silently along the highway, the traffic noise coming through the open window. Julian hated when he and Mia fought, especially when they were about to part, and as she kissed him goodbye at the airport terminal, her face descending in a frown, he promised her he'd do what she asked, which was to keep an open mind about the subject.

As the plane dipped beneath the clouds, Julian could make out through his window the tops of palm trees. He felt as if he were landing in a foreign country, though he'd been in the air only four hours.

Soon he was out in the airport terminal, that eye-rubbing sensation of being thrust beneath glaring lights, and now, in baggage claim, as the suitcases came trundling out, Carter emerged like a piece of luggage himself, revolving on the baggage carousel.

"Jesus, Wainwright, what took you so long? I was starting to get dizzy."

"I didn't know you were coming to get me."

"I had to fend off the security guard. A couple more revolutions and I would have been arrested." Carter was wearing a seersucker jacket, and he had on white linen pants and shoes to match. He had let his hair grow out, and he was sporting sideburns.

"Look at you," Julian said. "You're like something out of a fashion magazine." He stepped back and inspected Carter.

"So you approve?"

"Heinz, you're blinding." Julian grabbed his luggage. "Seriously, you didn't have to come pick me up."

"And allow you to get lost? There's no grid out here. You're not in New York City any longer."

"Carter, I live in the Midwest now, remember?"

"Though you keep insisting Ann Arbor's on East Coast time."

Carter wasn't the only one who couldn't recall what time zone

Julian was in. Julian's friends on the East Coast kept forgetting, too, to the point that he wondered whether it was intentional.

"I'm sorry Mia couldn't come," Carter said.

"She'd have loved to," said Julian. "But her dissertation adviser is back in town for the week, and you know how these things are. He's the lord and she's the serf."

"Does this mean I'll have to come visit Ann Arbor?" Since they'd moved to Michigan, Julian and Mia had been out to California twice, once to spend a spring break with Carter and Pilar, the other time for Carter and Pilar's wedding. But so far, at least, Carter and Pilar hadn't reciprocated. Julian spoke to Carter every couple of weeks and had been threatening to buy him a plane ticket. Failing that, he suggested he might try the opposite approach and start to call Carter collect.

Carter drove a convertible, and as he and Julian traveled north on 101, he pointed out the landmarks they passed, treating everything with a proprietary air. They passed Candlestick Park and the Cow Palace. San Francisco lay up ahead.

"Heinz, are you going to make me start calling you Esquire?"

Carter smiled. "Not until I get my degree."

"It's not like you need it. I suspect you could buy the law school at this point."

"You think?"

"You know, for someone as talented and lucky as you are, you don't make things easy on yourself."

So Mia had been right: Carter had ended up in law school. But his path there had been circuitous, for his relationship with Pilar was a series of negotiations, of offers and concessions back and forth. It had been Carter's turn when, after graduating from college, he and Pilar spent two years backpacking around the globe, and it was his turn, too, when they moved to California. But it was Pilar's turn when they applied to law school. She wanted them to go to Stanford Law School and, when they graduated, to practice together, maybe start off working for the public defender and eventually open their own criminal defense firm.

But a few months after applications were due, Julian received a phone call from Carter in the middle of the night. "Pilar got into Stanford and I didn't."

"Jesus, Heinz. I thought your record was as good as hers."

"It's better, actually."

"What happened, then?"

"I have no idea."

"So what are you going to do now?"

"I got into Berkeley Law School, at Boalt Hall."

"So Pilar will go to Stanford and you'll go to Boalt?"

"No," Carter said. "Pilar's going to Boalt, too. She insisted we do this together."

His first semester at Boalt, Carter explained, he treated law school the way he'd treated college. Sometimes he went to class and sometimes he didn't; often he slept until noon. One time the Civil Procedure professor called on him when he wasn't there, and when no one answered, the professor marked this down in his book. Another time, in Torts, the professor called on him when he hadn't done the reading and he answered anyway. Throughout college, he'd managed to talk about work he hadn't read and to do so persuasively; he didn't see why law school should be any different.

Then he got his fall grades. Two B's and two C's. Carter had never gotten a C before; even a B astounded him. For the first time in his life he'd failed at something, and fearing he'd been found out, he bought thick spiral notebooks and became the model of a diligent student, staying up late outlining his cases, raising his hand in class.

He did this for a full month, until he called Julian one night and said he was dropping out.

"You're dropping out of law school because of one semester of bad grades?"

"I never wanted to go to law school in the first place." Law school, Carter explained, had been Pilar's idea, just as everything he'd ever done had been urged on him by others: his mother, Pilar, these well-meaning women he'd hitched himself to and under whose exhortations he operated.

"So what are you going to do instead?"

"Some friends of mine are forming an Internet startup. It's called Signet, and they're developing a handwriting-recognition software that can read medical records, claim forms, and digital tablets."

"So you're going to join them?"

Carter nodded. "You know how I've always dreamed of becoming rich."

But Carter couldn't possibly have dreamed that, once the company had gone public, he would leave, selling his stake for seventeen million dollars. He was twenty-nine and wealthier than he ever imagined he'd be, and though years later he'd tell Julian how fortunate he'd been—he'd gotten in during the boom and out before the bust—he must have already sensed he was lucky, for no one deserved to make seventeen million dollars for three years of work.

Carter was wealthy enough to retire, and that was what his friends thought he would do, especially Pilar, who claimed to be as shocked as anyone else when he decided to return to law school. He went back, he told Julian, because he believed that dropping out in the middle of his first year was sufficiently shameful that earning a hundred and fifty million dollars wouldn't have made a difference. As he toiled down in Mountainview, where Signet's offices were housed, those two B's and two C's hung over him, and he believed they would continue to do so until he did something about them. So he returned to law school with his indignation intact, and with a resolve to make his professors rue the grades they'd given him. He would make the admissions office at Stanford regret its decision, too.

Now, two years later, he'd succeeded. "Number one in my class," he told Julian in the car, "discounting that fluke first semester. If only I'd set my mind to things from the start."

"But then you wouldn't have dropped out," Julian said, "and you'd be seventeen million dollars poorer."

They were on the Bay Bridge now and Carter said, "I've never told anyone this before, but whenever something good is about to happen, I think disaster will occur. It was that way with Signet. Once I decided to quit and we were working out my compensation, I was sure the company would go belly-up. And we were doing great. There was nothing to worry about." He was quiet for a moment, staring out at San Francisco Bay, where a bird had landed. "My father was on the Bay Bridge the day of the big earthquake. He drove across it fifteen minutes before it collapsed. And the next morning he was back up in his hot-air balloons. I'm the same way. Things don't scare me. But right now, I'm afraid this bridge will collapse and I'll die before I graduate from law school. As if becoming a lawyer was what I wanted to do in the first place." He pushed down on the gas and they accelerated, hurtling past the other cars toward the East Bay.

Commencement was taking place all across the country, but this was Berkeley, Julian thought. Growing up, he used to ride the subway to Morningside Heights and while away the hours on Columbia's College Walk, imagining, vaguely, that he was a campus radical and it was 1968. He'd been born in 1968, and he maintained a romantic's view of that time, especially of Berkeley, which he liked to think of as Columbia's West Coast cousin.

Now, as he walked up Sproul Plaza to Sather Gate, he was greeted by protestors and bullhorns, students thrusting leaflets into his hands. Migrant workers. Genocide in Africa. Graduate student unionizers. He passed Dwinelle Hall and the graduate library. Up the hill was the law school, and the tennis courts facing Bancroft Way.

He headed over to People's Park, site, as he imagined it, of mammoth protest, so he was disappointed to find that it was an abandoned field, home to a few panhandlers and a man in a wheelchair trailing a bag of empty soda cans, the metal clanking behind him.

It was seventy-five degrees out, he was wearing shorts and sneakers, and he wandered along College Avenue toward Oakland. He picked up an ice cream cone and stopped in a few stores, and before he realized it two hours had passed and he had to hail a cab so he wouldn't be late for dinner.

When he arrived, Carter was standing in front of the restaurant, wearing a black silk jacket and a tie.

"Am I late?" Julian said. "And underdressed?" He had changed into khakis and an Oxford shirt.

"Late, yes," said Carter. He didn't say anything about Julian's clothes. "I had to pull some strings. This wasn't an easy reservation to get graduation week."

Now, having been seated by the hostess, Julian unfolded his napkin on his lap. "So this is the famous Chez Panisse. Do you eat here often?"

"I've got my own chair here," Carter said. "Someday they're going to stuff it and put it in a museum."

"And you along with it?"

"If I'm lucky."

Shattuck Avenue was a busy street, but Chez Panisse was set back and felt secluded. Upstairs was the café, where you could get the poor man's version of the restaurant's food, though that wasn't for the poor, either. Carter read through the wine list appraisingly. Between him and Julian, a single candle bobbed in a glass.

"Isn't Pilar coming?"

Carter shook his head. "Pilar's too busy to eat. These big law firms own you."

A woman approached, and Carter rose to hug her. "Alice," he said, "this is Julian, my buddy from college. He flew out from Michigan to see me graduate. Alice is responsible for my good health," he told Julian. "I kid you not. She's made me look at the world in a whole new way."

Alone now, Carter said, "Do you realize who that was?"

" Alice?" said Julian.

"As in Alice Waters? Chef and owner of Chez Panisse? Spawner of a culinary revolution?" In college, Carter had subsisted on cheeseburgers, onion rings, potato chips, and chimichangas. He'd been contemptuous of anyone who regarded food as more than sustenance, and in this regard, at least, he had become the kind of person he'd once despised. He'd taken a couple of wine-tasting courses, and in his house, in a leather container next to the toilet, sat a pile of old issues of *Wine Spectator*. He'd befriended the produce buyers at Berkeley Bowl, and every Thursday when he shopped for groceries they would set aside a special basket for him filled with litchis, loquats, Pluots, and Apriums.

JOSHUA HENKIN

Chez Panisse served a prix fixe menu, and tonight it was grilled asparagus salad followed by pork shoulder, Chino Ranch carrots, and Jerusalem artichoke purée. Growing up, Julian had eaten with his parents in more expensive restaurants than this one, but his father was a meat-and-potatoes man who, though he found himself on occasion at Bouley Bakery or Le Cirque, was still happiest ordering a porterhouse at Peter Luger. Julian's mother was the same way. "So has this made you happy?" Julian asked Carter.

"Eating here?"

"Your new life. It's what you always wanted. To be rich."

"It hasn't made me *un*happy."

"But is it what you imagined?"

"Nothing's what you imagine," Carter said. "Anyway, I think happiness is beside the point."

"Oh, come on."

"They've done studies that show that when something good occurs people aren't as happy as they expected to be, and when something bad occurs they aren't as devastated. We each have a natural disposition we eventually return to. It's the best argument I've heard for the welfare state. Because it's for the truly poor that money matters. Meet a poor person's basic needs and you have an impact on his happiness. But once he reaches a threshold, the extra wealth doesn't make a difference."

"So you've been tilting at windmills all these years."

Carter shook his head. "I'm happy to have money even if it hasn't transformed me. As Mae West said, 'I've been rich and I've been poor, and rich is better.' "

"Yet it hasn't made you a Republican."

"You should know," Carter said. "You're rich and you're a Democrat."

"Some people would say it's because I can afford to be one."

"A limousine liberal?"

Julian shrugged. His father had tried to make him a Republican, but from the start, he'd felt different from his parents. In November 1972, his mother had taken him to the voting booth and let him

140

pull the lever, but she wouldn't allow him to vote for McGovern and he sulked all the way home. He was four: what did he know? But he sensed intuitively that he wasn't for Nixon. And four years later, he voted for Jimmy Carter in his school's mock elections, though his parents loathed Carter and made arch, knowing jokes about peanut farmers. "When I was in junior high school, my father would draw Laffer curves on my breakfast napkin. He was trying to teach me about supply-side economics. My father's a smart guy and he's irrepressible, but I wouldn't budge."

"When I was in junior high school," Carter said, "I didn't even know what a Laffer curve was."

"I knew all I needed to know," Julian said. "That Arthur Laffer was a Republican flunky. Apparently, he drew his curve on a napkin in a Washington, D.C., bar and trickle-down theory was born."

Carter removed a pen and drew a Laffer curve on a piece of scrap paper. The Signet logo was embossed on his pen.

"Why did you leave Signet, anyway?"

Carter shrugged. "For me, it's always been about getting there. But once I'm there, I become restless. With Signet, we made this great software, but then I wanted to know what came next."

"So now you go work for a law firm?"

"It's what's expected of me. Otherwise, why did I go back to school?" Carter looked down at his plate, which was empty now, just a small mound of gristle in the corner and a couple of fugitive gravy spots. If he didn't know better, Julian thought, if he hadn't become refined, Carter would have asked for seconds. He was a creature of appetite, he'd always been that way, and Julian was as well, the two of them with their hunger and their fast metabolisms. At the all-you-can-eat sushi place in Northington, they used to compete to see who could eat more. "What about you?" Carter said. "Are you still working on your novel?"

"Every day."

"You just get up in the morning and write? I don't think I'd have the discipline to do that."

"What do you mean? You started your own company."

"That was different. Other people were counting on me. I had deadlines and an office." Carter considered this. "I still miss it sometimes. Sitting around with everyone, shooting the shit." He was eating dessert now, scooping up his tangerine soufflé. A cup of tea sat in front of him, and he dropped a lump of sugar into it. "So how's your book going?"

"Glacially," Julian said. "It's like that joke about Joyce Carol Oates. Someone calls her up and her secretary says, 'I'm sorry, Miss Oates can't come to the phone right now, she's busy writing a book,' and the person says, 'That's okay, I'll hold.' Only with me it's the opposite. Rip Van Winkle wakes up twenty years later and I'm still writing my novel."

"Now, now."

"I've been at it almost ten years," he said. "I've got two hundred and fifty pages, though I've probably thrown out twenty for every one I've kept. I'm laying waste to whole forests."

"What's the book about?"

Julian hesitated. Even to Mia, he hadn't confided much; he didn't want to jinx himself. Growing up, he'd had a special cup he drank from and a lucky number, eight. When he watched the Mets at Shea Stadium in 1973, five years old, in the corporate box seats with his father, he always wore his baseball glove, less because he expected to catch a foul ball than because he believed it made the Mets play better. It had worked when he was watching them on TV. Writers, Julian believed, came in all types, but one way or another they were control freaks, and superstition was nothing if not an attempt to exert control. Besides, he thought a good novel resisted summary; it had to speak for itself. Still, he felt he owed Carter an answer, for Carter was his friend and he'd written fiction, too.

"It's about me," he said, "but pretty quickly it departs from fact." At the table across from them, the waiter had brought out another bottle of wine and was holding it up for approval. A pretty blonde in a short skirt and tights wove her way back to her seat, her heels clicking against the floor. "Remember how Professor Chesterfield used to say that everyone at college either writes what they know, which is a transcript of Friday night's keg party, or what they don't know, which is Martians? Well, according to him, you should write what you know about what you don't know or what you don't know about what you know. Keep it close enough to home that your heart is in it but far enough away that the imagination can take over. That way, you don't descend into solipsism."

"Are you succeeding?"

"I feel like I am. But then I lose confidence and think I need to shake up my life. You know, 'The writer has to live!' It's ridiculous. According to Flannery O'Connor, anyone who's lived until the age of ten has enough material to write about for a lifetime."

"So what are you worried about?"

He shrugged. "I keep telling Mia I'm going to quit teaching, but I have no idea what I'd do instead. I wish I had your balls. You decide to leave law school, and the next time I look up you're running a multimillion-dollar tech company."

"It wasn't quite that simple."

"You're not afraid to try something new." An image came to Julian of Carter feasting on something nauseous in a faraway land (bugs? grasshoppers? Carter had sent photos) and of Julian's last trip to San Francisco, when Carter had taken him to a restaurant and attempted, unsuccessfully, to get him to eat brains. Try everything at least once, Carter liked to say. A few years ago, scientists had discovered a novelty-seeking gene, and when Julian told Carter about it, Carter said, "That's me."

"Things are getting even more complicated," Julian said now. "Mia wants a baby."

"And you don't want one?"

"In theory I'm persuadable."

"But in reality?"

"I promised myself I'd finish my novel first."

"People with babies write novels."

"You sound just like Mia."

The restaurant was starting to empty out, and Alice Waters stood next to the kitchen, her hair tied up in a bandanna.

"What about you?" Julian said. "Do you and Pilar think about kids?"

Carter shook his head. "The Heinz dynasty stops with me. I have enough trouble taking care of myself."

"And Pilar's okay with that?"

"As far as I can tell."

Alice approached them. "Are you two sleeping over?"

Carter shrugged apologetically. "Julian and I were just catching up."

"I can give you a lift home."

"Okay," he said, "we can take a hint."

Then they were out into the night, Carter going north toward the Berkeley hills, Julian south to the hotel, walking slowly through the crowds on Shattuck, taking himself toward repose.

"Hey, you! Wainwright!"

It was Carter, shouting at him from his convertible. "You told me the Cheeseboard," Julian said.

"I also told you nine, and it's nine-fifteen. Which makes it afternoon your time. You're not in college any longer." Carter held a paper bag out the window, letting it dangle like bait. "Come on," he said. "Get in."

They headed west on University Avenue, the sun slowly ascending above the bay. On the corner of Sacramento, someone had opened a fire hydrant, and a group of teenagers was spraying passing cars. "It's supposed to hit eighty today," Carter said. "And eighty-five tomorrow. I'll be sweating in my cap and gown." A blind man stopped at the crosswalk, rhythmically tapping his cane. "Listen, can you fend for yourself for a couple of hours? I'll drive you into the city and you can wander around for a while. I need to take care of a few things."

Now, as they approached San Francisco, Carter silently ate his cheese roll. It seemed to Julian that he was turning in on himself, that he was less expansive than he'd been last night.

"Is everything okay?" he said. "You seem subdued."

"I'm just tired."

They parked in the Haight and walked along Carl Street and up into Cole Valley, then down the hill into the Castro. On Castro Street, all the cars were parked with their wheels turned to the curb and everyone drove with their emergency brakes. "It's the world's hilliest city," Carter said. "People drive even if they're going only a few blocks."

"But not you, Heinz."

"I'm like everyone else. I take the elevator to the third floor so I can work out on the StairMaster."

"And now we've left the car on the other side of the city."

"If we walk quickly, we can get back in half an hour."

"I thought you needed to take care of some things."

"I tell you what," Carter said. "You can come with me."

They walked back to the car, then drove silently along Clement Street, past the produce stands and the Chinese restaurants. They turned right on Park Presidio, and soon the wind was at their backs and they could see the Golden Gate Bridge. "I hate tolls," Carter said. "Three bucks just to commit suicide. People come from all over the world to jump from here." He looked out the window. "They've talked about putting up barriers to make it more difficult, but if someone's determined it would be hard to stop them."

They got off the bridge, then wound their way through the hills. On the car in front of them was a BILL BRADLEY FOR PRESIDENT bumper sticker. The tree branches canopied them, covering them in shadows. Carter made a left, a right, another right, and a left again. He slowed down and turned into a driveway. "I'll only be a few minutes," he said, and it wasn't until he was walking up the path to a modest A-frame house that Julian realized where they were. Sausalito. Carter's parents' house.

"Should I come in?"

"No need to," Carter said. "I won't be long."

But twenty minutes later Carter still hadn't returned. A bird called out; a couple of cars drove past. Julian heard voices through the open window, he saw a figure shimmering behind drapes, but then there was nothing. He had met Carter's parents just once, at Graymont's graduation, though he expected he would see them again tomorrow. At college, the only one who knew Carter's parents was Pilar. It was as if Carter kept them sealed away, bringing them out on special occasions only to return them to the closet.

Julian flipped on the radio, but all he could get was static. He leaned his head against the window and shut his eyes.

He was woken by the sound of Carter kicking up gravel, his friend, loaded down, walking along the path.

"Wainwright, I'm sorry. I didn't realize it would take this long." Carter was holding books and papers, and a pillow, and a carrying bag.

"Here, let me help you."

"I'm all right." Carter deposited his belongings in the trunk.

In the car now, he let the engine idle. He looked up obscurely at his parents' house. "There it is," he said. "The place I grew up."

"Yet you're not giving tours."

Carter tapped his feet against the brake. "You should know something," he said. "Pilar won't be coming to graduation tomorrow."

"Don't tell me she can't get off for something as important as this."

"The truth is, I've asked her not to come."

"I don't get it."

Carter laid his head against the steering wheel. "We're not together," he said. "We've separated."

"Carter, you're kidding me."

"I wish I were."

"When did this happen?"

"A couple of months ago."

"I had no idea."

"I was going to tell you last night. I tried to tell you. I've been staying with a friend until I find my own place."

"Are you getting a divorce?"

"We haven't started the proceedings, but it looks like it."

"Jesus, Carter, I'm so sorry."

Carter tapped his hand against the steering wheel. "You want me to tell you about it?"

"If you're willing."

Carter started the car and they drove in silence, up through Tiburon, Corte Madera, and San Rafael. All the cars were exceeding the speed limit, but Carter was driving faster than them all.

He pulled over to the side of the road. "I could give you all the usual reasons."

"What are those?"

"I spent too much time at work, and Pilar did, too. We started to take each other for granted. We didn't attend to our sex life." He looked down at his lap. "I mean, Jesus, everyone gets divorced. Why did we think we'd be immune?"

"It just never occurred to me."

"I thought we were too young to get divorced, but then I thought we were too young to get married and we did that. And sure, I'm only thirty-one and twenty years from now I'll probably think I was just a kid saying this, but I can see myself feeling the same way at fifty or sixty. Real life, the big decisions—those always seemed to be the realm of someone else, and I thought when my turn came I'd know it." Carter looked up at Julian. "You want to know the truth? I think Pilar and I shouldn't have been together in the first place."

"Oh, come on. You can't convince me of that. Mia and I—we were with you guys for four years." Julian recalled those early months together, the four of them playing cards in the dorms, and how, when Carter won, he would do hurdles over the couch where Julian and Mia were sitting, and Pilar, watching him, seemed in her heart to be hurdling, too. "If Carter has his way," Pilar said once, "I'll end up wherever he takes me." And this, Julian thought, was where he'd taken her. California. Separation. He couldn't believe it. If he'd been asked freshman year which couple would stay together, he would have bet on Carter and Pilar.

"I'm not saying I didn't love her," Carter said, "or that she didn't love me. I'm saying we weren't the right fit." Meeting Pilar, he explained, hadn't been that different from meeting Julian. He loved them both, and all right, he admitted it, they made him feel bad about himself. He wanted to be Pilar and it seemed she wanted him to be her, too; she made him into her project. "I was the rebel," he said, "and she was going to civilize me. The boyfriend on the motorcycle. *Épatons les bourgeoisie.* At dinner last night you asked how I feel about having all this money, but I could have ten times the money and it wouldn't change where I come from. Give me a little credit, Wainwright. The expensive clothes, the dinners at Chez Panisse, the friendship with Alice Waters? You think I don't know I'm compensating?"

Julian was silent.

"Last summer, I was working at this big law firm and one of the partners mentioned Toulouse-Lautrec. Now, I'd heard of the guy, but I didn't grow up going to museums, so art isn't my strong suit. Inadvertently I made clear that I thought the artist's first name was Toulouse. Not Henri de Toulouse-Lautrec, but Toulouse Lautrec, like Carter Heinz. Okay, so big fucking deal. But to me it was. Everyone was laughing, and I felt like saying, 'I know more than all of you. I speak more languages, I've been to more countries, I've read more books.' When I got home that night, I read up on Toulouse-Lautrec, and because I can afford it, I contacted an art dealer and bought one of his paintings." Carter looked up at Julian. "Not that you'd understand."

"Why not?"

"You don't know what it's like to have to prove yourself."

But Julian disagreed. He had spent his whole life trying to prove himself, especially to his father. Yale, summa cum laude. Head of the arbitrage division. His name at the top of the company hierarchy. Julian recalled a conversation when he was small, his father telling him that at a certain hour each day it was today in New York but in Hawaii it was yesterday, and soon his father was explaining to him about the sun and the earth and the speed of light—a conversation Julian found himself irretrievably lost in and that, even in retrospect, seemed to embody a storehouse of knowledge his father had that he would never possess. His father had gone to Yale, a school, he once explained, where everyone believed they were so good that even Yale itself didn't deserve them and where it was unfashionable to be happy, for happiness was the domain of the credulous and the callow. Yet his father had been happy at Yale, so happy, in fact, that growing up, Julian had come to believe his life would be incomplete if he didn't go there. But when it came time to apply he refused to do so, afraid he might not get in.

"The first time I visited Pilar's house," Carter said, "it was like I'd landed in a different galaxy. Pilar's father brought me into his study and showed me his memorabilia. An early draft, care of Ted Sorensen, of Kennedy's Bay of Pigs speech. A get-well card from Dean Acheson on the occasion of having his appendix removed. The stub of a Cuban cigar reputedly smoked by Castro himself."

Julian remembered. He'd visited Pilar's house once, and when only he and Carter were in the room, he reached into the glass case where the cigar was kept and inserted it in his mouth. "Groucho Marx," he said. "Fidel Castro."

"Put that back!" Carter said. Julian had never seen him look so terrified.

"After graduation," Carter said now, "Pilar and I were traveling from country to country, and for the first time I felt we were on the same footing. But then Pilar got into Stanford and I didn't, and that was a blow someone else might have shrugged off, but it was hard for me. I insisted we move to California, but it only alienated us from each other. We've been here for seven years now and Pilar still misses the East Coast. If only I'd taken that more seriously."

"You're saying you'd still be together if you'd gone east?"

"Coming west certainly didn't help things." Carter considered this. "It's good Pilar and I didn't open our own law firm. We'd have been terrible business partners."

"So it's really over?" Julian said, still not believing it.

"And the worst thing is my parents—my mother and father who are so fucking proud of me. Graduating from Boalt, getting Signet off the ground, and it's as if none of that matters."

"That's not true."

"Half the country is divorced and California leads the way, but it's never happened in my family. My parents see it as shameful, and in a way I do, too." Carter was staring out the window, and he had a heart-sick look on his face, as if he were trying to imagine how he could have done things differently. "You know what? I think people should marry their own."

"Their own what?" Julian said. "Race? Religion? Class?"

"Yes," Carter said. "All of it."

"That's ridiculous. Mia's Jewish and I'm not. Are you telling me we shouldn't have gotten married?"

"There are those who would say you shouldn't have."

"What would *you* say?"

"I'd say fundamentally you come from the same place."

"Our parents couldn't have been more different from one another."

"In the scheme of things, the distinctions are minuscule."

"So what are you telling me? That we all should just marry ourselves?"

"I think there's some truth to that."

"And what should you have done then? Married the daughter of another balloonist?"

But Carter, it was clear, didn't want to talk about this. He started the car, pulled out of park, and drove them back to the highway.

At graduation the next day, Julian watched Carter onstage in his cap and gown. Next to Julian sat Carter's parents, his aunt and uncle, a few childhood friends, and Max and Sander, Carter's cofounders at Signet. For an instant Julian caught Carter's eye, and Carter nodded, then looked away.

After the degrees were conferred, everyone hugged and congratulated him, and Carter's mother was crying, which made Carter cry, too.

Carter's uncle handed out cigars. "Now all this young man has to do is pass the bar. Then he can hang out a shingle."

Sander, Signet's CEO, said, "To Carter Heinz! The man taking the world's biggest pay cut!"

Carter introduced Julian to his family and friends, and everyone shook hands.

"Wainwright," Sander said. "So this is the Sugar Daddy."

Julian started to respond, but Carter's aunt broke in, holding a gift wrapped in a large box, and everyone was demanding that Carter open it.

Soon campus began to empty out. Strawberry stems and empty plastic champagne cups littered the green, and the chairs were tilted toward one another, a few of them having been toppled as people departed. A sanitation worker was stacking chairs and another was stabbing at refuse with a long, pointed stick, and Julian was reminded of the term "shit-picker," which was how Carter used to describe himself, cleaning his classmates' dorm rooms back at college.

Carter went off to change into a tuxedo, for tonight was the law school's black-and-white ball, the final dance after graduation.

When Carter emerged, Julian was on the steps, waiting for him. "The penguin cometh," Carter said.

"Congratulations, Heinz. You're a lawyer now."

"Not until I pass the bar."

"When does that happen?"

"The test's in July."

"Are you going to take it?"

"I might as well keep my options open."

Across from them stood the graduate library, where a professor was resolutely making his way up the steps, holding a stack of books in one arm like someone protecting a football.

"Look at that guy," Carter said. "Do you think he even knows it was graduation today?" Carter was still holding his cap and gown, and a breeze came through, sending the tassel flapping back and forth.

Julian said, "I'm so sorry about what's happened."

Carter nodded. He repeated Julian's words from senior year: the last two couples standing. He and Pilar had gotten married three years to the day after Julian and Mia; they'd chosen that date, he told Julian, because they'd thought it would bring them good luck. "Not that it should have made a difference. Who cares about a fucking wedding date?"

Julian was silent.

"Are you flying out tonight?"

"In a few hours."

"If it weren't for the dance, I'd drive you to the airport."

"Heinz, you've been more than accommodating."

A couple was tossing a Frisbee on the lawn, their German Shepherd running back and forth between them. Monkey in the middle, Julian thought, except the monkey was a dog.

"We can walk around if you want," Carter said. "I can help you check out of your hotel."

They left Julian's suitcase at the front desk and walked down Telegraph Avenue past the crowds. At People's Park, they stood outside the playground where Carter had played basketball with his law school buddies. The courts were unoccupied, but a ball lay on the far end beneath the basket.

"How about it?" Carter said. In college, he and Julian had played basketball together several times a week.

"Heinz, you're wearing a tuxedo."

Carter removed his tuxedo jacket and slung it over his back. "Now I'm not."

Julian pointed to Carter's pants.

"Those will have to stay on." Carter spun the basketball on his index finger, then transferred it to the middle finger and the one after that, going from finger to finger, hand to hand. "If law doesn't work out, there's always the Harlem Globetrotters." He made a couple of foul shots, then handed the ball to Julian, who did the same. Sweat stains blossomed across Carter's tuxedo shirt. "Should we play one-on-one?"

Julian took the ball out first and drove to the basket, but his reverse layup missed, and Carter followed with a missed shot of his own. For the next few minutes they went back and forth like this, the score locked at zero.

"Have you ever seen such ineptitude?" Carter said. "We've got the score of a soccer game here." But then Carter spun past Julian for a layup, and finally someone had scored a point.

They were thirty-one and they'd slowed down since college, but what they'd lost in speed and buoyancy they'd made up for in know-how. There was no shade on the courts, they were sweating immoderately, and when the ball came loose they both dove for it. On one missed shot, Carter slipped and fell on his rear, and now he had a dirt stain on the back of his tuxedo pants.

The score was tied at five, and at seven, and at eleven again. The first player to reach fifteen won. Julian would elude Carter and get an offensive rebound. He was a better jumper than Carter, quicker and lighter-footed, but Carter was stronger and he had a deadly outside shot.

Julian slapped the ground to encourage himself. Carter was breathing heavily. He kept wiping his brow with the back of his hand, and now some sweat had dripped onto the ball, which got away from him momentarily.

Carter backed in, using his strength, and he put up a little leaning jump shot that swished in.

"I need a drink," Julian said, and he walked over to the water fountain.

When he returned, he made a cross-over dribble to the left. He was a step ahead of Carter, he was going in for a layup, and Carter, coming at him to block his shot, kneed him in the thigh.

"Fuck." Julian lay on the ground, and when Carter bent over to help him up, he batted Carter's hand away.

"I'm sorry," Carter said.

"Jesus Christ, Heinz!"

Carter missed a jump shot from behind the three-point line, and when Julian fired off a shot of his own, it rolled around the inside of the rim like toilet-bowl cleaner before popping out.

Carter had tied his tuxedo shirt to the fence, and now he was wearing only his black shoes and pants, which he'd rolled up past his knees. He looked like someone about to enter the water, as if he were going fly fishing.

It was game point and Carter muscled in on Julian, but instead of spinning around toward the basket as he usually did, he propelled himself backward, lofting a fall-away jump shot that sailed over Julian's outstretched arms and went in.

"Game!" Carter was lying on the ground. "Call the paramedics. Hook me up to an oxygen tank." His tied-up tuxedo shirt blew languidly in the breeze, the cuff links jangling against the fence. "Good one," he said. "A couple of lucky rolls and it would have gone the other way."

Julian nodded noncommittally. Already he could feel his thigh tightening up. He pictured the plane ride home, returning to Ann Arbor at two in the morning, back from his friend's graduation with a charley horse.

A teenager shouted something from a passing car, but Julian couldn't make it out. He looked at Carter still lying on the ground. "That guy from Signet?" he said. "The CEO? What was that supposed to mean, calling me a sugar daddy?"

"Don't worry about it."

"I'm just asking what he meant."

"He wasn't even talking about you."

"Oh, really, Heinz? Do you know some other Wainwright?"

Carter put on his shirt. The tuxedo jacket, which he'd taken off before the game, was the one piece of clothing no worse for wear, and he put that on, too. He examined his reflection in the metal pole that held the backboard up. "Your father's the other Wainwright, if you have to know. He's the sugar daddy."

"What?"

"I talked to him at college graduation, and he said if I ever needed anything I should give him a call. So a few years later, when Signet was looking for investors, I sent him our brochure and our financial plan."

"And he invested in you?"

Carter shook his head. "He saw us as novices, a bunch of kids. But he told me he liked me and wanted to help us out. He gave us a loan of a hundred thousand dollars."

"Jesus Christ."

"And we paid back every penny of it, with interest. The fact is, he'd have done a lot better if he'd invested that money with us. By this point he'd have made it back tenfold."

Julian was looking at Carter, shaking his head.

"Wainwright, would you get off your fucking high horse? So I asked your father for help. Tell me you don't do that every day."

"Actually, I don't."

"Are you kidding me?"

"Do you realize how many times my father has offered to introduce me to a literary agent?"

"Your father knows nothing about literature."

"Maybe not, but he's a businessman, and I don't have to tell you he's well connected."

"But you're too high-minded to accept his offer."

"It's not a matter of being high-minded. It's just that, if I succeed, I want to do it on my own."

Carter laughed. "You've never done anything on your own. Your whole life has been one big loan from him."

Julian looked at Carter levelly. "I'm past apologizing for who I am. Jesus, Heinz, would you finally get over me?"

"I was over you years ago," Carter said.

Now it was Julian's turn to laugh. Christmas of freshman year, when Carter visited him in New York, there had been an hour when Carter was alone in the apartment, and when Julian came home he caught Carter stepping out of his parents' bathroom, where he'd been showering in their seven-nozzled shower. Who cares, Carter seemed to say, about a bunch of spigots, but Julian could tell, looking at Carter, that he'd never been so covetous of anything. Years later, when Carter and Pilar bought their home in Berkeley, Carter insisted on redoing the master bathroom. Seeing the bathroom for the first time ("It's not even called a shower," Carter told Julian proudly; " 'wet room' is the term of art."), Julian understood that Carter had renovated because of him, that so much of what he'd done in the years since college he'd done because of Julian. No, Julian thought, Carter hadn't gotten over him and, he suspected, he never would.

"You know what your problem is?" Carter said. "You've got your head stuck up your asshole. It's in so deep you can't see anything."

"Oh, is that right?"

"I fucked your girlfriend," Carter said.

"What are you talking about?"

"Back in college. Spring of senior year."

"You slept with Mia?"

"That's right."

Suddenly, Carter was bawling. He was lying on the ground with his head between his legs, and his jacket and pants were creased, as if he were a vagrant who'd slept in someone else's tuxedo. "God, Julian, I'm so sorry."

"You disgust me," Julian said.

"Forgive me!" Carter wailed. "Please!"

Julian heaved the basketball over the fence. Then he exited the playground and walked away, not bothering to look back.

He headed up Dwight and over on College, past the Greek Theater toward the Berkeley Hills. He could feel his pulse beating. He thought of freshman year, when he and Carter had discovered Mia. Page 47 of the Graymont freshman facebook. Mia from Montreal. But Carter was with Pilar already, and Julian was enthralled. "Okay," Carter said, "so you get first dibs." Though Carter had continued to covet Mia, coveted her the way he coveted everything of Julian's simply because she was his. There were times, Julian recalled now, when the four of them were playing cards and he would catch Carter staring at Mia in a way that unsettled him. It was how Carter smiled, the scar above his lip curling up as if it were smiling as well. One time he said to Carter, "So you want my girlfriend, too," and Carter, laughing, said, "Why not?"

But Carter was his best friend. How could he have done this to him? And how could Mia have done it? That assailed him above all else.

He walked up Euclid, past the Berkeley Rose Garden and Codornices Park. Across the bay stood San Francisco. He was still sweaty from the basketball game; he needed to change out of his clothes. He had a taxi to catch in half an hour. A breeze came off the water and he shivered. The sun had begun to dip, and he turned around and made his way down the street, heading back to the hotel.

It was two in the morning when Julian got home. The apartment was silent and dark, and when he turned on the light he could see through the open door to the bedroom, where Mia lay asleep, her back to him, her rib cage moving to the thrum of her respiration. He laid down his suitcase and began to unpack. His shoes creaked across the floor, though he tried to move silently.

He got into bed and attempted to sleep, but fatigue wouldn't come, just a hollow, pervasive ache. He told himself it was early still—it wasn't even midnight in Berkeley—though that wasn't it, of course; he'd been gone for just the weekend.

He watched the alarm clock numbers flip, the room shot through with a dull orange glow. There was a distant mewling, the neighbor's cat, its own insomnia accompanying his. The clock read four in the morning, then five. He thought of his childhood, of those early years, when he was three and four, when his parents placed a clock in his bedroom with the instructions that he wasn't to wake them until the little hand was on seven. He felt an unaccountable power, thinking he knew something Mia didn't, when the truth was the opposite: what he knew now she had known all along.

His lone hope was that it hadn't happened. That Carter was engaged in wishful thinking. That he was delusional.

He awoke an hour later, to Mia's touch. "Julian, sweetie, I missed you." She kissed him on the neck, the nose, the lips, the eyebrows. "How was your trip?"

"It was fine."

She kissed him again, wrapping her arms around his neck, but he pushed her away.

Then he told her everything.

She was silent as he spoke, her fingers drumming against her thighs, and he knew that what he'd held on to, the scant hope, was false. There had been no lying, no wishful thinking, no delusion.

"So it's true?"

She nodded.

Then there was more silence as she went to make herself a cup of coffee. She offered him some, too, but he refused, and now she was back in bed, the steam shrouding her. "I'm sorry," she said. "I truly, truly am."

"Is that all you can say?"

And in the midst of this, he looked at her, his wife, saw the wisp of hair dangling down her forehead, and he thought how beautiful she was and how much he loved her, and this made it even worse. "You slept with my best friend. You betrayed me."

"If I could take it back, I would. Really, Julian, I so wish it hadn't happened."

He'd wanted tears and chest-beating, her laying herself prostrate before him. Not that it would have made him feel better. But this distance, this equanimity, felt even worse. "Why did you do it?"

She was silent.

He was still in his T-shirt and boxers, and he felt curiously vulnerable half-naked in front of her, so he went into the bathroom and put on some clothes.

When he returned, she had gotten dressed, too. She seemed more composed now, though she had the damp, pallid look of someone who had been crying. There was so much more to say, but he had no idea what to tell her, and it seemed as likely that they'd spend the whole day locked in their bedroom in silence. "When did you sleep with him?"

"Spring of senior year."

"When, exactly?"

"Jesus, Julian, I can't remember the precise date."

"We got married senior year."

"I know that."

"Were we already engaged?"

"I don't think so."

"You mean we might have been?"

"No," she said. "We weren't."

"Did he come on to you?"

She hesitated.

"Did you come on to him?"

"In which case I'd be more guilty?"

He didn't answer her.

"Oh, Julian, I have no idea who came on to whom."

"How's that possible?"

"It was nine years ago. Think of what we've been through in the last nine years. My mother died. We got married. We made a home together. I barely remember what I was like at twenty-two."

"I remember," he said. "I loved you."

"I loved you, too."

"Then how could you have done this to me?"

She didn't have an answer for him.

"Where was I when it happened?"

"You were away, I think. Gone for the weekend."

"Where?"

"I can't remember." She recalled a difficult conversation with her mother—she'd gone back into the hospital, the cancer had gotten worse—a rain-soaked night, the campus derelict, the smell of Carter's aftershave, and his voice, a haunting laughter.

"Were you drunk?" Julian asked.

"As if that would excuse me? The truth is, I've repressed it. I don't find it very pleasant to think about."

"Well, I don't either."

"Yet you're pummeling me with questions."

He turned away from her now.

"It was nine years ago," she repeated. She wanted to tell him the statute of limitations had elapsed. But was there ever a statute of limitations on something like this? "My mother was dying, Julian. Doesn't that count for anything?"

It occurred to him that even if he managed to forgive her, he would always know that what had happened once could happen another time; he could never look at her the way he used to. He was ashamed to admit how credulous he'd been, but he'd trusted her so implicitly that when he'd tried to imagine her cheating on him he couldn't do it. She hadn't seemed like the cheating kind, and now that was gone, and along with it the notion that there was a cheating kind. He'd been so wrong about something so fundamental he didn't know any longer what to believe. "Our marriage has been a lie."

"Oh, Julian . . ."

"Listen to me," he said. "If you'd told me the truth when it happened, we wouldn't have gotten married. We probably would have broken up."

"Then I'm glad I didn't tell you."

"And married me under false pretenses?"

"I love you," she said. "I can't imagine my life without you."

"Until yesterday, I couldn't either."

A chill ran through her; the hair on her arms stood on end. She started to cry and he did, too, and she thought maybe she should leave and return at the end of the day. Perhaps then they would see things differently.

But when she came home that afternoon, Julian was back to where they'd been that morning. And she was tired of it. Tired of his accusations when she could offer no more than an honest apology, and since that didn't appear to be enough, maybe it was best if she didn't say anything. She sat in the kitchen eating leftover Chinese food, and Julian, with no appetite and nothing to say himself, simply watched her pick at her vegetables.

"I did something terrible," she said. "I'm not denying it. But are you going to hold it over me for the rest of my life?"

"I honestly don't know."

"Julian," she said, "we can work this out."

He wanted to embrace her, to tell her everything would be fine, but he couldn't because things weren't fine, and it occurred to him now, watching her, that they never would be fine again.

"So this is it?" she said. "You're leaving me?"

I don't know you anymore. He'd heard those words in movies, read them in novels, and he was a writer, his life was words, he had to be able to do better than that. But language, his one refuge, was failing him. He'd be miserable without her; he could see that. He was already miserable without her and she was still there.

Just three days ago, on the way to the airport, they'd been talking about having children. She wanted them; he knew that. But what she longed to tell him now was that it was him she wanted to have children with. Without him, children meant nothing to her. And if he was going to leave her, and if in five years, or ten, she was on her own, she couldn't see doing it by herself. Without him, her plans were meaningless.

He had the front door open, and she imagined he was waiting for her to haul him back. "Where are you going to spend the night?" He seemed capable of anything. She saw him on a bench in the Arboretum, camped out on the steps of Angell Hall, curled up like a bear beneath his office desk, his jeans jacket cloaking him. "Will you be all right?"

"I don't know."

Then he was out the door and down the hallway, a figure she watched through their bedroom window, diminishing in the shadows beneath the streetlights of Kerrytown, dwindling in the darkness.

The next morning, she canceled her therapy appointments for the day. The day after that she did the same thing, but on the third day she went back to work, and soon a week had passed and she realized he wasn't returning.

He must have stopped by when she wasn't there, because she came home one night to find his apartment key on the table and most of his belongings removed from his drawers. He'd left a note with the phone number where he was staying, but when she called him he was silent, and she was, too.

"Julian, can't you at least talk to me?"

"I don't have anything to say."

"But eventually?"

"I don't know."

She had never balanced her checkbook before, but she began to do so, keeping track of the checks Julian wrote and the money he withdrew, following him along the streets by the paper trail he was leaving. In their bedroom, she and Julian each had a dresser, but since he was taller than she was he'd taken the top drawers of each dresser and she'd taken the bottom ones. Now that he'd left, the sensible thing would have been to consolidate dressers, but she couldn't bring herself do that. So she continued to use the bottom half of each dresser and left Julian's drawers unoccupied.

The password for her bank card was Julian's date of birth, and the password for her e-mail account was the date they'd met. She could have switched passwords, but doing so felt like a bad omen; that way he would never come back. But she changed her screensaver, which was a photo of Julian eating scrambled eggs—he was smiling, holding his fork away from himself, as if he were waving the eggs at her—and replaced it with a photo of Olivia, looking up from her desk, in an apartment in New York City, which was where she was living now, trying to make a go of it as a dancer.

Their first night in Ann Arbor, she and Julian had arrayed candles about the bedroom and made love on their futon. "Sex in Michigan," Julian said. The Lower Peninsula of Michigan resembled a mitt, and the natives held up their right hand, palm out, to show you where in the state they were from. "I'm from here," Julian said, pointing to the base of his thumb, feeling already like a true Michigander.

"Enough with this old futon," Mia said. They'd slept on it in college; she wanted to get a real bed. So they placed the futon on the street, their first donation to Ann Arbor recycling or to some passing student who wanted an old bed, and went off to the store to buy a new one.

But the next morning their futon was still sitting outside, and the morning after that it was, too. Feeling sentimental about it, they hauled it back inside and folded it up in the closet. That was where it had been the last eight years, until now, convinced she could detect the smell of Julian on their mattress, she removed the futon. She'd been sleeping on it for a week now, slumped on the floor like a college student again.

She learned from a friend that Julian was subletting an apartment near Burns Park, and she started to walk there afternoons, hoping to catch a glimpse of him. One day she saw him in front of the college hockey rink. She considered crossing the street to greet him, but she didn't know what to say, and as she stood there watching him, he continued up State Street toward Packard, disappearing with the cars.

As the weeks passed, she did her best to accept her solitude. When the bills came she paid them immediately, and she felt a strength in doing this, for she had always relied on Julian to pay the bills. She went to the movies, and she drove into Detroit, which she had rarely done before. Once, she drove to Windsor, to Canada, across the Ambassador Bridge, trying to look at the world as bigger than she'd imagined it.

And in July, when Art Fair came to town, she spent a couple of hours every morning wandering among the exhibits. There were hundreds of booths and tens of thousands of people, and State Street was awash in curly fries and funnel cakes. Julian liked to say that for a week every summer all of Ohio and Indiana made a hajj to Ann Arbor. He and Mia used to barricade themselves in their apartment, almost, it seemed, as a kind of protest, and a couple of years they actually left town. Now, wandering among the booths, Mia saw her visit to Art Fair as part of her new openness, and she imagined Julian, wherever he was, sneering at the spectacle; she was happy not to be doing that this year. She felt that without him she was more willing to see the good in things, and she liked herself better for that, even if, despairingly, she still searched for him among the crowds.

Then, when she tired of this, she went for lunch at Park Avenue
Deli, where she would get the spinach and mozzarella sandwich and
drink a lemonade, and after that, she would head to Rackham to work
on her dissertation. Whenever she sat in front of the computer, she
was reminded of what Julian had said about writing, how inspiration
didn't matter, what you needed was to tie yourself to your chair, and
she heard his voice, as she so often still did, and she took this as reas-
surance. Once, wanting to hear his voice for real, she called the number where he was staying. But no one answered and in a way she was
relieved, and she went back to walking through Julian's new neighborhood, telling herself that if she saw him again this time she would
know what to say.

Spending time with Sigrid and Ivan, Francine and Saxton, and Will
and Paige, she felt acutely Julian's absence, and never more so than
when they went out of their way to include her in their activities, to
make her feel that she wasn't alone.

When somebody asked her what had gone wrong, she said, "It's
complicated." But it wasn't complicated. She'd slept with Julian's best
friend and he'd left her. It sounded so grave, articulated that way, but
it *was* grave, and it was the very gravity that had eluded her. She hadn't
told anyone she'd cheated on Julian because she knew people would
think she'd gotten what she deserved.

Finally, though, she told Sigrid. "It was nine years ago," she said,
"but that's no excuse, because Julian and I were already committed to
each other."

"Why did you do it?"

Her instinct was to say she didn't know. And the truth was she
didn't. The betrayal itself, when it came to her, when, as always, she
felt conscience-stricken, seemed to have been perpetrated by someone else. For that was how she remembered that year, from the
moment her mother was diagnosed right through the funeral, seven
quicksilver months when she couldn't own anything and she felt—
there was no other way to put it—inhabited. But in the last few weeks

some details had returned to her. A nighttime ride on Carter's scooter, the wind pummeling them, the feeling that he was taking her somewhere. Carter was going out with Pilar, but his feelings for Pilar, he told Mia, had nothing to do with his feelings for her, and he had a cool, poised logic she couldn't gainsay. Julian was, in fact, away—she remembered this now—home for the weekend to see some friends. And maybe that was part of it: she resented Julian for abandoning her while her mother was dying. Pilar was away, too. Carter with his persistence and his platitudes—"It doesn't have to be a big deal"—and he flattered her, sure, but she wasn't someone who was easily flattered. It was the way Carter made you feel guilty, how he could convince you that you owed him something. "It's the least you can do." Had he actually said those words? She had a sudden, glancing vision, Carter in her bedroom, pressing her against the closet where Julian's shirts hung, for there was a violence to the sex, coming from her as much as from him.

But guilt explained only so much. That spring, feeling helpless, seeing the tight, dour faces of the doctors, she'd watched her mother waste away. "What difference will it make?" Carter said, meaning the sex, and with her mother dying she thought he was right: nothing made a difference. All she could think of was that day with Carter in the co-op kitchen, and his words: "My mother had breast cancer." Of course he hadn't told her this before; she'd never been able to get a word out of him. He'd been six at the time; he couldn't remember much. But she didn't care; she wanted him to tell her what had happened, for the simple reason that his mother had been cured. That night, when Carter wanted to have sex with her, she thought maybe if she slept with him his luck would rub off. Failing that, she thought he would talk to her. But he didn't talk to her. He fucked her and he came and he rolled off her and fell asleep. And not knowing what to do, she fell asleep herself, only to wake up disgusted.

She was sitting with Sigrid outside the computing center, and for an instant she thought she saw Julian. But it wasn't him, just someone else queued up at the printing station. "I have to go," she said. But she just sat there after Sigrid had departed, staring vacantly ahead, and half an hour passed before she looked up and realized she had to be at the clinic.

Up in Montreal, she found her father at McGill, in the room where he taught his classes. She used to sit in the back of the room while he worked, sometimes even while he was teaching, doing her homework to the sound of chalk pressed against the blackboard, equations blooming across the slate. The day the building was unveiled, she'd been here with her parents for the celebration, and afterward she'd gone upstairs to see her father's new office, where she looked out the window at campus, holding a glass of champagne she'd drunk too much of, feeling the ground blur beneath her. "It's my new perch," her father said, and she felt as if it were hers, too. She'd probably done more homework in Rutherford than anywhere else in the world. She had a memory of an earlier building, of running through the corridors playing tag with her father, only to be scooped up by a stranger who turned out to be the dean of sciences, then being rescued by her father, who said, "It's all right, Warren, that's my daughter, Mia."

She watched her father now from across the room. He wore his signature outfit: the flannel shirt with the collar open, the jacket with the elbows patched. As a boy, he'd had to wear a uniform to school, and he'd done all he could to circumvent the rules, leaving the necktie unknotted, failing to wear the white shirt he was supposed to. It was the kind of transgression that would have gotten a lesser student in trouble. "Are you hungry?"

She nodded.

"Cheeseburgers?"

She smiled. It was her mother who hadn't permitted junk food in the house, who had read all the food and drink labels and applied the rule that any ingredient she couldn't pronounce wasn't to be consumed. So it was left to her father to sneak licorice to her, to buy her cotton candy when her mother wasn't looking, to allow her when she was ten to eat her favorite snack, SpaghettiOs straight from the can, to take her after school for cheeseburgers, which her mother disapproved of so close to dinner. At twelve and thirteen, when she became religious, she stopped going out for cheeseburgers with her father. She knew he missed this, and she did, too, even if she hadn't been able to admit it at the time. He had offered to take her to the Jewish delis in town to buy smoked meat, but the food there wasn't kosher. A couple of times they drove to Hampstead and Côte Saint-Luc to get kosher meat sandwiches, but in the end she felt it wasn't worth the drive, and it was always a school night, anyway, and she had homework to do.

It had been years now since she'd kept kosher, but she didn't like cheeseburgers anymore. Perhaps it was a relic from when she'd been religious; she'd lost the taste for them. Still, she was happy to join her father while he ate, glad to be back home visiting him.

In the bottom of a closet, she found an old T-shirt of her mother's with a name tag sewn inside the collar. When she went to summer camp, she'd been required to have name tags on all her clothes, but she disliked name tags and refused to let her mother sew them on her clothes unless she sewed them on her own clothes, too.

Her father still had his old datebooks, even his old checkbooks, from as long as thirty years ago. Every summer, when they did their big housecleaning, her mother would put those checkbooks aside in the hope that he would finally agree to dispose of them. But he was always returning them to their marked boxes. Her mother had called him a secret sentimentalist, and though Mia had never thought of him that way, she realized now that it was true.

She found a pile of unmarked cassettes. "What are those?"

"They're what Mom sent me when she was in Greece. We communicated by tape that summer."

"You were apart?"

"Summer of 1964," he said. "Mom was doing research."

"You never told me that."

"You see?" he said, smiling at her. "And you thought you knew everything."

She touched the top cassette. Her mother's voice from thirty-five years ago. She'd have liked to listen to one of those tapes. But they weren't meant for her, and the longer she stared at them the more she was convinced her mother wasn't really on them. She could imagine events from before she was born—World War II, the red scare, the Cuban missile crisis—but her parents themselves, going on dates, "courting each other," as her father liked to say: all that confounded her.

She didn't want to look at the photo albums—where could she begin?—but there were a few loose photos of her mother as a girl. Mia was astonished by how much she resembled her mother. Babies were said to look like their fathers, evolution's way of encouraging men to stick around, but she had done things in reverse: she had looked like her mother when she was a baby and now, years later, she resembled her father. The clump of dark curls, the long, narrow face, the cleft like a brand on her chin. Though some people thought her parents looked alike, and she supposed that over time they had started to.

"Who's this?"

Her father smiled. "That's the guy who tried to break Mom and me up."

"Another suitor?"

"In a manner of speaking." On their first date, her father said, he had gone to her mother's apartment to pick her up. A photograph of a young man hung on the wall above her desk—a boyfriend, Arthur Mendelsohn presumed, and he wondered why she'd consented to go out with him. He almost didn't ask her out a second time, but he ran into her in the rain in Harvard Square, and because she was just standing there allowing herself to get wet, he assumed she was waiting for him to ask her out again. "What about your boyfriend?" he said. "That photo above your desk?"

"Him?" her mother said. "That's Paul Klee!"

Apparently, as a young man Paul Klee had cut a striking figure, striking enough almost to have derailed Mia's parents' relationship before it even started.

"And you still have that photo?"

Her father shrugged. "I didn't see fit to throw it out."

"You've kept everything, haven't you?"

"I suppose I have."

He was quiet now, and she was, too, the way they often were together. Her mother had done most of the talking; she acted as a go-between for the two of them. "Have you heard from Julian?"

She shook her head. She'd spoken in generalities—there had been problems in the marriage—and it saddened her to talk this way, but she didn't know how to go about it differently. Her father believed in solutions, or at least in the possibility that there was a solution, and now, as she implied through her silence that there wasn't one, he seemed not to know what to say.

She bent over to do her laces.

"Look at you," he said. "Tying your shoelaces with two loops."

"It's how you taught me."

"I did?"

She must have been three, four at most. He'd always been eager to start her early; it had been true with everything. "Two loops were easier," she explained. She hadn't had the fine motor skills at that age.

"And now?"

"I guess I've gotten used to it." She recalled an anniversary her parents had celebrated. How old had she been? Five? Six? She'd picked roses from the neighbors' garden, and when her parents found out where the flowers had come from, they made her apologize to the neighbors. But she'd always suspected they were secretly pleased. They didn't like the neighbors, a sour, misanthropic couple. Years later, when they moved out, it became a joke that she'd chased them away, that she'd done the whole neighborhood a service.

"Dad, what do you do on yours and Mom's anniversary?"

"I think about her," he said.

"I do, too."

"I know," he said. "You call every year."

She was silent.

"It's the burden of the elder child, isn't it, to take care of the parents."

"Oh, Dad, I don't take care of you. I haven't even managed to live in the same country."

"You remember birthdays and anniversaries."

"Remembering isn't hard."

"Maybe not, but Mom and I were eldest children ourselves, and we swore when you were born that we'd do our best not to turn you into a dutiful daughter. And despite our good efforts, look at you."

"I'm not so dutiful."

"You're here."

She understood he was talking about Olivia. "If it's any consolation, she doesn't call me much, either."

"So I shouldn't take it personally?"

"No, Dad."

He got up to prepare dinner. Once, before he was married, he'd heated a can of peas in the oven only to have it explode. He'd been known to live off frankfurters for weeks at a time. He looked thin now, but he always had; she was glad to see he was eating.

He poured them each some wine, and she gazed at him now through her wineglass, the undulating shape of him, her father. On the kitchen counter lay a page of equations. He was busy at work; there was nothing to worry about. Except, she knew, he was worried about her.

Finally, Julian came back for the rest of his belongings. She was standing in the kitchen when he arrived, unsure of what to say. "How are you?"

"I'm okay," he said. "You?"

"I'm okay, too."

She fixed herself a piece of toast, searching for a conversational gambit, and when she couldn't find one, she wandered into the bedroom and sat down. This was her home. Though really it was *their* home, and now that he'd left, she felt as if none of it belonged to her, as if she'd been squatting for years and the police had been called. "I hear you're living in Burns Park."

He nodded.

"Will you be here in the fall?"

"Probably," he said. "I've agreed to teach again, but I don't know."

"What do you mean?"

"I'm thinking of taking a trip. Maybe going overseas. I've never really traveled before."

"Of course you've traveled. Your parents took you to tons of places."

"I mean without my parents."

"What about our honeymoon?" she wanted to say. "And our cross-country trip that summer in college?" He couldn't leave her, not like this, leave not just her home but the state she lived in, perhaps the very country.

He took out his checkbook to pay the bills. Watching him sign his name, she realized that beyond the heartbreak there were practical concerns, for everything that had been his had been hers, too, and though everything that had been hers had been his as well, he'd had so much more than she had.

"Don't worry," he said, as if he knew what she was thinking. "I'm not going to fight you over money."

Her heart lurched: was he going to ask for a divorce?

Then he was in the closet, methodically taking what was his. Later she would convince herself she'd seen moistness around his eyes, but what struck her at the time was his abject dispassion. She'd expected accusations, a rehashing on a minor scale of what had come before, but what she got instead was a lump for a heart, the rigid cast of his back as, carrying a trash bag like a vagrant, he made his way out the door.

She agreed to go for coffee with a friend of Sigrid's, an anthropology graduate student who had recently gone through a breakup himself. Sitting across from him, she feared he would talk about his ex-girlfriend and that she would have to reciprocate and talk about Julian. But, to his credit, he was as circumspect as she was. For a moment, she looked at him and thought he was handsome, with a long, sloping face and dark eyes, and she allowed herself to think he was interesting. She could understand why Sigrid had set them up; in other circumstances she might have been attracted to him.

Later, though, she grew depressed: she was thirty-one and going on dates. In spare moments, she wondered about old boyfriends, Glen, for instance, whom she'd gone out with in high school and who was now living in Indiana, having married a woman who had grown up there. She recalled a German exchange student she'd met when she was fifteen, how everything between them in their brief relationship had been fraught with import for the simple reason that he spoke such poor English and she spoke no German and it took so much effort for them to communicate.

But it was Derek she thought about most, Derek, whom she'd met when she was eighteen. She was taking off a year before college, working as a nanny to two French children, and it was in a café in Aix-en-Provence that she saw Derek for the first time, standing in line with his knapsack of groceries.

"You're too young to be a mother," Derek said, seeing Claudette and Emile trailing behind Mia.

"You're right," Mia said. "I'm their au pair."

Mia introduced the children to Derek, and then, realizing she hadn't done so already, she introduced herself.

Derek spoke to her in his clumsy French, until it was determined that she knew English, too, that English, in fact, was her first language. Derek's English was clumsy as well, but in a different way from how his French was clumsy. He sounded as if he'd learned English from an elderly British lady, which, it turned out, he had. "How do you do?" he said. "I'm pleased to meet you."

Sitting across from Mia, Derek said, "Do you think the baby needs his diaper changed?"

"It's possible." Mia reached into her bag and removed a diaper.

"Wait," Derek said. "I'll do it. I'm good at changing diapers." He laid Emile across the table and moved him from side to side, as if he were basting a turkey. "Not so bad," he said when he was done.

Mia wasn't sure what Derek meant, whether he was saying that changing diapers wasn't so bad or that he wasn't so bad at doing it. But since both were true, she said, "You're right."

"My brother has children," Derek explained. "You have to be careful when you change the boys. They pee in your face."

After that day, Derek would come to the café to look for Mia. He asked her to tell him when she would be there, but she rarely knew in advance. Emile napped irregularly, and sometimes Claudette had a play date. Occasionally Mia would be allowed to borrow the family car to take the children to parks and museums in nearby towns, and sometimes on longer excursions, to Lyon, for example, where she would walk with Claudette and Emile through the different neighborhoods, past the men hawking wares on the street. She enjoyed these trips, liked having the children to herself, discovering a city that was new to all three of them. Most of all, she liked being behind the wheel of their parents' Peugeot, the shifting up and down from gear to gear, the activity of driving. Other times, however, without the car, consigned to a house that wasn't hers, pressed into the company of two toddlers, she found herself growing lonely. She was by nature a solitary person; in high school and before she had always preferred to remain on the periphery. But it was one thing to be on the periphery voluntarily, another thing to have no choice in the matter. Now, in Provence, she longed for companionship. She would walk past the café, hoping Derek would be there, always glancing in as she went by.

Derek had long, fragile-looking fingers, and the image Mia kept was of him scooping his hands through a barrel of mangoes. He looked like a schoolboy carrying his groceries in his knapsack. On that knapsack, like a heraldic coat of arms, was a patch with the words "Derek and the Dominos" on it.

Mia would come to the café at eleven in the morning and find Derek waiting for her. And at two. And at four-thirty.

"I thought you were a student," she said.

"I am."

"Are you playing hooky?"

"What's that?"

"Don't you go to class?"

"Sure I do." Derek removed his folder and showed Mia his notes, as if she were the professor checking his homework.

His name was Takeshi in Japanese, which was, Mia thought, a long way from Derek, but here in Provence with all these English-speaking foreign students he wanted a name English-speakers could pronounce, so he chose Derek, after Derek and the Dominos. Derek loved American rock music. He was always asking Mia about obscure American bands, and every time she didn't know one he looked at her with a mixture of disbelief and disappointment. It was as if he thought that being proximate to the United States, having grown up in a country that actually touched it, Mia had a knowledge of American music that wasn't available to him.

They read *The International Herald Tribune* together, Derek scanning for news about Japan. He told Mia about Prime Minister Nakasone and the Japanese economy. He spoke adoringly of Japanese cuisine, and of his own mother's cooking, which was, he said, what he missed most about home. "I want to take you out for sushi," he said.

"But I don't like sushi."

"Are you a vegetarian?"

"No," she said. "I just don't like fish."

But Derek still wanted to take her out for sushi, so they agreed to go and Mia would eat the vegetable sushi.

The following week, when they went out, Mia and Derek ate asparagus sushi and shiitake mushroom sushi and a plate of oshinko, Japanese pickles, though Derek, apologetically, also ate some fish.

And the next morning when he saw her at the café, he had a present for her.

"Sushi earrings!" Mia exclaimed. Each one was a plastic shrimp pinioned to a bed of rice.

"Just don't eat them," Derek said.

Mia introduced Derek to the family she worked for and to the other people she knew in town. "This is my friend Derek," she would say, and Derek would stick out his hand and say, "I'm pleased to meet you."

But afterward, once the person had left, Derek became taciturn and morose. "Why do you always tell people I'm your friend?"

"Because you are my friend."

"I don't want to be your friend," he said.

"Why not?"

Derek was silent, and in that silence Mia waited for him to say what she realized she'd been waiting for him to say for some time now. "I want to be more than friends."

"Oh, Derek."

"I like you."

"I like you, too, Derek."

"But you don't want to be my girlfriend?"

"No."

"Why not?"

She could have told him she wasn't attracted to him, but why wasn't she attracted to him? At the university, the American girls herded after him, seeing the gentleness Mia saw in him and finding him exotic as well, so different from the boys they'd gone to high school with. But Derek didn't wish to be thought of as exotic. And he wasn't drawn to these American girls, though in his own way, doing so with as much humility as the circumstances would allow, he let slip to Mia that these girls were interested in him, hoping that the knowledge that other girls liked him would make Mia like him, too. But it didn't work. Mia tried to imagine Derek in Japan, wondered whether in Kyoto he would seem as unprotected as he did in France, or whether, speaking his own language, he would have a layer of guardedness he couldn't muster here. All she knew was that in Aix, talking English, Derek spoke with so little artifice it should have been enough to make her like him. But it didn't. "I don't know why."

In Mia's experience, when you told a guy you didn't like him he tried to convince you you did; he turned your feelings into a subject of debate. But Derek, thank God, didn't do this. It wasn't everything or nothing—he was still willing to be her friend—and Mia was so relieved that the next time she saw him, standing outside the café with his knapsack of groceries, she allowed him to kiss her. It was just a kiss, she figured; it wasn't a big deal.

But to Derek it was. He took it as a sign that Mia had reconsidered, and when it became clear that she hadn't, he grew disconsolate. "I think I love you," he said.

"Please, Derek, don't say that."

"I *want* to say it."

But Derek couldn't get Mia to say it back, and when he discovered, finally, that there was nothing he could do to make her love him, he became angry. "I think there's something wrong with you."

Mia's heart pitched. She had heard these words before. Boys were always falling in love with her and she was always not quite falling in love back. It had happened with Glen, whom she did love but whom she hadn't managed to love as much as he loved her. Being with Glen, Mia began to wonder whether there really was something wrong with her; maybe she was incapable of love. The possibility so unnerved her that she agreed not to break up with Glen, hoping that over the summer she'd learn to love him the way he wanted her to. And when it didn't happen, when she felt about him the kind of vague admiration she'd felt for some time now, she told herself she was distracted and perhaps when she returned from France things would be different. It was enough to allow her to feel she wasn't lying when she explained to Derek that she had a boyfriend back home.

"You never told me about him," Derek said.

"You never asked me."

"Do you love him?"

"Yes," she said.

"Don't you think if you loved him I'd know about him? Wouldn't he always be on your mind?"

But how much on someone's mind did a person have to be in order for you to love him? Mia suspected this was a dense question, and that anyone who asked a question like this was automatically disqualified from loving someone else, and from being loved in return.

"So you don't love your boyfriend, either," Derek said, and Mia let the accusation stand.

After that, she and Derek saw each other less. It was March, and she would be leaving France in a few months. They still occasionally got together at the café, but there was a remoteness between them that hadn't existed before, and she didn't know what to do about it.

The week before she left, she realized she'd never heard Derek speak Japanese, and suddenly it seemed like the most essential thing. "I want to hear you speak your language," she said.

"Why?"

"Please, Derek, I'm asking you a favor." She felt like a voyeur, as if she were grabbing something that wasn't rightfully hers.

"What do you want me to say?"

"Whatever you like." She was afraid he would tell her he loved her, that he was going to say it in Japanese. But it would have been all right if he did, since she didn't understand Japanese, and for a moment she actually wanted him to say it. Fleetingly, she thought she loved him, too, and the fact that she felt it, even if briefly, filled her with tremendous relief.

Then Derek began to speak. He spoke whole sentences in Japanese, for how long, Mia wasn't sure, but it felt like minutes, and it was ravishing.

"What did you say?"

"I said I hope you enjoy college."

"But you spoke for so long. Please, Derek, tell me what you said."

"I want my sushi earrings back."

"But you gave them to me." She took hold of the earrings as if he might grab them from her.

"It was nice to meet you, Mia."

"Nice to meet me? Is that one of the phrases you learned in your English class? Nice to meet me, Derek! You act as if we didn't spend the whole year together."

"What difference does it make? I'm leaving, and so are you."

"So is this goodbye?"

Derek nodded.

"I'm not leaving for another few days," she said. "We could see each other again."

"I have exams to study for." Derek reached out to shake her hand, and not knowing what to do, she took it.

The day before she left, she found a piece of paper in her mailbox with Derek's name and address on it and the words "Write me" in his handwriting. He must have gotten hold of her address, too, because a few weeks after arriving at Graymont, she received a letter from him.

When she came to college, she had a singular goal: she was going to fall in love with someone. But at college, love felt elusive to her. Boys trailed after her the way they had in high school, and without even realizing it, she carried herself with just enough aloofness to make her seem doubly appealing. That first month at school, she slept with someone from one of her classes, but it felt almost obligatory—a rite of passage: she'd made it to college—and she didn't sleep with him again.

Her first semester, she took calculus, linguistics, anthropology, music appreciation, and—her favorite—introductory Japanese. Late at night, she would sit in the library carrels memorizing her kanji, thinking of Derek as she did so. He had taught her a few Japanese phrases, enough to make her feel the language wasn't foreign, at least for the first hour of the first day of class, until she realized it was. But she was improving. That was one of the gratifying things about learning a language; it was easy to trace your progress. By November, she could actually speak some Japanese. She even wrote a letter to Derek composed entirely in Japanese. It was filled with mistakes, no doubt, but it was a Japanese letter, written in a script that until recently had been no more familiar to her than cuneiform. It was hard to keep up with Derek. For every letter she wrote him, he wrote three. Sometimes she felt she should give up writing him entirely; she needed a less prolific Japanese pen pal. Then, in the spring, she met Julian. Those first weeks, she felt beyond the exuberance a pleasing vindication. So people had been wrong: she *could* fall in love. It was as if Derek himself intuited this, for his letters stopped coming, and she stopped writing him, too.

Now, in Ann Arbor, she thought of Derek again, sweet, fragile-fingered Derek walking along the streets of Aix. She wanted to write him, but she'd misplaced his address years ago. She knew him, besides, as Derek, which wasn't his real name.

Then, one night at three A.M., she remembered it. Takeshi. Takeshi Moriyama. She tracked down his address.

> Dear Derek,
>
> It's Mia. Do you remember me? We were friends in 1985, in Aix-en-Provence. We spent the year together. . . .

A month later Derek wrote back.

> Dear Mia,
>
> Of course I remember you. So much has happened since 1985. I live in Kyoto and teach economics at the university. Perhaps I can see you sometime in the United States. Occasionally I'm invited to give lectures there. My son loves America and I've promised him a trip to the U.S. someday. I've never been to Michigan but I've been to Chicago. Maybe we can meet in between.
>
> In Friendship,
> Takeshi (Derek)

A son, Mia thought. So he'd gotten married. Why did this surprise her? She couldn't have expected him to wait around, when she'd given him no reason to do so, when, at eighteen, she'd barely let him kiss him, when he was living in Japan, a country she'd never been to, when she hadn't been in touch with him for years. Vainly she thought, *Come visit me, Derek. Oh, Derek, take me back.* Walking along State Street she started to cry, and she was still crying when she ran into Julian.

"Mia, are you all right?"

Then she realized that the blond woman standing next to him, the woman who had just stopped laughing at something he said, was

Trilby. His ex-student, and he was sleeping with her: it was so obvious they might as well have announced it.

"Is something wrong?"

But she didn't answer him. She just ran across the diag, continuing to cry, until she was out on East University.

Iowa City, Iowa

"Do you have your paint roller?" Henry asked.

Julian shook his head. "I didn't realize I was supposed to bring one."

Henry stepped inside the house, and when he returned he was holding a large box of tools out of which he produced a paint roller.

"Overalls," he said, checking Julian out. "Last night I wouldn't have imagined you in this getup, but in the clear light of day you look like a real farmer."

"I figured I'd wear something I wouldn't mind getting dirty. I'm telling you, I've never painted a house before."

"It's easy," Henry said. "You just dip the roller into the paint and apply it."

Julian shrugged. "Don't say I didn't warn you."

Julian didn't really know Henry, but then he didn't really know anyone in town yet; he'd been here only three weeks. Yesterday afternoon, he and Henry had been up in workshop together, and they'd both been eviscerated. Yet Julian had liked Henry's story, and he figured if the class could be wrong about Henry, they could be wrong about him, too. And this was how a friendship had started. Your enemy's enemy was your friend.

Henry was thirty-one, which made him almost Julian's age, whereas much of the first-year class had only recently graduated from college.

And Henry was a doctor. He'd been a surgery resident ("You think workshop was bad? You should see what assholes surgeons can be") and he'd been headed for life as a surgeon when he decided if he didn't pursue what he loved he'd never forgive himself. So he left his job in San Francisco and applied to the Iowa Writers' Workshop. This was another thing Julian admired about Henry; he'd given up something in order to come here, whereas most of their classmates had given up nothing. Julian liked Henry, besides, liked the fact that he was painting his landlady's house, which he thought bespoke humility. But Henry said he didn't see it that way. He was trying to save money (his landlady was cutting him a deal on the rent), and painting houses was physical and he enjoyed physical things; he'd already conscripted Julian to play tennis with him.

Henry stood on the top rung of a ladder, pressing his paint roller against the house. Julian stood on a ladder, too. They were painting the back of the house, and then, when they were finished, they would move around to the front.

"Workshop got pretty ad hominem," Henry admitted. "When the stakes are low, the fangs come out."

In his written comments, the instructor had made clear how much he liked Julian's story, but in class he'd been less forthcoming, and he'd done nothing to intervene when the discussion turned spiteful. He simply sat there as if enjoying the display, curious to see how tough Julian was.

So this was Iowa, Julian thought. Though he understood there might be special animus toward him and Henry. Henry already had a literary agent, and Julian had recently published a short story in *Harper's*. He'd also been featured over the summer in *The Village Voice*'s "Up-and-Coming Fiction Writers" special. He and seven other young writers had been flown to New York, where they posed for photographs on the steps of the New York Public Library and were asked questions about their writing habits and their literary influences. There was no way to answer such questions without sounding like a pompous ass, and Julian hadn't acquitted himself any better than the others had. This had been made clear to him when, just days after his arrival, he learned that two of his new classmates had hung his photograph from the *Voice* above their mantel and were lobbing darts at it.

Now they'd exacted their revenge.

Henry said, "So are you depressed?"

"My depression is so deep I can't begin to describe it. And workshop is the least of it."

"Let me guess," Henry said. "Female trouble?"

Julian nodded. "Female trouble" was the phrase Julian's grandmother had used to describe menstruation. Though that wasn't what Julian had in mind right now. It had been over a year since he and Mia had split up. Fifteen and a half months, to be precise. There would come a day, he hoped, when he wouldn't mark time by how long they'd been separated, but he was beginning to wonder if that would ever happen. He hadn't wanted them to communicate—he found speaking with her too painful—though he'd sent her his contact information in case she needed to reach him. He hadn't brought up divorce and neither had she, though that, he understood, was the next step. There was common-law marriage, where a couple lived together for so long they were considered married. He, on the other hand, could see himself heading toward a common-law divorce. He imagined himself at fifty, perhaps not even knowing where Mia lived, still with his marriage license secreted in some drawer, still, despite his best efforts, in love with her.

"I know what you mean," Henry said. "My girlfriend's back in San Francisco. If I'd stayed there, we'd still be together."

"She didn't want to move here?"

"She would have if I'd asked her to. But I couldn't get myself to do it. What if she didn't like it here? Hell, I'm not sure *I* like it here. So we decided to leave things open. You know what leaving things open means? It means you're broken up by Thanksgiving." Henry put down his paint roller. "I don't know what I'm doing in this place. Do I really need to be in another writing workshop?"

Julian wasn't sure what he was doing here, either. In fact, if one thing appeared to unify his classmates it was that already, after three weeks, everyone seemed to wonder why they had come to Iowa.

Julian leaned his hands against the ladder, looking at Iowa City from where he stood, at the clusters of wood houses set back from campus. Henry lived on Fairchild Street, and Julian on Gilbert. All these street names he still had to learn, another town to discover. How random for the Writers' Workshop to be in Iowa; how, he wondered, had it ended up here? Though there was cachet, he understood, in moving to a town you wouldn't otherwise have lived in. Off to the hinterland. A kind of snobbery in reverse.

But it wasn't snobbery that had brought him here. It was the fact that he needed to get out of Ann Arbor. On his fifth anniversary of teaching, when a friend jokingly bought him a cake, he went directly to the composition office and handed in his resignation. It had been three months at the time since he and Mia had separated, and he hadn't written another word of his novel. "Lost your muse?" someone said, and he nodded, though that didn't really capture it. He thought he had writer's block, but then he sat down and wrote a short story, and he finished it in three weeks. He finished another one a month later. That was the story he'd published in *Harper's,* and while he was proofreading the galleys, his editor, learning of his predicament, suggested he consider going to the Iowa Writers' Workshop, where she herself had gone.

At first the idea struck him as absurd. Going to graduate school, doing more of what he'd done in college, with classmates just out of college themselves, had the sordid aspect of returning to junior high school. It wasn't that he thought he had nothing to learn. He just didn't think he had much to learn from graduate school, especially a graduate school as competitive as Iowa. ("There's nothing to do there," someone once told him, "except be mean to each other.") Some people went to Iowa to make connections, but he had grown up in New York and was already connected. Besides, he wasn't interested in making connections. This was a species of arrogance, he understood: he believed the connections should come to him.

And in a way, they had. For his editor at *Harper's* had called the director of the Writers' Workshop and told him to look out for Julian's application. And Julian, who hadn't yet decided to apply, finally agreed to do so. He couldn't have been working on his novel any less than he already was. And Ann Arbor was where he'd settled because of Mia; he needed to move somewhere else.

That was how he'd ended up where he was now, on a ladder next to Henry, two of the twenty-five chosen, painting Henry's landlady's house. Henry had a broad, open face and features that suggested curiosity; his hair was thinning, and it was so blond you could see his pink scalp beneath it. "That's why I wear a baseball cap," Henry explained. "I've never met anyone who burns as easily as I do. And my father's a dermatologist, so he'd kill me. He already wants to kill me just for coming here."

"Let me guess," Julian said. "He thought being a surgeon was a better idea."

"Who wouldn't?" Henry rested his baseball cap on the roof. A ribbon of sweat traversed the inside of the cap, where his forehead had been. "How about your parents? Do they wish you were doing something else?"

Julian laughed. "They don't have a problem with the Iowa part. My father thinks I've finally gotten into Yale."

Down Fairchild Street, Julian could see someone from the Writers' Workshop making her way toward campus. She was a second-year student; he recognized her from an orientation event at the English and Philosophy Building, or maybe from one of the happy hours. The University of Iowa was a big school, but it was a good deal smaller than the University of Michigan, and here, at the Writers' Workshop, the MFA students stayed to themselves. You could find them at the Mill or the Foxhead or Prairie Lights Bookstore, but in the end, there were only so many places to go searching for them.

Julian had gotten paint on his overalls, and on his shirt, too. Henry was speckled and spattered himself, and the house appeared no better. It looked as if a gigantic ice cream cone had dripped down the side of it.

"You better hope your landlady doesn't show up now."

Henry dipped his paint roller into the can and tossed some paint against the wall. "It's a lot like writing," he said. "You get it all down on the page and then attend to the mess."

Julian had once heard an analogy made between writing and architecture. You had to lay down the foundation before you focused on the molding. But he went about things differently. He revised as he went along. Every sentence had to be right before he moved on to the next one because each sentence grew organically from the one that preceded it. For him, the foundation *was* the molding.

"It's like the potter at his wheel," Henry said. "Throw down the clay and let it spin."

"Don't tell me you're a potter, too."

Henry shook his head. "It's just what I've heard." He descended the ladder and dropped his paintbrush to the ground. "Should we call it quits?"

Julian nodded.

On the porch, Henry handed Julian a glass of iced tea. He served them each a tuna fish sandwich, and then, having finished off the iced tea, he removed from the fridge a couple of bottles of beer. He popped open a bag of potato chips, the hiss of air diffusing across the porch. "Where are you from originally?"

"New York," Julian said. "Though the last place I lived was Ann Arbor." He looked up at Henry. "How about you?"

"I grew up in Hanover," Henry said. "And then I went to Dartmouth. You'd think I'd have had more imagination."

"I've never been to Hanover," Julian said, "but I suspect it might be my next stop. I've been making a tour of college towns."

"How long did you live in Ann Arbor?"

"Nine years."

"Can you imagine living here for nine years?"

"Right now, I can't imagine living here for nine weeks."

"I hear Ann Arbor's a nice place," Henry said.

"It's all right. The problem is, everyone's either twenty or fifty. You hit your thirties and you're not sure what to do. You end up sleeping with your students."

"Is that what you did?"

"In one case. Though she wasn't my student any longer. I was on the rebound. My wife and I had just split up." He'd been hopeful about Trilby, and he could tell that she'd been hopeful, too, but in the end they'd been disappointed. Another time, another place, other circumstances: he really had liked her. It had been five years since she'd been his student, but they'd never been able to get past that; what had started as one thing hadn't managed to become something else. Or maybe it had simply been too soon. He had slept with a couple of other people, kindhearted, attractive women who took a sincere interest in him and he'd thought he'd be able to do the same for them. He'd managed to get himself into bed with them, but that, he learned, was the easy part; it was everything else he failed at. That was another reason he had come to Iowa City. To try again with someone else, knowing he wouldn't run into Mia.

He was in Henry's study now, where in the middle of the desk sat an old typewriter. "Do you actually write on that?"

"Sometimes," Henry said. "Word processors have their uses, but I'm suspicious of them. The screen makes things look neat before they actually are."

Julian pointed to a box. "Is your novel in there?"

Henry nodded.

"Will you bring it in to workshop?"

"It's done," Henry said. "My agent will sell it or she won't. It's time to move on to other things."

"I was working on a novel myself," Julian said. "That's why I came to Iowa. To try to get back to it."

"Will you be showing it to class?"

"First I have to finish it. And after yesterday, why show anything to those jerks?"

"They're just jealous," Henry said. "They're not the ones who were published in *Harper's*."

"It's just one story."

"What about that spread in *The Village Voice*?"

Julian shrugged. "The world is full of prognosticators." The feature in the *Voice* had called him promising. It was how Professor Chesterfield had described him, what countless others had said about him over the years, and every time he heard the word he thought of what Cyril Connolly had said: "Whom the gods wish to destroy they first call promising." He was thirty-two now. When was he going to fulfill his promise?

Henry said, "It's never a bad sign when people hate your work. It shows you inspired passion."

"Is that what you told yourself after you were up? That you must be on to something if they were so vicious to you?"

"I tried to," Henry said. "But sure, it hurts." He picked up the box that held his novel. It looked as if he were going to open it, but he just hefted it to his chest and returned it to the floor. "If it counts for anything, I really liked your story."

"Thanks, Henry." *Harper's* had liked his story, too. They had considered publishing it, but ultimately decided it needed more work, so they returned it to him, hoping he would revise and resubmit it. He'd been working on it over the summer, and he'd brought the revised version in to workshop to see what his classmates thought. The story was quiet; all his work was. Perhaps it was a matter of differing aesthetics. There had emerged in American fiction a strain of excess, he believed, a group of knowing authors whose every sentence seemed to shout, "Look how smart I am." He had nothing against muscular prose; it was the flexing of those muscles that he objected to, and, along with it, a disregard for character, which, for him, was what fiction was about. He'd been at Iowa only a few weeks, but already he could detect a clique of students for whom character was beside the point. "You're a good guy, Henry. People told me I wouldn't like anyone at Iowa, but I like you."

Henry laughed. "I like you, too, Julian."

"On the other hand, the last friend I made in a writing workshop slept with my wife." Julian hadn't spoken to Carter since that day in Berkeley, more than a year ago now; it seemed possible they would never speak again. He tried to tell himself it didn't matter, and certainly, compared with losing Mia, it didn't. But then, without expecting it, he would find himself thinking about Carter. He'd be reminded of him, often by people who were nothing like him, the way, standing next to Henry painting his house, he found Carter coming to mind.

Carter had been his best friend, and now he was gone, too; one loss compounded the other.

"Well, I'll do my best not to sleep with your wife."

Julian laughed. "That's probably a good idea."

The house was only half painted. And there was the inside, which Henry had neglected to mention until now. "Do you want to come back tomorrow?"

Julian smiled. "With a friend like you, I'll never get any writing done."

"It's best to be overscheduled," Henry said. "Too much time on your hands and a person becomes lazy."

"Of course you would think that. You went to medical school."

"Is that a yes?"

"I'll let you know tomorrow morning. It depends how much writing I get done today."

Julian walked down Fairchild Street, and he was a block away, on Church, when he realized he was still holding Henry's paint roller.

When he returned to the house, he found Henry on the ladder again, attending to a wall.

"It's yours," Henry said. "My token of gratitude. Maybe you'll find some use for it."

Julian laughed. "My house is already painted. I rented it that way."

But Henry had turned around and was going over a trouble spot. *More revision,* Julian thought. The heat spread across Henry's shoulders, the brim of his baseball cap shielding him from the sun.

Second semester came, and Julian's spirits lifted. He had come to Iowa to write, and he'd never been anyplace where people cared so much about writing. How easy it was when you were laboring on your own to feel that what you were doing was frivolous. But at Iowa there was no doubt that writing mattered, and he allowed himself, in the company of other writers, to believe that nothing was as urgent as crafting a good sentence, as creating vital characters.

He had sold another story to *Harper's,* the one that had been attacked in class last semester, and though Henry told him he should gloat, he didn't want to. The other workshop members, as if appreciating this, appeared to hold him in greater esteem; even the two classmates who'd used his photograph as a dartboard congratulated him on his success.

This semester, the director of the Writers' Workshop was his instructor. There were twelve students in class, and only once they were seated would the instructor make his solemn entrance. The instructor told the students that at the beginning of a story the writer hands the reader a backpack. He places certain objects in that backpack, telling the reader to keep them in mind, and if the reader gets to the end of the story and it doesn't matter what's in that backpack, the reader feels cheated. Julian thought about that analogy as he wrote. He watched admiringly as the instructor dissected a story, and though he himself wasn't exempt from criticism, it was clear that the instructor respected his work, and this meant a great deal to him.

After workshop, he joined his classmates at the Mill for hamburgers, pizza, and pitchers of beer, and on Saturdays he participated in the weekly softball games, fiction writers against poets. That year, one of the visiting instructors organized practices the day before the games, and Julian went out on Friday afternoons to shag fly balls with him. He reminded himself of the legacy of Iowa, how when the Writers' Workshop was founded it had been held in Quonset huts in the parking lot of the student union. He listed to himself, like a litany, the people who had studied at Iowa—Wallace Stegner, Flannery O'Connor, Raymond Carver, Andre Dubus—young writers like him, who had become successful; placing himself in their company, he felt buoyant.

At times, however, feeling lonely and beset by the cold, relying on his list of writers to buck himself up, he wondered again why he had come to Iowa. The previous week, he'd been at a party where a fistfight had broken out over Nathaniel Hawthorne, and though he hadn't been part of the fight, he felt sullied by it, embarrassed by the fact that he fraternized with people who threw punches over Hawthorne and, worse, were proud of it.

And, sure, he'd had two stories accepted at *Harper's,* but he hadn't been able to get back to his novel, which was why he had come to Iowa in the first place. Then his classmates would bring him up short again with the glee of their judgments—why did being cruel make people so happy?—for the class had been vicious to Henry once more, over the opening chapters of his new novel. Henry's novel was great, Julian thought; their classmates were just jealous.

After workshop, playing pool with Henry at the Foxhead, Julian was even more upset than he would have been if his own work had been attacked. "I hate everyone here," he said. "I'm thinking of dropping out."

Late one night, unable to work, he called Professor Chesterfield. They hadn't spoken in years, but Professor Chesterfield was the one who had encouraged him, and Julian needed his advice.

"How are you, Wainwright?"

"Terrible."

"What's wrong?"

Julian didn't know where to start. He and Mia had separated. He was living in a town he didn't like, among classmates he found mean-spirited. He'd stopped working on his novel. "Did you get an MFA?"

"No," said Professor Chesterfield. "They weren't as popular back then."

Of course they weren't, Julian thought. Hemingway hadn't gone to school to write; neither had Faulkner. For years, novels had been written without writing workshops, and everyone had done just fine. "My wife and I split up."

"That must raise the stakes," Professor Chesterfield said. "It's what happened with my novel. There wasn't enough room for both it and my wife."

Julian wished he could have said the same thing, that he and Mia had split up over his novel. Not that it would have made him feel better. But infidelity? How paltry, he thought. How inconsequential.

As the semester wore on, he started to skip the public readings at Prairie Lights and attend college basketball games instead. One cold February night, the snow collecting in drifts on Dubuque Street and along the banks of the Iowa River, he went to see Iowa play the University of Michigan. Sitting in the crowd with the Iowa fans, he heard the chants of "Let's go Blue!" He listened to the Michigan fight song being played, and he thought of the games he'd gone to with Mia and he felt wistful and alone.

Michigan won and he went home happy, but later that night his mother called, and as soon as he picked up he could tell she was crying.

"Dad's gone," she said. "He left me."

In the elevator of his parents' building, Julian said a quiet hello to George. George had been at the helm since Julian was a boy, and now, as he rode silently to his parents' apartment, he felt as if he were being transported to his own funeral. He had his key, but he decided to knock. When his mother didn't answer, he rang the bell.

It was noon, but his mother was still in her bathrobe, and her hair looked as if it had been branded on her forehead.

"Mom."

She hugged him.

Out! Out! Out! The first words he'd ever spoken, yet when he arrived at college, when he'd finally gotten out, he was surprised to discover that he was homesick. He hadn't been close to his parents; or the way that he'd been close to them, especially to his mother, had encouraged him to run. But he'd never known where to run, or how to return. Though he'd always held out the hope that someday they'd be closer. He would go away and do the things he needed to do, and in his selfishness, his indifference to his parents, he would freeze them as they'd been when he was a child. Now his father had left his mother, and what he felt more than anything was that his parents were mortal; they were going to die. He was a boy again, the toddler into whose room his mother would come at night, when he called to her in his nightmares, when he cried out for milk. "When did things go wrong?"

"We've had problems for years," she said. "You must know that."

He didn't and he did. He recalled his parents fighting, and himself beneath the covers, ostensibly asleep, putting a pillow over his head. His father not home yet, ten o'clock, eleven o'clock, sometimes after midnight, his mother waiting up for him before finally turning in herself. For a time, he feared his father wasn't coming home at all, but then he'd be there the next morning eating his half-grapefruit and reading his *Wall Street Journal* and Julian would feel foolish for having been worried. His father was a workaholic, but then all his friends' fathers were workaholics, and so many of his classmates' parents had gotten divorced that, by comparison, his own parents' marriage had seemed tranquil. True, there had been another group, whose parents had stayed together until the children left for college, with a rash of divorces freshman year, but his parents hadn't fallen into that category, either. They'd hung on, and he had come to assume they always would. "Is someone else involved? Does Dad have a girlfriend?"

"Not as far as I know." His mother looked up at him. "I almost left him years ago."

"Why didn't you?"

"It's not easy to leave. Dad was a good provider, and I've always been terrified of being poor. When I was a girl, my father lost his job. He was out of work for nearly three years."

"I didn't realize that."

"The economy wasn't doing well, and jobs were hard to find, even for attorneys. My parents had been living beyond their means. There was a boat, some fancy clothes, too much jewelry, and too many expensive vacations, and my parents piled up a lot of debt. The creditors were calling, but my parents did everything to keep up appearances, and I inherited that. I put myself through Wellesley working three jobs, but my friends were the rich girls, and I was so good at hiding how poor I was I almost convinced myself it wasn't true. Then I met your father. He appealed to me, Julian, a good-looking young man from a prosperous family, and as sure as I was standing there, he wasn't going to pile up debt the way my father had. And I was right about that. Not that there haven't been sacrifices. I had dreams of following my father into law. Of becoming the first female lawyer in our family."

"But Dad wouldn't let you?"

"It was just understood that I would stay home. And I was all right with it. I've always been willing to compromise."

"Perhaps too much?"

"By nature I'm an accommodator. Though the real compromise was the original one. I'm a romantic at heart, and even at twenty-two I knew marrying your father wasn't the romantic decision."

"You're saying you didn't love him?"

"I did, but he's a certain kind of person, and I'd be lying if I told you I didn't realize it from the start."

She took him into her bedroom, where she opened his father's dresser drawers. The underwear was gone, and the socks and undershirts. The trousers had been removed from the closets; the shoes were missing. As a boy, Julian used to take out the shoe trees and clomp around in those shoes, pretending to be his father, wanting to be him, even trying on his suit jackets, though his hands reached only as far as the elbows. He would grab his father's briefcase and walk around the living room, someone with a purpose, going somewhere. For years now he'd been hesitant to enter his parents' bedroom, and when he did he felt a quickening of breath. All those drawers and closets. The secrets contained within. And now his father's dresser drawers were empty.

"Back in college, there was this man I used to flirt with who worked at the local diner in Wellesley. He was a musician from Belgium, his English wasn't good, but I could have seen myself falling in love with him."

"But you didn't?"

"Dad came along and I went with him."

"And you think you'd have been happier with the other guy?"

"Not necessarily. It's just easy for me to see different paths."

He wanted to tell his mother to stick it out, but he himself hadn't stuck it out, though his parents had begged him to give Mia another chance. What, he'd thought then, did they know about marriage, his parents who had been married longer than he'd been alive but whose marriage had occurred—did all children tacitly feel this way?—for the sole purpose of bringing him into existence? They'd sat with him in this very apartment trying to understand what had gone wrong with Mia, and how could he explain it to them when he couldn't understand it himself?

His mother looked up at him. "I thought I was ready for this to happen, but you're never ready. Nothing could have prepared me for the moving truck, or for going into our bedroom and seeing his empty drawers."

"I'm so sorry, Mom." He'd learned more about his mother in the last hour than he'd known his whole life, though no doubt she would have told him years ago, if only he'd asked. "Where's Dad staying?"

"He's renting an apartment on Fifty-eighth and Park."

It occurred to him, as if for the first time, that he was going to see his father again.

"I had this idea when you were small that I'd run off to Paris and start a new life. What a borrowed fantasy that was, some schoolgirl's idea of romance."

"Why didn't you do it?"

"What would I have done with you? I wasn't about to leave you and move across the world."

"I would have come along." And for an instant Julian allowed himself to imagine it, too, life on the lam with his mother, living in Paris in some garret, getting by, the two of them.

"You wouldn't have stood for it. Besides, you were always making fun of my love of the French. You thought I was putting on airs."

"You weren't?"

She shook her head. "Paris was where Dad and I first traveled."

"On your honeymoon?"

She nodded. "We went out dancing, and we spent afternoons people-watching at Café les Deux Magots. But it wasn't just the honeymoon, because every time we went back to Paris this more sprightly person emerged. A version of him appears whenever we travel. When Dad left, I wanted to say, 'Give me a call when you retire.' I have this idea that we could be happy if work weren't hanging over him, but work will always be hanging over him, and if he ever retires, which he won't, it will still be hanging over him, the fact that he isn't doing it any longer." She thought for a moment. "I like to enjoy myself and it's hard for Dad to do that. That's been the fundamental difference between us."

"And will you be able to enjoy yourself now?"

She cast him a saturnine look; those dark green eyes could bore a hole in him, could still, when she was fifty-nine, catch the attention of a man across the room. When she was six months old, Julian's grandmother was told how lovely her daughter was; maybe she should be in advertisements. Those long days at the playground, the diaper changes and tantrums, praying for the naps to last longer, the dull hours waiting for her husband to come home so she could make dinner for him. On a lark, she sent in a photo, and Julian's mother was chosen for a laundry detergent billboard. Constance Wainwright, née Prescott, the Downy baby. There was talk of entering her in beauty pageants, but Julian's grandfather wouldn't countenance it; he thought beauty pageants were déclassé. Yet that was the image that came to Julian now, his melancholy mother in her beauty queen crown, coasting along on a parade float.

"For years I felt such responsibility for him."

"Shouldn't he have felt responsibility for you?" An image came to Julian from years ago, his mother lying on the couch late at night, her stockings bunched at her feet so her skin looked like an elephant's, one boot off and one boot on, his melancholy mother waiting for his father, listening for the sound of a key.

"You don't think he kept up his end of the deal?"

"Do you?"

"He wasn't abusive, certainly."

Julian laughed.

"You're saying that's a pretty low standard?"

"Isn't it?"

"I suppose. But he never raised his voice to me, and he was always concerned for my comfort. The only thing I hold him responsible for is how he was with you."

"I turned out all right." And he thought this was true. Though he also felt as if he were going to cry.

"I want you to know Dad always loved you, even if he wasn't able to show it."

"Look at you," he said. "Still defending him."

"I'm loyal to a fault," she admitted. "And Dad is someone who inspires loyalty. He's quite vulnerable, don't you think?"

"If he is, I've never seen it."

"That's because if he showed it, he'd fall apart."

"Why?"

"It has to do with his brother, I'm sure."

"The phantom Lowell?"

"He wasn't a phantom."

But Julian had always thought of him that way. The dead brother. Run over in the driveway when the ball rolled onto the street. His father standing there, watching it all. If only things had been different. But things hadn't been different, and to envision his father as someone else was, at a certain point, fatuous. "He left you, Mom. Isn't it time you got angry at him?"

"I am angry at him. But what you don't understand is I've been angry at him for years now, and I'm tired of it." She was standing next to the living room window, where a set of French doors opened onto the balcony. Julian recalled being a toddler, when she used to hold him on that balcony after his father left for work and they watched the planes descend to LaGuardia. And when his mother fed him, she would imitate a plane, saying, "Zoom, zoom, zoom, into the landing field," moving the spoon like a propeller into his mouth.

"I passed Dalton the other day," she said. "It was three-thirty in the afternoon and all the students were leaving. I had a moment when I expected you to walk out the door."

Dalton. He'd gone there from kindergarten through twelfth grade. He'd always liked school, yet what he recalled most distinctly about Dalton was waiting for classes to let out. College had been easy by comparison. In high school, he'd woken up at six-thirty in the morning, whereas in college he often didn't rise until noon. He complained about Ann Arbor and Iowa City, but when he and Mia had driven cross-country he insisted they stop in every college town they passed.

Mia used to say he was a walking college tour. One time, he told his mother, they drove through North Carolina and stopped in Raleigh and Durham and Chapel Hill until finally Mia said, "Enough!"

"Was she bored?"

"It was more than that. She associates college with her mother getting sick. Besides, she's never liked college towns. They're too one-industry for her."

"Yet she took you to Ann Arbor."

"She's a contradiction, isn't she?"

"I guess it's hard to go to graduate school in a place where there's no school."

He followed his mother into the living room, to the couches and chairs on which he'd reclined as a child tossing a tennis ball to himself. He'd always had a ball in his hand, sometimes a real ball, sometimes a makeshift one he'd fashioned out of newspaper. He would spend hours firing it into the wastepaper basket, always to the accompaniment of some sportscaster's voice regaling the audience with his feats. Back then, he couldn't walk anywhere without tapping a doorpost; everything was an improvised gymnasium.

He had fixed himself a peanut butter and jelly sandwich. Standing across from his mother, he held the sandwich out.

She smiled at him.

"What?"

"I thought you were giving me your sandwich crust."

"Is that what I used to do?"

"You don't remember? Once I forgot to remove the crust, and you brought it home and handed it to me."

"As a souvenir?"

"More like a rebuke. I'm always saying a mother never loses her peach pit instinct. Even with a grown son, you have to stop yourself from sticking out your hand when your child finishes a piece of fruit."

"Was I difficult?" he asked.

"No," she said, laughing. "You were bewitching and sweet. Easy words for a mother to say, but in your case they're true. I'm afraid I was the difficult one."

"Oh, Mom." He remembered being small, that love affair between mother and son. She used to take him to the boys' department at Bloomingdale's after school and buy him sweaters, neckties, and little-boy dickeys, sending him shuttling back and forth to the fitting room. And afterward, seeing him in his new clothes, she would lavish kisses on him, saying, "I could just eat you up."

"It's hard being an only child. If Dad and I had had more children, it would have spread the burden out."

"But you chose not to have them."

"I wouldn't put it that way."

"What do you mean?"

"When I got pregnant, I miscarried."

"I thought you didn't want another baby."

She laughed. Her pregnancy with him had been easy, she said, but after that she kept miscarrying. "It happened six times. Finally Dad convinced me it was overwhelming us."

"I'm so sorry." He'd believed his bunkbed, which still stood in his old bedroom twenty-five years later, was a consolation prize, when his parents, as much as he, he realized now, had longed for someone else to fill it.

"It was years ago," she said. "And we had you. Quality is more important than quantity."

Memories alighted on him. Playing gin rummy with his mother before he went to sleep. A daffodil petal falling gently to the floor. Sitting in the lobby when it was snowing out, reaching into the doorman's coat pocket for sucking candies while outside his parents were warming up the car for him, his father in a fur hat and gloves, brushing snow off the windshield, his mother with her own scraper, brushing snow, too, his parents next to each other like windshield wipers themselves, their arms moving up and down.

He arrived at his father's office, an expanse larger than many Manhattan apartments, and all glass, with views that made him feel as though he were descending in an airplane. My kingdom, Richard Wainwright called it self-deprecatingly, but there was nothing self-deprecating about the office. In the framed letters and photos on the walls, Julian's father was standing next to a sequence of New York City mayors, Lindsay, Beame, Koch, Dinkins, and Giuliani, as if they were lining up to greet him. His father's office was gigantic, the way Julian had once thought of his father himself, Julian's head level with his father's waist, the days of standing in the bathroom watching his father shave as if trying to uncover some secret. He was the bearer of his mother's genetic heritage, tall, wispy, delicate-framed, and despairing of this, he had, at fourteen, started to lift weights. Then, at sixteen, he realized with a start that he was taller than his father, though he still didn't have his father's stumpy neck. "Are we going out to eat?"

"I thought we'd stay in."

A blond woman brought in sandwiches, and sushi, and plates of roasted vegetables, and fruits and nuts, and a silver bowl with Beluga caviar. It was enough to feed the floor, but it was just the two of them, him and his father. He knew he would eat a sandwich and his father would, too, and he'd have a little sushi and then, like a bear, he'd forage among the nuts and berries. But most of the food would go uneaten, and Julian, recalling the starving in this country and around the world, the homeless man he'd given a dollar to this morning, thought, *What a waste.* There they were again, the indignation and sanctimony. The lectures he'd given his father about water preservation, the silent breakfasts when he was in high school, his father clipping out articles from *The Wall Street Journal* while he clipped out articles from *The Nation* and *The Progressive,* the two of them communicating like this for years, unable, it seemed, to talk to each other.

"I appreciate your coming home," his father said. "I know Mom does, too."

Julian nodded.

"You flew in?"

"I drove. All the flights were booked."

His father had wanted to see him, and in a way Julian had wanted to see him, too, but now that he was here, he didn't know what he'd been hoping for.

His father got up and stood by the window, and Julian, not sure what else to do, joined him. And he realized, standing there, how accustomed he'd grown to seeing New York City from up high, from his parents' apartment, from his father's office on the thirty-eighth floor, so that now, when he thought of New York, it was as if he were always flying over it.

Below them, the pedestrians moved along Fifth Avenue, spattering the sidewalk like paint.

"It makes you feel tiny," his father said.

But Julian felt as if he were nothing at all.

"You look good," his father said, touching Julian's jacket sleeve. When he was a boy, Julian always wore a suit to his father's office because his father thought he should look like a man in this world of men. Julian's grandfather had made Julian's father do the same thing, and so they'd carried on this sartorial tradition from one generation to the next. Now, when Julian didn't own a single suit, when all he had was a tattered blazer, he had worn a jacket to his father's office, having found one in his bedroom closet last night. Once, when he visited his father at work, he arrived to see streamers tacked to the walls, and a sign that read, WELCOME, JULIAN, and when his father introduced him to his colleagues, someone said, "Don't look now, but here comes the new head of arbitrage." His father took him for lunch to the rooftop garden and gave him one of his business cards, and for a time Julian wanted nothing more than to have a business card of his own. His father had hoped that he'd go into investment banking, and for a second now Julian wished just that, that he'd gone to Yale and studied economics, that he'd been able to be his father's son.

His father wore a tormented expression; it frightened Julian, for he'd never seen that look before. He saw that his father, the most solitary man in the world, was also terrified to be alone. His mother was wrong; his father wouldn't have left her if there hadn't been someone else. "You have a girlfriend, Dad, don't you?"

His father hesitated.

"Fuck," Julian said.

His father began to speak, then stopped.

"So it's true?"

"It's not why I left Mom, if that's what you're asking."

"You two were together for almost forty years. Don't you think you owe her something?"

"I owe her a lot," his father said. "But am I obliged to stay with her when neither of us is happy?" He pulled on his jacket sleeves. For his birthday once, Julian had bought him a pair of blue jeans, but they looked too much like a costume, and he never wore them again. "It's not what you're thinking," he said. "She's not half my age, and she's not a bimbo."

No, Julian thought, he couldn't imagine his father with a bimbo, though the truth was he couldn't imagine him with anyone at all, not even with his mother, though he also couldn't imagine him without her. It occurred to him for the first time how implausible it was for his mother to have fallen for him in the first place.

His father removed a card from his desk drawer. It was thin and white, like a credit card with nothing printed on it. "I was in Laos last month."

Then Julian understood. Years ago, when his father traveled on business, he would bring home the key from the hotel room he'd stayed in; the corporate mogul was filching hotel keys for his son. Julian had keys from Hong Kong, Malaysia, and Taiwan, from Peru, Botswana, New Zealand, and Zimbabwe. He kept the keys in his desk, and when his father was away he'd take them out, trying to imagine where he was.

"I want you to have it," his father said.

A hotel key card. Because even in Laos, in Luang Prabang, in sleepy cities just starting to embrace industry, hotels didn't use real keys any longer; they used plastic key cards, and you didn't even have to steal them, they were disposable. "Tell me about Lowell, Dad."

"Who?"

"My uncle," he said, and how curious that word felt emerging from his mouth, for he'd never really had an uncle, not one related by blood, at least.

Seeing his father's eyes mist over, he said, "It's okay, Dad. You don't have to talk about him if you don't want to."

"What do you want to know?"

"You probably don't remember much."

"I was only four when he died."

"Did he look like me?" And it wasn't until he said those words that he remembered his mother having told him this. The thought came to him, hauntingly, that he was his dead uncle reincarnated.

"At least in the pictures I've seen of him."

His father's lip quavered, and Julian thought, *Please, Dad, don't cry.* He'd never seen his father cry, and he wasn't sure he could endure it now, sitting across from him in his office. He got up to go.

"Wait, son."

Julian stood opposite him as if commanded to.

"What I remember came afterward. My parents turned the house into a shrine to Lowell. When people asked how many children they had, they said two, and it was years later. Where was my brother? He was more alive to them dead than he'd been when he was alive, certainly more alive to them than I was."

It had been his father's ball Lowell had chased, an errant throw or kick, a four-year-old's exuberance, and Lowell had gone after it, rushing toward the oncoming car. Julian didn't know how he knew this, but he did. When he was a boy, his father had refused to play sports with him; he said he wasn't athletic. Yet there were glints of memory, a teenager hitting a tennis ball against a church, his father catching it as he walked by. His father chasing the bus when he was late to work, running from Sixty-third Street to Sixty-second Street and overtaking it, the fleet-footed sight of him moving like an antelope. Was his father an athlete, after all?

Julian stood up to shake his father's hand, and his father reached out and they were hugging. But they got tangled in the arms, so they started over, and this time they were gripping each other. It was as if they were inventing a new mode of affection, waving their arms up and down, two elephants in a tussle, and it wasn't until they had separated, not until Julian was out of his father's office and into the elevator, dropping precipitously from the thirty-eighth floor, that he started to cry.

It was eight-thirty in the morning when he arrived in Ann Arbor. A town of students, where the streets were abuzz long past midnight, but at this hour everyone was asleep. It was February, and the roads were snow-covered. He trod tentatively, feeling like an interloper, when, he realized, he'd been gone only six months, and except for his friends, no one would have found his presence remarkable.

At Shaman Drum, he scanned the New Fiction shelves, then picked up a *Michigan Daily* from outside the store. He headed down State Street, toward Hill and Packard, silently reciting the street names, as if to make sure he hadn't forgotten them. He cut back up Monroe, past the law school and across the diag, passing Angell Hall where, no doubt, his old office was occupied by someone new.

It was eleven o'clock when he reached Mia's apartment. She had moved out of their place on Kingsley Street and was living on the Old West Side. He'd looked her up this morning when he got to town and saw that she was listed on Fountain Street. He himself was still listed on Granger, where he'd last lived, and also, inexplicably, at their address on Kingsley. In Ann Arbor, it seemed, there was no erasing you. And in other places, too, for back in New York he was still served jury notices every couple of years, and no matter what he did he was unable to convince the city that he wasn't a resident any longer and hadn't been one since he'd left for college. Year after year the courts kept calling, until eventually he stopped answering the letters. He half expected to find a policeman at his door one day, ready to extradite him to New York.

He rang the bell but no one answered, and he was reaching into his bag to write a note when he heard footsteps on the stairs.

"Julian?" Mia said. "What are you doing here?" She was standing outside now, and she took a step back, as if to regard him afresh. "You look terrible."

He laughed.

"No, I mean . . ."

"I've been driving all night," he explained. "I was home in New York. I'm on my way back to Iowa."

"You must be exhausted."

"I am."

"Do you want to take a nap?"

He hesitated.

"You're thinking why would I trust you alone in my apartment? The world's biggest snoop? The truth is, I don't have a lot of secrets. And the ones I have, I can part with." She held out her keys.

"I have another idea. Do you want to grab lunch?"

She laughed. "So, I get it. You need to leave town in order to have lunch with me? If I'd known, I'd have sent you away ages ago."

They found a table at Red Hot Lovers, home to the world's largest condiment selection. Julian piled relish on top of onions on top of barbecue sauce on top of pickles. He smiled at Mia. "You look good," he said.

"You're just not used to seeing me in a skirt."

"Or in makeup."

"It's my nod to the work world. It's how I remind myself I'm an adult." She looked up at him. "How are you, Julian? How's Iowa?"

"Savage."

"Is your writing not going well?"

"My novel is stalled. On the other hand, I've been writing stories."

"And you're happy with those?"

He reached into his bag and removed a copy of *Harper's*. It was the issue with his story in it; his name was printed on the front cover.

"Oh, Julian!"

Now, emboldened, he told Mia that *Harper's* had accepted another story of his. Yet even as he said this, he felt a queasiness overtake him, as if he'd spent some capital without realizing he was doing so.

"It sounds like you're the star of the program."

"The program is filled with stars." He touched his face, where there was several days' growth of beard. Often he went a week without shaving, though for a time he'd had a full-fledged beard. His accidental beard, he called it; all his beards had begun that way. He might still have had that beard, but Mia hadn't liked it, so he'd consented to shave it off. "What about you? Are you here for the long haul? Putting down roots?"

"You mean do I finally vote here?" Mia was a dual citizen, and when she and Julian moved to Michigan she refused to switch her registration because she insisted she was in Ann Arbor only on a layover. Now that layover had lasted almost ten years. Finally, she'd relented: she was officially a Michigander. "And do you know what happened? As soon as I established residency, I reached a breakthrough in my dissertation. I was going to be on the fifteen-year plan."

"But you're not any longer?"

"I'll be defending next month."

"Mia! Congratulations!"

"I'm even thinking of marching at commencement. It's in the football stadium. Do you remember when we went to football games together?"

He smiled at her: did she think he had forgotten?

When they finished eating, they walked on Washtenaw, then up past the tennis courts to the Arboretum. Mia had taken up running when they moved to town, and sometimes Julian would run with her in the Arb. He was a good athlete, but he was partial to sports that involved balls, and eventually he tired of running, so he walked while she ran. "I'm power walking," he would say, which sounded to him like an oxymoron, at least as he had come to understand power walking, which involved swiveling your hips and swinging your arms and generally making an ass of yourself. So he walked as unpowerfully as he could, and then he sprinted to catch up with Mia, and soon they started the process all over again.

Now they cut past hedges and bramble. Julian plucked a leaf and smelled it, the way at the produce stands in New York's Chinatown he liked to raise the unfamiliar vegetables to his nose. His jeans were fraying at the cuffs, which was where they always went first. It happened that way with Mia, too, though, unlike her, he would continue to wear his jeans until there were holes everywhere, until there was practically nothing covering him.

A squirrel halted in their path, moving from side to side, as if hoping to get them to dance.

"We're explorers," he told Mia. "Think of me as Ferdinand Magellan."

"And who am I?"

"Mrs. Magellan," he said. "Francine."

"Was that really her name?"

"Franny for short. Ferdinand and Franny Magellan."

When they used to walk together, they would occasionally wander off onto private property. It always concerned Mia, traversing ground they weren't supposed to be on, but Julian told her not to worry. It wasn't as if someone would shoot them.

"You never know," she'd said.

One time, Julian took out a squirt gun and sprayed her. "A trespasser has to defend himself."

"Be careful," she said. "Somebody will think it's an actual gun and they're liable to shoot you for real."

Now, back on campus, she told him she had to go to the library. "I need to check my footnotes. It would be a shame not to graduate because I mispaginated the thing."

He stood opposite her.

"So is this it?" she said.

"What?"

"I assume you have to leave."

"I had to leave days ago. I already missed my turn in workshop."

"Why aren't you back in Iowa, anyway?"

"It's a complicated story," he said.

"Will you at least take a nap before you leave?"

He must have really been tired, because when he awoke it was seven o'clock and dark outside. He recalled childhood naps like this one, lying beneath a mohair throw, waking up unsure of where he was. Mia lived in a studio, and across from him sat her futon—though he realized now it was their futon, the one they'd slept on in college. He'd gone right to sleep in her apartment. He'd been too tired to snoop, though he also felt it wasn't his right to do so. He didn't, in the end, want to know her secrets. It felt like enough of a secret that he was here.

"Are you feeling better?" Mia stood across from him, holding open a Zingerman's shopping bag. "I got you some sandwiches," she said. "And a cherry scone and a peanut butter cookie and a Key lime bar and some fresh-squeezed lemonade and a loaf of Parmesan-pepper bread."

"You got me bread?"

She held up the loaf of bread. "Wasn't Parmesan-pepper your favorite?"

He used to memorize the weekly bread schedule and show up at Zingerman's when the Parmesan-pepper arrived. Then he would go home and make a sandwich for Mia and bring it to her office.

"I figured you'd have the leftovers when you got back to Iowa. Ply your classmates with them."

They ate dinner together at her little dining room table facing the boxes of herbs on the windowsill: rosemary, thyme, sage, oregano, chives. Out of necessity, she had begun to cook, and she thought of Julian as her inspiration, recalling how he'd started to cook when they got to Ann Arbor and had become quite good at it. And he was the one who had purchased the window boxes, who tended to the herbs back in their apartment on Kingsley, who, when she came home, could be seen with them lined up on the kitchen counter, happily conducting his experiments.

"So this is your home," he said.

"It's not exactly palatial."

"No, but it has character. Everywhere you've lived has."

She smiled at him.

"Why? Don't you like it here?"

"I wouldn't have minded a larger space, but the price is right." She hesitated.

"What?"

"I was thinking about how when we moved to Ann Arbor you wanted us to live in a real house."

"What's wrong with a real house?"

"Nothing, but I was worried about money. And then you left me, Julian, and even our apartment on Kingsley was too expensive for me."

"Is that why you thought money was tight? Because in the back of your mind you believed things might not work out?"

"No," she said. Though it was true, she thought, that she'd never felt his money was hers. When they got married, he had wanted them to join checking accounts, but she refused at first. It took years for her to acclimate to having married someone rich, and those initial months in Ann Arbor she kept a secret log of everything she spent, trying, vainly, to live off her student stipend. "Anyway, I'll be moving in July."

"Where to?"

"New York."

He laughed.

"What?"

"I thought you hated New York."

The truth was she liked New York, but it had been hard to muster much enthusiasm for it when Julian was being so enthusiastic himself. Now she was the one moving there, while he, to her surprise, hadn't returned. Was that, she wondered, the reason she'd chosen it? Because, no matter what happened, he might end up back there? No, she thought, she wouldn't acknowledge it. She'd stopped waiting for him long ago.

She would be working at a clinic at NYU, she said, seeing patients suffering from post-traumatic stress disorder. Bosnian refugees, displaced Somalis, a few regular old traumatized Americans. She would do that for a couple of years; then she hoped to open a private practice. "It won't be easy," she said. "There are more therapists in Manhattan than in Vienna. But my adviser knows people in New York, so I should get some referrals. The University of Michigan casts a wide net."

"Go Blue!" he said.

She smiled.

"Is Olivia still living there?"

She nodded. "That's another reason I'm moving. I want to spend time with her."

"Has she been dancing?"

"As much as she can." Olivia had been an understudy with Mark Morris, and when someone from the troupe went down with an injury, she'd gotten to perform at BAM. Their father came in for the performance, and Mia flew in, too. But Olivia had been injured herself. In the last year alone, she'd separated her shoulder and blown out her knee.

"She's five foot eight," Mia said, "which is too big for a dancer. Too big for a dancer, she likes to say, and too small for a model. And not pretty enough for either."

"She's pretty," Julian said.

"Of course she is, but she doesn't see it. And now she's going out with a married man. Kincaid's fifteen years older than her, and he has a wife and three daughters. Does she really want to be involved with someone like that, out of all the guys in New York?"

"Have you tried talking to her?"

"Of course I have, but she won't take my advice." Mia was in the kitchen now, and on the wall across from her hung a backward clock. The one read eleven and the eleven read one; left and right were reversed. It had been a gift from Olivia for her twenty-first birthday, and she'd kept it all this time, transporting it from apartment to apartment. "When you left me, Julian, Olivia started to call regularly for the first time in years. But in the end, she saw my splitting up with you as another example of my good fortune. Do you know why? Because at least we didn't have kids. From the minute she was born, she's thought of me as the lucky one, and whatever happens, she simply incorporates it into what she already believes."

"She sounds like a philosopher," Julian said. "Never let a fact get in the way of a theory."

"So I've decided to stay quiet. I just watch her carry on her affair and fritter away her inheritance."

"Is that what she's doing? Frittering it away?"

"Spending it, yes." Though Mia supposed "frittering it away" was uncharitable. Olivia gave dance lessons, and occasionally she still picked up waitressing shifts. But that wasn't enough to support yourself in New York, and realistically, she wasn't going to be dancing that much longer.

214

"And you?" Julian said. "Are you still sitting on your inheritance like it doesn't exist?"

"It's two hundred thousand dollars," Mia said. "It's not going to support me for a lifetime."

"Right now, it sounds like it's not supporting you at all."

"You're right. And here I am complaining my apartment is too small when I could have done something about it."

"But you didn't."

"And you went along with me, Julian. Paying more of the bills when we split up, letting me convince us I was poor. I don't want to spend the money for no good reason, but it's as if there couldn't be a good enough reason in the world." She sat down on the couch. "This is crazy. We haven't spoken in I don't know how long, and all I can talk about is me, me, me. How are you, Julian? How's your family?"

He hesitated.

"Is something wrong?"

"My parents have separated," he said. "They're getting divorced."

"Oh, Julian."

As a boy, Julian used to play Twister with his father. How anomalous it had been to see his father contorted like that, Saturday afternoons, the few hours when he wasn't at work, and Julian knew he would have his father nearby as long as they were playing Twister together. Because his father wasn't going to let him win. But as bullheaded as his father was, Julian was more so, and with each spin, his mother, the designated spinner, intoning her instructions, he knew he wouldn't permit himself to fall and eventually, if he was steadfast, his father would capitulate. And when he did, when he tumbled to the mat, perspiring, his tie sweeping across the floor, he looked up at Julian still crouched on the mat and said, "I admire your stubbornness, son."

And this was what his stubbornness had wrought. He'd gone off to Iowa City, a town with no draw for him, no history save for the history of the Writers' Workshop, to classmates who saw themselves as his competitors and who left him no choice but to see them as competitors, too. He'd lost everything, everyone important to him. He'd lost Mia and he'd lost Carter, and now his parents were getting divorced and he'd lost them, too.

"Can I ask why they separated?"

"It wasn't a happy marriage," he said. "I figure they should have split up twenty-five years ago." He wiped his face with a tissue, then forced out a laugh. Sugar tears: he was crying the remains of his Key lime bar. "When your mother was dying, Mia, I wished it was happening to my mother instead. Because, I thought, if it was my mother, sure, I'd be upset, but I didn't think it would be so terrible. I was twenty-one. I thought I was done with her, and with my father, too."

How little they'd known then, she thought. And not much more now. The way your parents could surprise you.

"You liked my parents," he said, "didn't you?"

It took her a while, she admitted, but her affection had grown for them. Julian's mother, especially, had been a solace to her after her own mother died. Occasionally, the two of them would talk on the phone even when Julian wasn't there. And then Julian left and she lost his parents, too. She recalled a spring afternoon, a few hours spent shopping with Julian's mother, strolling along Madison Avenue. Her memories of shopping, the good ones, at least, always involved her mother. Men didn't understand this, the intimacy you felt when shopping with your mother; she didn't fully understand it herself. But she marked that as a time when things opened up between her and Julian's mother, when she felt more welcomed by his family, and she felt more welcoming herself.

She looked up at the clock. "It's almost ten," she said. "I don't want you driving through the night."

"I'll be okay."

"You can sleep on my couch. You've already staked a claim to it."

She flipped on the TV, and they sat in front of it watching but not really, letting the sounds sweep over them.

"Did your parents really keep the TV in the closet?"

She nodded. The status quo ante, she thought. She could hear her father's voice, see him fiddling with the antenna he'd made from that clothes hanger.

"I thought of calling you on your birthday," he said. He'd been born at four-fifteen in the morning, and every year on his birthday his parents used to wake him up in the middle of the night so they could sing "Happy Birthday" at the moment he was born. He'd worked at Bennigan's one summer on Cape Cod, and when it was a customer's birthday he would bring out a piece of cake with a single candle on it and the waiters would sing the Bennigan's song. "Happy, happy birthday, may all your dreams come true. Happy, happy birthday from Bennigan's to you." It was the same song he'd sung to Mia every year on her birthday.

"Why didn't you?"

He didn't know. Pride, he imagined. Or fear. The conviction that he'd end up in her apartment, which was where he'd ended up anyway.

That night, he slept on the couch still wearing his clothes, and Mia was on the futon, in her clothes, too. He'd fallen asleep to the sound of her breathing, and he didn't even notice that they'd left the TV on.

When he awoke the next morning, she was at his side, holding orange juice and toast with marmalade.

"Are you just going to keep feeding me?"

"Isn't that what a hostess is supposed to do?"

He leaned over and kissed her. He was still lying on the couch and she was sitting next to him, and now, when they separated, the toast was stuck to her elbow and marmalade was smeared across his brow.

She stood up, and he did, too, and they kissed again, without the acrobatics.

"Does this mean you'll consider taking me back?" He tried to sound offhand, but his heart was thrashing against his rib cage and he didn't know what she would say. You left someone you loved, and eventually they stopped loving you back. For all he knew, she had a boyfriend.

"Do you want to spend the day with me?"

"I could be your research assistant," he said. "I'll check your footnotes for you."

"And after today?"

"I'll find another task."

She made a show of considering it. He had forced her to wait this long; she was going to make him wait a little longer. There was still more to talk about, in any case. Not that she had any doubt.

She had her coat on and she was out the door.

"Where are you going?"

"To the library," she said. She was already down Fountain Street and he was following her, doing his best to keep up.

New York, New York

It was a gigantic building, thrust above the East River, and at the Sixty-eighth Street entrance, where Mia went in, the taxis were navigating around the parked cars and the people in line waiting for the valet. At the information desk, she asked for the Greenberg Pavilion and was directed through a doorway and down a hall to a bank of elevators next to which hung an enormous portrait of Mr. and Mrs. Greenberg staring down at passersby.

She checked her reflection in the elevator doors. She was late. She had taken the express train uptown, and since the local hadn't been waiting at Fifty-ninth Street, she had decided to walk from there. On days when the weather was good, she ran on the paved path between the Hudson River and the West Side Highway, heading north from the West Village, past the meatpacking district and Chelsea and up beyond the turnoff to the Lincoln Tunnel. Other times, she ran on the city streets themselves. Twenty blocks to a mile, everyone said; the taxi meters confirmed it. But the avenue blocks, going west to east, were four times as long. Third Avenue, Second Avenue, First Avenue, York Avenue, the East River: this was a mile in its own right. She could have run, but she was in her work pumps and a skirt, carrying her bag, and she didn't want to be perspiring when she arrived—though, having walked at a brisk clip, she was, anyway. It was warm, besides, unusually so for April. She removed her sunglasses and placed them in her bag.

In the waiting room, she flipped through *Us Weekly*. This was the second time in a week that she'd read *Us,* for a just few days ago Julian had brought home a copy someone had left on the subway and deposited it in the magazine bin in their bathroom. She had never read *Us* before, and what she'd wanted to know, leafing through it, was whether *Us* was more like *People* or like the *National Enquirer.* What she meant, she told Julian, was did it pay lip service to the truth, however much it traded in gossip and innuendo, or did it disregard the truth, like the *National Enquirer,* which reportedly had a large budget reserved for libel settlements?

"The truth," Julian snorted. He was working as the assistant to a literary agent. He read the slush pile, passing on the promising material to his boss; he answered the phone, mailed contracts to authors, helped with first serial and subsidiary rights, and fed Lulu, the office cat, who spent most of her day asleep on the boss's desk square in the middle of a pile of manuscripts. Julian's boss knew he wrote fiction, and though she was partial to fiction herself—she represented a number of accomplished novelists—what editors were looking for, she told Julian despairingly, was the truth.

But whose truth? The truth of that reporter who'd been let go by the *Times*? The truth of George Bush? Of the Gulf War? The publishing world was in the midst of a memoir craze, and many memoirs crossed Julian's desk. The people who wrote them had led exquisitely painful lives, but this didn't automatically make them writers. "I suffer, therefore I am," Professor Chesterfield had said, and it remained true more than fifteen years later. At Iowa, one of Julian's instructors had complained about passive protagonists to whom bad things happen and who remain inert throughout the story, never making a choice, never *doing* anything, and so they lack moral complexity. Richard Nixon stories, Julian's instructor called them. Mistakes were made. But who made these mistakes? Who was responsible? Such were the manuscripts Julian read at the agency and brought home at night, occasionally reading a few lines aloud to Mia.

Mia went into the bathroom, careful not to upset the urine samples. When she emerged, the receptionist gave her some forms to fill out.

"Is this your first time here?"

It was.

Her medical history was unexceptional, and so she put check mark after check mark in the "No" box, feeling a palpitation nonetheless. She signed her signature at the bottom, releasing the doctor from responsibility for things she wasn't sure doctors should be released from, but now wasn't the time to argue. "You don't accept insurance, do you?"

They didn't. But the receptionist agreed to take Mia's insurance card anyway. Perhaps her insurance company would offer her partial reimbursement for services administered out-of-network.

"Is there a water fountain here?"

She was pointed to one.

Her tongue was dry, her throat parched. She drank lengthily, and almost as soon as she was done she needed to pee again.

Out the window, she glimpsed a narrow swatch of the East River. Bedpan Alley, this part of the city was called; along York Avenue everyone seemed to be wearing a white coat, a photo ID clipped to their breast pocket. Ambulances patrolled the streets, their lights flaring, a siren going on and off. Just last week a doctor had been mown down by an ambulance. Killed in the line of duty. Memorial Sloan-Kettering was a few blocks away, and the Hospital for Special Surgery. And New York Presbyterian, where Mia was now. Although she was *at* the hospital, she wasn't *in* the hospital, she reminded herself. She was just here for a doctor's appointment.

Across from her a woman, perhaps seven months pregnant, was drinking a smoothie, and a few seats away sat another pregnant woman, reading a fashion magazine. A coincidence, Mia thought, before she realized, rebuking herself, that of course it wasn't a coincidence; she was in the waiting room for ob/gyn. A girl in her late teens emerged crying from the office, followed by a boy roughly the same age. A technician walked purposefully past them, carrying vials of blood down the hall. On the table next to Mia lay a stack of pamphlets with the words THINGS YOU SHOULD KNOW written across the cover. One of the pamphlets was about chlamydia, another about AIDS. A nurse emerged and called someone's name, and Mia, anticipating, stood up, but it was another patient being asked to come in.

She turned the pages of *Us* with dutiful solemnity. She and Julian lived in the West Village, home to many of New York's movie stars, and just last week, when they were out to dinner, Matthew Broderick had been sitting at the table across from them, and it took Mia several moments to realize who he was. She had never thought of herself as out of touch with popular culture, but she was beginning to wonder whether this was so. The joke back in graduate school had been that there was no point in therapists' going to the movies because their patients had already ruined the endings for them. But Mia was finding she had a different problem. She hadn't heard of many of the actors her patients mentioned. A friend of hers read *People* cover to cover every week. It was her version of pornography, her friend said, but flipping through *Us,* reading the tales of heartbreak and betrayal, of divorce and weight gain and plastic surgery and palimony, Mia was less aroused than bored, and so she put the magazine away.

She looked out the window, past the East River to Queens. She'd been to Queens a few times recently, out to dinner in Astoria, Flushing, and Jackson Heights, but the borough still bewildered her. Sixty-fifth Street next to Sixty-fifth Avenue next to Sixty-fifth Place: it took a cartographer to understand Queens. Besides, she was still discovering Manhattan. She'd been living in New York for three years now, but she still approached it with the glow of a newcomer; she was glad to see she hadn't used it up.

That last semester in Ann Arbor, she'd finally abandoned hope that Julian would return to her, and then he was there, sharing her tiny apartment with her. She'd been planning to stay with Olivia in New York, but Olivia didn't have room for both her and Julian, so while Mia finished her dissertation, Julian flew to the city to check out rentals. My own private real estate agent, she called him.

When Julian first said he was joining her in New York, she assumed he was taking a leave of absence from graduate school, but he quickly made clear that he was dropping out. "It's what I've wanted to do from the moment I got there."

After a week in Ann Arbor, Julian returned to Iowa and left a rent check for his landlady; he didn't even consider asking for his security deposit back. Then, having collected his belongings, he stopped by Henry's house to say goodbye.

"So this is it?" Henry said. "A semester and a half is enough for you?"

"Life calls."

"It's probably for the best. It wasn't pretty in workshop last week."

Julian had forgotten. When his mother had called to say his father had left her, he'd departed Iowa City without telling anyone, and he was up in workshop the following week. Apparently, the class had discussed his story anyway. "They acted as if you were there," Henry said.

"Which is just the reverse of what they usually do," Julian said. "Most of the time, they pretend you're not there even when you are."

Henry smiled.

"So they hanged me in effigy?"

"Pretty much."

"It's to be expected, I guess."

"Don't worry," Henry said. "You'll have the last laugh."

"You will too, Henry. I'm counting on you."

It was late August when Julian and Mia moved to New York, just weeks before the Twin Towers fell. Welcome to New York City, Mia thought. Someone else might have turned around and left, but if anything, the attacks drew her closer. She and Julian were leaving for work when the planes blew up, and from in front of their apartment building they could see the smoke and hear sirens. In the days and weeks afterward, Mia walked around the city, stupefied. She and Julian volunteered at a shelter a few blocks from where they lived, and they brought pizzas late at night to the Ground Zero workers. Standing in the midst of it all, she felt that she was already an official resident, that she'd been placed on the fast track to becoming a New Yorker.

"At least it can't get any worse," Julian said.

He was right—though, a month later, Mia was standing on a

crowded subway platform when suddenly everyone began to run for the exits. Did somebody have a gun? A bomb? She ran along the platform and up the stairs, but when she got outside and asked people what had happened, no one seemed to know. She scoured the newspapers the next day and couldn't find anything. It must have been a false alarm. A case of spontaneous panic. She never would find out.

In the weeks after that incident, she started to walk more, and to run on the streets, for running, she found, was her preferred mode of transport. She would go from neighborhood to neighborhood, her own internal taxi meter clicking, glancing up at the Flatiron and Puck Buildings, discovering a city that now felt like hers.

She had spent that first year working at the clinic at NYU, treating people with post-traumatic stress disorder (now there were the Ground Zero workers to attend to as well), and then, as she'd planned, she opened a private practice. And maybe it was true that there were more therapists in Manhattan than in Vienna, but there were more patients as well. She came home one night and said to Julian, "You know what? I'm supporting myself."

"Hell," Julian said, "you're supporting me."

But it was because Julian was rich that, once the lease on their apartment ran out, they were able to purchase a brownstone on Perry Street, a couple of blocks from where they lived. "Let's buy a building," Julian said, and that word, "building," seemed right to Mia, for he might as well have said, "Let's buy the Chrysler Building," owning a home was that foreign to her.

It had been a year now since they'd bought their brownstone, but Mia still liked to recall the day they moved in, Julian upstairs propping the doors open, the movers, an Israeli and two Mexicans, at her side, communicating in a medley of Hebrew and Spanish. Across the street stood the bakery she'd soon be getting coffee from. Everything that surrounded her felt like props that had been erected solely for the enactment of her new life. All that had happened until now had been simply a prelude.

Then the movers were gone, and it was just her and Julian amid the piles of boxes and the furniture in bubble wrap. "This is our home," she said.

Julian smiled.

"Our home, our home, our home, our home." She couldn't recall having been this happy.

Yet in the months that followed, she kept waiting for something to go wrong, and now, sitting at the doctor's office, she was convinced it had. A girl of about fourteen entered the waiting room, her mother at her side. Mia recognized the look on the girl's face, for when she herself had been that age she'd visited the gynecologist for the first time, and though she couldn't have imagined going on her own, it seemed even worse to be accompanied by her mother. She had a boyfriend at the time; they wouldn't have sex for another year, but she was fitted for a diaphragm that day. At heart, her mother was a prude, but she had considered it her duty not to be one, and so she'd gone out of her way to be open about sex with Mia. Though Mia hadn't wanted to talk about it with her. To this day, she felt that sex was about separation from your parents, and she thought that if she ever had a daughter she would spare her the talks her mother had given her, the effort she'd made to appear liberal and broad-minded, the copy of *Our Bodies, Ourselves* that had appeared at her bedside the day she turned fifteen.

In the examining room, she was given a gown and told to undress. "How are you today?" the nurse said.

Mia, dreading the companionship of strangers, did her best to be polite while hoping to discourage further exchange. "I'm fine," she said, though the truth was she'd been agitated all day, sufficiently so that she'd contemplated canceling her therapy sessions. She hadn't, because she believed doing so was irresponsible and she prided herself on not missing appointments. Besides, she thought seeing patients would distract her. But it hadn't in the end.

The nurse removed the blood pressure kit. She was big-boned and stout, a redhead of about forty-five who had the bustling, efficient manner of the competent. She rolled up Mia's sleeve.

"Will we be doing it here?"

The nurse laughed. "As opposed to outside?"

What Mia meant was would they be doing it where she was now, sitting on the examining table with her legs dangling down. She'd read that the most accurate way to gauge blood pressure was with the patient in a chair, feet on the floor. Dangling your legs required more exertion and contributed to falsely elevated blood pressure readings. But she said none of this. Her blood pressure tended to be on the low side of normal, and now, when the nurse began to pump, the machine read a hundred over fifty-three, which was, in fact, the low side of normal.

Alone now, Mia waited for the doctor. Her clothes were folded in a pile on the chair. She'd placed her underwear beneath her skirt so it wouldn't be visible when the doctor came in, though she knew the doctor would be seeing her naked. But she wanted her clothes to appear presentable whether they were on her or not. Dozens of pale hairs clung to her skirt, and she did her best to remove them, even searching through her bag for a lint brush, but she seemed to have forgotten it. A black skirt. A Yellow Labrador puppy. Though all her clothes, no matter what their color, were covered with dog hair. And the furniture, the floor, everything. She had complained to Julian about it, but she'd wanted the dog as much as he had. They'd been talking about a puppy for a few years now, really since the time they'd moved to New York, and once they became homeowners and there was no landlord to get in the way, they began to consider it in earnest. They'd joked that it would be training wheels for a baby. They would have a house and a dog. Welcome to the life of the bourgeoisie. As if they hadn't been part of it all along.

She and Julian were thirty-six now. Julian had returned to his novel, he was finally making progress, and they had agreed that in a year, whether he had finished it or not, they would try to have a baby.

But they'd never done anything about getting a dog besides stare in the windows of the pet stores they passed, watching the puppies wrestle with one another. "Impulse buy?" she'd said to Julian once. But they never would have gotten a puppy from a pet store; those dogs came from puppy mills. Still, they gazed desirously at the Collie and Golden Retriever puppies that seemed to grace every catalogue that arrived in the mail, as if the dogs themselves were screaming, "Buy me!"

And then, a couple of months ago, Julian ran into an old high school friend at the supermarket, and when he glanced inside his friend's shopping bag he saw a Yellow Labrador puppy asleep inside it. The dog was six months old and fully house-trained. His friend was looking for a good home for him.

"You mean I can have him?" Julian said.

"He's yours."

So it had been an impulse buy, after all. And Julian hadn't even had to buy him.

They quickly learned, however, that anyone who thought a dog was training wheels for a baby had never actually owned a dog. If anything, Mia thought, a baby might be training wheels for a dog. That first morning, she came back to their bedroom to find that the puppy had eviscerated their pillows. And on the bathroom floor lay a puddle of urine. "I thought you said he was house-trained."

Julian rubbed the puppy behind the ears. "He's probably just nervous. At least he made into the right room."

Later that day, when Mia came home from work, she found Julian and the puppy on the living floor surrounded by dog paraphernalia. The biggest item was a crate, which stood fully assembled, and by its sides was an assortment of stuffed toys, all with noisemakers in them. There was a collar, a Frisbee, and two bowls. There were sterilized bones flavored with chicken and liver, Nylabones flavored with beef, and what Julian claimed were pigs' ears. There were—Mia couldn't believe this—dog goggles. "Doggles," said the package. "To protect your dog from sun, wind, and debris." Julian had bought a book of names and a pile of index cards; when he found a name he liked, he wrote it on the front of the index card, and on the back he wrote the name's etymology and history.

"What are you saying? I choose a card and that's the name we give the dog?"

"If we like it."

"And if we don't?"

"We try again."

Mia picked a card. "This isn't a name. It's a biography."

"Flip the card over."

"Leila?"

"It's from the Arabic chapter."

"You bought a book about Arabic dogs?"

"It's not a book about dogs. It's a book about names. There's an Arabic chapter and a Welsh chapter and a Korean chapter and a Polish chapter and a Slovakian chapter. Thirty-five thousand names in all, Arabic ones included."

" 'Leila,' " Mia read. " 'Derived from the Arabic Leila—night, dark beauty—or the Persian Leila—dark-haired. Used in George Byron's poem 'The Giaour.' " Julian, isn't Leila a girl's name?"

Julian admitted that it was.

"But this dog's a boy."

"True."

"How about we eliminate the girls' names?"

"You're giving up some good ones."

"Like what?"

"Tusa. Native American name. It means Prairie Dog. But we still have the Native American Kangi Sunka, which is male and means Crow Dog. Or Elaskolatat, also Native American, also male. Then there's the Scandinavian Dag. As in Hammarskjöld. Alternatively, we could give him a Japanese name."

"Why would we do that?"

"Because I love sushi."

"You're going to *eat* the dog?"

"We can call him Hideo," Julian said, "which means excellent male, or Yukio, which means snow boy, or Ozuru, which means big stork—"

"How about Cooper?" Mia said.

"Why Cooper?"

"Because I like the name."

So it was decided: Cooper it was.

Now, though, sitting in the doctor's office, her legs sticking to the paper on the examining table so that two blotches of sweat were imprinted on it in the shape of her thighs, Mia thought how foolish they'd been. Because now, with what was about to happen, maybe they couldn't handle a baby *or* a dog.

She got down from the examining table, scolding herself. Nothing was about to happen. She had no idea.

On the wall across from her hung a poster of a woman's insides, the vaginal canal and fallopian tubes, the uterus and ovaries. She felt as if she'd been photographed for everyone to see, turned inside out like a pair of trousers. She thought of fifth-grade health class, the boys in one room, the girls in another room down the hall, the damp scent of mothballs as the girls, in their knee socks and sweaters, sat staring at the screen on the chalkboard, the taste of humiliation on their breath. She recalled anticipating a throat culture, that long toothpick like something you'd spear marshmallows with, and then the doctor's voice, "It's over now, wasn't that easy?," his hand sliding into his coat pocket where a lollipop was secreted. She'd always been afraid of doctors. She still was, though she was a doctor herself. A different kind of doctor, but then therapists could be the scariest doctors of all. Though she'd never felt that way about her own therapist, only about medical doctors, which was how she felt now, wishing she weren't here.

There was a knock on the door and she started. "Who is it?" She cinched the tie on her gown.

"Dr. Kaplan," a voice said. "May I come in?"

"Oh. Yes." She'd forgotten. The doctor and nurse saw you undressed, but they didn't see you *getting* undressed. They knocked on the door, as if this were your office, not theirs. Not that she didn't appreciate the gesture.

"Emily Kaplan," the doctor said. "It's nice to meet you."

Mia slid off the examining table and shook the doctor's hand. Then she mentioned the friend who had recommended her, another patient of Dr. Kaplan's. Dr. Kaplan smiled in acknowledgment, and Mia waited for her to say something, but she didn't respond and a moment of awkwardness settled between them.

Dr. Kaplan appeared about forty, and she had straight blond hair cut bluntly above the shoulders, a small face, and light blue eyes. She was wearing street clothes: a pair of khaki pants, a white shirt open at the collar. "Are you here for a regular checkup?"

"No," Mia said.

Dr. Kaplan glanced up.

"I think I have a lump in my breast. At least, that's what it feels like."

"When did you discover this?"

"Yesterday. I thought I might have been imagining it, but I check my breasts every month and this feels different. My mother died of breast cancer," she added.

"When?"

"Fourteen years ago."

"How old was she when she was diagnosed?"

"Fifty." Mia corrected herself. Her mother had been forty-nine when she'd been diagnosed, fifty when she died. She still couldn't believe it. It had all been over in less than a year.

"Do you know whether she was pre- or post-menopausal?"

Mia shook her head. "Does it make a difference?"

"It can. Pre- and post-menopausal breast cancer often have different characteristics."

"I could ask my father," she said.

Dr. Kaplan nodded. "This may very well turn out to be nothing, but it would be good to know in any case." She started to stand up, then sat down again. "I'm sure this is quite frightening for you, but you should know that with breast cancer there are many false alarms."

"Benign lumps?"

"There are a lot of those, certainly. And I've had patients who thought they had a lump who turned out to have nothing at all. Breast tissue can be quite dense."

Dr. Kaplan administered a breast exam, moving painstakingly around the tissue, beginning at the center of the breast and moving to the sides, up toward the armpits, where the lymph nodes lay, starting with the left breast, then the right. At one point she stopped and went over the same spot several times, and Mia wanted to say, "Did you find something?," but the words wouldn't come out.

She had been in the shower when she discovered the lump, and she was too agitated to do anything at first. Perhaps, she thought, it was simply the angle at which she had approached the breast, or the temperature of the water. Also, she was expecting her period soon, and her breasts got tender before she menstruated. But this wasn't tenderness she felt. She thought of calling Julian, but he was already at work, and she was too frightened to tell him. When she got out of the shower, she checked again, and this time she immediately called a friend who came from a family of doctors and asked for the name of the best gynecologist in New York. That was how she'd ended up at Dr. Kaplan, who had a three-month waiting list for an appointment but who, thanks to Mia's friend, found her a spot the very next day.

Dr. Kaplan was conducting an internal exam. She had Mia's feet in the stirrups and was placing the speculum inside her. Maybe, Mia thought, she didn't have a breast lump, which was why Dr. Kaplan could focus on something so mundane. Or maybe she did have a breast lump and Dr. Kaplan was checking for other problems, too. What if she had cancer and it had already spread? But she could ascertain none of this because she was dry-mouthed, mute, lying with her legs spread, while Dr. Kaplan, steadfast, silent herself, went about the business of examining her.

Mia got dressed quickly and left the gown on the chair before realizing there was a bin in which to deposit used gowns. The piece of paper on which she'd been sitting still had her sweat stains on it, and she wanted to get rid of that, too, but she didn't know what to do with it.

Down the hall in Dr. Kaplan's office, she sat staring at the diplomas on the wall. Dr. Kaplan had graduated from Princeton and NYU Medical School. She'd done her residency and internship at Brigham and Women's Hospital in Boston. There was a photo of a girl on the desk, blond like Dr. Kaplan, about seven years old, but there were no photos of a husband. Maybe, Mia thought, Dr. Kaplan was divorced. Maybe her husband had died, maybe there had never been a husband, maybe she was gay, maybe she'd had the child on her own, maybe it wasn't her child but a niece, or a cousin.

"You're right," Dr. Kaplan said. "You have a lump in your breast."

"Are you sure?"

"It's quite small. Less than a centimeter." Dr. Kaplan held out her thumbnail and bisected it. "It could easily prove to be nothing."

"Even though my mother . . ."

"There are lots of benign lumps out there, but it's the malignant ones, understandably, that get all the press. That said, I think we should have it checked out."

"Get a biopsy?" This, Mia thought, was how it all started. You found something suspicious and you had a biopsy. With a shudder, she remembered that call from her father senior year of college. *Something's wrong with Mom.*

"It's done over in Oncology," Dr. Kaplan said. "They should be able to fit you in at the beginning of next week."

"I can't get it done today?"

"It's already four o'clock."

"How about tomorrow?" She couldn't endure having to wait. She wanted the lump out, whether it was malignant or not.

Dr. Kaplan left the office, and when she returned she said, "How does ten o'clock tomorrow morning sound to you?"

"Thank you," Mia said. "I truly, truly appreciate it." Then she was out of the office and through the corridor, back into the pitiless heat.

At home, she watered the plants and put in a load of laundry. She wandered around the house, from the first floor to the second to the third, walking from room to room as if to make sure the house hadn't rearranged itself, her footsteps reverberating across the hallway, the white and black squares like on a gigantic chessboard. She could hear Cooper barking downstairs. When they got him, Cooper was supposed to be confined at first, and then, slowly, if he wasn't having accidents, he would be granted greater access to the house. But every time they increased his space he wanted them to increase it more, and he would place his paws up on the gate that was designed to pen him in. Finally, they succumbed and gave him the run of the house.

She took him for a walk, down Perry Street and over onto Hudson, where she tied him to a parking meter outside the supermarket. She picked up some lamb chops for dinner. She wanted to indulge in the rituals of normalcy—dinner, a bottle of wine; maybe later she and Julian would have sex—and somewhere, between all that, she would have to tell Julian what she'd discovered. He would end up assuring her the lump was benign because at his core he was optimistic, but also because she worried about health and he tried to balance her out. He liked to accuse her of hypochondria, and she had to concede he was right. After her mother died, she'd cut back on meat and processed foods and started going to the gym several times a week. But she remained anxious about her health. Once, finding a rash on her leg, she had been convinced she had Lyme disease. When Julian pointed out the odds against this—they'd been living in Ann Arbor at the time; there were no deer ticks on State Street—she was only half reassured. Just to prove she could do it, she went for months without reading the Science *Times,* which had been the section of the paper she read most carefully. She bullied herself into not worrying and, to her surprise, it worked. A semester would pass and she'd realize she hadn't been concerned about her health, that she'd gone back to how she'd been before her mother died, with the casual, unthinking trust of the vigorous. But then something would happen and she couldn't even pinpoint what—an article she'd read, a phone call from her father in Montreal, sometimes, as far as she could tell, nothing—and she'd be back to where she'd been months before, obscurely, distantly fretful.

Now, a block from home, she saw her neighbor approaching. He was a young, prematurely graying man whose name she could never remember. He seemed not to recall her name either, for whenever they passed each other they would smile exaggeratedly, as if trying to compensate for something. He had a dog, too—Buddha, a white creature so tiny Cooper didn't know what to do with him and he had to be reminded Buddha wasn't a ball. When Cooper and Buddha played, Mia and Buddha's owner talked about dog things. But alone, they acted lost. It was that way with dog owners in general. When you saw them without their dogs, you didn't know what to say. It was as if you had run into them naked.

She laid out the lamb chops on the kitchen counter and made a salad. Then she took a bath, descending beneath the bubbles, cleansing herself of the grime and perspiration, hoping to wash away the breast lump itself, which, like someone testing a toothache, she palpated when she got out.

Someone had left a message on the answering machine, and when she heard Julian's voice, telling her he loved her, she started to cry. She lay down on the floor with Cooper next to her, wiping her face with his ears.

By the time Julian got home, she was dressed. The Last Supper, she told herself dramatically, but she couldn't pretend she felt otherwise.

"Guess who called today," Julian said.

"Who?"

"Professor Chesterfield. He finally finished his novel. He's looking for a new agent."

She sat down on the sofa, staring glumly at him.

"Is something wrong?"

She shook her head.

"Are you sure?"

"I'm just tired."

She went upstairs and lay down, turning on the radio to some classical music in the hope that it would soothe her. In the bathroom, she washed her hands and face, scrubbing her pores until her cheeks shone.

"Mia?" he called out. "Are you all right?"

"I'll be down in a minute."

But when she came downstairs, she found Cooper in the kitchen with the lamb chops in his mouth.

"Jesus Christ, Julian! That was supposed to be our dinner!"

Cooper dropped the remains at her feet, then continued to ravage them, moving from one lamb chop to the other as if unable to decide which appealed more. At least she'd caught him in the act. According to the dog books, if you didn't catch your dog in the moment of transgression he wouldn't understand what you were upset about. But even in the moment of transgression, Cooper appeared unrepentant. He seemed too stuffed to care.

"Look what your dog did," Mia said, and she let out a litany of complaints, about how everything revolved around Cooper, his walks, his feeding schedule, how he lay in the hallway, immobile as a sack of grain, as if daring you to step on him, only to rise suddenly to thump his tail against your knee. His toys made appearances all over the house, under the bed, between the sofa cushions, in a whimsical rite of burial and disinterment. She had never seen a dog so obsessed with food. The sound of her pouring out her vitamins resembled Cooper's food going into his bowl, so she was forced to take her vitamins out of Cooper's earshot; otherwise he would bark. Just the other day, she'd fished inside her pocket to give a homeless man a quarter and she'd mistakenly given him one of Cooper's treats. Another time, she or Julian had left treats in a pocket, and when the clothes came out of the wash everything smelled like stew. Julian had taken to dressing Cooper up, not in dog clothes, but in political placards such as BONES, NOT BOMBS, which Cooper had worn dutifully around his neck to a gay rights rally, though what bones or bombs had to do with gay rights she had no idea. Cooper, cave dweller that he was, liked to lie beneath Julian's desk, the bottom beam of which he would maneuver himself under as if doing the limbo. Man and his dog, Mia thought, and she, as co-owner of that dog, wasn't allowed to say certain words in her own home, lest Cooper misunderstand. "Hurry up" was forbidden because that was what they said to Cooper when he was supposed to pee, so if they said it in the house he would pee on the floor. Forbidden, also, were "walk," "food," "outside," and "park"—she couldn't even ask Julian where he'd parked the car without Cooper, their hapless dog, starting to bark, so she was reduced to searching for synonyms, or whispering the words, or saying them in a different language.

"Jesus, Mia. It's just a couple of lamb chops. I'll go out and pick us up a pizza."

She started to cry. "I have a lump in my breast."

"What?"

Through the window, she could see Perry Street buckle, the sidewalk folding in on itself. Everything looked flat, as if the city were a sheet of paper out of which the pedestrians had been fashioned and everyone was falling through it. "Julian, I might have cancer."

Julian's lip shook. He reached out to steady himself. *No,* she wanted to say. She needed him to be unwavering. She was crying now, and he was doing his best not to cry himself, and only barely succeeding.

"Am I going to be all right?"

"Of course you are."

"How do you know?"

"I'm sure of it."

"I just wanted us to have a normal dinner, and now I've gone and ruined that, too."

"We can still have dinner." But Julian simply stood in the living room and she did as well, and now she was telling him she wasn't hungry.

"You have to eat."

"I don't want to."

"I'll go out and get you whatever you want. Chinese, Thai, Italian, you name it . . ."

"I just want you to stay with me."

"Of course."

She went into the kitchen. "What about you? Are you hungry?"

"I'm fine."

"You shouldn't starve because of me."

"Mia . . ."

She placed the salad bowl on the floor, and having forgotten utensils and failed to make a dressing, she doused the greens with oil and vinegar, pouring them on like kerosene. Slowly, with their hands, they picked at the lettuce leaf by leaf, olive oil coating their fingers. Then she removed a quart of vanilla ice cream, and they hacked away at it as if with pickaxes, managing to get little clumps onto their spoons. But they weren't hungry, and so they left the rest on the floor for Cooper to eat.

They lay in bed that night, unable to sleep, and the following morning when they got up they took a cab to the hospital.

Back at home, Julian did his best to keep himself diverted. One minute he was transported on the billows of his own hope; the next he was downcast. Three days passed, and Mia hadn't heard from Dr. Kaplan. Maybe the results had come back already and Dr. Kaplan had been too busy to call. Julian told Mia that a delay might be good. No need to rush if the lump was benign; it was a malignant lump that required swift attention. Half the time they wanted to get it over with, to learn the news no matter what it was, and more than once, Mia picked up the phone to call the hospital, only to think better of it.

Professor Chesterfield's manuscript had arrived, and for the first day Julian simply left it in its packing.

When he finally opened it, he handed the manuscript to Mia. "Four hundred and seventeen pages," he said despairingly.

"Is that too long?"

"If anything, it's too short." It was 2004, eighteen years since Julian had first studied with Professor Chesterfield, at which point Professor Chesterfield had already been working on his novel for more than twenty years. It was a forty-year project, Julian realized, which came out to ten pages a year. At that rate, it had better read like Joyce, but when he sat down with it, he found the novel uninspiring; fearing he wouldn't love it, he decided he was going about things wrong, dipping into the book for a few pages, then laying it down. He half suspected, fretful as he was, jumping up with Mia every time the phone rang, that if he'd been reading Joyce himself he wouldn't have been drawn in, and so he put the manuscript away, believing he had to read it under different circumstances, so as to be fair to Professor Chesterfield.

One night, Julian and Mia caught a movie at the Angelika, and afterward they ate dinner at an Italian restaurant, sharing a chicken dish and pasta, shouting to each other over the noise. The next day they met after work to play racquetball, and when Mia thought Julian wasn't trying, she said, "Hey, don't take pity on me!" and she whacked the ball as hard and as low as she could, hitting several consecutive winners and reaching game point before Julian came back to beat her.

Later that night they had sex, and when Mia came she was elated, feeling this was her body and she was fine, though she understood it meant nothing, that, vigorous as she felt, when it came to cancer by the time you didn't feel healthy it was generally too late and it was only when you still felt good that you had a chance.

Exactly a week after her biopsy, the phone rang, and it was Dr. Kaplan. "How would you like some good news?"

Her heart, her whole body launched. "The lump is benign?"

"The lab results came back an hour ago. You're fine. Your pap smear was normal, too."

She was crying. "Thank you, thank you, thank you."

"I had nothing to do with it," Dr. Kaplan said.

But Mia felt that Dr. Kaplan *did* have something to do with it, that in a way she'd saved her.

"While I have you on the phone," Dr. Kaplan said, "I think you should start getting regular mammograms. We recommend forty for most women, but because of your mother I would start you now. And women with benign lumps have a slightly elevated risk of malignancy. It's nothing to be too concerned about, but it should give you extra incentive to pay attention."

"Oh, I will."

"One more thing. Am I right in thinking you're Jewish?"

"Yes," Mia said. "Why?"

"I assume you know about the Ashkenazi Jewish breast cancer genes. We call them BRCA1 and BRCA2."

"I've heard of them."

"Well, before you get worried, I'd say you're not a very likely candidate." The two genes, Dr. Kaplan explained, accounted for only about five percent of breast cancers, and most women who carried the gene had more than one close relative with the disease. "Your mother was the only immediate family member to have breast cancer, right?"

"That's right," Mia said.

"What about on your father's side?"

"My great-aunt had breast cancer. But that was years ago. I never even met her."

Dr. Kaplan paused.

"Why? Does it make a difference?"

"Most people don't realize it, but the gene can be passed down from the father's side, too. Still, I'd say it's unlikely. Your father's family doesn't have an extensive history, either. On the other hand, your mother was diagnosed relatively young, so we couldn't rule it out."

"And if I had the gene?"

"You'd have a greater than eighty percent likelihood of developing breast cancer and a fifty percent likelihood of developing ovarian cancer." In a way, Dr. Kaplan said, the ovarian cancer would be more worrisome. There was a pretty good chance of catching breast cancer early, but by the time ovarian cancer was diagnosed, it was usually too late.

"So what would my options be?"

"If I had the gene," Dr. Kaplan said, "I would certainly get more regular checkups. Mammograms two or three times a year, along with an annual MRI." Some women took Tamoxifen, Dr. Kaplan explained, but it remained to be seen whether the drug was effective at preventing gene-linked breast cancer. Researchers were learning that "breast cancer" was an imprecise term. There were a number of different kinds of breast cancer, each with distinct cell makeups and disease mechanisms. It almost made no sense to call them the same disease.

"Don't some people get mastectomies?" Mia asked.

"That's right," Dr. Kaplan said. "They do it prophylactically. It's the best way to ensure you won't get breast cancer. Though I don't have to tell you that's a drastic step. Still, if you've seen one, two, three people you love die . . . And a prophylactic double mastectomy reduces your chances to almost zero."

"*Almost* zero?"

"I know," Dr. Kaplan said. "You'd think with a double mastectomy you should get a money-back guarantee. But it's next to impossible to remove all the breast cells." Still, Dr. Kaplan said, with a double mastectomy a person could feel pretty safe. As for ovarian cancer, what she recommended was that anyone who tested positive and was past her childbearing years seriously consider having her ovaries removed.

"Well," Mia said, "this is all very cheery."

"In the end, it's a personal decision. How much risk can you tolerate and what kinds of risks? How much do you want to know about things over which you have only limited control?"

"Let me think about it," Mia said. Julian had come home, and greeting him at the door, Cooper was wagging his tail so hard he was wagging his whole butt. Julian seemed to know who had called, for when Mia smiled at him he jumped in the air. And when she got off the phone he popped open a bottle of champagne and they decided to go out and celebrate.

Temperate weather, a delicious meal, feeling robust when she awoke in the morning, the throb of her heartbeat as she ran beside the Hudson, the traffic speeding by her. She noted these things now and was grateful for them. Her subway stalled, she got a ticket for double parking, and she didn't care. She was, she realized, a survivor cliché, and she hadn't even survived anything.

"My unflappable wife," Julian said. "From now on, I dub you Mellow Mia." He walked about the house imitating her, though he looked less like someone mellow than someone asleep, for his neck lolled and his knees buckled and he seemed to have lost all muscle tone.

But after a few weeks had passed, it became difficult to recapture the dread, or the relief. Things went back to how they'd been before. She submerged herself in work. She went out to dinner with Julian. They played racquetball. They saw friends. But there remained a pall: that she might have the breast cancer gene. Late at night, after Julian had gone to sleep, she would surf the Web, trying to find out whether she had anything to worry about.

She learned that nearly a million Americans carried one of the mutations, which meant that in the population at large the odds were about one in four hundred. But among Ashkenazi Jews the odds were one in forty. What was more, in one study, out of 104 women who had been found to have the mutation, half had no known family history of breast cancer. In almost all those cases, the gene had been passed down silently by the woman's father.

On the phone with her father, Mia said, "Did anyone besides your aunt have breast cancer, Dad?"

"A cousin of mine had it in her thirties," he said. "But they caught it early and she was cured."

"But no one else?"

"I don't think so."

"You aren't sure?"

"How can I be? I've never stayed in touch with extended family."

He was right, Mia thought. She had friends who were close with a large family tree, second cousins, first cousins once removed, everyone descending for an annual family reunion. But her family had never been that way, and her father, at least, looked at extended family with near distaste, as if the very category of "cousin" had been foisted on him. He found blood ties, except for those of immediate family, abstract, a curiosity, and he saw no reason to fraternize with people he had little in common with simply because they shared a great-grandfather. His extended family was the family of physicists; those were the people he wished to spend time with.

"What about Mom? Was her cancer pre- or post-menopausal?"

Her father didn't respond.

"Dad, did Mom reach menopause before she got sick?"

"I don't know."

"Wouldn't you remember if she had?"

"It's been ages now, Mia, and we had much more pressing things on our minds than whether Mom had reached menopause."

"I understand."

"Is everything all right?"

"Yes." For years now, her father had resisted going to doctors. He had a superstitious regard for the medical profession; he believed if you paid attention to doctors they'd pay attention to you. He'd been proven right, he believed. Mia's mother had held doctors in high esteem and it hadn't done her any good; he, on the other hand, had remained healthy. Since her mother had died, it had fallen on Mia to watch over her father's health, and it was all she could do, miles away, to get him to go for his annual physical. She hadn't told him about the breast lump. In fact, the only people she had told were Julian and Dr. Kaplan. She was a private person, and she didn't want anyone to worry about her, especially not her father, alone in Montreal.

She had a couple of hours off from work, so she stopped by Olivia's apartment in Alphabet City. Olivia's place was small, but it was so uncluttered and sleek that it always looked as if she'd just moved in. "You're amazing," Mia said. "How do you keep the walls so white?"

Olivia shrugged. "I guess I make things sparkle."

She did, Mia thought. Olivia and her feng shui. At the center of the living room, across from the couch, sat a brass Chinese trunk, and on the wall beside the window was an ebony side table on which stood a slender glass vase holding a rose. Aside from that, there was little furniture in the room and the walls were bare. Everything was understated, which made sense, Mia thought, for when Olivia had been mentioned in *The New York Times,* in a review of her dance troupe's performance, the reviewer had written, "Olivia Mendelsohn glides across the stage with such economy of motion she appears not to be moving at all."

"Anyway," Olivia said, "Kincaid likes how I keep things here."

"Immaculate?"

"No dirty dishes in the sink, no kids' underwear to pick up, no Parcheesi pieces lodged between the sofa cushions." She subsided onto the sofa, frowning. "You must think I'm crazy."

"For keeping house for someone you don't even live with?"

Olivia shook her head. "I keep house for myself. Still, I can't help thinking I'm a feminist's nightmare."

"Oh, Ol, that's not true. You're living alone and supporting yourself. You're doing what you love."

"Mia, I'm going out with a married man."

"But you love him, don't you?"

"Absolutely."

Olivia had been with Kincaid for four years now, and long ago Mia had resolved to stop judging her for it. Who was Mia to judge, in any case, when she had slept with her husband's best friend and nearly lost him over it, when for a time she *had* lost him? Kincaid had promised to leave his wife, and the fact that he hadn't made Mia doubt he ever would, but then she didn't know Kincaid—not well, at least: his relationship with Olivia was, of necessity, secretive—and if Olivia believed Kincaid would leave his wife, Mia was determined to believe it, too.

It was noon, and Mia had called to see whether Olivia wanted to get lunch, but Olivia was still in her sweatpants—she'd been waitressing late last night—so they agreed to have lunch at her apartment.

In the kitchen, Olivia slathered cream cheese on a couple of bagels and placed blueberries in a bowl. A long mirror hung in the hallway, and she stopped in front of it to examine herself. "I hate this," she said. "I'm losing my looks."

"You were saying that when you were twelve, Ol."

"But this time it's true."

Olivia claimed she had a bump on her nose and that her chin was misaligned, but Mia could see none of this. Neither, apparently, could men, who had been drawn to Olivia when she was younger and who were still drawn to her; Kincaid wasn't the only one who had pursued her.

"Remember that *Newsweek* article that said that a single woman over thirty-five is less likely to get married than be killed by a terrorist? And that was in the days before there were terrorists."

"You aren't thirty-five yet," Mia said. "And they disproved that study," Mia said.

"Okay," Olivia said, "so I'm being retrograde." She sat down at the table. "Sometimes I think Kincaid is with me because I'm the path not taken."

"Because you're a dancer?"

Olivia nodded. "Frustrated artists are attracted to me." Apparently, Kincaid had been a painter once, but there had been pressure on him not to pursue his art, first from his parents and then from his wife, who believed that painting was ultimately an indulgence. He'd considered architecture and graphic design, but he had ended up in investment banking. Then there were kids and bills, the usual things, and he was locked into something he found soulless. "He says I followed my dream," Olivia said.

"Well, you did."

"I just wish he wouldn't romanticize me."

"Think of it as a compliment."

"Kincaid wishes he'd done what I've done, and what do I want? Domesticity. Jesus, Mia, I want to cook for him."

"There are worse things than that."

"I love to cook, but it's lame to cook for yourself, and when Kincaid and I are together, he wants to go out."

"And you don't want to?"

"Sometimes I do. But more often, I just want to stay home and watch TV with him."

Olivia retreated to her bedroom, and when she came back she was holding a picture of her and Kincaid. It was a strip of three photos, the kind taken in a drugstore booth, and it made Mia think of her sister from years ago, Olivia with her arm draped over some boy's shoulder, lipstick smeared across her mouth. "And when we do go out," Olivia said, "we have to go someplace where Kincaid won't run into anyone. A few weeks ago, we had reservations at this Italian restaurant I love, but he needed to cancel a couple of hours before because he forgot it was his wife's birthday. I was torn between being furious at him for blowing me off and thinking, *What kind of jerk forgets his wife's birthday?*"

Olivia was standing by the window, looking out at the traffic. Her hair, which had always been lighter than Mia's, was even lighter now, for she'd begun to highlight it, but aside from that, she looked as she always had. When they were girls, Olivia used to ask Mia to pinch her stomach, but there had been nothing to pinch—that was the point—and there still wasn't. Even through her sister's sweatpants, Mia could make out the muscles in her calves. Olivia had been born a month early, had pounded her way out, their mother used to say, and

Mia recalled leg-wrestling with her, lying on her back on the floor opposite Olivia and grabbing on. She could hardly remember a time when she'd been stronger than Olivia. Already when she was seventeen and Olivia was twelve she'd landed feet-over-head when she leg-wrestled her. "Have you thought of breaking up with him?"

"Of course I have."

"But?"

"I love him, Mia. I really do. And . . ." She looked up. "Oh, God, I can't believe I'm about to say this."

"What?"

"He treats me well."

"What's wrong with that?"

"It's the world's most revolting statement, don't you think? It's what every woman says about her boyfriend, as if they can't hope for more. It's mercenary, too, because what a woman usually means when she says a man treats her well is that he takes her out to nice restaurants and buys her expensive gifts."

"Is that what *you* mean?"

Olivia tapped her knife against the plate, and the *ping* reverberated through the apartment. "It gets hard after a while not having money. It isn't romantic anymore."

"I understand."

"Do you?" Mia had married rich, Olivia liked to say, and when Mia claimed that that hadn't been her intention, Olivia said that was precisely her point; it was another example of Mia's good luck.

Olivia poked at the blueberries on her plate. "I was surprised when you called today," she said. "I wondered what the reason was."

"Does there have to be a reason?" Mia lived only a few miles from Olivia, yet she could go for weeks without seeing her. "You can stop by whenever you want to," Olivia always said, and Mia said the same thing. But Olivia never stopped by. When they saw each other, Mia initiated, and whenever Mia called, Olivia assumed it was with a purpose.

"Olivia, do you know about the Ashkenazi Jewish breast cancer gene?"

"It sounds vaguely familiar."

"There are two genes, actually, and if you have one of them you have a better than eighty percent chance of developing breast cancer and a fifty percent chance of developing ovarian cancer."

Olivia nodded noncommittally.

"I thought you might mention it to your gynecologist." Through the front door, Mia could hear a cat meowing, the sound of paws moving down stairs.

"I don't have a gynecologist," Olivia said.

"You don't?"

"I was seeing someone for a while, but he retired, and I haven't gotten around to finding someone new."

"You really should."

"Mia . . ."

Long before their mother had died, Mia had acted like a second mother to Olivia; now that their mother was gone, she was even more that way. Mia thought of her mother's words in the hospital. "Swear to me you'll take care of Olivia." Olivia didn't like it when she acted this way, and neither did Mia, but she couldn't help herself. "I'm thinking of testing for the gene."

"Why? You don't know Mom had it."

"But she might have. Or Dad might have it. A father can pass it down, too."

Slowly the information seemed to settle on Olivia, and she appeared agitated. She turned on the TV and flipped through the channels.

"Please, Ol, listen to me."

Olivia turned off the TV. Sitting on the couch next to Mia, she looked like a child again, retreating into herself. "You're saying you want me to test, too?"

And it occurred to Mia that she did want Olivia to test, that if they tested together it would be less frightening.

In the kitchen, Olivia opened the cabinets, and Mia could see their mother's old china, each plate protected by a piece of green felt. The artichoke plates were there, too. They looked like an experiment in topography, with a trough at the center in which the artichoke sat, and surrounding it additional troughs for the sauce and leaves. It had been a wedding gift from a graduate school classmate, and it had symbolized to Mia her mother's squandered career, how she'd sacrificed her ambitions on the altar of the dinner party. As a teenager, out of protest, Mia had refused to eat artichokes, and Olivia, who wasn't protesting, had never developed a taste for them. Yet the plates were front and center in Olivia's kitchen, and Mia wanted to ask her for one, though she had no idea what she'd do with a single artichoke plate—probably what Olivia had done with the rest of them, which was leave them in the cabinet unused. There they were, Mia thought, the dishes Olivia mooned over, hoping to serve dinner to Kincaid.

"What if you test positive?" Olivia said.

"Then I'll have a tough decision. There are drugs I can take that might lower my risk. Or I could get a double mastectomy."

"Just chop your breasts off?"

"I wouldn't put it so violently."

"Well, it *is* violent, don't you think? Mia," Olivia said, her voice softening, "would you really do that to yourself?"

Mia was quiet. She had no idea what she would do.

Outside, on the fire escape, two pigeons had landed. They stood side by side, looking out at Avenue B.

Olivia got up to water the plants. She bent over each pot, then moved on to the next one, and from where Mia sat, it looked as if she were bowing to them.

Olivia put down the watering can. "I just don't think I can take that test." She looked up at Mia. "It would be useless information, anyway, because I can't see myself getting a mastectomy."

"Even if you had the gene?"

"Tell me something," Olivia said. "If you had the gene and you got a mastectomy, would Julian stick by you?"

"Of course he would."

"Because I'm not so sure about Kincaid."

"You're saying he'd leave you?"

"I just don't know." Olivia started to cry, tears rolling down her face, falling onto her plate next to a mound of leftover cream cheese.

"Olivia, honey." Mia laid her hand on her sister's arm, but Olivia swatted it away.

"And if I tested positive and didn't have the mastectomy, I'd spend the rest of my life worrying. I worry so much already. When's the next audition? Will I land the part? What if I get injured again? Will Kincaid leave his wife? Will I get married to him? Will I be able to have children?"

"You want children?"

"I might."

"You never told me that."

"But how can I even think about children when I'm barely getting by on my own?"

"Well, if you did have children . . ."

"You're saying wouldn't I want to spare them what we went through with Mom?"

Mia nodded. Sitting next to Olivia on the couch, feeling the leg of her sister's sweatpants brush against her, she said, "If this test had been around twenty years ago, Mom might be alive today. Do you know how old she'd be?"

"Sixty-four." They always called each other on their mother's birthday, and now that Mia was living in New York they went out for drinks to commemorate it. Sometimes they didn't even talk about their mother, but they knew without having to say so why they were there.

"Don't you think about her, Ol?"

"Only all the time." Olivia opened her jewelry box and removed a locket. It was a photo of their mother, so small it was hard to make out, but Mia recognized her, unmistakably.

Staring at that photo, Mia thought of her and Julian's wedding, her mother in a wheelchair at that point, her father pushing her down the aisle. It was the last time the family was together; three weeks later, they would gather for her funeral. "Olivia," she said, "I found a lump in my breast."

"You what?"

"But I'm okay," she said. "It was benign."

"Jesus, Mia, you scared the shit out of me."

"Imagine how much I scared myself."

Olivia was sucking on her arm, and Mia recalled Olivia as an infant crying herself to sleep, how she used to suck on her forearm to comfort herself. And in the morning, when their mother went in, there would be little mouth marks on Olivia's arms from where she'd been sucking.

"Mia," she said, "what happened between us?"

"What do you mean?"

"Remember when I was small and you would guard my room against intruders? You didn't even want to let Mom and Dad in. You told me you were my real mother and Mom and Dad were just the hired help."

Mia laughed.

"I was crazy about you," Olivia said. "What little girl doesn't worship her big sister? But then you went off to college and left me with Mom and Dad. I don't think I ever forgave you for not going to McGill."

"Oh, Olivia."

"I thought of calling you at school, but what was I going to say? 'How are your classes going?' I wasn't interested in my own classes, let alone in yours. 'Have you met any boys?' Well, you'd met Julian and that was that, and I wasn't going to ask about your sex life."

"You could have."

"I was fourteen, fifteen, going through my sullen period . . ."

Mia remembered. She had come home with Julian one vacation and found Olivia holed up in her bedroom with a "Witness Protection Program" sign on the door. For a week, Olivia refused to talk to anyone in the family. One night, she showed up at dinner with a towel covering her head and the words "Ignore Me" taped over the towel.

"Then Mom got sick, and she and Dad were so preoccupied I could have disappeared for a month and they wouldn't have noticed. I thought it would be easier once Mom died, but it was worse afterward. It was just me and Dad, and we never got along."

"He was hard on you growing up."

Olivia shrugged. "He was all right."

"Herr Doktor Professor," Mia said. It was what they used to call their father, a man who wore no necktie to work, who hoped that if he dressed informally his students would find him approachable. But it hadn't worked. His students were intimidated by him, and in a way his daughters had been intimidated, too, even Mia, on whom the burden of his expectations fell. Even now, she thought, he still hadn't gotten over the fact that she hadn't gone into physics. Psychology, with its fuzzy intricacies, its emotions blooming like mold, was too soft for him. Everything she was doing that wasn't what he was doing, he'd assumed was simply a phase. She recalled those nights at the Montreal Forum, how he liked to list the Canadiens hockey players they were watching, Guy Lafleur and Jacques Lemaire and Guy Lapointe and Ken Dryden. Then he would move back in time to the Canadiens of the sixties and fifties and earlier, from Serge Savard and Jean Béliveau to Maurice "The Rocket" Richard, and when he said Richard's name he would whistle like a rocket.

"You should have seen what he was like after Mom died," Olivia said. "It was my last year of high school, and I thought if I didn't come home and make dinner for him, he'd starve himself."

"And I was in Northington," Mia said. Not that she hadn't been mourning, too. But she was miles away, having started her marriage, and Olivia was home, taking care of him. "I should have come back more often."

Olivia shook her head. "You came back plenty. Certainly more than I would have." She looked up.

"What?"

"Remember how when you were moving to New York the plan was for you to stay with me?"

"I was looking forward to that."

"I was, too. And even once things worked out between you and Julian, I thought we'd spend more time together."

"Why didn't we?"

"I wish I knew. Your door has always been open to me."

"Your door's been open to me, too, Ol. Look at me. I'm here."

"But you're the one who's made the effort. It's like it's enough for me to know that I can see you anytime. And now you tell me you had a lump in your breast, and it makes me realize we're going to die someday and I don't want to die not having been close to you."

"We can still try."

"I don't know . . ."

"What do you mean?"

"I want to be close to you, Mia, but I've wanted to be close to you for so long and I haven't been able to do it." Olivia removed a Popsicle from the freezer and took a bite of it. It was cherry flavored, and a red smudge bloomed beneath her nose, as if she'd misapplied her lipstick.

Picking at the blueberries on her plate, Mia thought of their mother, the fruit czar, who years ago, when they were small, used to count the berries she gave them. She was a stickler for impartiality, and she wanted to make sure the girls got the same amount. Though Mia, five years older than Olivia, would sneak extra berries when her sister wasn't looking. And years after that, she would sneak them back in the other direction, like someone paying off an unacknowledged debt. She put on her jacket.

"You have to go?"

She nodded.

"Here," Olivia said, removing another Popsicle from the freezer. "Take one for the road."

She unwrapped it.

"Red Dye Number Two," Olivia said. "Remember how Mom wouldn't let us eat that? No maraschino cherries? They caused cancer."

Mia smiled dolorously.

She walked up Fifth Street, and when she turned around she could see Olivia's fire escape. When she first went to school, her mother would stand at the window holding Olivia and they would wave at her as she departed. And years later, when she left for Graymont, they'd been waving, too. When she pictured her family, what she thought of was leave-takings, and here was another one; she'd never been good at saying goodbye.

When she got home, she made an appointment with the genetics counselor. And the following week, accompanied by Julian, she went to the hospital to have her blood drawn.

.   .   .

When the results came back, she was required to retrieve them in person. She sat beside Julian in the same waiting room they'd sat in three weeks before, and the geneticist emerged to greet them.

"Have a seat," the woman said.

Mia sat in the chair facing the geneticist's desk, and Julian stood behind her.

The geneticist looked down at Mia's file. "I wish the news were better. You tested positive for BRCA1."

"I have the breast cancer gene?"

The geneticist nodded.

"There must be a mistake." She had tested to rule out the gene, not to have it.

The geneticist, shaking her head, regarded her kindly. "These tests are extremely accurate."

"How accurate?"

"They're practically foolproof."

Julian took her hand.

"What you need to remember," the geneticist said, "is that this doesn't mean you're going to get breast or ovarian cancer. Every person is different, and there's still a lot we don't know."

So this was why they told you in person. Because in Mia's case there was so much more to talk about, more geneticists, more doctors, more experts to consult. But she didn't want to talk to any of them right now; the only person she wanted to be with was Julian.

She must have stayed at the hospital for another hour, taking down phone numbers, getting referrals. But later she would recall none of it. The only thing she would remember was embracing Julian, and afterward the walk home, from the Upper East Side down to Perry Street, five miles, she ventured, but she refused to take a cab. They walked, slowly, cheerlessly, passing thousands of people along the way, but it was as if the streets were desolate, for they didn't notice anyone as they moved from block to block, making their silent way home.

Northington, Massachusetts

"Julian Wainwright!" a woman shrieked. She took Julian in a hug, but before he could determine who she was, she had extricated herself and was doing her best to catch up with her friend, who was running down Rigby Hill in stiletto heels, her pocketbook slamming against her.

"Who was that?" Mia asked.

"I don't know."

"She certainly seemed to know you."

Men in seersucker jackets and women in sundresses dotted the lawn, some with children in tow. A volleyball net had been erected in Allenby Field, and two barefoot couples were swatting a beach ball over it. One of the women was wearing a bikini top with the words "Class of 2000" masking-taped across her spine.

It was June 2005, Julian and Mia's fifteen-year college reunion. They hadn't attended a Graymont reunion before; at their five-year reunion they'd been living in Ann Arbor, and at their ten-year reunion they'd been separated. Now they were back together and only a few hours' drive from Northington—though, in truth, Julian had been surprised when Mia suggested they go, and surprised, too, that he acquiesced so readily. They were getting older, he thought, and more sentimental.

Towels had been folded on the dormitory beds and little mints placed on the pillows, as at a hotel. There was a fan in the room, and Mia turned theirs on high and placed herself in front of it.

Now, having unpacked, they wandered through campus and into town. Megan's Muffins was gone, as was McNulty's Cleaners. Northington Paper and Copy was still there, and so was Store 24, but most of the businesses had changed hands, perhaps, Julian thought, several times over.

"Where's the Bison Bar and Grill?" he asked. It was where he and Carter used to go for cheeseburgers, where Carter and Pilar had gone on their first date.

"It's a cell phone store."

"And Burgher's Burger?"

"Gone, too."

And where, he wanted to know, was Mr. Kang's produce store? And Mr. Kang himself? In place of the produce store stood a real estate agency. Mia asked a few passersby what had happened to the Kangs, but no one seemed to know.

"I used to be friends with the Kangs," she told someone, though really it was Julian who had been friends with them. But she felt as if she had, too, if only vicariously.

At the co-op where they'd lived senior year, they found a group of construction workers patrolling an empty lot.

"Don't tell me," Mia said. "You're putting up condominiums."

"A bank," said one of the construction workers. "The students need somewhere to put all their cash."

They sat down on a park bench; Mia was exhausted. It was fourteen months since she'd found her breast lump, a year since she'd tested positive for the gene. It wasn't simply that she measured time this way; it was that she couldn't recall how she used to feel, before everything was fraught with peril. When she'd tested positive, she'd wanted to schedule the surgeries immediately, but Dr. Kaplan told her not to rush. "At least take a few weeks to decide," she said. "You're unlikely to come down with cancer in that time."

So Mia stayed up late talking with Julian, flipping through the articles she'd copied. There was some evidence that pregnancy was protective against breast cancer. Nursing was supposed to be protective, too. "I thought you wanted to have a baby."

"I do," Julian said.

She looked up at him. "On the other hand, we could adopt."

Finally, after weeks of vacillating (she even proposed, half seriously, that they flip a coin), she announced that she wanted to have a baby.

"You mean through sex?"

She laughed. "Yes, through sex."

How incongruous it was, not just the act of unprotected sex but the very fact of wishing to get pregnant when for so long she'd hoped she wouldn't, when back in college her period had been late a couple of times and she'd been frantic. Perhaps that was why she hadn't given thought to infertility. She'd spent so many years afraid she was fertile, it was hard to change course now.

But three months elapsed, and she realized she had no right to be complacent about getting pregnant, that having the gene didn't earn her a pass.

She called Dr. Kaplan, who told her it was too early to panic. "It takes six months for the typical thirty-year-old to get pregnant," Dr. Kaplan said. "And you're thirty-six, so there's probably nothing wrong with you."

But there *was* something wrong with her. She had the breast cancer gene, and every month she didn't get pregnant was another month she could get sick. She watched her diet and tried to get more sleep, but when two more months passed and, despite having used home ovulation tests, she still hadn't gotten pregnant, she became abject.

Finally, after six months of trying, she returned to Dr. Kaplan, who agreed to send her to a fertility specialist. "But I'm warning you," Dr. Kaplan said. "The doctor is going to put you on Clomid."

"What's wrong with that?"

"Nothing, necessarily. But there's a suspected link to ovarian cancer. It hasn't been proved, but in general, you don't want to take these drugs unless there's a good reason."

The last article Mia had read suggested she had a fifty-four percent chance of developing ovarian cancer. How much worse could her odds be?

Finally, like an alcoholic, she drank half a bottle of Robitussin. The theory was that cough syrup thinned the mucus in your body, and a woman's cervical mucus needed to be thin so that sperm could get through it. But as Mia stood in the bathroom with the bottle of Robitussin pressed to her lips, aware that no studies had proven a connection between cough syrup and fertility, she felt like a crackpot.

Yet almost as soon as she and Julian started to try again, she felt a low-grade queasiness she couldn't account for; even if she was pregnant, it was far too early for morning sickness.

"Maybe you're just anxious," Julian said.

"About what?"

"Your special lunch?" Julian had just emerged from the shower, and he stood before Mia in his towel, dripping water on the floor.

"Oh, come on." Julian was talking about Derek, she realized. Derek from Japan. He was visiting New York with his son, and she'd arranged to have lunch with them. Her Japanese boyfriend, Julian called Derek, and the more she resisted, the more he poked fun.

The last time Mia saw Derek, they were nineteen, and it was as if she'd overcompensated, for she imagined him now in his fifties instead of his thirties. So when she saw him again, standing in front of a bodega on Eighth Avenue, she was doubly surprised to see he'd hardly aged. His hair was graying at the temples, but other than that he appeared just as he had, his cheeks pale and unmottled, his bangs falling across his face. "Derek, you look exactly the same."

"You do, too," he said, and he shook her hand.

When Derek had said he was bringing his son, Mia had imagined a boy of seven or eight, but the young man next to Derek appeared sixteen.

"We're visiting universities," Derek explained. "Rodney wants to go to school in the United States." He rested his hand on his son's shoulder. He's just like me when I was his age. He's already given him-self an American name."

Mia looked at Rodney, then at Derek. "You have a son who's going to *college*?"

"I got married young."

"So did I."

"But you don't have a child who's ready for college?"

Mia smiled sadly. "I don't have children at all." She reached into her bag. "Here," she said, "let me buy you a drink," and she returned from the bodega holding three cans of Coke, and they stood on the street corner drinking them.

"Tell me about yourself," Mia said to Derek. "What does your wife do? Do you have other children besides Rodney?"

"It's just me and Rodney," Derek said. "I don't have a wife."

"You're divorced?"

"Actually, my wife died."

"Oh," she said. "I'm so sorry."

She got discomposed after that, and it seemed for the next couple of hours she didn't know what to say. So she contented herself with wandering around Manhattan with Derek and Rodney, taking them to South Street Seaport and the Empire State Building, talking about the differences between Columbia and NYU.

Eventually, though, Rodney tired of adult company and left Mia and Derek alone in Central Park. Runners loped around the reser-voir; a girl on a skateboard whizzed past them. A unicyclist juggling bowling pins emerged from behind the bend, and a crowd gathered to watch him.

"It's New York," Mia explained. She sat down on a park bench next to Derek, and soon a flock of pigeons approached them. One was picking at something by Derek's feet.

"It's funny," Derek said. "Rodney's always telling me I should feed the pigeons. He says I need to relax."

"Do you?"

"Probably. I work too hard. It's true of men of my generation. Maybe of men of all generations. But Rodney swears he's going to be different. That's why he wants to come to college in the U.S. He thinks university students in America have more fun. They sleep late and drink more beer."

"There's some of that," Mia said, remembering her students at the University of Michigan.

"I guess if you don't drink beer at college, when are you going to drink?"

"So you're not worried?"

Derek shook his head. "Rodney will probably find he's more serious than he realized. Away from my influence, he'll turn out just like me. It's what happened with me and my father."

"Is he an economics professor, too?"

"No," Derek said, "but temperamentally we're the same." A group of preschool children walked past them, everyone in pairs, holding hands. "Why? What kind of work do you do?"

"I'm a psychotherapist," Mia said.

"Is that what you studied in college? Psychology?"

She shook her head. She'd taken a psychology course her sophomore year, but half of what she learned seemed so obviously true she wasn't sure why anyone bothered to teach it, and the other half seemed just as obviously false. Everything felt as if it were straight from a psychology textbook, which shouldn't have surprised her, because it was. "My mother died, and I started to see a therapist myself. Before that, I hadn't considered it as a career."

"Are you a good therapist?"

Mia laughed.

"Why? Has no one asked you that before?"

"Not so directly." And she remembered now how forthright Derek had been, and how it had disarmed her.

She said, "People make fun of therapists for projecting themselves as a blank screen. The patient asks them a question, and all they can say is, 'What do *you* think?' But I've got the opposite problem. I'm too quick to say what's on my mind. It's the product of being a big sister. I'm a know-it-all. She looked up at him. What about you, Derek? Are you a good economist?"

He shrugged. "Sometimes I think I'm too good. Remember in France, when we went out to eat, how quickly I could calculate the tax? You taught me that phrase, 'the three R's.' Reading, writing, and 'rithmetic. I was good at them."

"But especially arithmetic?"

Derek nodded. "Economics was the easy path for me. I have a friend who was a stutterer when he was a child and he ended up becoming a politician. Compared to him, I'm a coward."

"Why?" she said. "What would you have been if not an economist?"

"A musician, maybe?"

"I didn't know you played music."

"That's the point. I don't. But I could have tried. It would have been a challenge."

Mia laughed.

"But no," he said. "I've been happy professionally."

"But not in other ways?"

"My wife died," he said. "It's hard to get over something like that."

Mia thought of her father, who seemed to have recovered from her mother's death. He went to work every morning. He had friends. Most of the time he appeared happy. But it had been fifteen years since her mother had died, and he still thought of her every day. He'd told her this once and it startled her. Though she didn't know why. She thought of her mother every day, too.

"I have a colleague whose wife was killed in a plane crash, and less than a year later he got married again. I guess some people fall in love easily." He looked up at her. "What about you?"

"Do *I* fall in love easily?"

"Tell me about Julian," he said. "He's a fiction writer?"

She nodded.

"And you love him?"

She laughed. "Yes, I love Julian. We had some difficulties—we were separated for a while—but things are better now." She looked up at Derek. "How long ago did your wife die?"

"When Rodney was three."

"So you raised him on your own?"

Derek nodded. "And now he's getting ready to go to university. It's not easy when they leave. That year in Provence, my mother cried at the airport when I left, and I thought, *What are you crying about?*"

"And now you understand?"

"Absolutely." Derek glanced at his watch. He'd agreed to meet Rodney, he told Mia, at the Metropolitan Museum. Mia had to leave, too, but she decided to walk him partway there.

Above them, the sun emerged from behind the clouds, and as they made their way across the open meadow, Mia could see Fifth Avenue, its majestic apartment buildings lined up like gift boxes. "So you never remarried?"

"I almost did," Derek said. "But Rodney was twelve at the time, and he and my fiancée didn't get along. In the end, she wasn't right for me."

"And now?"

"Now I sort of have a girlfriend."

"Sort of? Does your girlfriend know you feel this way?"

"Look who's talking," Derek said. "You were Miss Sort Of yourself."

"What do you mean?"

"You sort of had a boyfriend, too. What was his name? Glen?"

"How do you remember that?"

"You made an impression on me."

And an image came to Mia of Derek tossing a mango from hand to hand, the two of them weaving through the streets of Aix, Derek on his way back from class, carrying his knapsack of groceries. She wondered what would have happened if she'd let herself love Derek. She imagined herself in Kyoto, mother to his children, and for a moment it seemed as possible as the life she'd lived, as any path she might have taken. "Do you still like Derek and the Dominos?"

He nodded. "How about you? Did you ever learn to eat fish?"

"I'm afraid not."

"Then how am I going to host you in Japan?" Derek gave her his business card and he was off, his gaze focused on something in the sky, but all Mia could see was a flock of birds.

She cried out, "If Rodney comes to college here, have him look me up!"

"I will!" Derek said.

She ran after him. " Derek, I'm pregnant!"

She had no idea how she knew this. But two weeks later, when she took a pregnancy test, she barely had time to celebrate with Julian because she was already feeling nauseated. It usually took a month for morning sickness to set in, but with her it had been almost instantaneous.

Now, five months pregnant, at her college reunion, she found that nothing about her pregnancy had gone as she'd anticipated. She'd assumed she would be one of those trim pregnant women, someone with a little bump for a stomach, but she could see now that this wouldn't be so: she'd already gained fifteen pounds, and much of it was in her face. She was famished all the time, yet the food she craved also repulsed her. And only in the past week, well after the end of her first trimester, had the nausea begun to subside. In these middle months—the most endurable trimester, everyone said—she was still so tired she often went to sleep as soon as she got home and didn't wake up until the morning. What she felt, above all, was despondent; she was carrying something alien inside her. This must have been what post-partum depression felt like, only hers had arrived months early.

At particularly bad moments, she wondered why she'd wanted a baby at all. She'd always liked children, and she still looked forward to the holiday cards that arrived every year from her family in Aix; Claudette, unbelievably, was in university now; Emile would be starting next year. Some of her patients were children, and she enjoyed the play-acting and board games, a therapy through indirection that was altogether different from how she worked with adults. Yet when she tried to recapture what she'd felt just months ago, that instinctive, seemingly chemical urge to reproduce, it was as if she were remembering someone else. She recalled what it had been like for her mother to get sick, and she thought she had made the wrong decision. She should have had her ovaries removed. Then, if they wanted to, she and Julian could have adopted.

But there was nothing to do about that now. She lay in her underwear, perspiring, on the dormitory bed, and no matter how many times she showered she couldn't get comfortable.

Other reunion classes had returned as well, but only the class of '90 was treated to a special convocation by the president of Graymont, who, having taken office their freshman year, was now going back to teaching. "I came when you came and I leave when you return. I look out at you today from this podium, a hundred and eighty strong, and I'm proud to say I've watched you grow up."

As if to disprove this, someone made a farting noise.

The president listed his accomplishments. He had doubled the endowment and overseen the creation of a Latino studies department and an African American studies department; a new library had been built; in the last five years, Graymont had graduated more Rhodes Scholars per capita than any other college in the country. "But this isn't about me," the president said. "This is about you."

The students roared.

"Among you are lawyers, doctors, artists, musicians, writers, and entrepreneurs. But I want to single out for special mention those students in the class of 'ninety who have, in good Graymont tradition, taken paths that are a little more offbeat."

"Where's Tuckahoe?" someone shouted. Cameron Tuckahoe had been the rumored baker of the hash brownies that had gotten the dean of admissions stoned.

"We have a former member of the United States Olympics Luge team," the president said.

"God bless you, Baker!" someone called out.

Back in college, Ted Baker had prepared himself for the Olympics by leading his team to the gold medal in the Graymont Bong Olympics, which involved running up ten flights of stairs while stoned.

Soon the president finished speaking, and everyone dispersed across the quad. Julian greeted Michael Manheim, who fifteen years ago had come to graduation in a gorilla suit. (Jimmy Carter had gotten an honorary degree that day, and Michael had tried to place a wreath of bananas around the former president's neck before being apprehended by the Secret Service.) Since then, whenever Julian thought of Michael he pictured a gorilla, so that now he was half startled to see him upright, looking every bit as human as the rest of the class.

"People expect me to have grown hair on my back," Michael said. "And do you know what? I have."

Julian wasn't sure he wanted to hear this.

"And on my shoulders and coming out of my ears."

Or that.

Paisley McDonald was talking with Norman Stevens, and next to them was Astrid, from Professor Chesterfield's class. Astrid had undergone a transformation since graduating from college. "I'm a 'do-me' feminist," she kept saying, which meant, if Julian understood her, that she was a sex-loving feminist, not a sex-hating feminist.

A child zigzagged across the lawn, searching for her parents. According to the Class of '90 Survey, sixty-eight percent of the class was married and fifty-six percent had children. People were swapping photos of their children, and Tom Monroe, who stood in the shadows of Christ Church talking to Alison Thompson and her husband, was passing around a photo not of his child but of a missing child from a milk carton—as a teenager, Tom had collected, as he liked to say, "the whole series"—which prompted Alison to say, "Tom, you're sick."

"Do you know who I am?" someone asked Julian. It was Cara Friedberg, from Professor Chesterfield's class.

Julian shook Cara's hand.

"I hope you don't remember that story I wrote. The one about the girl breaking up with her boyfriend at the pizza joint?"

Julian admitted that he did.

"Anyway, I want you to know I've gotten a lot better. A story of mine is being published this fall."

Soon Julian was off to say hello to other classmates. But quickly he tired of this, for no sooner had he exchanged a few sentences than he found he had little else to say; everyone gravitated toward a bland nostalgia. So he decamped to the other side of the quad, to wander around campus alone.

Outside Andrews Hall, he picked up a copy of *The Graymont Alumnus* and flipped to the Class Notes. The students who submitted to Class Notes were the same ones who in college, full of good cheer, could be seen walking backward across campus wearing the maroon ribbons given them by the admissions office and leading a tour of prospective college students. The world could be divided, Julian thought, between the people who submitted to Class Notes and the people who didn't. A few members of his class had already died, and they were by and large people he'd liked. That was the way alumni bulletins worked. The people you disliked were accomplishing things, and the people you liked were dead.

The next morning, taking a break from activities, he felt a tap on his shoulder.

"Don't say anything," Carter said.

Julian was sitting under a tree, and he rose to greet Carter. "Well, this is a surprise. You weren't on the list of people attending."

"And if I had been, you probably wouldn't have come yourself." Carter was wearing a white T-shirt, chinos, and running sneakers, and he was sporting a couple of days' growth of blond beard. He looked older, Julian thought, though Julian must have looked older, too; he hadn't seen Carter in six years.

And there it was. Carter's voice. The guy who could imitate a loon so well even the loons thought he was one of them.

"Anyway," Carter said, "I've come back so you can spit in my face. Or punch me, if you'd prefer."

"It's too late," Julian said.

"In that case, can I talk to you?"

Julian nodded.

"But not here, with all the glad-handing and back-slapping. I've never been to a reunion in my life, and it pains me to break my record."

They passed Pickens Hall and McMillan Library, and now they stood looking up at the registrar's office, where Mia had worked after graduation. "The funny thing is, I never thought of you as the reunion type, either."

"I'm not," Julian admitted. "But Mia and I met here. I've become nostalgic in my middle age."

"Is that how you see yourself? Middle-aged?"

"A lot has happened."

They stopped in front of the statue of Theodore Graymont, abolitionist hero and educational reformer, founder of the college in 1878. Freshman year, Carter climbed that statue and painted a Native American headdress on Theodore Graymont's head while Julian snapped photos.

Now Julian asked Carter what he remembered about college.

"I remember getting drunk and vomiting at the foot of that statue. And I remember that Theodore Graymont had four children— Wendell, Elizabeth, Margaret, and Clarence- and two more who died at birth. At least, that's what the tour guides said."

They walked across the lawn past the president's house. "President Vickers is retiring," Julian said. "He gave a speech to us yesterday. He came when we came, he leaves when we return . . ."

"So he's still an idiot."

"Pretty much."

Carter stopped walking. "I don't want to do this."

"What?"

"Shoot the shit. Not that you aren't my favorite person to shoot the shit with. But that's not why I came here."

"Why did you come?"

"To apologize," Carter said. "And to tell you how lucky I was to have you as a friend."

"Heinz . . ."

"When I heard that you and Mia had separated, I fell into the worst funk, and I didn't come out of it until you'd gotten back together."

"So you've been keeping tabs on me."

"I think about you every day," Carter said. "I've had other friends over the years, good friends, mind you, but it's not the same. I suspect it's been ages since you've thought about me, and I'm not going to stand here beating my chest over something you probably don't care about any longer."

"I do care about it," Julian said. Not the fact that Carter had slept with Mia. He'd let go of that, finally, when he returned to her; at a certain point it was time to move on. What he cared about was that Carter was here. And though he didn't think about Carter every day, he thought about him, in fact, quite infrequently, he'd had to endeavor to reach that point. And seeing him again made Julian realize he *had* been thinking about Carter, even as he'd convinced himself he hadn't been.

"I'm truly, truly sorry for what I did. I'm sorry, also, for having been such an asshole it makes me wonder why you were my friend."

"Heinz, come on."

"Seriously, have you ever met anyone with such a big chip on his shoulder?"

Julian laughed.

"What did I have to complain about? I got a scholarship to prep school and college. I graduated from an excellent law school, and before I was thirty I was handed seventeen million dollars just for showing up to work."

"You should give yourself more credit."

"I spent so much of my life feeling aggrieved I didn't know what to do without my indignation." He looked up at Julian. "Listen to me. I sound like I've been in therapy."

"Have you been?"

"Sylvie—my girlfriend—convinced me to go into it."

"And you've become a believer?"

"It's worked for me. Or maybe I should say it's working. What about you? Have you ever seen a therapist?"

"I see one every day," Julian said. "And best of all, she doesn't charge."

"Mia?"

"It's the women who save us from ourselves."

Carter smiled. "So now I'm done," he said. "If you want me to go, I'll go."

And when Julian didn't say anything, when he made clear through his silence that he didn't want Carter to go, Carter said, "Stay right there. I just have to tell Sylvie I'll be a while longer."

"She's here?"

"We're going camping in the Berkshires," Carter said. "We decided to make a trip of it."

Carter sprinted across the quad, and when he returned he and Julian walked farther through campus, past the sciences building and Danforth Gym, where they used to play basketball together. Freshman year, between games, Julian would practice his vertical leap in the hope that he could learn to dunk a basketball. He was six foot one, and at eighteen he'd been able to dunk a tennis ball, and he could do no better at twenty-one. Then began the slow process of diminishment. At thirty, with a running start, he could barely touch the rim, and now, at thirty-seven, he couldn't even do that. He still played pickup a couple of times a week, but he kept spraining his ankle and twisting his knee. Someone seemed to be telling him to hang up his sneakers.

They stood now inside Thompson Hall, in the room where Professor Chesterfield had held his class. Carter sat down in one of the chairs. He placed his feet on the desk and closed his eyes, mimicking what he'd been like in college.

On the blackboard Julian wrote, "Thou shalt not confuse a short story with a Rubik's Cube."

"Chesterfield's commandments," Carter said.

"He's gone," said Julian.

"Retired?"

"Dead. You didn't hear?"

Carter shook his head.

"I spoke to him a couple of months before he died. I was working at a literary agency, and he called to say he'd finished his novel. He wanted us to represent him."

"Did you?"

"The book was terrible. Not the writing itself, which was more than adequate, but the characters. It was as if they'd lived as hermits for the last forty years, which probably shouldn't have surprised me. Chesterfield had talent, but the book made me realize that it takes more than talent and it takes more than luck. Sometimes a writer's personality gets in the way. Chesterfield wasn't sufficiently self-aware, which I know can be said of all of us, but in his case it tanked his novel."

"So you didn't take him on?"

Julian shook his head. "What's worse, my boss made me write the letter. You'd think I would get some perverse pleasure out of that. You know, toppling the father, and I'm a toppling-the-father kind of guy. But it made me sick. I thought my letter was going to kill him, but by the time it got to him he was already gone. He had a heart attack while sitting at his typewriter, at work on his next novel."

And now, as if in homage, Carter pointed from chair to chair, naming the students in Professor Chesterfield's class: Rufus, Astrid, Sue, Cara, Simon, the whole bunch of them.

"The man was dedicated to his craft," Julian said. "And he helped me. I'm not sure I'd have continued to write if it weren't for his encouragement."

"You call what he did encouragement?"

Julian shrugged. "I guess he was the right fit." Sitting down next to Carter, he said, "I ran into Astrid yesterday. And Cara came over to say hi to me. She's still apologizing for that story she wrote."

"Twenty-three pages of breaking up with your boyfriend at a pizza joint?"

"And now a story of hers is being published. So you see? There's hope for everyone."

"Even for you?"

"You're asking about my novel?"

Carter nodded.

"Are you ready for this? I sold it!"

"Jesus, Wainwright. And you waited this long to tell me?"

It was in the midst of everything else that he'd found out about his book, and he immediately fell into a depression. He told Mia and his parents, he told a couple of friends, but they all reacted with more excitement than he felt, so he decided to stop telling people; they would learn about the book when they saw it in the bookstore. It was the lot of the writer, he thought. At least, it was his lot. To feel unrecognized for so long, he didn't know what to do when someone finally paid attention. Though he had to admit he'd been briefly elated. And, more than that, relieved. At long last, he could think of himself as a writer. As if to prove that, he immediately sat down and began a new novel, which, he swore to himself, wouldn't take as long as this one had.

"So tell me the whole story," Carter said.

"What's there to tell? I signed a contract and they gave me some money. Now it's up to the gods."

"Did your boss sell it for you?"

Julian shook his head. "I signed on with another agent. I was about to quit anyway, and I wanted to be represented by someone who didn't know me. To have the work speak for itself."

"You always were a purist, weren't you?"

"I suppose."

They were outside now, sitting on the steps of Thompson Hall. Dark clouds hung overhead; there was talk of rain.

"So is this what's making you middle-aged? Your great success?"

"There have been other things, too," Julian said. "Mia's pregnant."

"That's not good?"

"It is. But it's been hard. Mia's five months in and she's still feeling sick. She's back at the dorms now, vomiting, for all I know."

Then Julian told Carter about the breast cancer gene. How for a while it had seemed they wouldn't have a baby and Mia would have her ovaries removed. How she would have a prophylactic double mastectomy as well. "But we decided to wait."

"Until after she gives birth?"

"Probably until she's done nursing. Though I suppose there's a chance we'll try for another child. Who knows? Maybe she won't do the surgery at all. I tell myself there are a million ways to die. We live in lower Manhattan, the world's favorite terrorist target. Still, this feels different. I already have dreams that Mia's dead and I'm taking care of the baby on my own."

It started to pour. The rain pummeled campus, to the accompaniment of lightning and thunder. Every few seconds the quad lit up, and now, as people ran for cover, Julian and Carter heard screams from across the field. Julian recalled a summer on Martha's Vineyard when he got caught in a thunderstorm with his father and how, they later learned, lightning had struck the bench where they'd been sitting just minutes before the storm began. "What about you, Heinz? Don't tell me all you do is go to therapy."

Carter smiled. "I do need to find ways to fill my time."

"Have you been living off your wealth?"

"I did that for a while, but I grew tired of it. I'm good at doing nothing when people want me to do something, but when no one cares what I do I end up becoming bored. So I went to work for the public defender. Which is funny, because that was what Pilar wanted us to do."

"Except she didn't do it herself."

"No," Carter said. "She went for the money. She recently made partner at her law firm."

"So you're in touch with her?"

Carter nodded. "She's still in San Francisco. All those years she complained about missing the East Coast, and then she decides she likes California after all. She's getting married again, to an East Coast transplant just like her. The state is overrun with them."

"And what about you?" Julian said. "Are you still at the public defender?"

Carter shook his head. "I left a couple of years ago."

"To do what?"

"To write fiction," Carter said sheepishly. "I finished my novel last month."

Julian laughed. "How typically nonchalant and savant-ish of you, Heinz. I've been working on my book for fifteen years and you churn yours out in no time."

"That doesn't mean it's good."

"Oh, it's good," Julian said. "I'm sure of it." He looked up at Carter. "So what other surprises do you have in store for me?"

"Sylvie," Carter said.

"Tell me about her."

"You can see for yourself. She'll be back soon with the kids."

"The *kids*?"

Carter laughed. "It's not what you're thinking. They're Sylvie's kids, not mine, though they've started to feel like mine as well. Tess and Delphine. They're thirteen and eleven."

"Teenagers?"

"What can I say? I fell in love with an older woman. Sylvie will be forty in the fall."

"And you're a stepfather?"

"Not officially, though that will come soon enough. We're talking about a wedding next summer. Sylvie would like me to adopt the girls, and the sad thing is their father wouldn't care. He's your typical dead-beat dad, sees them maybe once every couple of years."

The rain had stopped, and now, in the parking lot, Julian met Sylvie and her children. Then they trooped over to the dorms to see Mia.

They found her watching TV when they arrived, sitting up in bed. "Carter?" she said. "Is that really you?"

"None other." Carter took her in a hug.

"You mean you're talking to each other?" Mia said.

Julian smiled. "I guess we are."

"And you're talking to me, too," Carter said to her.

Introductions were made, and Carter was saying he wished they could stay for dinner but they needed to pitch tent before dark. "Promise me one thing," he said. "That it won't be another six years before we see each other again."

"I promise," Julian said.

Sylvie said, "Can we get you guys out for a June wedding? How old will the baby be then?"

"Eight months," Mia said.

"Good. At that age, they just sleep through the trip. It's when they get to be like these two that they start to cause trouble." She poked Tess and Delphine in the ribs.

Watching Carter and Sylvie load the kids into the car, Julian thought of senior year, shuttling the group of them from the co-op to class, everyone piling into the Wainwrightmobile. And later, wandering through town, he would see Carter, with Pilar at his back, zipping through the streets on his scooter. "Do you still drive a motorcycle?" he asked.

"Shhhh," Carter said. "Sylvie doesn't want me to corrupt the girls."

"It's too late," Sylvie said. "He's corrupted them already."

"Though he could be more original." This was Tess, the thirteen-year-old, from the back of the car.

"Listen to her," Carter said. "This is what I've signed on for." He turned on the ignition.

Julian and Mia waved at them, and they waved back. Then the car was off, kicking up dust, disappearing from the parking lot.

Up in Montreal, on the anniversary of her mother's death, Mia lit the yahrzeit candle with her father. She had stopped being religious before her mother got sick, but when her mother died she sat shiva for her and during the year of mourning she went to synagogue a few times to recite the kaddish. Her father had never remarried. For a couple of years he'd had a girlfriend, Abigail, also a physicist, whom he'd met at a conference in Berlin, but she taught in southern California, where her ex-husband still lived and where her children, already grown, had settled, and she wasn't inclined to move to Canada. And Mia's father wasn't interested in returning to the United States, especially not to California, forever tainted by the Vietnam War and Ronald Reagan calling in the National Guard in 1968. You reached a certain age, Mia thought, and it became harder to compromise. Your brain hardened. Or your heart. So his relationship with Abigail consisted of weekends, vacations, academic conferences, and phone calls, and under such circumstances it flared out, cut off in the end by Abigail but without much regret from Mia's father. There had been a few other women, and a period when he succumbed to the entreaties of his colleagues' wives to set him up with their friends and coworkers, with their divorced cousins. But the truth was he didn't like to date. With his focus on work and his irregular hours—he was at his desk at four in the morning, and he would sleep during the day when he didn't have class—he was suited to stay single.

Besides, Mia thought, he hadn't really intended to marry again. He had led her to believe that marrying someone else would have meant betraying her mother. Mia didn't think so; she'd have liked to see her father remarry. But over the years he'd grown more loyal to her mother. The further away their marriage got, the more it became encased in the hard shell of myth. They had spent all their time together, he told Mia. When he was away at conferences he would call her mother three or four times a day. Mia remembered none of this. Early in their marriage, her father had assumed he'd be the one to die first; in contemplating this, he had also imagined Mia's mother's remarrying, and he hadn't liked the thought of it. By staying loyal to her after her death, he convinced himself she'd have done the same.

Forty years ago now, her mother had moved with her father to Montreal, had done what was expected of her, following her husband without complaint or regret, though she, too, had been a graduate student at Harvard. When she left Cambridge, she forgot her dissertation in her apartment and had to have it mailed to her by the new tenants. Although she said she would work on it in Montreal, she never did, leaving it in a drawer for the next twenty-five years and settling into the life of a faculty spouse. After she died, Mia's father took her dissertation out of the drawer, and though it was only half finished, he had it bound. Six months after her death, her voice remained on the answering machine because he refused to erase it until, creeped out by the sound and by the idea that she was still in the house pretending to be alive, Mia convinced him to tape a new message, though not before he had removed the old tape and placed it in a shoe box for safekeeping.

Now, when Mia visited, her father would take out the old family photographs, and they would promise each other that this year they would place them in albums, because that was what her mother would have done, and every year they forgot to do it, or decided not to, as if hoping she might come back and do it herself.

In many ways, he was a better father now than when she was a girl. Children confounded him; he didn't know how to treat them except as small adults. When Mia was four, he bought her an abacus and attempted to teach her the multiplication tables. He'd even tried to teach her to stand, holding her up when she was just six months old and slowly, gently letting go. "Balance," he said. "Come on, sweetie, balance."

His papers were still spread throughout the house. His work was in string theory, which, from the little Mia understood of it, held that matter was composed of strings so tiny they made atoms look like monstrosities. At her request, he'd given her a popular book on string theory—"string theory for poets," he called it—but even that she didn't understand, so she gave up and asked Julian to read it for her, but he didn't have any better luck with it. When her father was young he'd shown great promise; there had been talk of a Nobel Prize. But his research hadn't produced the results he'd hoped for. With physics, if you didn't break ground by the time you were thirty-five you were considered washed up; it was like being a ballerina, or a professional athlete. Another person might have become bitter but, if anything, he'd grown more even-tempered over the years, and more forgiving, too, as if his own failures had awakened him to those of others. He'd recently described a colleague as kind, and he'd meant it as a compliment. "Kind," "nice," "pleasant," "friendly": these had always been terms of disparagement in his eyes, but now that he was getting older, he joked that he'd gone soft. And he had. If not soft, exactly, then softer.

His books were strewn about the living room in what he liked to call constructive disorder. The whole house was in disorder, but he preferred it that way. This was another advantage of living alone: no one cared how you kept your possessions. He had a long-standing habit of leaving half-filled drinking glasses about the house, but whereas Mia had once taken this as an invitation to her mother to clean up after him, now she understood it as something else. He didn't care whether the glasses were cleared. Like a bachelor, which was, she had to admit, what he'd been for fifteen years now, he let the dishes collect until no clean ones remained and then he embarked on a single burst of dishwashing. Things took care of themselves that way.

He rested his hands on the grand piano. "Do you remember your lessons?"

She did.

"You were good."

She laughed. "Dad, I was terrible."

"Maybe you gave up too soon."

She didn't think so. Her piano teacher, Mr. Clendennon, had made her memorize scales. Piano should be like finger painting, she'd thought then; children should be allowed to enjoy themselves. She still felt that way. She'd never understood the rush to seriousness; there was time for that when you got older.

But her father disagreed. He believed everything you did you should do seriously.

"The first time I met Julian he asked whether I was related to Felix Mendelssohn. I think he was hoping for a famous girlfriend."

Her father laughed.

"Did you ever play piano, Dad?"

"No," he said. "All I was interested in was physics. And when I wasn't doing that I was watching ice hockey. I was always very focused."

"Do you regret that?"

"It's who I was," he said. "Who I am." He sat down on the piano bench. "Mom used to play."

"As a girl?"

"And when she was older. The last year of her life she started to play again."

"Is that why you kept the piano all these years? Because of Mom?"

"I suppose." He took out a sheet of music. "You used to sit on it. Remember?"

She thought she did. It was hard to know what she remembered and what she'd been told so many times she simply believed she remembered it. She used to take the sheet music out of the piano bench and sit on it. No one knew why; she liked to sit on things. When she was a toddler she wanted to sit where the adults sat—she refused to be placed in a booster seat—so her parents put telephone books on a chair and seated her on top of them. At six, she saw *Peter Pan,* and for a year after that she *was* Peter Pan, dressed like him, refused to answer to any name besides Peter. She remembered these things, but they came back to her like cumulus clouds, as if she were descending through something she could no longer see. At times it seemed to her that her only clear memories were from the year her mother was sick. Everything before felt like the blueprint for a life she hadn't lived. She gravitated to people who had lost a parent, drawn instinctively by their grief before she'd even learned of it.

She and Julian had been on their honeymoon when her mother died. She had wanted to delay the trip, but her mother insisted they go. From Chamonix, from Lyon, from the Loire Valley, she called home every day. She called again from Nice, called her mother's private number in the hospital room, and when she asked for Joan Mendelsohn the person said, "Who?" That was how she found out her mother was gone. Died the night before and already her room had been given away. She had never forgiven herself for not returning home sooner, for failing to come back to say goodbye.

"You look beautiful," her father said.

She laughed. "Dad, I'm six months pregnant. I've never looked less beautiful in my life." But the truth was she was starting to feel better. She was less a victim of her appetites; she was no longer going to bed at seven at night.

"We found out it's a boy," she told him. The night before the amniocentesis, she hadn't been able to sleep. She had almost decided not to find out the sex, but the prospect of not knowing seemed worse. When she got the news, she started to cry. She'd prayed for a boy; she'd practically begged for one. Because though a man could develop breast cancer, the odds were so much worse if the baby was a girl.

She still hadn't told her father about the gene she carried. She would, eventually, but not until after the baby was born. She wanted him to be a grandfather first, to celebrate without worrying.

But she had told Olivia. She'd gone to her sister's apartment, and when she said she'd tested positive, Olivia hugged her and started to cry, frightened for Mia, relieved for herself. Because Olivia had found out, too; after all that, she'd gone in and tested.

"You're negative?"

Olivia nodded.

"Oh, Olivia." She had never felt such unbounded relief.

Later, she said to Julian, "What's Olivia going to do now? How's she going to think of herself as the unlucky one?"

"She'll find a way."

And the following week, Kincaid told Olivia he wouldn't leave his wife, and Mia was back to consoling her again. It was the role she'd played for as long as she could recall, the role of the older sister, and she suspected she would play it for the rest of their lives, into their fifties and sixties if she was lucky enough to get there.

She stood next to her father in the kitchen, drying the dishes he'd washed. In the living room, the grandfather clock chimed. These were the long days of summer, and the sun hung high overhead.

"How's Cooper doing?" her father asked. "Is he ready to be displaced?"

Who knew what Cooper was ready for? The books she'd read advised her to send a receiving blanket home from the hospital so the dog could get used to the baby's smell. And to spend time alone with the dog when she first returned. She doubted she'd have the energy for any of that. Cooper would have to manage. Sweet Cooper. The small things came back to her, how he did a little jump when you brought out his food, and then, when he was done eating, how he would return to his bowl, once, twice, three times, four times, to make sure he hadn't missed anything; he was, she liked to say, an obsessive-compulsive dog. How he watched TV with them, his ears perking up when a fellow canine appeared on a show, and he would run over to the TV and thump his tail against the screen. One time, he kept sliding on his butt across the pavement, and when she took him to the vet, she didn't know what to put under "Reason for Visit." Then, on the row above her, she saw another dog with the same condition, for which the owner had written "butt slide." And two rows above that another dog as well. "Butt slide." It was an actual medical condition, and when the vet examined Cooper she said, "It's his anal sacs."

"That's right," Mia said, as if she'd known this herself and had simply neglected to mention it, as if she'd realized dogs had anal sacs in the first place. Cooper. Julian's dog. Her dog. Their dog together. The things a person learned to love.

Out her father's window, she could see the street-sweeping truck. "There it goes," she said. "The great garbage Zamboni reshuffling the trash." At the hockey games her father had taken her to, the Zamboni would move up and down the rink, wiping the ice clean between periods. She'd always looked forward to the Zamboni; it had been her favorite part of the hockey game.

"I might visit for Thanksgiving," her father said.

"You?" she said. The great anti-American? Her father had stopped celebrating Thanksgiving after the Gulf of Tonkin.

"You could make us a turkey," he said. "Or we could make one together."

The yahrzeit candle burned on the windowsill. It was designed to last twenty-four hours, but it usually burned longer, and she always stayed up with it into the next night, until the wick had extinguished. She had a collection of old yahrzeit glasses, burned-out candle holders she kept in the storage closet, each candle scooped out like a dark and toothless mouth, the contents of some macabre fun house. Six months after her mother died, that winter in Northington the first year of her marriage, she decided on an impulse that she wanted to say kaddish. It was late, and cold outside, and the doors to the local synagogue were shuttered, so Julian drove her in the darkness through the snow, from town to town across Massachusetts, searching for a synagogue service, but they couldn't find one. In Springfield, she stood outside on the synagogue steps and recited kaddish while

Julian held an umbrella over her head. He said kaddish, too, stumbling through the transliterated Hebrew, mourning a woman he'd only just gotten to know but whom, in his own way, he had come to love.

Now, standing next to her father, Mia watched the yahrzeit candle on the windowsill, the flame flickering across from them.

Epilogue

It's four in the morning, and Julian sits in the living room in the dark, holding the baby on his lap. Mia has been nursing, so when the baby is hungry it's her turn, and the rest of the time it's his. When he's awakened in the middle of the night, Julian will say, "I think the baby's hungry," and Mia, still asleep, will murmur, "Come on." But there's been no arguing tonight; she fed him less than an hour ago.

The baby's five months old, and sometimes he wakes up only once a night, but tonight he's been up every couple of hours, so they're up, too. The world can be divided, Julian thinks, between the sleeping and the sleepless; he feels a new alliance with nighttime workers, with insomniacs across the globe.

He's been staying at home, relieved by the babysitter a few hours a day so he can write. And Mia's hours have been good; she has been seeing fewer patients. Julian's mother takes the baby one day a week, and sometimes Julian's father comes over after work so Julian and Mia can catch a movie.

Around the time the baby was born, Julian's father and his girl-friend broke up. "It was too soon after Mom," he said, and now, in the wake of becoming grandparents, Julian's parents have been talking on the phone again. "I think he's getting ideas," Mia said, but Julian doesn't want to hear about it. Now, whenever his mother says she's spoken to his father, Julian holds his breath. "Tell me it's about the grandson," he wants to say, and so far, thankfully, that's all it's been.

The baby has started to cry, so Julian turns on the light and reads to him. Gorillas, horses, monkeys, sheep: he can't find a children's book that isn't littered with them. You would think he and Mia lived on a farm, but were it not for Cooper, the baby's only experience with animals would be the squirrels in the park and the occasional fugitive rat seen in an alleyway.

Across from him, on the bookshelf, sit ten copies of his novel. They arrived yesterday from the publisher. The official publication date is next month. And last week Carter called to say his novel is going to be published, too. "A wedding present," Carter said.

And, for Julian, a baby gift.

Not until after he came back to her did he tell Mia the truth: that he'd stopped working on his novel when he left her and hadn't been able to return to it until he came back. It went to prove that writers didn't need to be unhappy; in his case, at least, the opposite was true. In college, he and Mia used to laugh at acknowledgments pages, those doddering professors thanking their wives for typing their manuscripts and keeping the kids at bay. Mia's mother used to say that she'd refused to take a typing course lest she become like the women of her mother's generation, who, if they worked at all, were consigned to the life of a secretary. Not that Mia has to worry about that. Still, she half prides herself on her clumsiness at the keyboard. She may be a writer's wife, but she isn't about to think of herself as one.

And now, when he looks up, Julian sees her standing across from him. "What are you doing up?"

"I couldn't sleep," she says. "I'm overtired."

The baby is on his stomach, lying in his diaper with his arms and legs spread out, as if he's been strip-searched. He's smiling now, staring up at them.

"He's beginning to recognize us," Mia says. "He's starting to distinguish between friend and foe."

She goes into the kitchen, and when she returns she's holding a brownie and a can of Reddi-wip. It's her four-in-the-morning snack.

She thought her cravings would be gone, but nursing has brought its own cravings. She sprays some Reddi-Wip onto a plate and takes a spoon to it. "Don't even start with me." If she's going to feast on whipped cream, Julian likes to say, she might as well eat the real stuff, but she prefers her whipped cream in a can.

She holds her palm out to Julian; she's showing him the Michigan mitt. And there it is, a dollop of whipped cream at the base of her thumb, where Ann Arbor lies. Her Michigan husband, she still calls him.

And now, she thinks, *Look at us here.* She means in New York, of course, with their baby, but also in their home, which she's still getting used to. Once, when she was a girl, her mother rebuked her for spending five dollars on lunch, and for weeks after that she would stand incapacitated in the deli line, unable to order anything. Her mother would tell her about her own mother, who had reused old dental floss, hanging it over the shower rod to dry. So it shouldn't surprise her that it's taken her a while to grow accustomed to her new life, and she hopes Julian won't begrudge her an occasional moment of guilt.

Though she's making slow progress. Finally, she has dipped into her inheritance. She has opened a college savings plan for the baby, and she has set up a scholarship fund in her mother's memory, with her and Olivia as the trustees.

On the coffee table sits a ceramic plate with the baby's name and birth weight printed on it. Nine pounds, eleven ounces. Labor was hard going, and Dr. Kaplan thought she might have to do a C-section, but she managed to twist the baby's shoulders around, and out he came. Richard John Wainwright. John after Mia's mother, Joan, and Richard after Julian's father, and after his grandfather and great-grandfather before him. It was what Julian himself was supposed to have been named, what he would have been named if his mother hadn't insisted on naming him Julian.

Richard is fair-haired and blue-eyed; he looks like neither Julian nor Mia. Mia has joked that they took the wrong baby home, which got Julian sufficiently anxious that he checked their hospital bands to make sure they all matched. Later, looking at photos of Mia as an infant, he saw that she, too, had been fair-haired. And her mother had blue eyes, as does his. All the Richards of the world must have been babies once, but now, in 2006, having a baby named Richard makes Julian feel as if he's fathered a fifty-year-old. He tried Ritchie for a few weeks, but it sounded too much like a character in a cartoon strip, so he's taken to calling him Buddy, or Kiddo.

Dandling his son on his lap, he says, "May he grow up to be a banker."

"Is that what you want?"

"Whatever makes him happy."

"Maybe he'll be a veterinarian," she says. "He certainly has taken a liking to Cooper." The affection is mutual, for when she comes home she finds Cooper licking Richard's face. Sometimes she and Julian will place Richard on Cooper's back and Cooper will walk around the living room with a paternal care they haven't seen him display before. And Richard, laughing, will kick Cooper's sides. He seems to think Cooper is a horse.

"Just as long as he doesn't become a writer."

"Why?" she says. "Your life hasn't been so bad."

No, he admits. It's been pretty good, in fact. "I just don't want him to write about me."

"The way you wrote about me?" Julian hadn't allow her to read his book until yesterday, when the first copies arrived from the publisher. She stayed up late reading it, and her first reaction was that he'd written their story. Except he'd also made things up.

"Write what you know about what you don't know," Julian said, "or what you don't know about what you know."

"Which did you do?"

"Both, I guess."

The baby has started to cry again, and this time he's hungry. Mia has left her nursing pillow upstairs. My Brest Friend. A name so insulting she almost didn't buy the pillow, but everyone insisted it was worthwhile. She's wading through the swamp of puns and cuteness, made to feel like a child herself. It's something she has grudgingly learned to tolerate, as she tolerates the middle-of-the-night feedings. Sleepily, she carries the baby upstairs.

Alone now, Julian closes his eyes. He hears a car idling outside the window. A dog barks, and soon Cooper is barking, too. Then there is silence. *So this is it,* he thinks: *my novel.* He'll have to wait to see what comes next. Curious Julian, Mia calls him, because their first month together he snooped through her closet and he hasn't been able to live it down. He hears a voice in the bedroom and, indistinct as it is, he imagines his son is talking already. At least Mia is, and so, with the lights still out, everything dark, the house blanketed in shadows, he follows the sound, his dog dutifully trailing him, and heads upstairs to see what's going on.

Acknowledgments

I owe a great debt to many people. Ian Twiss, Jason Dubow, and Beth Berkowitz read an initial version of this novel and offered invaluable insight. I am especially grateful to John Fulton, whose comments on two early drafts of this book were instrumental in setting me on the right path. A thank-you, as well, to M. J. Rose for her generosity and wise counsel. I have been fortunate to be published by Pantheon/Vintage, a writer's dream of a publisher. I owe a particular debt to Marty Asher, who championed this book from the start, and to Dan Frank and Janice Goldklang for their great and unswerving support. Thank you to my wonderful publicist, Liz Calamari, and to Chris Gillespie, Altie Karper, Archie Ferguson, Jolanta Benal, Wes Gott, and everyone else at Pantheon and Vintage. A special thank-you to my agent, Lisa Bankoff, who fought for this book from the day she got it and who has been, from the moment I signed on with her, a brilliant agent and a loyal friend. Finally, I want to thank my editor, Lexy Bloom, without whom this book would be a pale version of itself. Lexy's intelligence, passion, and commitment went far beyond anything I could have hoped for; I'm so lucky to have her as my editor.

My parents, Alice and Lou Henkin, and my brothers, David and Daniel, have supported me with their love and friendship, during the writing of this book and from the start. A thank-you, as well, to my new family: Alisa Henkin, Sammy Henkin, Dahlia Henkin, Sharon Berkowitz, Jerry Berkowitz, Randi Berkowitz, Jon Regosin, Talia Berkowitz-Regosin, and Shachar Berkowitz-Regosin. Finally, to my daughters, Orly and Tamar, who have enriched my life more than I could have imagined, and to my wife, Beth, whom I ran into on a rainy night in Manhattan ten years ago. I have lived a fortunate life, but that was the greatest fortune of all; without her love, none of this would matter, not this book or anything else.

ABOUT THE AUTHOR

Joshua Henkin is the author of the novel *Swimming Across the Hudson,* which was selected by the *Los Angeles Times* as a Notable Book of the Year; his short stories, essays, and reviews have appeared in numerous journals and newspapers. He teaches at Sarah Lawrence College, Brooklyn College, and the 92nd Street Y in New York City. He lives in Brooklyn and can be found online at www.joshuahenkin.com.